Dreams Are Forever

Requests for permission to make copies of any part of this work should be
mailed to Permissions Department, Llumina Press, PO Box 772246, Coral
Springs, FL 33077-2246

3/09 Amazon $13.45

ISBN: 978-1-60594-205-6 (PB)
      978-1-60594-206-3 (HC)

Printed in the United States of America by Llumina Press

Library of Congress Control Number: 2008909691

Dedication

To the

Shawneetown Community High School

Class of 1956

Rivers are the perfect streams
For barefoot boys and endless dreams
Humming birds and honeybees
Floating logs and pecan trees

Boyhood is the perfect time
A jaunt through carefree life sublime
Without a dollar or a pence
A boy is richer than a prince

Acknowledgments

My thanks to the many friends and relatives who read the first draft and made excellent suggestions for improvement. Thanks also to Stephen Matthews for his legal advice, to Ruby Allen, one of my favorite artists, for the cover art, and to Duncan Carson of Hal Leonard Corp. for his help with the process of acquiring permission to use the song lyric excerpts.

Acknowledgments for use of these excerpts follow:

Pledging My Love
Words and music by Don Robey and Fats Washington.
Copyright 1954, 1955 SONGS OF UNIVERSAL, INC. Copyright renewed. All rights reserved. Used by permission.

Memories Are Made of This
Words and music by Richard Dehr, Frank Miller and Terry Gilkyson. Copyright 1955 (Renewed 1983) EMI BLACKWOOD MUSIC INC. All rights reserved. International copyright secured. Used by permission.

Unchained Melody
Lyrics by Hy Zaret. Music by Alex North. Copyright 1955 (Renewed) FRANK MUSIC CORP. All rights reserved. Used by permission.

I Hear You Knocking
Words and music by DAVE BARTHOLOMEW and PEARL KING. Copyright 1955 (Renewed). EMI UNART CATALOG INC. All rights controlled by EMI UNART CATALOG INC. (Publishing) and ALFRED PUBLISHING CO., INC. (Print). All rights reserved. Used by permission from ALFRED PUBLISHING CO., INC. and J. ALBERT AND SON Pty. Limited.

Chapter 1

1945

L ying in a shell hole in the mud, Paul screamed until he was hoarse. "Medic! Up here! Medic! Help me! Bobby, help me! Bobby!" The background noise of battle drowned out his frantic efforts. His feelings of desperation were becoming hard to manage. Alternating between panic and hopelessness, thoughts were racing through his head.

My God, they can't hear me. I'm going to bleed to death if they don't find me. The tourniquet...it's as tight as I can get it. Still some bleeding. Got to make it stop. Water is all gone. So thirsty. Need to quit whining, take action. But what? Funny, my leg doesn't hurt as much. Think it's getting numb. They can't hear me. Can't walk, can't even crawl. Oh, God, this can't be happening. I'm going to die. No, don't think that way. Don't think like that.

He rested his mind for a moment. Tears ran down his face. Then the thoughts continued.

Oh, God, what should I do? Need to send Eleanor a note. A farewell note. Need to do that now. Might pass out soon. What can I write on? My diary...rip some pages from my diary.

He pulled the diary from the large rectangular pocket on his right pants leg and opened it. Ripping a page from it, he began writing. His usual artful penmanship gave way to a small jagged scrawl.

Okinawa
April 9, 1945

Dearest Eleanor,

Afraid I've let you down. Promised to return w/o a scratch, but have bad leg wound. Will lose left leg. Trouble stopping the bleeding. By myself last few hours.

This letter may never get to you, I pray it does.

Landed on this place on Easter. Easy for a while. My buddy Bobby & I doing fine for a couple days. Then had trouble. Japs all dug in. Big explosion near me & Bobby. Don't know what happened to Bobby. Gone. Think most our guys pulled back down the hill. Can't move. Yelled so much--no one answers.

May not make it, Love. Remember, love you more than anything. Tell Dak will always be my special boy. Love to baby too. May die, but spirit will be with you, my dreams are forever. God bless all.

Love

Paul
Dakston Paul Leventhal III
Pfc U S Army
77th Infantry Division

He ripped another sheet from his diary and wrote some instructions.

ATTENTION
ANYONE WHO FINDS THIS
PLEASE SEND TO
MRS. ELEANOR LEVENTHAL
SHAWNEETOWN, ILLINOIS
UNITED STATES OF AMERICA

He was getting very weak. Some tears dropped on his letter. He didn't care. He folded the paper and wrapped it with the cloth he had cut off his mangled leg. He was puzzled for a minute about how to protect his note until it was found. Then he pulled out his Prince Albert tobacco can, dumped the tobacco in the mud, and slid the note and instructions into the can. Stashing the can in his helmet for protection, he felt momentarily better. *Trouble seeing,* he thought. *Maybe I should rest for a minute.* He closed his eyes.

Chapter 2

1956

Dak Leventhal woke early and stretched his leg muscles. He had learned to do that without displacing the brown plaid flannel sheet and three old quilts that kept him warm in his cold room. It was still dark as he looked out the window next to his bed to see the streetlight on the levee. The tiny rays of light from it danced through the ice crystals on the inside of his window to produce a fuzzy golden glow. As he heard the town clock strike six deep-throated bongs, he knew it was time to get up. And though he briefly considered rolling deeper into his feather bed and dozing a bit longer, he gave up that idea. Jumping out of bed with a shiver, he jerked his frigid jeans over his long legs, flung a red flannel shirt over his shoulders, grabbed his shoes, and ran down the stairs. As he passed his younger sister's adjoining room, he yelled, "Nancy, get up!" Why was it, he wondered, that he always had to pee more urgently when it was cold.

As Dak opened the noisy sliding doors to the warm part of the house, he savored the woody smell of bacon frying and the swish, swish, swish noise of flipping hot bacon grease onto a skillet full of eggs.

"That you, Dak?" asked his mother, not really expecting an answer. "Get that toast out before it burns and put some more in. I swear if I make breakfast a thousand times, I'll never get everything ready at the same time. Where's your sister?"

Dak was washing his hands in the cold water in the wash pan. He took a deep breath as he splashed his face. Drying himself with a clean towel made from a feed sack, he said, "She'll be here in a second." He didn't actually know she was coming, but she usually did when he called her by name. A couple minutes later, Nancy stumbled through the sliding doors, still in her fuzzy pajamas. She yawned and held her hands palms forward toward the pot-bellied stove. Her hair was a mess, and she looked as if she had used her last ounce of energy just getting down the stairs.

The three of them sat down to eat, but Nancy complained that there was no jelly for the toast. She looked utterly unable to get up from her chair, so Dak scooted his chair over far enough to open the ice box door and grab the jar of blackberry jelly. Dak, at 17 years and 6 foot, 2 inches tall, had a reach that saved many steps.

"Eleanor, do I have this year's jelly or is this some of that ol' sugary stuff?" Dak asked while stirring it with his spoon. He sometimes called his mother Eleanor, which irritated Nancy but got no reaction from Eleanor, and sometimes called her Mom.

"It's from the blackberries you and Johnnie David picked last July," she said.

"Well, I hope it's the good stuff, because I almost got bit by a copperhead pickin' them," replied Dak. No one responded to his little drama, so he raised the jar and squinted. "Yeah, it says right here on the jar, 'Shawneetown's Best Blackberry Jelly, personally canned by the famous Eleanor Leventhal in July 1955,' so it must be good stuff." His spoof got no attention either, so he dropped the subject and took a big bite of egg.

Every morning after breakfast, Dak took the table scraps to the back yard for his dog, Alex. Alex was a six-year-old frisky black and white mixed terrier who loved Dak greatly. Dak had chosen his full name, Alexander the Great, after he finished reading a book about the great man. Alex was a very happy dog, and he launched Dak on a cheerful course almost every morning.

There wasn't a lot of time to spare. Dak had to get ready for school and walk a couple blocks to Gene's Grocery where Buck Dawson stopped the old International school bus at 7:30AM sharp every school day.

It took Dak only a few minutes to brush his teeth and shape his flattop. Then, he grabbed his lunch bag, threw his mother a kiss and playfully thumped Nancy's nose. As he went out the sliding doors, Nancy yelled, "Bye, Dak, and quit thumping my nose." Having produced the desired effect, he was quickly out the main door and down the steps. Then, laying his left palm on a fence post, he swung his narrow hips forward over the fence and was on his way to Gene's.

He loved his sister Nancy, but saw her as a 12-year-old pest, a likable pest, sometimes a fun pest, but nonetheless a pest. She loved to be wherever Dak was, especially if Dak's best friend Johnnie David was there.

Nancy was at an age where she almost always had a crush on someone. Johnnie David was often that someone, though it changed from day to day. She liked Johnnie David's athletic figure, his low-pitched voice, his big brown eyes, and his irreverent attitude. Even so, she thought he was a bit lazy. Johnnie David liked joking with her, but he never considered it flirting because Nancy was just too young to be of any serious interest to someone of his age. So Nancy could horn in whenever Johnnie David and Dak were hanging around at their house, but both Johnnie David and Dak considered her presence an inhibitor on their free discussion of girls and sex and a hundred other topics.

Dak liked most of the people in his class, and though he didn't often say so, he also liked most of the teachers. Sure, there were some of each who would be offensive from time to time. He regarded that as an acceptable thing as long as it wasn't too irritating and didn't last too long. Judy Savoy, for one, could be a real pain when she started putting on airs and telling how rich her banker daddy was. Dak realized that this was just an attempt to gain some semblance of respect from classmates who were not impressed by her stumpy body and bad case of acne. Sadly, it never worked.

As the bus crunched its way through the gravel at the back of the high school and came to a noisy stop, Dak saw Johnnie David walking in the back door of the building. Dak knew this meant that Johnnie David had talked his dad into letting him take the family car to school. It was a '48 Ford, and its black bulbous body had suffered some considerable rust damage as well as assorted dents and scrapes. It also had some strange white

bubbles between the layers of the windshield glass. Notwithstanding all of this, it moved pretty well and had a good radio.
That was enough for Johnnie David and Dak.

Dak hurried in and bounded down the concrete steps to the
lockers three at a time. Then he remembered that Mr. Jordan, the
principal, had practically threatened the boys with their lives if
he caught them running on the steps. This had followed a near
lawsuit when Donny Branch had done the steps in record time
only to run head-on into Judy Savoy at the bottom of the stairs. It
had caused a bloody mess. Dak continued in an orderly way to
the locker area and, walking up behind Johnnie David, sharply
thumped his right ear from behind. This caused an apparently
violent reaction in which Johnnie David whirled around and secured a headlock on Dak. Dak immediately yelled, "I give up!"

Punching Johnnie playfully on his right shoulder, Dak said,
"Don't leave without me today. I'm ridin' with you."

"Not a chance," Johnny responded with a silly smile, but Dak
knew he was in.

Dak and Johnnie David had only a couple classes together.
One of them was American History II, which covered the period
from the beginning of the Civil War until the present. Dak's
classmates all knew that he loved history. Even though most of
them thought it was a bit weird, sometimes they couldn't help
getting caught up in his enthusiasm. Johnnie David had once
told Dak, "Man, you almost live that stuff." It was true. Last
month, Dak had gotten into the Battle of Chancellorsville very
deeply. When he told Johnnie David about Stonewall Jackson
being accidentally shot by friendly fire after a masterful move
against the Yankees, he became very excited. Johnnie David had
said, "Hey, Dak, it was a hundred years ago! What does it matter?" But a couple weeks later when Miss Hurd, the history
teacher, gave an essay question on the fate of Stonewall Jackson,
Johnnie David surprised her with a pretty good description of
the event. Not as good as Dak's description, of course, but
Johnnie actually scored an 83 on the test. Dak, as usual, received
a 98 with congratulatory remarks by Miss Hurd.

Miss Hurd almost always found some reason for not giving a grade of 100. "We don't pretend to be perfect," she said once when Erma Johnson protested that she had absolutely nothing wrong on her test, "and we can't expect ever to get a grade of 100."

During the previous week, Miss Hurd had announced that each student would be required to prepare a term paper on a subject related to the history of Shawneetown. This was an exciting prospect for Dak, but Johnnie David felt it was a little ridiculous. "What is there about the history of this beat-up old town that anyone would want to write about?" he asked.

Miss Hurd had offered some topics for consideration, such as, *Lafayette's Visit to Shawneetown*, *The Conviction and Hanging of Joe Peck Smith* and *No Loan-Chicago is too far from Shawneetown*. Dak had chosen to research a long-abandoned mansion just north of town called Ellsworth Place. He submitted the title, *What Really Happened at Ellsworth Place?* J.D. said he could answer that without any research. "It went to pot," he said. "It went to pot and ended up being a good place for high school students to go have a few beers without gettin' caught."

J.D. had submitted the title, *Was Shawneetown really Camp Breckenridge's Brothel?* Camp Breckenridge was an Army camp just across the river a few miles, and its young soldiers often took their time off in Shawneetown. They sometimes drank too much and tried to find local girls to relieve their homesickness. J.D. was actually pleased when Miss Hurd rejected that title because he didn't know how he would do the necessary research. Still, it allowed him to ridicule the whole exercise in a back-handed way, and that, of course, was the whole idea. Miss Hurd also disapproved his next title: *Was General Posey the Illegitimate Son of George Washington?*

"Johnnie David, can't you select some subject that doesn't have to do with illicit relationships?" she asked.

"What's wrong with illicit relationships anyway?" J.D. replied. She didn't answer, but did approve his third title. J.D. explained that *The Honeymoon of U. S. Grant in Shawneeetown* had real potential.

"At least they were married," she muttered.

Miss Hurd asked Dak to be the editor of the '56 yearbook. Dak, incapable of saying no to anyone, took the job even though it meant he would have to stay after school a good many days. He wasn't sure how he would get home after doing this. It would not be easy because the high school was about three miles from town, and his mother had no car.

Dak's family hadn't had a car since Dak's father, Dakston Paul Leventhal III, had left for the War in 1942. They had sold the family car to save money. Their plan was to get another one as soon as they could after his return from the War. As it turned out, he never returned. He was killed in action on Okinawa in 1945, or so his buddies thought, though the body was never actually recovered.

Dak's father had received a short leave before shipping out to the Pacific when Dak was only five years old. Dak didn't remember his father very well because his father left for the war when Dak was so young. On their final day together, everyone gathered at the train station. Dak's father shook hands with his friends and hugged all the relatives. Then he embraced Eleanor and Dak a long time while tears ran down their cheeks. Waiting as long as he could, he finally picked up his duffle bag and stepped up into the train. They never saw him again. Eleanor had unsuccessfully strained to see a glimpse of him through the steamy windows of the train. She kept expecting to see his face and a final wave goodbye. Maybe he would throw them a kiss or flash a thumbs-up sign. Instead, the locomotive gave a loud hiss and a guttural belch before slowly moving out of the station. As it chugged down the tracks, it became smaller and smaller and then it disappeared altogether. Eleanor was left sobbing and hugging Dak. Sadly, this day was burned into her memory and it left her with a feeling of frustration and loneliness that never entirely went away. She would only find out a month or two later that she had gotten pregnant during his visit.

From the day of his dad's departure, Dak often wished he had a father. He longed for someone to teach him how to hunt, how to swim, and how to drive a car. Sometimes, he desperately needed someone to be there when he had problems that only a man would know about. He would go to his room and look at the yellowish-brown picture of his dad for hours. In the picture, his dad wore an army uniform and had a slight smile and dark eyes that seemed to be looking directly at the viewer. Dak would wonder what his dad was like and what life would be like if he had lived. Did he have a good sense of humor? Was he talkative? Was he a hard worker? Would they be able to take long vacations if his dad had lived? When he asked Eleanor these questions, he never found the answers satisfying. It was also a frustration for Dak that the US Army had never recovered his dad's body. Other people would go to Westwood Cemetery just west of town to see the graves of their loved ones, but Dak never could visit his dad's grave. He often checked out the big book about World War II in the school library and studied the section about Okinawa. He would try to imagine how his dad had fought, how he had died, and what had happened to his body. In his younger years, he had fantasized that his dad was single-handedly fighting a hundred of the enemy soldiers and beating them all, only to be killed by a kamikaze aimed precisely at him.

After school, Dak explained to Miss Hurd that he would not be able to work on the yearbook today. This was a disappointment to her, because it was her role to supervise the preparation of the yearbook, and she looked forward to staying with Dak and working with him on the first set of pictures. She would never show it except in the most subtle ways, but she loved the way Dak talked and his great enthusiasm for everything he did, as well as his cheerfulness and unexpected sense of humor.

Miss Hurd was 38 years old and had never been married. She found that one of the great benefits of teaching was contact with the brighter minds of the next generation. Occasionally, there had been a physical attraction to one or another of the students, but she would hardly admit this even to herself. She would go to any length to avoid giving such an impression to others. The fact that Dak's athletic-looking body, unblemished skin, ultra-white teeth, and smiling eyes combined with his dark brown flat top in a very favorable way was not a factor for her, she told herself.

When Dak reached his locker to stash away his books, he noticed an unmarked envelope taped to his locker door. Knowing that several students thrived on practical jokes, he assumed this was part of yet another one. He jerked the envelope from the locker and tucked it into his shirt pocket. Then he returned his books to his locker and joined Johnnie David in the graveled area that served as the high school parking lot. As Johnnie David moved the old Ford out the school driveway, throwing gravel in the air, he turned the radio to KXOK. At that moment, the station had Gogi Grant singing *The Wayward Wind*. Dak liked the song but was in a talkative mood right now, so he reached over and turned the knob as far down as he thought Johnnie would allow.

"Hey, J.D., what say we go huntin' Saturday?" Dak asked. "I heard Buck Dawson tellin' somebody on the bus that squirrels are thick as fleas this year."

Johnnie David liked going hunting and he liked Dak's company, so he knew he was going to say yes. Still, something in him told him to stretch this out a little. "Ain't the river flooded over the woods up there?" he asked.

"No," Dak replied. "The water is not high this year like usual, and you can walk all over the Uppers."

The Uppers was a long stretch of beach along the river north of town where swimming was good in the summertime. The beach area went back fifty feet or so from the water at that time of year before reaching a small cliff that went nearly vertical for ten or fifteen feet. Above that was the flat cornfield. Along the way, there were small streams every mile or two that flowed into the river, and near these streams there were woods that made for good hunting. However, in the wintertime, this whole area was often flooded. Sometimes, the entire region south, north, and east of town was flooded. In those times, the town was protected only by its levee, which made a big "U" shape, with the top of the "U" meeting some hills in the west to complete the protection of the town. Dak had just been over the north levee last weekend to see how high the river was. He knew that right now the water was low, even though they were in the middle of the winter season.

"Okay," said Johnnie David, looking over at Dak. "Let's go huntin', but I spent my last dollar for gas this mornin'. Do you have a few extra .22 shells?"

"I do have some extras," said Dak, "but they come at a price, which you may not want to pay."

"What price?" Johnnie said.

"The price is you have to listen to my latest stuff. My latest piece of history."

"That's not the kind of piece I'm most interested in," said Johnnie, "but it's a deal." He stopped to let Dak out at his home.

"You might do better with that kind of piece if you weren't so darned ugly," Dak said. He smiled and slammed the car door before Johnnie could respond.

As Dak walked toward the house, he remembered the envelope which he'd found taped to his locker. He pulled it from his pocket, ripped it open, and removed the single sheet of paper it contained. He stopped in his tracks as he read the neatly typed message:

Pick a different topic for the term paper.
If you do not, you will be sorry.

Dak still thought it was a joke. It had to be a joke. Why would anyone care what topic he chose for his term paper? But as he thought more about it, it seemed to him an unlikely joke. He was unable to envision any way that it could be funny. He decided to keep quiet about it and see what he could learn. *No*, he thought to himself. *This is definitely not a joke. Whoever did it will probably show their hand in some way if I just ignore it.*

Chapter 3

The Discovery

As Saturday morning dawned, Johnnie David rode up on his old Western Flyer bicycle. Since his kickstand was missing, he leaned the bike on the pump scaffold at the back of Dak's house. By habit, he pushed the horn button on the side of the bike's tank to make a silly little beeping noise. This was a ritual that, though he had done it hundreds of times, still somehow seemed humorous to him. This time, no one even heard it except Alex, who ran to J.D. and repeatedly jumped in the air to greet him. This was a ceremony that Alex performed for any visitor whom he recognized as being a friend of Dak's.

"Alexander the Great!" J.D. said as he ruffled the hair on the dog's back. At that moment, Alex felt an urgent need to scratch a particular place on his neck, so the ceremony was over. J.D. took his worn rifle off the handlebars of his bicycle and positioned it in the corner of the porch, barrel up. As was his habit, he opened the back door and walked in with no warning. Eleanor did not allow Alex to enter the house. However, he knew how to nose open the side gate to the yard and could go anywhere else he wanted. He made it a policy to stay in the yard every morning until Dak delivered the table scraps. He would devour the scraps, do some rituals for Dak, and immediately start his rounds, which took him all over the town. This morning, he continued a serious sniffing activity that J.D.'s arrival had interrupted.

Eleanor was in the kitchen opening a quart jar of tomatoes that she had canned last summer. Looking up with mock surprise, she said, "Why, Johnnie David, I haven't seen you since last Sunday. How are you doing?"

"Well, I'm doin' okay, Mrs. Leventhal. That is, I'm doin' okay as long as Dak has some extra rifle shells. We're goin' huntin' this mornin'," he said, "and I don't have any shells."

"Dak said you were," she responded as Dak walked in with a dirty brown hunting coat, his rifle, and two boxes of cartridges in his hand. Eleanor thought the old hunting coat, which had belonged to Dak's father, made Dak look so mature.

"J.D., here are your cartridges." Dak pitched the small box across the kitchen table. "I hope hollow points are okay."

"Okay with me," said Johnnie David, "but the squirrels may complain a little!"

"Probably not," said Dak, "because you probably won't even get close enough for a hollow point unless you've improved."

"Now, you boys be careful," Eleanor said. "You remember the accident last year when the Miller boy was killed. Just make sure you don't point your gun at anybody."

Dak's mind briefly flashed back to that snowy day a year ago. Donny Branch had raced up breathlessly on his bicycle and, talking much too fast, said, "Jerry Miller's been shot! Fonzo and Jerry were out huntin' and tried to get a shotgun shell unstuck! The dang thing went off! Oh, it was awful! I think Jerry's dead!" Dak felt a shock run through his chest into his gut just like it had last year when Donny told him about it. Dak had played basketball with Jerry Miller and joked with him about his small stature: "Hey, Jer, why don't you pass the ball up here where us big people are?" It didn't seem possible that Jerry was gone.

"We'll be careful, Mom, don't worry," Dak assured her. "We'll be real careful." She knew they would, but somehow the painful scene when Dak's father had boarded the train to go to war moved through her mind as the boys walked off toward the levee. She had an unusually close relationship with Dak and shuddered to think how she would ever deal with it if she lost him.

As Dak and Johnnie walked down the other side of the levee toward the Uppers, the sun was bright in the eastern sky, reflecting on the broad river as waving silver ribbons. A small brown dog scampered down through the brush chasing something that the boys couldn't see. At the bend in the river just north of town, a barge was moving south producing waves that shone in a white "V" on the surface. Dak loved this particular view of the river. He said, "You can see why they call it the Beautiful Ohio, J.D." When Johnnie David gave him a puzzled look, Dak realized that J.D. was looking at the same thing, but wasn't seeing what he was seeing. He decided to skip it.

As the two boys reached the sandy beach of the Uppers, Johnnie David picked up a flat rock and skimmed it across the water at the greatest speed he could manage. It bounced six times before sinking into the river. Deciding not to try to beat that, Dak instead picked up an old deflated volleyball which had floated in, did a jump shot from an imaginary centerline and yelled, "He made it!" as it hit the water exactly in the imaginary basket.

It was Johnnie David who brought up the topic of girls. "Hey, what do you think of Marie Sanders? I was watchin' her cheer at the ball game the other night...watchin' real close... and she has some fine legs," he said with enthusiasm. "Some really fine legs."

"She's pretty nice, I'd say," Dak commented. "She has this tiny waist and lots up above that makes her figure just about perfect. When I see her, I sometimes get this urge to just walk up and hug her, to rub my chest against hers. Ain't that crazy?"

"No, I don't think that's crazy." Johnnie said.

"But, you know what I like best?" Dak asked. "It's ankles. I just hate big clubby ankles. They should be slim and shaped like Michelangelo had personally sculpted them."

"Well, Dak, I don't know anything about Michelangelo, but this girl has a fine body, I'll tell you that. She smiles at me every day in Study Hall, and we talk all the time. The last time was before the ball game last week. Boy, she is something. What do you...do you think she's okay?"

"Hey, are you real interested in Marie, J.D.? I mean, are you goin' to take her out? Or is this just another one of your fantasies?" asked Dak. "If you're askin' if I approve, I give her five stars. Like Eisenhower or MacArthur. She's pretty, she's smart, and she's friendly. Oh, and she can sing like everything. She's great! Go for her, man!"

"I probably am, if she'll go with me. If I can get the car next Friday night. If I can get some money. If I can figure out some-place to take her. Hey, it ain't soundin' too good, is it? But you know what, Dak? You shouldn't be comparin' her to some ol' bald army general. She's a nice girl."

J.D. had said "nice girl," but Dak thought he really meant "nice body." In some vague way, that was discomforting to Dak who knew Marie was genuinely a nice and talented person, not just a great body.

There was more talk about other girls. They thoroughly dis-cussed and, in some cases debated, each of them. Dak liked more what he called the "fresh" look-- clean, bright, and wholesome with a light sprinkling of freckles. Johnnie David favored the sexy look-- shapely, long blonde hair, and a sultry expression that says, "I want you."

"How a girl looks is important," Dak said, "but her personal-ity is a big part of it too. I want to know what she's thinkin', what she's feelin', what she cares about, what she's interested in, what she wants to do with her life."

"What she wants to do with her life? Who the heck knows that? I tell you what...I can put up with any personality if they look good enough," J.D. countered. "What does it matter what they are sayin' if they look like Marilyn Monroe?"

J.D. talked about the girls as if he was comparing cattle, a practice which Dak found simultaneously unfair and humorous. Then J.D. started describing his fantasies. Some of these were so outrageous that they brought Dak to full-scale laughter as he visualized each one. Dak had heard some of J.D.'s fantasies be-fore and knew J.D. was oversexed, but had not realized to what extent until just now.

"I wouldn't throw any of them out of bed," Johnnie David laughed.

"Your hormones are about to get you, J.D.," said Dak, "You're right on the verge of a hormone explosion!"

"Hey, man, I've done exploded," J. D said wistfully. "I just need Marie to calm me down again."

Dak decided it was best to change the subject, as amusing as he found all this. Besides, they were coming upon a creek and wooded area where they might be able to shoot a few squirrels.

"Johnnie David, let's go in the woods here and see if we can find something to shoot," said Dak. "This looks like the place. It's probably swarmin' with the little critters."

Johnnie David was having a hard time clearing his mind of his current thought processes, but after a few seconds, he seemed to recover.

"Hiyaaaaaa," he yelled so loudly that he startled Dak. "Let me load up this here rifle, and let's shoot some dang meat for supper! Y'all know I'm a hungerin'," he said in mock hillbilly.

Dak frowned at all the noise and said, "If you were really a hillbilly, you'd know not to make so much noise when you're huntin'."

They walked up the creek a short distance and stopped under a large pecan tree. There were some pecans on the ground, mostly broken open or at least showing teeth marks from the squirrels. "Let's sit here quietly for a few minutes and see what we see," Dak whispered. They leaned on a big fallen limb and began loading their rifles. When they had just finished loading, they heard some squirrels barking. The noise seemed to be coming from the next tree over, so they both moved quietly in that direction. As they grew closer, they could see two squirrels chasing around the tree trunk.

"Wait till they hesitate," whispered Dak, "and then you take the high one, and I'll take the low one." The squirrels paused for just a moment, and that was all the boys needed. J.D. shot first, followed a split second later by Dak. One squirrel fell to the ground and didn't move at all, but the second one fell about twenty feet from the boys and, apparently only addled, ran directly for J.D. If he had had time to think, J.D. wouldn't have been scared by a squirrel. However, the speed of the animal, in what appeared to be an attack mode, startled him so much that he let out a strange yell and leaped into the weeds. In the process, he tripped over a vine, dropped his rifle, and landed with a thud on his back.

Dak tried to control his laughter as he walked over to help J.D. to his feet. When he got there, he extended his hand, but was laughing with such abandonment that he didn't have the strength to pull J.D. up. Instead, J.D. pulled Dak down and, feigning anger, rolled on top of Dak and began pummeling him violently. Dak quickly extracted himself from J.D. and stood up but continued to laugh for several minutes.

"I trust that entertained you sufficiently," said J.D. "And that now we can get on with our huntin'."

"Well, I guess so," said Dak wiping his eyes with the sleeve of his hunting coat. "Boy, this will make a good story: 'Man attacked by injured squirrel, knocked off his feet.'" The thought of telling this to their classmates set Dak off on another round of laughter.

"Where did the stupid squirrel go?" J.D. asked.

"I don't know where yours went, but here's mine," said Dak as he picked up the other squirrel.

"Yours?" J.D. yelled. "That's the one I got. If you were a better shot, the other one would be dead too." After looking extensively for the addled squirrel, the boys gave up and moved on.

Up the creek a bit farther, J.D. spotted another squirrel and took a shot at it, but it ducked at just the right moment. While Dak was razzing him about missing it, another one appeared on a lower limb. J.D., in an almost continuous motion, raised his rifle, fired it at the squirrel, and dropped it to the ground. As the squirrel fell, he thrust his left arm out in an expansive gesture, moved his right hand to his waist, and took a deep bow toward Dak. Then, he ran over to get the squirrel where it fell.

"That's not too bad, Johnnie," Dak said, laughing, "not too bad at all."

J.D. flashed a silly smile and said, "At your service, sir. Do you have anything here that's a challenge for a man like me?"

The boys came to a tree trunk lying across the creek in what appeared too neat a way to have just fallen in that position. At any rate, it seemed solid, so they walked across it and jumped off on the other side.

Walking back toward the river, they didn't hear or see another squirrel all the way. To get back down to the sandy area next to the river, they had to jump off an embankment that was eight or ten feet tall. After tossing the rifles and the squirrels down, Dak leaped immediately. J.D. had never liked heights and wasn't sure he wanted to jump. Then, thinking more about the soft sand at the bottom, he leaped and landed in such a way that his feet and butt hit the ground simultaneously.

"God, that was graceful, J.D." said Dak. "Maybe you should be in gymnastics." Actually, J.D. was more athletic than Dak, but sometimes hesitated before taking a risk. Dak usually did not.

As they wandered further up the sandy beach, Dak stopped to see a large bird in a tree above the embankment. At first, he thought it was an American eagle, maybe because he had spotted one before in this area. He soon realized that it was just a hawk. As he was lowering his line of sight down over the embankment, something else caught his eye.

"Look at that, Johnnie David. What do you suppose that is?" he asked.

"Don't see anything, Dak. What did you spot?" J.D. responded, visually scanning the area.

"Well, I'm just wonderin' why there would be sawed planks stickin' out from that embankment. See them there?" asked Dak.

"Ahh, yeah, that is odd, isn't it?" J.D. said as he walked closer to the embankment.

Jutting out of the ground about five feet from the top of the embankment were four planks, each of which was maybe twelve inches wide by one inch thick. Two of these planks were aligned with the wide part parallel to the ground, and the other two, at the edges of these, were aligned with the width of the board running vertically. All four were a dark gray color and had rotted off at the ends.

The two boys walked closer to the planks and looked at them for maybe a full minute without saying a word. It was as if it were all their brains could do to process the information before them. Finally, Dak said, "Hey, these are definitely sawed planks. Somebody sawed them a long time ago. They're right in here with all these roots sticking out of the ground where the river has washed some dirt away. I bet nobody ever noticed them before. They had to be buried here a long time ago."

Johnnie David climbed up on a cottonwood root to get close enough to touch the planks. "Hey, these planks were the sides and bottom of some kind of box. Maybe somebody buried treasure here. Hot dog, maybe there's gold in there," he said.

Dak was thinking along another line. "No, J.D., I bet this is a coffin. Look at the width and height. They're just about right for a coffin. Do you suppose it could be?" he asked.

As they were pondering their find, J.D. heard something and, looking over at Dak, whispered, "I hear voices coming from up the creek apiece. Let's get away from this for now, and we just won't say anything about it if anybody comes down here. Don't really want to share all that gold."

"Right," said Dak as he wandered nonchalantly down the sandy beach toward the river. J.D. picked up an old piece of driftwood and, moving away from their discovery, tossed a mussel shell in the air and hit it hard with the driftwood stick. "Home run!" he shouted and ran around the first two of an imaginary set of bases.

Sliding noisily down the embankment was a group of three boys. It was Neil Bonham, his younger brother Tyson, and some kid neither Dak nor J.D. knew. They were about 13 years old and were just out exploring for kicks. Dak and J.D. were courteous.

"How are you doing, guys?" asked Dak. "Aren't you gettin' pretty far from town?"

Dak and J.D. wanted the boys to move on so they could look more closely at their find. The boys didn't see it that way.

"We're going to set up a little camp here on this sandy spot. We have our lunch, and we have a beer we're going to drink. Wish we had another. We'd give you one," said Neil proudly.

"You guys shouldn't have beer," said Dak. "Where'd you get that?"

"My grandpa got it for us," Neil said with a pleased look. "He would've got us two if we'd had the money, but Tyson lost some of our money. So this is it."

"Why don't you head back toward town to set up your camp?" asked J.D. "You probably should be on the other side of the creek before you get soused."

The boys had made up their minds. "We won't get soused. We're just going to eat and have our beer and then mess around awhile," said Neil.

Giving up for now, Dak said, "Okay, well, I guess we better get on back to town, J.D. See you guys around."

As they crossed back over the tree trunk that spanned the creek, Dak talked in a low voice. "We've got to come back up here and dig to see what it is...no tellin' what we might find. Do you think we have to report it to the sheriff's office?"

"No way," Johnnie David responded. "Why would we have to report it when we don't even know what it is?"

"Yeah, right," Dak responded. "Let's just keep it a secret until we have a chance to get back up here with some...with a spade. We'll also need some small tools. You know how archaeologists use real fine tools to avoid messing up the find."

"Man, I can hardly wait. It could be treasure. It could be a body. It could be something somebody stole and buried. We might be rich!"

"Or it could be a piece of an old barge," Dak suggested.

"Naw, it's something better than that," J.D. replied.

Dak was accustomed to being excited by things like this that might have some historical meaning, but he was surprised that J.D. was so enthusiastic. "It could even be important from a historical standpoint," he said. "We just have to keep it quiet and hope Neil and the boys don't see it."

As they were walking back toward town, Dak decided this might be a good time to tell Johnnie David about his latest piece of history. He reminded J.D. of the deal they had made earlier that, in exchange for the gift of some rifle cartridges, J.D. would listen to it. J.D., in mock despair, protested that he had only used three cartridges and would gladly return the others. "Mercy, mercy!" he said. "Anything but that!"

Dak knew, of course, that J.D. was joking and that he was actually mildly interested in hearing the latest info. Dak seemed to always be discovering some juicy tidbits from the history of the area that were fascinating to him and slightly interesting even to J.D., who was anything but a scholar of history.

"You know ol' Miss Mattie Lott," Dak began. "Well, she's 97 now and all by herself, so I go up on my bicycle maybe once a week to see about her. She sometimes needs me to go to the store for her or something. We became pretty good friends, and we talk about ol' times and stuff. She seems to like me. So, the other day, we were sittin' in her porch swing and talkin' about slavery, and she says she wants me to see something she's got. Well, she drags out this ol' wooden box. It has a beat-up leather cover all around it with a whole bunch of papers and some pictures inside. The stuff's mostly all written by hand and real yellow and all, and it's something between a diary and a log of things that happened. There was so much of it that I could hardly carry the box. She says it was written by her Aunt Mariah, who is long since dead."

"So, what's it tell about?" asked J.D.

"I'll get to that in a minute," Dak replied. "The thing is, she was just showin' it to me, and I thought it was real interestin', so I asked if I could borrow it for a few days. She hesitated, but then she looks over at me with a big smile and puts her shaky hand on the side of my head. Then she says I can take it as long as I take good care of it and bring it back in a while. She says she wouldn't want it damaged or anything, and I promised it wouldn't be. She said her Aunt Mariah would roll over if something happened to the ol' papers or pictures."

"Yeah, Dak, but what do the papers say?" J.D. asked.

"You'd never believe what I found in those old papers, J.D. This is almost beyond belief," said Dak. "I don't know if ol' Miss Mattie had ever read them or not. I don't even think she can

read, because when I get her mail, she always has me read it to
her."

"Well, I'll never know if you don't quit talkin' about it and tell
me," replied J.D. "Let's have it!"

"Okay, you know about the Ol' Slave House out by Equality,"
Dak continued. "Well, Miss Mattie's Aunt Mariah lived there for
some years when she was young. She was some cousin of the
people who ran it, and so, when her mother died, she lived there
with them. This was back in the mid 1800's."

"So, it tells all about the Ol' Slave House?" asked Johnnie.

"Yeah," Dak responded. "It was called Hickory Hill then and
was something of a plantation like the ones in the ol' South, but
here it was in Southern Illinois. They made their money more
from sellin' salt from the salt works than they did from farmin'
or raisin' animals. The salt works was a bunch of springs that
gave real salty water. They would gather this water, put it in big
kettles, and build a fire under them. When the water boiled
away, they just had salt left. It took a bunch of people to cut trees
to get wood to burn. It was a lot of work."

"So, what did they want with all that salt? Just to put on stuff
they cooked to make it taste better?"

"No, no," Dak responded, "salt was real scarce, so they could
sell it for a lot of money. People used salt and smoke to cure
their meat, so it would last all winter and not spoil. It took a lot
of salt, and there weren't any other salt springs for a long way."

"Well, okay, but that's not really so fascinatin', Dak. Sometimes, you kind of get carried away with...," J.D. said before he
was interrupted.

"No, no, Johnnie, that's just background," said Dak. "Be pa-
tient with me! Now what's good is what this ol' aunt of Miss
Mattie's said about what happened at the plantation. She told of
them capturin' slaves that had been freed from the South and
makin' them work in the salt springs. And she told about them
capturin' runaway slaves and doin' the same with them."

"But I thought Illinois was not a slave state. That's what you
told me. So, how could they do that?" asked J.D.

"They couldn't legally, but there were some things that made it really easy to do," said Dak. "For one, a slave who'd been freed by his master was a free man as long as he had papers showin' he had been freed. But they would capture the freed slaves and then burn their papers. Without the papers, they weren't legal in the state, and they were at the mercy of whoever had them."

"So you mean that if somebody kidnapped them and burned their papers, and then they ran away from their kidnappers, they were illegal, and they couldn't move around how ever they wanted in the state?" asked J.D.

"That's right. That's what the ol' lady wrote. And there were also the runaway slaves who escaped their masters in the South, and made their way north. They were captured too. By this law they had back then, the 1850 Fugitive Slave Act, sheriffs were supposed to catch any of these slaves they could and return them to their rightful owners in the South. But the guys at Hickory Hill captured them and kept them. Or, sometimes, if they got more than they needed, they would take them down the river and sell them. I guess that's where the expression 'sold down the river' came from."

"How would they capture these black people?" J.D. wondered. "They ain't just goin' to go with you because you ask them to."

"Okay," Dak was gathering enthusiasm, "They did it in various ways. Sometimes, they would catch a family travelin' and just take them at gunpoint. Sometimes, they would trick them by pretendin' that they were goin' to help them get to somewhere safe."

"What a deal!" J.D. replied. "So they get free work done at their salt springs, and there wouldn't be anything the slaves could do about it."

"The man who ran all this was named John Crenshaw. He was big in the Methodist Church and gave lots of money, so some of the people thought he was a real upstandin' person." continued Dak. "But some lawman got onto him and charged him with kidnappin'. He denied everything. And the slaves were just property like a cow, so they didn't have the right to testify against a white man. And also, there was not much sympathy among the white people for slaves anyway, so he got off and continued doin' it."

"Hell, Dak, that's really wild! That's even better than your story last month about the river pirates at Cave-in-Rock."

"That's not all," said Dak. "She also told about how the third floor of the plantation house at Hickory Hill had cells in it for keepin' some slaves. I didn't get all of why they kept some in the house and some at the salt works, but they also had a breedin' room on the third floor."

"A breedin' room?" said J.D. "Maybe I should have been a slave. I can pretty well guess how that worked."

"Yeah, I expect you would like to imagine how that worked. That's about your speed, you maniac," Dak said jokingly. "But, seriously, they had this young slave who was picked because he was very big and well built, and they found he often produced boys. So they would bring a slave woman up and put her in his cell with him. His job was to get her pregnant. And if he didn't at least try, he was punished. His name was Bob Wilson and he had been a stud slave in Virginia earlier when he was only a teenager. Crenshaw had made a trip to Washington, D.C., for something. On the way back, he stopped at a plantation in Virginia and bought Bob, just especially for being a stud. Ol' Aunt Mariah said they would sometimes put a slave girl as young as eleven in with Bob, and they would hear some screamin' before it was over."

"Wow!" was all J.D. could manage.

"Anyway," Dak continued, "when they got a surplus of slaves, they'd take them down a back road to the river and load them on a boat. Then, they would go down river to Natchez or New Orleans and sell them. Sometimes, they made an arrangement in advance with some plantation owner to meet them at some appointed place along the river to buy the cargo."

"Dak, do you still have the papers from that Aunt Mariah, or did you take them back to Miss Mattie?" asked Johnnie.

"I still have them. I hid them under my bed so Nancy or somebody wouldn't find them. I have to take them back soon, though, and I haven't read even a tenth of all that's there."

They were still talking about Hickory Hill as they reached the top of the levee coming back into town. Alexander the Great saw them from a distance and ran enthusiastically to their side. Arriving there, he performed one of his better welcoming ceremonies. "Good dog," Dak said as he patted Alex on the shoulder. "I guess you've finished your rounds for the day. What's that on your neck?" Dak kneeled next to Alex and saw that a small envelope was taped to the dog's collar.

"Looks like somebody gave Alex some mail," J.D. said.

"I guess," Dak replied. "Whoever put it there sure didn't spare any tape." It took a few minutes to pull all the tangled tape loose so that the envelope could be removed. Then Dak opened the unlabelled package and retrieved a single folded piece of paper with the words:

Change the topic or the dog will die.

Dak handed the note to J.D. without comment.

"What kind of crap is this?" J.D. said. "What does this mean? What topic? Who's this from?"

"I have no idea who it's from," Dak replied. "I didn't tell you, but there was a note taped to my locker at school saying I should change the topic of my term paper or I'd be sorry. I thought it was a joke at first, but I don't know. Can't imagine what this is about."

"Whoa!" J.D. said. "What is the topic of your term paper?"

"It's about what happened at Ellsworth Place, remember?"

"Oh yeah,"J.D. replied. "Why would any body care what topic you write about? It must just be a joke."

"I'm not sure. It's not a very funny joke when they say Alex will die. Do you think I should be worried about it?"

"Naw, not really,"J.D. said. "It's probably just some silly freshman playing a stupid trick. On the other hand, you never know."

"Let's keep it quiet and see if we hear anything," Dak said. "I don't want to worry Mom with it and I don't want it to get around at school. I don't want Alex to get hurt either, but I can't believe anyone would hurt Alex to get me to change my term-paper topic. That's just stupid."

Chapter 4

Cold Brown Water

O n the day following their great find on the Uppers, Dak and Johnnie David were greatly disappointed to see heavy rain. "Well, Dak, this throws a wrench into our plan to do some important archeological work today," J.D. said wistfully. "That was going to be fun, too. Sellin' gold would probably be a lot of fun."

"Yeah," Dak responded, looking as always at the bright side, "but we can still try to figure out what the planks might be and get prepared to dig when the weather is better. It might even be a good thing that we don't get in a big hurry. We can plan it better. And, J.D., it's probably not gold."

The sky was heavy with a uniform dark gray cloudiness that hung low as far as the eye could see. The temperature was near freezing, and the wind bent over Eleanor's lilac bush so much that she thought it would break. To make matters worse, there was little let up from morning until night.

Although this was the first day of rain in two weeks, the way it was raining reminded Eleanor of the winter of '37. In that year, the river had started swelling in December and continued into January and February. Each day had seemingly brought more rain than the day before. She remembered that the rains had been heavy upstream all the way to Pennsylvania. The river level had grown higher and higher until it was near the top of the levee which protected the little town. The townspeople had gotten very worried about an area of the levee that was showing signs of weakness. They knew that if the levee broke, a great wall of water would roar through the town, causing great destruction and death. To avoid that, they had decided to move their families and their furnishings to higher ground and let the water into the town slowly. The resulting damage was still extensive. For the most part, though, the homes had remained on their foundations and could be cleaned and re-plastered after the waters receded. This was an unpleasant memory for Eleanor and,as she moved her mind back to the present, she was comforted by the thought that such a thing was unlikely this year because it had been relatively dry in the fall.

• • •

Two weeks later, the rains continued. Eleanor knew that Miss Mattie Lott lived in a house that was actually on the outside of the north levee. It had one end on stilts and the other firmly planted in the soil of the levee. While there was no concern at this point about the house flooding, she thought Miss Mattie might be a little depressed by all this dark weather.

"Dak, I wonder if you should get your raincoat on and go see about Miss Mattie." Eleanor said. "She has been all by herself since these rains started and I'll bet she would be real glad to see you. She might need something from the store, and she could even be sick."

"I'll go see about her," Dak responded. While his tone seemed to indicate this was a chore, the truth is that he actually looked forward to seeing Miss Mattie because he wanted to talk about what he and J.D. had found on the Uppers. He had thought of little else since their discovery. Also, he needed to start his research on Ellsworth Place and Miss Mattie might know something about that.

"Can I go too?" Nancy said in a voice that seemed to acknowledge that a negative answer would be forthcoming.

"Nancy, there is no need for you to go. You might catch a cold. Let's let Dak take care of it," Eleanor replied, to Dak's great relief.

Dak pulled his bicycle up on Miss Mattie's long porch, shook the rainwater off his coat, and shivered a little as he knocked on the heavily weathered door. He could see through the dirty glass that she was moving toward the door carrying a miniature kerosene lamp. While electricity was available to Miss Mattie, she usually used kerosene lamps because she was accustomed to them and thought they were cheaper.

"Good morning, Dakkie," she gushed as she put her hand on his cheek. "I'm so glad to see you. It's so nice of you to get out in all this weather to come see me. I was just thinkin' you might come by this mornin'. Come in and sit over here next to the stove."

Dak walked in and awkwardly gave her a hug. She seemed so tiny and fragile. He could smell onions, pepper, and what?--maybe it was beef--all of which overpowered the kerosene odor from the lamp. He inquired about how she had been and whether she needed anything from the store. It turned out that Mrs. Tolbert from the Ladies' Church Aid had brought her a piece of beef and some bacon, so she was doing fine and needed nothing from the store.

Pleased that he wasn't going to have to battle the wind and rain all the way to the store, Dak decided this was the time to discuss the great find with her. "Miss Mattie," he began, "If I tell you somethin' secret, would you not tell anybody?"

Miss Mattie had a puzzled look. She was wondering if something was wrong, but she said, "Why, sure, Dak. What is it?"

Dak enthusiastically explained what he and J.D. had discovered on the Uppers. He then repeated the story in different words to make sure Miss Mattie understood. She sat expressionless, like her mind had escaped the current time and place, until he asked her if she had any idea what it could be. Then, she took on her puzzled look again.

"Why, I don't know, Dak," she began. Thoughtfully looking down at a smear on her apron as though that might give her some inspiration, she said, "I suppose it could be something the river pirates buried back in the early days. They stole a lot of stuff from flatboats going downstream, and it was rumored they buried some for safekeepin' at times. But they were mostly down at Cave-in-Rock or at Ford's crossing, though. I doubt it was them." Dak was relieved that her mind hadn't really wandered too far.

Mattie thought a little more but was distracted as the stew she had cooking began making a bubbling noise. She went to move it off the hottest part of the cook stove and returned with another idea. "There were some guerillas they used to talk about.

Did some raids from over in Kentucky in the War Between the States. You know, they weren't a part of either of the armies. They just raided and hurt people and stole what they wanted. Some of them came across the river here, and there was a fight, so they used to say." She seemed to lose her train of thought. Dak decided to just be quiet and let her get through it.

After what seemed a long time to Dak, she continued. "Course, I was just a little girl, so I don't remember it myself, but my daddy talked about a skirmish up above town after some of the guerillas burned some barns and stole some horses. I remember he said they killed an ol' man named Jenkins and used his blood to write somethin' about killin' Lincoln on the side of a house. Maybe they were rebels or sympathized with them. They needn't shoot up this town though because there were lots of folks here that liked the rebels. Anyway, my daddy said he was part of a posse that shot some of them guerillas and just put them in a pine box and buried them in the ground up the river apiece. I don't know just where. He said some townspeople came up to see the dead bodies before they were buried."

"Miss Mattie, do you think that what we found could be them dead guerillas?" asked Dak. "I mean if it turns out that our find is really a coffin."

"Well, it's possible," she said as she looked out the window at the pouring rain. "I just don't know. Then there's also another thing. You know, there were some freed slaves that were captured here, and some folks had big fights about that. I know Aunt Mariah used to talk about them. I don't remember just what it was about, but they had trouble lots of times. Some was down on the river and maybe on riverboats. Course, Aunt Mariah, she lived out on Hickory Hill for a few years, so she knew all about that stuff. I wish she was still with us, so you could ask her. And I'd really like to see her anyway," she said sadly.

"Well, let me ask you this, Miss Mattie, did you ever read all that stuff your Aunt Mariah wrote that you loaned to me?" asked Dak. As soon as he had said it, he realized he should have kept his mouth shut. He had told J.D. that he thought Mattie couldn't read, and yet, momentarily forgetting about that, he blurted this out. He really respected the old lady and liked her too. The last thing he wanted to do was embarrass her.

"Oh, no, I haven't read it," she said quietly. "I guess I never told you, Dak, but I never learned to read any more than my name and a few words. I always wondered what Aunt Mariah's papers said, but I was too embarrassed to ask anybody to read to me. Of course, I wasn't sure what it said that Aunt Mariah might not want to get out. That's why I loaned it to you after all this time, because I know I can trust you to do the right thing with anything that's in it."

Dak felt simultaneously awful that he brought it up and proud that Miss Mattie trusted him so much. "Well, Miss Mattie," he said with great respect, "you don't need to be embarrassed about that. You did right about it. And if you let me keep those papers some longer, I'll keep readin' them, and if I find anything you'd want to know, I'll tell you, okay?" he asked.

"Why, yes, you keep them as long as you need. But don't lose them or let anything happen to them," she said. "There is another thing I've been meanin' to mention to you. I should have told you this before you read any of Aunt Mariah's papers. I know that your daddy, Paul, died in the Pacific in World War II and that your granddaddy, D. P., died back around 1930 before you were born, so you maybe never heard much about your great granddaddy. But he was..." she trailed off.

"He was what?" Dak asked.

"Well, Dakkie," she was choosing her words carefully. "You know I'd rather do anything than hurt your feelings. But I know how interested you are in ol' times, and so I know you'd want to know about him. When I was a girl, your great granddaddy was a pretty big man around this town."

"Is that right?" Dak said.

"Yes," she continued. "He was the largest land owner around, and he had this big home in the country and another one in town. He was pretty tough. Not too many said anything bad about him if he could hear it. He was a handsome man. He looked a lot like you, dark and tall with piercin' blue eyes, and always dressed real nice. Nobody was better on horses, and he had a beautiful white horse named Savannah. He cut a pretty figure when he rode into town." She moved her right hand through the air as though she were stroking the horse. "He was also supposed to be a sharpshooter, but he never joined with the Union Army. Some people said it was because he paid not to. They said he was a rebel sympathizer, and I know Aunt Mariah said he sometimes showed up at Hickory Hill. Maybe it was just to pick up some salt. I don't know. So, well, I didn't want you to be surprised or anything if you find some mention of him in Aunt Mariah's papers."

"Thanks, Miss Mattie, for tellin' me that," said Dak. "I've heard some of that before. I understand he maybe cut some corners. But that doesn't bother me too much. Just because I have the same name as my dad and my grandpa and my great grandpa doesn't mean I'm the same as them. We're all different."

As Dak stepped back out onto the porch, the rain on the tin roof was like the roll of a thousand little drums. "Sure you don't need anything?" he yelled above the noise.

I'm okay," she said. He couldn't hear, but knew what she said. As he was leaving, she pointed proudly to the firewood she had stacked on her porch for the winter.

• • •

By the following Monday, the rains had become intermittent, and it had gotten colder. Dak was again riding home with Johnnie David and was anxious to explain all he had learned from Miss Mattie. When he jumped into the car, Johnnie already had the radio on, and Doris Day was singing *Que Sera, Sera*.

"Hey," J.D. said as he lowered the volume. "I've got to tell you about me and Marie." Dak was a little frustrated because that wasn't what he was going to talk about, but on the other hand, he really wanted to hear how it had gone with Marie.

"Oh, yeah, did you take her out Friday?" Dak replied. "Tell me about it!"

J.D. decided to play it a little coy. "Well, I don't know whether you deserve to know or not. What've you done for me lately?"

"Well, okay, if you'd rather talk about ol' Miss Mattie than Marie, fine with me. Matter of fact..."

"Okay, you win. So last Friday, my Dad let me use the car, and Marie agreed to go see a show with me, so I was all fixed. There was some gas in the car, and I had a couple dollars that my aunt gave me for my birthday. So, I go by and pick up Marie at her house, see, and man, did she look fine. I was a little nervous, but her dad was real nice. He just said, 'Don't drive too fast, Johnnie,' and I said I wouldn't, and I didn't--well, depends on what's too fast--but anyway, we went to the show, and they had *The Searchers* playin'."

"Oh, I'd like to see that," Dak interrupted. "John Wayne and Natalie Wood are in it. Donny said it's a great story."

"Well, I guess I didn't get too much out of it because we sat in the back. I put my arm around her, and I was tryin' to whisper things in her ear and all. She got all interested in the show and started sayin' how she liked Vera Miles and how pretty the scenery was and everything. Then she wanted some popcorn, so I had to go get that. Before long, the show was over."

"Yeah, the show was, but the evenin' wasn't," said Dak, anticipating what was coming next.

"Well, I drove down by the lower levee... you know, where that little road goes over to the ice house...and we parked there for a little while. The moon was bright, and I was tryin' to think up some scary story to tell her so she would scoot over real close to me, but I couldn't think of one."

"You couldn't think of a single scary story?" Dak asked.

"No, I guess I was a little flustered. Anyway, after we talked for a few minutes, I kissed her a couple times. Man, can she kiss. And then we kissed some more, but before long, she said she was a little hungry and could we go up to Ann's Cafe. God, I hated to leave, but she was sort of insistent. So I took her there, and we had a hamburger and a shake. Then she had to go home.

Course, when we got to her house, I kissed her again, and I really made this one count! So that was it. But she's really fine. I'm takin' her out again whenever I can."

"Hey, man," Dak said happily, "I'm proud of you. You did real fine. Just wait till next time!"

"Yeah," J.D. said, somehow relieved that Dak hadn't made fun of his efforts, but realizing at the same time that Dak almost always gave encouragement, not criticism. "Yeah," he said again, "Just wait till next time!"

Dak finally had the chance to tell Johnnie David all about the conversation with Miss Mattie. He included every detail about the river pirates, the guerillas, and the skirmishes over the captured slaves.

J.D. listened carefully and speculated about all the possibilities. His favorite idea was still buried loot from the river pirates.

"I don't know when we'll ever be able to get up there and do some diggin'," Dak said. "The river has really been comin' up. It's way past the level of our find. I sure hope it doesn't wash away in the high water."

"Probably not," J.D. murmured, although that thought had not crossed his mind until that minute.

• • •

Dak had gotten very serious about the yearbook and was staying after school two days every week. Miss Hurd, sensing that Dak was embarrassed about not having a ride home when he stayed to work on the yearbook, had mentioned that she would be driving that way often to visit a friend and that she could give him a ride each time. In fact, there was no such friend, but it worked for Dak, and Miss Hurd was glad to do it.

Dak felt that the yearbook was all about the students, especially the seniors. He thought it should reflect the accomplishments and dreams of each in some way. His idea was that every student had some high points, some particular source of pride, or some very fond memory from high school. He called them their "finest moments" and was determined to reflect these in the yearbook. So he took the opportunity, whenever he could, to talk individually with each student and figure out what it was that should be in the year-book to make it meaningful. This wasn't really very hard for Dak because the class wasn't very large and he knew everyone well from their years together. Not only that, but Dak had this unusual fondness and empathy for almost everyone in the class. This gave him an extraordinary feel for their dreams and aspirations.

"If you were to lose every memory from high school but one," he had said to Mary Webster, "what would it be?"

"Oh, Dak, you ask the most ridiculous questions," Mary had responded. But when pressed, she finally said, "I guess it would be that standing ovation I got in the middle of the play after I did that trumpet solo." She blushed a little as she said it.

"Yeah, that's it! That was really something. You were great." He wanted her to look back thirty years later and see this picture show-ing her, for one brief shining moment, as the center of everything, her light blond hair sparkling under the spotlight, her face so full of expression, her silver trumpet bowing to her mastery, the crowd all standing and clapping. Except for that one picture in the yearbook, no one but Mary would remember that moment thirty years later, but with the picture, no one could forget. It was her crowning glory and it would be in a prominent place in the yearbook.

"Miss Hurd, I think we need to highlight this picture of Danny Slager makin' the big free throw. Where can we put it? He only played a few minutes all year, but he made the winnin' point in the biggest game of all," Dak said. Miss Hurd at first re-sisted Dak's efforts, thinking them excessive, but eventually she understood what he was doing and became a convert.

At their Thursday after-school session, Miss Hurd and Dak had made good progress with their layouts. When they had fin-ished for the day and were putting the pages in the storage cabinet, Miss Hurd put her hand on Dak's arm and said there was something she had been meaning to tell him.

"Nothing bad, I hope," Dak replied.

"Well, not bad, no...it shouldn't affect you at all." Miss Hurd had a sad look about her. "I'm going to be leaving the High School next year," she said quietly.

"Leaving? Why?" Dak was astonished. "Miss Hurd, you *are* this high school. How can you leave? Why?"

"I really think I need a change. It's the..."

"But what could you do that would be better than this?" Dak couldn't imagine.

"Dak, I'm thirty-eight years old, and I've taught at four schools so far. And, well, after all these years seeing the kids come in as excited freshmen, all giddy and silly and full of non-sense, and then develop over the four years into these more serious and caring and thoughtful seniors who look back over their four years like it was a lifetime... like it was the most impor-tant thing that would ever happen to them...and then to watch them leave to go out into the world so full of vigor and enthusi-asm and wonder at what the world has to offer ...well, it's so moving."

"I hadn't thought of it that way."

"At the end of the year, though, they are all out trying to live their dreams. They are trying to live their dreams, but I'm start-ing all over again with a new class of freshmen. The sparkling faces from last year, the best and the brightest we've produced after four years, well, they are all gone. Graduation for the sen-iors is a great celebration for them, and I'm so happy for them. But for me, it's not the start of something. It's the end of some-thing. You always think, well, we'll stay in contact. But, Dak, that's not the way it works. They are gone. They are gone for good. They are gone off to college, off to the Air Force, off to De-troit or Seattle or somewhere to take a job some uncle in some remote corner of the country has found for them. But they are gone. And I am, in some sense, all alone as I go into another bor-ing summer and just wait for the new school year to start."

Dak noticed a tear trickling down her cheek and then felt a sadness creeping into his own thoughts. He first wondered how she could be sad about such a happy event as graduation, but then he understood. Miss Hurd's life was her students, especially her senior students. She felt a part of them. She had helped make them what they were. She tried so hard to give them a full appreciation of the best that literature and history had to offer. She tried to make each one into a better person, one who would go out into the world to a fuller life. But when they left, she felt suddenly lost and lonely. She had no other close friends. And, so it was that every spring, a little of her died.

"Miss Hurd, I think I understand," Dak finally said. He instinctively turned toward her and hugged her tightly, putting her head up against his shoulder. She had never needed a hug so badly nor felt so consoled and comforted by anyone. She loved the feel of his body against hers, and she just wanted this hug to continue forever. It was somehow the fulfillment of longings she had held since she first started teaching. She hoped that Dak didn't see the tears in her eyes. She thought to herself that Dak is always looking for everyone's finest moment. Well, this was hers. What could be finer than to be hugging one of her best students, right at the peak of his high school development? What could better exemplify what her heart was all about? Finally, she thought how inappropriate it would look to others that she was standing there in a classroom hugging one of her students. But, even then, she didn't want to let him go. If someone saw them, she knew they would never understand that it was actually the most appropriate thing that had happened to her in many years. And now, she didn't care what they thought.

"Thanks for understanding, Dak," she said as he slowly pulled away from her. "And please don't tell the other students that I'll be leaving yet. I'll tell the class when the time is right."

"Sure thing," Dak said. He started out the door, but then he turned and looked back at her. "Miss Hurd, could I ask you a question kinda...uh, confidentially?"

"I suppose," she replied, hoping he wasn't going to ask anything about school business that she shouldn't share.

"It's about the term-paper titles," he said. "Do you know of any reason why anyone would want me to change mine? You have them posted in the room and so everyone knows what everybody else is researchin' for their paper. I've gotten two threatenin' notes saying I should change my subject."

"Threatening notes?" Miss Hurd said. "Goodness! Why, I have no idea why anyone would care. Maybe I should get Mr. Jordan involved in this."

"No, please don't do that," Dak said. "I noticed some other people have changed their titles. Was that at your request?"

"No," she replied. "Well, I asked J.D. to change his because I thought he had picked inappropriate subjects, but the others just changed their minds about their subject matter."

"Okay," Dak replied. "Thanks for the help on that and please don't tell anyone about it." He turned and walked out the door.

• • •

When Dak arrived home, Nancy ran out the door to meet him. She was carrying a small white kitten. "Dak, Dak, look at my new kitty! Ain't she the sweetest thing? Mr. Barton's cat had a litter, and he asked Mom if I would like this one. I'm callin' her Mamie, you know, after the first lady. Look how she runs!"

"Oh, wow," Dak responded as they walked in the door to the house. "She's pretty cute! I hope she gets along with Alexander the Great." He reached down to pet the kitten, but it ran effortlessly across the room, sliding on the linoleum floor as it tried to come to a stop.

"Johnnie David is in the other room waiting to see you," Nancy announced and, holding her kitten, stayed not more than two steps behind Dak.

"J.D., you're even uglier than last time I saw you," Dak said playfully. "How's the water level over the levee today?"

"Not good. It's still gettin' higher. Would you believe the gauge reads a little over 49 feet? It's about three-fourths the way up the levee. Must be washin' out a lot upstream, it's so muddy. And, man, is it movin'."

Dak seemed a little surprised. "It just keeps comin' up even though the rain has stopped," he said. "Guess that's because it's still rainin' in Cincinnati."

"Well, anyway, we ain't going to be diggin' in that loot for awhile, looks like," said J.D. "But I do have some good news. Marie is goin' to the ball game with me Friday night."

"Way to go, J.D. Maybe you're not as hopeless as I thought. Are you gettin' your dad's car?"

"Yeah, I had to bargain my life away to get it. Soon as there is a nice warm day, I have to paint the porch. I'll be workin' off all my promises for a year, but I got it!" replied J.D.

"J.D., I take that back about you bein' ugly and hopeless. You could actually be a movie star as far as I'm concerned. So, what say I ask Melodie Lerner and we tag along to the ball game? We'd be in the back seat, and you could pretend to be our chauffer while we make out." Dak knew J.D. would never turn him down.

"What's in it for me?" J.D. responded with a nonchalant look.

"Well, maybe I could give you some free ideas on how to improve your makin'-out skills. Marie tells me you are a little deficient in that area. After a few short lessons, the babes will be beggin' you for a date even if you were ugly...which you ain't, because I need to ride with you."

"Hey, I've got to go," J.D. said. "I just came to tell you the good news. I thought maybe you'd want to hitch a ride."

"How about you pick up me and Melodie at her house at six on Friday? I'll ride my bike over there, and you won't have to make like a bus." Dak was a little afraid J.D. would pick up Melodie first and he wouldn't be able to make an appearance to her parents.

"Que será," said J.D. He had been using that phrase to mean the same as "okay" lately. Dak wasn't sure that was legit, but he got the point.

A little later, as they were eating dinner, Nancy took a big drink of milk and with a full white mustache, said, "Dak, what loot was J.D. talkin' about while ago?"

"Loot?" Dak asked and tried to think what exactly it was that J.D. had said. He hoped J.D. hadn't talked too much about it in front of Nancy because if she knew, it wouldn't take two hours for every 12-year old in town to know about it.

"I hope you boys didn't rob a bank or something," Eleanor joined in.

"Uh, yeah, that's it. It's the bank we robbed. If you see ol' man Savoy runnin' around here, just tell him I left town with the money." Dak appreciated the opportunity his mother had given him for a diversion, and he promptly changed the subject. Nancy knew she had been outmaneuvered but couldn't think of any way to get the truth, so she dropped it.

"Speaking of Mr. Savoy," Eleanor said, "did you know that his first wife and I were good friends?" It was her attempt to get good conversation going at the dinner table.

"No, can't say as I did." Dak yawned.

"Well, she was French. He took a vacation to France back in the thirties and met her there. She later visited here, and eventually they were married. She was a very nice lady, very refined, and she was so pretty with her very long, slightly reddish hair. Her name was Josephine Ingres, and Dak, you would be interested in this part. She was a descendant of Lafayette on one side and of the famous French painter Jean-Auguste Ingres on the other."

The name Lafayette did arouse Dak's interest. "Do you think she really was a descendant of those people, or was she just pullin' your leg?"

"Oh, I think she was," Eleanor replied. "She had family heirlooms from both sides. She was really proud of that. She had this big ceremonial gold sword that had been presented to Lafayette by Washington or somebody...and she had a painting which she said had been done by Ingres. She showed them to me on more than one occasion."

"Really?" Dak said doubtfully. "What painting?"

"Well, it was called Baronne de Rothschild, I think. It was an exquisite painting of a distinguished lady in a beautiful pink satiny gown. It was a large thing, maybe three feet by five feet and, of course, seemed out of place in their modest home."

"So was she Judy Savoy's mother?"

"No, Dak, they didn't get along well. I don't know what the problem was. She eventually returned to France. He later married Judy's mother, Harriet."

Dak thought about that for a few seconds. "You ever write her or anything? I mean if she was a good friend."

"Yes, I wrote her. She and I had planned to make a quilt together, but she left town very abruptly. She didn't even come by to say goodbye. I was so surprised. I asked Mr. Savoy for her address later, and he gave it to me. I wrote, but she never answered. I really shouldn't say this, but it made me wonder if he intentionally gave me the wrong address. I always had the feeling that he didn't like me befriending Josephine. Actually, he didn't seem to like anyone befriending Josephine."

• • •

On Friday afternoon, Nancy had taken her new kitten to her friend's house. Dak was taking a bath in the tub out in the laundry shed, getting ready for his big date. He ran from the shed to the house with only a big towel around him and selected a nearly new blue-plaid flannel shirt and his only pair of khakis to wear for the evening. As he put his clothes on, he noticed that he had left his belt in the laundry shed with his dirty clothes and ran back out to get it. When he emerged from the shed, he heard a screaming noise.

"Help, somebody help! Help!" The sound seemed to be coming from Nancy's friend's house near the levee. It was a child's voice, but did not sound like Nancy. At first, he thought it was just some kids playing, but then he heard it again, and it sounded real to him. Dak quickly jumped on his bicycle and sped to the levee, where he came to a sliding stop not far from the screaming little girl. It was Nancy's friend Linda, crying uncontrollably. "It's Nancy," she yelled, running up the levee. Dak quickly ran ahead of her to the top of the levee, and there he could see it all. It was Nancy out on a limb, over the swirling brown floodwater, trying to reach the kitten which was even further out on the limb. Dak ran to the base of the tree to assess the situation.

"Nancy, don't go any further. It's going to be okay," he said firmly, trying to remain calm. "Are you hurt?"

"No, Dak, I just scratched my leg. I need to get Mamie! Why is Linda crying?"

"Nancy, now Nancy, listen to me," Dak yelled and then realized he was sounding excited. He had to calm it down. "Nancy, we'll get Mamie, but first we've got to get you back on the ground. Just be very still for a minute, okay?" He quickly inspected the limb. He could see that it was a dead branch of a live elm tree. The tree's trunk was just at the edge of the water. The limb was nearly horizontal, which explained how Nancy had gotten out so far. She had just laid face down on the limb and then pulled herself forward with her arms.

Dak's mind was whirling. He could see that she was about twenty feet out over the swirling water. Given the slope of the levee, the water would be maybe twelve feet deep if she fell off. The dead limb had lost its bark and didn't look very strong. He felt sure it would not hold his weight if he were to climb out to rescue her.

"Linda, honey," he said, trying to calm Nancy's friend. "Please go get someone to come help. Tell them to bring a rope. Go on, now! Hurry! Tell them Dak needs help!" The little girl, still crying, disappeared over the levee.

He considered going himself to get help, maybe a ladder with a couple people to hold it or a boat. Then he decided he had to stay so that if the limb were to break, he could attempt to save her. Nancy, unafraid, began moving further out the limb toward the kitten.

"Stop, Nancy! Nancy, please stop!" He could see the limb bending downward a bit. "Do not move any further out the limb. It could break!" He had not wanted to scare her with that message, but felt he must say it to stop her from going further.

"Nancy, listen to me." He decided he had to risk trying to get her to move back toward the tree's trunk. "I want you to move very slowly, back up toward me. Don't try to turn around and don't make any quick motions, but..." At this point, he heard a slight cracking noise, and the limb dipped a little below horizontal. Dak's hands were shaking. He was desperately trying to think of a solution to this seemingly unsolvable problem.

"Nancy, I need you to scoot back on the limb toward me...real slow like. Don't make any sudden motions. Don't jump around! Don't try to turn your body around. Leave your head on the outer end of the limb and your feet toward me. Come on now, start scootin' back toward me. Move very gently!" Dak's hands were shaking even more now. He began thinking how to handle the situation if the limb were to break completely. He knew the current was strong, and the water was icy cold and muddy.

Nancy finally scooted her body back toward Dak, but only a few inches. "That's it, be very gentle," Dak encouraged her. He heard another little cracking noise in the limb followed by a slightly louder one. A pain went through his chest like the one he had experienced when Donny Branch had told him about Jerry Miller being accidentally shot.

"This can't be happenin'," he thought to himself, as his mind raced through other actions he could take. But what he said was, "Come on back, very gently. That's it."

It was not clear what triggered it, but Nancy suddenly seemed to understand the gravity of her situation. "Dak, I might fall in the water! Dak!" she screamed. He could see the fear in her face as she began sobbing. "I'm scared, Dak! Help me! Help me, Dak! Oh, Dak, I might fall! Help me!" She was near total panic.

Dak tried to soothe her, to calm her. "No, no, Nancy, it will be okay. Nancy, try not to cry. Try to be calm. Keep movin' real gentle like, back toward me. Come on, keep movin.' Keep movin' very slow like. Nancy, I need you to stay calm and keep movin'. Keep it slow and easy."

Nancy had moved maybe eight or ten inches back on the limb, when Mamie decided to head for higher ground. The kitten jumped for another limb playfully and climbed further up the tree.

Why hadn't Linda returned with help? It seemed forever to Dak since she had left. "Come on back," he said to Nancy.

She made an awkward move, and then he heard a loud pop. He knew the worst had happened. The limb had made a clean

break, and as Dak watched in agonizingly slow motion, it came
down with a splash into the swirling water, Nancy and all.

Dak dove into the water and swam as fast as he could to the
limb, which was drifting rapidly downstream with the current.
He could see that Nancy was holding onto the limb, but he did-
n't think she could hold on long in the shockingly cold water. He
grabbed the limb, but as it was too small to serve as a floatation
device for both of them, he held with one hand and swam with
his other hand and legs. He yelled for help, but no one seemed to
hear him. He yelled again. The water was so cold on his body
that he began shaking violently. He tried to ignore that and concentrate on the job he had to do.

"Nancy, hold onto the limb!" he screamed. As if in a trance,
she said nothing, but seemed to be holding on tightly. Her lips
were purple, her face white. He knew that if they drifted into the
center of the river, their chances were very slim. The current was
swifter than Dak had supposed. He yelled for help again and
then screamed as loud as he could to try to attract some attention. He wondered whether they could really make it. He began
to feel sorry for Nancy and himself as his tears mixed with the
muddy water. He was beginning to feel numb.

Then, he could see that they were going to pass under a low-
hanging willow limb. He knew he had to try to grab it and stop
their rapid movement further out into the river. He positioned
himself in the water in front of Nancy so that if he could grasp
the willow limb with one hand, he could grab Nancy with the
other. As they got closer, the limb looked higher than it had from
a distance. Still, he decided to try. He took a deep breath and
held it while he dove under and then jumped upward as high as
his body could possibly manage. He thought at first he would
get it, but his hand peaked just a couple inches below the limb.
As he came back down into the water, he went under again.
When he came up, he moved again to Nancy's limb, feeling
numb and hopeless. Tears were streaming down his face.

And then he saw it. It was ol' Sid Snyder in his fishing boat,
motoring directly toward them. He had never seen a more beau-

tiful sight. Although Sid was open throttle, it seemed to Dak it was taking forever for the boat to get closer. For the second time today, he felt he was watching events in slow motion. Actually, Sid came a little too fast and threw a large wave of water over both Dak and Nancy.

Dak moved forward along the floating limb to grab Nancy so he could help get her into the boat, but she released her grip on the limb before he had a firm grasp on her. She slipped from his icy hands and went under the brown swirling water.

Dak was determined to take any risk to try to save her. Since she had momentarily disappeared, he began using his legs to comb for her. He knew he was close to where she had gone under, but he could not see her. Quickly diving under the murky water, he still could see no trace of her. In fact, he could see nothing at all. "The water is too muddy," he murmured to himself. With his head out of the water now, he began visually scanning for any bubbles or other evidence of Nancy. Then, as if by some miracle, Nancy grabbed Dak's right leg. Though it pulled him under water for a moment, he was able to reposition himself so he could swim and hold Nancy. As their heads popped out of the water, Sid quickly moved the boat closer to them and extended an oar to Dak. Dak pulled close to the boat as Nancy coughed deeply.

It was more difficult than they thought to get Nancy up into the boat, but after several tries, they did it. Then, with a final burst of energy, Dak pulled his own body over the edge of the smallish boat as Sid leaned over the other side to keep it from capsizing.

"Oh, thank you so much, Sid. Thank you so much. God bless you, Sid. I thought we were goners. Oh, God, thank you so much, Sid!" Dak was almost incoherent, and the tears were still coming. "Man, you are the greatest! Oh, man, thank you Sid! Oh, God. I didn't think we were going to make it! Awwww, God, Sid, we would have died if you hadn't come! We were close! I don't know how to thank you, Sid."

Sid was a quiet man and hardly knew what to say. He just smiled and gave Dak an awkward pat on the back. "Glad I was here, Dak," Sid finally offered in a matter of fact tone of voice, but Dak could see by Sid's expression that he was very moved by the event.

Nancy was still coughing loudly, and Dak wrapped his arms around her to try to warm her a bit as they both shook uncontrollably. Sid removed his coat and placed it over Nancy's shoulders. Then, he moved the boat rapidly toward the levee. The breeze produced by the boat's speed was so cold that it took their breath away. When they reached the levee, several people who had gathered there offered their coats, which Dak and Nancy accepted immediately. Their teeth were chattering so hard that Dak worried it would break them, but he could not make them stop. Eleanor had heard what had happened and was running for the levee. She saw them about a minute before she reached them. As she hugged them both, she broke into sobs of relief.

When they reached their house, Eleanor quickly got dry clothes and blankets for them, sat them on the floor before the fireplace, added another log, and then sat with them. They didn't talk at all. They just sat and hugged for a long time. Finally, the shaking stopped, and they felt very tired. Then, Eleanor got up and made hot chocolate for them and with a wide smile, said, "Oh, thank God you are both okay! This is a wonderful day! You are both okay!"

At about 6:30 PM, Johnnie David stopped his car in front of Dak's house and told Marie that he would be back in just a minute. He ran in Dak's house and saw Dak and Nancy sitting on the floor in front of the fireplace, a blanket around them, their hair still wet.

"What's goin' on, Dak? Thought you were going to meet us at Melodie's. She ain't too happy with you. I'd say you didn't make any points with her dad, either."

"Oh, no!" replied Dak. "Awww, I forgot all about it!" He slapped his hand on his forehead.

"You're tellin' me you forgot our date we been plannin' all week? Dak, are you losin' your marbles?"

"I don't know Johnnie, I may be. I'm real sorry. I had a little problem in the river. But I'm sorry. Oh, man, what will Melodie think of me? What will her dad think of me?"

Johnnie David was clearly perplexed. "Are you goin' or not? It's late, and Marie's waitin' in the car."

"Not tonight, J.D. Hey, I'm real sorry, but I better stay here tonight. I'll tell you all about it when we have time. And I'll explain it all to Melodie." Dak was warm now and didn't feel physically sick, but his mind was a whirlwind of questions mixed with reruns of the events in the water. What could he have done to get her off that elm limb? After she was in the water, what could he have done to get her back to the levee quicker? How could he have jumped high enough to grab that willow? What would he have done if they had been pulled by the current into the center of the broad river? Why did he almost lose Nancy after Sid arrived? Why had he cried so much? He felt confused and inadequate. Besides, he was exhausted.

J.D. seemed deeply frustrated that Dak would just sit there in front of the fireplace and refuse to go with them. "Well, it's your call," he said, and slammed the door behind him as he exited.

Chapter 5

Ellsworth Place

After spending some time with Nancy and Eleanor that Friday night, Dak went to bed early and slept for eleven hours.

When he woke up, he was sore, achy, and hungry. Eleanor waited until she heard his footsteps upstairs and then put neat disks of pancake batter on the hot buttered griddle that sat on the cook stove. "Here's our hero," she said as he walked in the sliding doors to the warm part of the house.

Nancy, who had gotten up an hour earlier, had a runny nose and a headache. Handkerchief in hand, she smiled sheepishly at Dak and said, "Sorry if I caused you a lot of trouble, Dakkie. It's just, I had to save Mamie." She tended to call him Dakkie when she felt she owed him something or wanted to show appreciation. "Did you know that Linda's mom brought my kitty home last night after you went to bed?"

"She did? I'm glad you got her back, Nance-baby. She's a cool cat!"

Dak was neither proud nor ashamed of his performance in the river the day before. His feelings of confusion and inadequacy were gone. By now, he knew that he had done everything possible to save Nancy. Still, he wondered how silly he looked to Sid when he was crying. He felt a little embarrassed about that.

"Man, those pancakes look good! Give me about four." Dak knifed a big hunk of butter onto the hot pancakes and lavished maple syrup over the combination. Seven pieces of bacon and two eggs completed his meal. After breakfast, he took the table scraps out for Alexander the Great. Seeing no evidence of Alex in the yard, he called a few times. When Alex didn't appear, Dak concluded that he had started his rounds early this morning.

When Dak returned to the kitchen with the scraps, he explained that Alex was not in the yard.

"Well, that's unusual. He is almost always here for breakfast," Eleanor replied. "Maybe Alex found a female friend."

As soon as he could get himself cleaned up, Dak bicycled to Melodie's house, hoping to repair any damage done on that front. Melodie's mother answered the door and explained icily that Melodie was in the back yard trying to repair her roller skates. Dak walked around the house and could see from Melodie's expression that she was not a happy person. He didn't know whether he or the skates were the source of the problem. It didn't take long to find out.

"Hi, Melodie," he said, trying a cheerful approach. "How are you doing?"

"Well, it was a little boring around here last night when you didn't show up, Dakston," she said sharply. "I was a little...a little humiliated. How could you just not show up? Marie and J.D. waited for a while. Then Marie tried to console me...but, I was just..." She started crying. Dak walked over and started to hug her, but she pulled back.

"You could at least tell me why you didn't come!" she screamed.

"Okay," Dak said, trying again to embrace her. This time, she let him put his arms around her. "Melodie, it was an accident in the river. Nancy fell in, and I had to go in after her. I thought we were both goin' to die. Mom and Nancy were so upset, and I was freezin' to death. I should've come over after I got warm, but I didn't. I'm sorry." How could he explain to Melodie that the accident had so shaken him that nothing else seemed important at the time?

"Well, you could have let me know something happened," she snapped.

"Yes, I should have come over and explained it last night. I messed up. I'm sorry."

Dak was enjoying the feel of his body against hers and could sense that she was getting past the feelings of hostility. He loved the shine of her honey-colored hair and the fresh, clean scent of her body.

"And I can't get my skates to work," she blurted out. "I'm about ready to throw them away, but I was supposed to meet Marie up at the park to skate this afternoon."

Dak looked at the skate, struck it sharply on the big iron kettle that sat nearby, and slid the sticking piece to a different position. "There," he said. "There's nothin' wrong with your skate."

As Melodie was examining the skate, her father walked out the back door of the house. "Dak, I'd like a few words with you," he announced ominously.

Dak was thinking this was a little much, but what he said was, "Yes sir."

Walking out of Melodie's earshot, Mr. Lerner said, "Now, son, what happened here last night was unacceptable. Somebody said you fell in the river or something, but be that as it may, I don't want you treating Melodie that way any more. Were you drinking or something?"

"Oh, no sir, it was an accident involvin' my little sister, sir. She fell in the river. I had to go in to get her."

"Well, that's fine, Dak, but did that disable you or something? You couldn't make it over to say you had a problem? I don't think you did right by Melodie." He was adamant and seemed to be getting agitated.

"Well, sir, you have my apology, and I told Melodie how sorry I am," Dak offered. "I know I should have come over last night. I'm sorry I didn't. I guess that's all I can say. I'm very sorry."

"Apology accepted," said Mr. Lerner. "I told Melodie that she isn't to see you for a month. Then we'll take it from there."

"With all due respect, Sir," Dak said, "I intended no slight of Melodie. She is real special to me. I would never intentionally hurt her. I don't think it's fair to say we can't see each other."

"Well, that's my decision. I think you had better tell Melodie good-bye and be on your way."

Dak walked back over to Melodie and, explaining what her father had said, hugged her again and said good-bye."I'll be seein' you at school," he said. He tried to smile.

Feeling that he had blown the situation with Melodie and her dad and feeling bad because he wouldn't be able to date her for awhile, Dak decided he would go home and discuss the events with Eleanor. Then he would talk with J.D. When he reached home, J.D. was there, and Eleanor had explained in detail all that had happened on the river the day before.

J.D. got up when Dak walked in the door and said, "Dak, ol' boy, that was some feat yesterday, and if it weren't for you bein' so darned ugly, I'd say we ought to have your picture put in the paper. Hell, I...pardon me, Mrs. Leventhal...I think not many people would have pulled that off. If I didn't know you better, I'd think you were some kind of hero or somethin'."

Dak smiled lamely and said, "Thanks, J.D., but I'll be lucky just to have people speakin' to me. And, I'll have you know that line about ugly belongs to me. Man, I really blew it with Melodie and her dad."

"They will get past it before you know it," J.D. said.

"Dak, have you seen Alex yet?" Eleanor asked. "I'd like to get these scraps out of the house before we attract ants."

"No, I guess he's still out on his rounds," Dak replied.

• • •

On Tuesday, Miss Hurd was having an exam over the last six weeks in American History II. For Dak, this was fun. It was the chance to do something imaginative, provided the questions were not all of the true/false or multiple-choice variety. He much preferred essay questions that gave him a chance not only to demonstrate knowledge of the subject, but also to provide some original ideas and some speculation on the subject.

J.D., as usual, sat right behind Dak. Even though J.D. borrowed Dak's notes after each class and copied some of them into his own notebook, he still found it beneficial to have a clear line of sight to Dak's notes and exam papers while class was underway. He would position his desk and his body accordingly, especially for important tests. This was fine with Dak, whose philosophy was that it's what you learn that counts, not what grade you are given. If J.D. could get some information looking at his papers, then J.D. was probably learning something in the process. J.D.'s philosophy was a little different. It was that if he could make a better grade by looking at Dak's papers, well, that was good, and what harm was done?

Dak at first wondered whether Miss Hurd knew that J.D. was doing this, because it was a clear violation of her instructions to the class. Eventually, Dak was sure she knew, yet she never said anything. He wondered what that meant. Did she just feel it didn't matter? Did she let it go on as a personal favor to Dak and J.D.? At any rate, J.D. usually did pretty well on the tests, and this one was no exception. Dak made a habit of sliding his completed papers to the left side of his desktop to make them more visible to J.D. while he continued to work on the ones on the right.

Miss Hurd had a tendency to walk around the room during exams. In the few seconds after she passed Dak's desk and before she turned around at the end of the aisle, J.D. found he could get answers to four or five multiple-choice questions. He tended to get the true/false and multiple-choice questions almost all correct. Copying from Dak on essay questions was much more difficult, and so he was more on his own for those. Dak's frequent discussions with J.D. outside of class helped this situation. J.D., knowing he would do poorly on one of the essay questions, decided a humorous approach was best. He wrote, "You'd have to check with Dak to get the real skinny on that!" Miss Hurd was not amused. She gave him a zero on that question and a written comment, "A serious student doesn't make remarks like this on an important test." The most interesting part of all this to Miss Hurd was that J.D. was actually a bright person and could certainly have done well on his own if he had been interested and willing to study. Unfortunately, neither of these conditions was met.

In addition to the exam, it was one of the days when Dak had to stay and work on the yearbook after school. He had come up with some great ideas for recognizing the contributions of some of the students who didn't normally get much attention. He reviewed these with Miss Hurd, and she bought them without reservation. She had gained such confidence in his work that she hardly questioned him anymore. Today he did a great layout on how Jimmy Richards, a student primarily interested in agriculture, had saved a lamb that was on the verge of death. Jimmy had done this after the veterinarian gave up on the sick animal.

When they were finished with the layouts for the day, Dak mentioned to Miss Hurd that his mother and sister would not be home until later this evening. They were going to a mother-daughter banquet that the Four H Club was holding.

"Why don't you come to my house for dinner?" asked Miss Hurd. "It won't be much, but I've got chicken vegetable soup that I cooked last night. I'll warm it up. It was actually pretty good."

Dak was not sure of the propriety of this, but Miss Hurd said it would give them a chance to discuss some other ideas she had for the yearbook. He could think of no reason not to, and, besides that, the soup sounded tasty.

When they entered her small house, she said, "Make yourself comfortable, Dak. I'll wash up a little and put the soup on the stove."

While she did that, Dak looked around the room at pictures on a table and on the wall. He didn't recognize anyone in any of the pictures. Before long, she reappeared looking fresh and cheerful.

"Dak, I think the yearbook should have a page somewhere giving recognition to the editor," she said. "It could explain what you tried to do, how you worked to show every person's finest moment. And we could have something showing your finest moment. What would be your finest moment, Dak?"

"Oh, no," said Dak. "We couldn't do that. It would seem so...so self-servin'. No, I couldn't face everyone if I did that. I'm the one who has to get the least coverage. It would be like a politician counting the votes."

"Aww, Dak, there you have vetoed my best idea!" she responded.

The room fell silent for a few seconds. Then Dak asked, "Miss Hurd, do you still plan to leave at the end of the year?"

"I'm afraid so, Dak. It just has to be that way. I don't know exactly what I'll do. I may go back to Moline where my relatives are and work in the family business. I have to leave Shawneetown. I have to get out of the cycle of getting close to people and then seeing them all go away. I just can't take it emotionally," she said.

"Yeah, I understand. It's just that..."

"It's just that what, Dak? That I could continue to be a good teacher for many years until they put me out to pasture? Don't you see that the better the quality of the education I give the students, the more I lose when they leave? It is just that much more painful when they go away at the end of their senior year." She was getting teary.

Dak thought he should change the subject, but he wanted to try one more thing first. "Miss Hurd, the students love you, and they'll think of you all their lives whether you ever see them again or not. You have had your influence on all of them. They will never forget you. And the thing is that this town needs you."

To Dak's astonishment, she broke down into sobs. *Oh gosh,* he thought to himself. *What have I done now? How will I get out of this?*

He gently scooted over on the sofa and put his arm around her to console her. It was what came naturally. Then, Miss Hurd surprised Dak again by putting her arms around him and burying the side of her face in his flannel shirt. She was squeezing him with an intensity that made Dak a little uncomfortable. At this point, he became a bit worried but thought to himself, *What's the harm...if this makes her feel better, what's the harm?*

This went on for some time, with Dak lightly patting her on the back to comfort her. She seemed to Dak to be deeply depressed. Finally, he said, "It sounds like the soup is hot in the kitchen. Think we should see about it?" As he said it, he slowly separated from her.

"Oh, okay," she said. "You'll pardon me for getting too emotional."

"Of course, think nothin' of it," he said. "Wow, does that soup smell good."

During dinner, Dak was careful to stay on upbeat subjects and as soon as they were finished, he said, "Oh my, Miss Hurd,

I'd better be gettin' home. I've got some chores to do before Mom gets back."

Resigned, she held his hands and said, "Dak, we're going to have the greatest yearbook ever, and it's all due to you!" Then she drove him home.

When Dak stepped out of the car and said good-bye to Miss Hurd, he expected Alexander the Great to offer a welcoming ceremony complete with a dance on his back legs. Instead, Alex was not there at all. Dak was not too concerned because there were times when Alex was missing in action. One time, he was gone for three days before arriving home smelling like dead fish. It was not the absence so much as the threatening note that caused Dak to be a little worried.

• • •

The next morning, Alex was still missing. Dak was beginning to think the worst had happened, but kept telling himself that it was too early to be overly concerned. He tried to think about other things and was so busy during the school day that Alex only crossed his mind a couple times.

After school, it was a different matter. There was still no trace of Alex, so Dak jumped on his bicycle and rode around town looking for him. He asked several people if they had seen him. He even went to the Uppers and hiked around calling the dog's name. It was all to no avail. When he returned home, he told Eleanor he was afraid Alex was dead.

Eleanor put her arm around Dak's shoulder. "He will probably be around in a day or two," she said. Sometimes, dogs get caught up in a romantic relationship and are gone for a while."

"A while, yes," Dak said. "But it has been too long and nobody has seen him."

"Well, let's give it another day," she said. "I think he'll show up."

"We need to talk about the possibly of your going to college next year," she said in an all-too-transparent effort to get Dak's mind off Alex. She had had two years of college herself and had always hoped that Dak and Nancy could go. The problem was that with the death of Dak's dad many years ago, her budget was very modest and could not cover all the costs of college. In fact, she had to be careful just to make ends meet, even without college expenses.

"I looked into what all the college expenses are," said Dak. "It gets costly when you consider everything. Since Dad was killed in the war, I can get tuition and fees covered by the GI Bill, but there will be so many other costs. I might be able to get some cash scholarship. Also, Mr. Jordan says he'd suggest that I go to the bank and ask about college loan possibilities. He knows people from last year who got loans that way. They can be paid back after college when I get a job."

Eleanor looked very pleased. "I think it is a good plan, Dak. Why don't you go ahead and apply to the college for admission and apply for as many scholarships as are available?"

"Yeah, but that's not enough, Mom."

"I know, I know. You and I could go together to see Mr. Savoy at the bank to see what's possible in the way of a loan." Eleanor was beaming at the possibility Dak could go to college because she knew he could excel.

• • •

The next morning, Dak was so worried about Alex that he went into the back yard before breakfast to check on him. Finding no trace of him, Dak called his name and walked to the front yard. There was no response. He called several more times. Then as he opened the front gate, he noticed. There was Alex, in a heap, lying just outside the gate. When Alex didn't leap to his feet for a welcoming ceremony, Dak knew there was a problem. He kneeled to see if he could help, but realized immediately that Alex was dead. The body was already stiff.

Dak felt a deep sadness as he picked up his dog's body and carried it to the back yard. He sat the body down near the laundry-shed door where Alex had liked to sleep. Then he sat down on the ground next to the body and rubbed his hand through the fur. "He was such a happy dog," Dak said, though there was no one to hear him. "He was so pleasant and gave only joy to anyone who saw him. In his few years on earth, he brightened the lives of several people, especially me. Without Alex, things will be a little less cheerful in this town."

Eleanor stuck her head out the back door. "Dak, are you coming for breakfast?" she yelled. Then she saw him sitting next to Alex. "What's the matter?" she asked.

"Alex is gone," Dak said as his voice broke. "He's been killed." He moved his hand through the fur once more, then rose and went into the house.

Eleanor was astonished. "What happened to him?" she asked as she put her hand on Dak's shoulder.

"I'm not sure," replied Dak. "There is no sign of injury. I suppose he was poisoned. What kind of deranged monster would kill a joyful dog like Alex?" Dak ate only a piece of toast for breakfast and then buried Alex in the back yard. At school that day, all he could think about was Alex and who could have done this. After school, he made a wooden cross, wrote "Alexander the Great, 1949-1956" on it, and placed it in the ground above the body.

Dak sat looking at the cross and thought he could probably have saved Alex by changing his term-paper topic. *Why would anyone care that much?* he asked himself. *There must be something really dark in the history of Ellsworth Place. Well, they won't win this one. I will find out about it. I won't quit. I will never quit now. I will find out. I'll do it for you, Alex.*

• • •

A few days later, Dak and Eleanor visited Mr. Savoy at the bank. Eleanor had always thought him a strange looking man. Short of stature and heavy set, he was balding and had eyes that seemed somehow too far down on his face. He stood and motioned them into his office and listened to Dak's plan. After adjusting a gray tie that looked like body oil had soiled it years ago, he coughed, lowered his head so that he was looking at them over his glasses, and said, "Well, there probably will be no problem arranging such a loan. Why don't you come back when admission to the college has been granted and the scholarship won?" As they were preparing to leave, he mentioned that his daughter, Judy, had already applied and been accepted at the college. He chuckled as he added, "Of course, Judy won't be requiring a scholarship or a loan." Eleanor gave a perfunctory smile.

And then Mr. Savoy said something else: "Dak, you are a nice-looking boy and I hear you're pretty darn smart too. You'd be a good match for my Judy. This is your chance, too, because Judy was just telling me she doesn't have a date yet for the Junior-Senior Prom. You know, a lot of young people have good opportunities to make it in this world. They just don't make the right decisions. I have a feeling you're smart enough to understand what's in your own best interest. I think you'll do the right thing. Good luck, Dak, and come see me when you've got the other arrangements made. I'll do what I can for you."

"Thank you, Sir, and I will be back," Dak said as they were leaving. But as he reflected on Mr. Savoy's words, he wondered what exactly the message was. *Surely he wasn't saying my loan depends on whether I take Judy Savoy to the prom,* he thought to himself.

Dak kept rerunning the words through his mind. As soon as they were well out of earshot of Mr. Savoy, Dak asked Eleanor how she interpreted those comments. To Dak's surprise, she said, "Well, Dak, I don't think he was exactly saying your loan depends on it, but it was clear that he would look favorably upon your taking Judy to the prom. It sure wouldn't hurt your chances, and it is so important. And, of course, Melodie's dad won't even let you see her right now, so I'd say she isn't a good bet for the prom."

"Mom!" Dak was raising his voice. "This is a matter of principle. I will not take Judy to the prom under a threat. Judy is okay, a little obnoxious sometimes, but okay. But this is not about Judy. It's about principles. I will not be blackmailed into takin' her to the prom." Eleanor had only rarely seen Dak angry, but this was one of those times.

"It's okay, Dak," she said. "It's okay. We'll figure out something." Eleanor clearly thought that Mr. Savoy was posing a condition for granting the loan.

With that, Dak got very quiet and didn't bring the subject up again.

• • •

When Dak told J.D. about Alexander the Great, J.D. was very surprised.

"Oh, God, that's awful," he said. "Awww, I shouldn't have told you not to worry about the threats. I'm sorry, Dak. I couldn't imagine anybody would really kill ol' Alex."

"Oh, no, J.D., it's not your fault. The threats bothered me a little, but I kept thinkin' nothin' like that would happen. Nobody would be that screwed up. But they are. Somebody must be scared and worried about me diggin' into the ol' mansion's history. I think I have to change my term-paper topic now. If I don't, they may come after Nancy or somethin'. I can't take that chance. But I'll tell you this: I will find out what happened at Ellsworth Place. They won't stop me from that. I won't do it out in the open, but I will do it. Just don't tell anybody, J.D."

"You got it, Dak. I'll help if I can."

The next day at school, Dak changed his term-paper topic to *Slavery in Shawneetown*. He erased the old topic on Miss Hurd's board and wrote the new topic in large letters so no one would miss it.

• • •

In the springtime, the floodwaters recede in the Ohio River valley and let summer show its birth pangs. The water, still above summer stage but slowly and surely declining, sculpts the shape of the river to its summertime configuration. Eventually, it will expose the sandy beaches. The more daring of the children begin taking off their shoes to experience once again the pleasure of soft soil under bare feet. But it is really too early, too chilly.

For Dak and Johnnie David, it all meant that they could walk to the edge of the embankment on the Uppers, but when they looked down, they could not yet see their find. In fact, they couldn't even be sure whether it was still there under the remaining water, or it had washed away. They wondered if those dark gray planks that reappeared so often in their imagination might now be drifting somewhere down around Vicksburg or Natchez along the mighty Mississippi.

"Well, hell, are we ever going to get to dig up our gold?" J.D. asked loudly, trying to communicate with Dak without turning down the radio in the Ford. Elvis Presley was doing such a fine job that he just couldn't bring himself to restrain the volume.

> Now since my baby left me
> I've got no place to dwell,
> Down at the end of Lonely Street
> at Heartbreak Hotel.

"Johnnie David...here, let me turn this down a little...man, you've got to quit expectin' that we're going to find gold, because we're probably not. But the water is comin' down pretty good now. In a week or two, we can probably do some diggin.' Tell you what we could do now. We could go froggin'. The water is off the bar pits now, and I'm thinkin' we could get a sack full of bullfrogs." Dak not only loved to eat frog legs, but he also enjoyed the sport and adventure involved in frog hunting at the snake-ridden bar pits.

The bar pits had originated with one of Roosevelt's WPA projects conducted back in the early 1930's. The objective was to raise and strengthen the levee around the town and make it safe from any future flooding. A lot of soil was needed for the project. The approach taken was to excavate several large holes of various shapes and depths, all in one area, and let them accumulate water. In a few years, these holes became large ponds and came alive with a great variety of plant and animal species that like stagnant water. In particular, the turtles, frogs and snakes were numerous, and long strands of dark green mosses thrived along with the willows.

"Hey, man, that's a good idea!" replied J.D. "Let's do that Friday night. Oh, and if it's okay with you, I'll ask Donny Branch to go with us. He was sayin' the other day he'd like to go froggin' sometime."

"Sure thing," replied Dak.

• • •

On Friday night, Donny Branch showed up at Dak's place, ready for high adventure. He said he had gone by J.D.'s place, only to learn that J.D. would not be going frogging as planned. J.D. had suggested that Dak and Donny go ahead by themselves.

"Okay," Dak replied. "Let's see, do we have everything? Looks like you have a good flashlight. I have this carbide light and the gig. This ol' grass sack ought to hold whatever we catch, and right here I have some apples and cookies my mom sacked up for us." Both boys were wearing long sleeved shirts to protect them from mosquitoes and hip boots to prevent snakebites. Rain was forecast for later in the evening, but the boys thought they could get a big batch of frogs before the wet stuff came.

Arriving at the pits, they observed that the water level was higher than in the summer as a result of the area being flooded just a couple weeks earlier. Donny thought that would make it easier to gig the frogs because they would be closer to the paths, not so far down the slopes into the pits. It turned out that there weren't many mosquitoes.

As darkness fell across the pits, a whole new world of sounds began. A chorus of insects of various kinds provided a backdrop for the deep, low-pitched croaks of the bullfrogs. Owls could be heard a little further away saying, "Whoo, whooo?" and various other night animals made sounds which neither Dak nor Donny recognized.

"Hey, it is really dark here tonight," Donny observed. "No moon. No anything. If our lights burn out, I don't know if we can even stay on the paths."

Dak wasn't worried. "Yeah, it's cloudy. That's why it's so dark. But this carbide lasts a long time."

"It's not very bright, though," Donny observed.

"Bright enough," Dak promised. "Bright enough to keep us out of the snake pits...uh, I mean the bar pits." It was obvious that both boys had snakes on their minds. For Dak, this added to the adventure, the thrill of it all.

About that time, a loud splash just to their right startled both boys.

"What the hell was that?" Donny cried.

"Just a big bullfrog jumpin' into the water because we're makin' too much noise. We're scarin' them before we even spot them."

After surveying the landscape with their lights, the boys spotted only a raccoon eating something that looked like a fish. They began focusing their lights as best they could on the line where the water met the muddy shore, because the frogs typically sat right at the edge, ready to jump at any hint of a threat. Donny got the six-foot long gig pole firmly in his grip so that he could thrust the three-pronged device into the back of a frog on a moment's notice.

"There's one now," whispered Dak, stopping his light on two shining eyes perched right at the edge of the water. "I'll keep the light on him real steady. You go around that willow tree and gig him from that side."

Donny moved very deliberately, being very careful not to step on a twig or to do anything else that might scare the frog. When he finally got into position, he made a quick motion of the gig just a half-second after the tricky frog jumped several splashes out into the water.

"Crap," Donny said. "Crap, crap, crap! That was frogus gigantus, too."

"No problem, we'll get the next one. Maybe I didn't have him blinded well enough with this light. Let's switch lights. Yours is brighter."

Walking on down the path, Donny heard a noise directly in front of him while he focused his light on the water line. Quickly shifting the light onto the path, Donny yelled, "Holy Moses! Hoooooly Moses! Look at the size of that snake! Man, look at that dude slither down into the water. God, he was right in front of me!"

"Shhhhh! Don't make so much noise. You'll scare all the frogs."

"Hey, Dak, that was a huge snake! I have to shine my light on the path as we move along. Man, if I had stepped on that monster, you'd probably be carryin' me home by now. Did you see that? We don't need a gig. We need hand grenades."

"Donny, only the water moccasins are poisonous. There are lots of big snakes that ain't poisonous. They just keep eatin' these big frogs, and of course, they get big too." Dak didn't seem much concerned about the snakes by now. "There's one thing you have to remember, though. If you gig a snake, make sure you gig him close enough to his head that he can't arch up and reach your hand on the other end of the gig pole. Otherwise, he might bite your hand, even if he's gigged."

"Yeah, well, thanks a lot for that great advice, Dak," Donny replied. "I mean thanks a dang million, but I probably ain't going to be giggin' that many snakes, especially any serpent that compares favorably in size with a friggin' tyrannosaurus rex. Hey, man, these things can kill you."

"True," Dak replied without concern. "Some of them can, but if you give them a chance, most of them, they'll slither away from you. They don't want to die either. The real cottonmouth water moccasin is the poisonous one. They can be large, sometimes seven-feet long and big around. The reason they're called cottonmouth is they have this real white mouth when they open it. And, they've got vertical pupils in their eyes instead of the round ones other water snakes have. They're sometimes a little aggressive. Scientific name is Agkistrodon Piscivorus."

"Oh yeah, sure! Hold still Mr. Snake, Mr. Kistrodon Pissychorus, while I check the color of the inside of your cute little mouth. And, if you wouldn't mind, sweetie, look right here at my light so I can check the orientation of your pupils. I just want to make sure you're not some venomous giant reptile monster that's just a tiny bit aggressive. All you other nice snakes with those cool round eyes...well, you just go right ahead and pass through my line here. Yeah, you can just go on over there and say the 'Pledge of Allegiance' or something. Give me a really big break, Dak!"

"Don-baby, there's the mother of all bullfrogs," Dak replied quietly. "I've got your light right in its eyes. Shift around and get it."

Donny, quickly shifting his mental focus, carefully checked first for snakes and then for twigs in his path as he moved down and thrust the gig into the back of the frog with a loud splat. "Got him!" he yelled.

"Great! Okay, pull him up and put him in this bag," Dak ordered.

"Yetchttt! God, I messed up the mother of all frogs pretty bad with that gig, Dak. Oh, man, look at that."

"Yeah, I don't suppose she's feeling any pain anymore. They do keep kickin', though. Hope the smell of the blood doesn't attract too many cottonmouths." Dak said this with a smile, knowing the effect it could have on Donny.

"Yeah, let's keep the population right here real close around us down to something manageable, not more than a few dozen or so." Donny said. He rolled his eyes, but Dak couldn't see it.

After a little more than two hours at this, the boys had about twenty large frogs and no snake bites. A couple of additional unnerving, unidentified noises and one additional clearly identified monster snake left Donny edgy. Then, it began sprinkling rain. They could see lightning off in the distance, and they could hear a low-level rumbling of thunder.

"We better get to some cover," Donny suggested. "What say we go to that ol' abandoned mansion across the road?"

"You mean Ellsworth Place?" Dak asked. "Hey, why not? It's such a neat ol' antebellum home. I'd love to explore it. The only reason I haven't already is because of those big 'Posted-No Trespassing' and 'Trespassers will be prosecuted' signs. Chances are nobody would see us at night. Let's go over there."

As they approached the old abandoned mansion, they could see that it was in even worse condition than they thought. Four huge gnarled trees in front of the house gave evidence of how long it had been since this place was in its prime. Many of the windows were broken, and some were covered with rusty corrugated roofing sheets. Almost all the paint was gone from the exterior wood, and the shutters were sagging or gone all together. Strangely enough, most of the shutter dogs were still in place. The huge two-story columns were missing some of their concrete plaster, leaving orange bricks showing. The boys went first up the stairs to the front porch to get out of the rain. On the porch was a large broken rocking chair from a long ago era, lying on its side, with leaves and debris all around it. As they approached the front door, they saw that it was intact, but the door handle and locking mechanism had apparently been taken. The heavy door moved slowly back and forth under the ornate fan window above, recognizing the slight breeze, and making an almost continuous squeaking noise.

"There is something about this place," Dak said enthusiastically. "It captures the mood, the feelin' of the antebellum South. It's north of the Mason-Dixon, but it was made for colonels and swords and beautiful belles with hoop skirts, cannons firin', slaves all around, dashin' horsemen, waltzes and mint juleps, bales of cotton, crepe myrtles and jasmine, duels and Spanish moss, and..."

"Okay, I get your point, Dak," Donny said. "This was one fine home. But why do you suppose the front porch was so high off the ground?"

"Because this area isn't protected by the levee, so it floods up to some level most every February," replied Dak. "So I guess they made the first level their basement. That makes this main floor quite high and the second floor even higher. Wow, look how thick these walls are!"

Entering the front door, they could see with their lights that the center hallway extended all the way to the back of the house. At the back, there was a set of double doors, presumably going out onto a back porch. In the middle of the big hallway, there was what must have been a beautiful spiral stairway that curved gently to the left and then back to the right as it gracefully made its way to the second floor. Now it had several broken balusters and a newel post that leaned about fifteen degrees off vertical. On the walls, painted on some kind of cloth, was a barely visible scene from somewhere in Europe, probably Paris. There were no furnishings to speak of left in the hallway. There was a couple of old wooden boxes and the remains of an antique grand piano that, because it had one leg missing, sat at an angle on the floor like a wounded animal. The ivory strips had been taken from most of the keys. Overhead, the plaster was missing from several areas of the ceiling, but a molded flowered circle, which had apparently once graced a large chandelier, remained.

Donny's flashlight was getting weak, but the carbide light was still going well enough to light their way as they entered the large room to the left of the entranceway. A loud flapping noise startled them both as a few bats flew out a window. They had come from an oversized carved-marble fireplace on the outer wall of the room. On the floor, there were three bales of hay, probably the result of a farmer using this room to store hay. The boys wanted to enjoy their visit to the old house, but there was something heavy and just a little scary about the place. Dak decided to try to lighten things up a little.

"Well, Donny, will you join me for dinner this evening? You will? Well then, let me call Rasmus and tell him we're ready to be served." Dak spoke with a southern accent as he arranged the hay bales next to one of the windows covered by corrugated metal roofing. The three bales became a table and two chairs. Taking out two red apples and two large cookies from his bag, he placed them on the table of hay and announced, "Dinnah is served, Gentlemen."

Dak turned off Donny's flashlight to preserve what little battery power they had left. He placed the carbide light on the center bale of hay and said, "Dinnah will be by candlelight this evenin'."

Dak and Donny had built up a strong appetite with all the night's activities, so the apples and cookies seemed very tasty. "Wish I had a beer," Donny said. "I should have had a beer before I came out here. It would have helped my nerves."

"I'm sorry, suh, we have no beer this evenin'. Shall I get you a glass of Chardonnay from the cellars?" Dak said, still doing the Rasmus bit.

"Hey, Dak, you think this place is haunted?" asked Donny, ignoring Rasmus. With that, Dak gave up on Rasmus and began speculating about who the original inhabitants of the house were and what might have happened to them. Donny said there was some old rumor that there had been some murders at the house a long time ago, but he could not remember any of the particulars. Dak, who was usually up on almost anything historical that had happened in the area, notably did not know either, though he had also heard the rumors. He started to say that he would look at Aunt Mariah's papers to see what he could find there, but then it occurred to him that he was not to reveal the existence of the papers.

Whatever this house's secrets are, I hope to dig them out," Dak said.

"Will they let you do that?" asked Donny. "I bet they want to keep everything a big secret."

"Who is 'they' and why would they want to keep it a secret?" Dak asked. He was hoping Donny might know something and might shed some light on the warnings he'd received in the envelopes and who had killed Alex.

If Donny knew anything, he wasn't saying. "I don't know," he replied. "But...I'd let sleeping dogs lie. You shouldn't mess with stuff like that."

"Why not?" Dak asked. "If there were murders here, I'd like to know."

"Maybe it's best to let the past keep its secrets," Donny said.

"Well, if the past keeps all its secrets, we never learn anything," Dak replied.

At some point during the conversation about the house and its background, Dak thought he heard a noise. "What was that?" he asked quietly.

"I don't know, but I heard it, too. It sounded like...uhh...someone walkin'. Was it upstairs or on the front porch?" Donny was getting edgy again.

Before Dak could answer, they heard a second noise. This one was more like a scratch.

"Oh, hell, Dak, I know I heard that. What's going on?" Donny whispered with a touch of panic. And then there was another noise, this one like a weak moan.

"Maybe it's some animal," Dak said very quietly. He was not easily panicked, but he was feeling a bit scared by these very real noises.

"Dak, think we should turn off the carbide light? I mean, if there is someone here, they can see us, but we can't see them."

As Dak reached for the carbide light, a sudden, very loud noise startled and shocked both boys. Dak, light in hand, jumped instinctively back toward the fireplace wall while Donny let out a loud cry that was something like, "Whaaaaaas?" and ran toward Dak. They then realized that the noise was a heavy banging on the corrugated steel roofing that was on the window just a couple feet from them. They looked at each other with a mutual expression of fear, but it was soon replaced by a further shock as someone or something holding a piece of the rusty steel in front of it moved in the door toward them. There was no noise at all. Whatever was moving the ugly piece of steel just moved slowly and steadily toward Dak.

Dak made a kind of whimpering noise, and then, as Donny looked on in horror, he ran at full speed toward the sheet of steel and kicked it with all his strength. The steel fell backward with someone or something under it. As Dak jumped back, he noticed that Donny appeared to be having an attack of some kind and fell to the floor holding his chest. Dak shook with fear as adrenaline slammed his nerves.

When the sheet of roofing began to move, Dak had no idea what to expect. As he moved back from it, he saw a leg and then a full body roll out as the steel fell to the floor. "God, it's J.D.!" he gasped. Although J.D. was laughing, he was also holding his left arm with his right one. "Ouch, Dak, you didn't have to kill me. I was only tryin' to give you a little thrill. Hey, I think you bruised my arm."

"Oh, God, J.D.!" Dak shouted. "Man, are you crazy? You just about scared us to death. Man! If we'd had a gun, we might have shot you! You shouldn't do that!" Then, Dak looked around and saw Donny on the floor gasping and grabbing his chest.

Dak leaped to Donny's side. "Oh, no! Oh, no! J.D., Donny's got a problem! I think he got too scared. May be a heart attack! Quick, let's do something!"

J.D. seemed frozen and didn't say a word.

Dak leaned over and pulled on Donny, who rolled over into his arms, face up. Donny's eyes came open and rolled upward until Dak could only see white. Then his eyes closed, and his body slumped. "Donny! Donny! Open your eyes, Donny! J.D., we've got to do something! Oh, God! What are we going to do?"

"Let him die," said J.D. "Hell, you can't save the whole world. Don't worry about it, Man!" With that, Donny's body miraculously rose up from the floor. As Dak's chin dropped in surprise, both J.D. and Donny began laughing with such gusto that they could hardly stand. Dak realized in a few seconds what had happened, that this whole thing had been planned by J.D. and Donny. Still, he had not entirely recovered from the multiple shocks of the last few minutes. He just stood there, mouth open, for a few more seconds. Then, when J.D. bent way over with pangs of laughter, Dak gave him a swift, very hard kick to the backside. J.D. fell forward to the floor, still laughing. Shifting targets, Dak attacked Donny with a lunge that knocked him to the floor and left Dak on top of him. Dak then began pummeling Donny with the paper bag that contained two apple cores and two oatmeal cookies. Finally, Dak just rolled over on the floor on his back and also began laughing. For perhaps a full minute, the three boys lay on the floor laughing, partly because it was so funny, and partly because it relieved their tension.

After a few minutes of recovery time and banter, the three boys decided to explore the first floor a bit before they left the old mansion. Donny was carrying the bag of frogs and Dak the gig and carbide light as they moved into a smaller room that looked like it might have been a food preparation room, though not really a kitchen. Dak explained that most of the antebellum homes had their kitchen in a separate outside building so that if it caught fire, it didn't burn the mansion. There was a door that seemed to be stuck shut. After Donny jerked it open, they could see it led to stairs down to the mostly-above-ground cellar. Arriving in the cellar, they noticed that the floor was made of large squares of sandstone, which had been shaped to have a flat surface. Years of foot traffic had apparantly worn their surface smooth. The cellar had obviously flooded recently and had a layer of mud on one end.

"What's this?" asked Dak, pointing with his foot to a rusty steel ring that was secured to the stone floor with a steel pin. "Looks like it's been here forever, part of the original building."

"Here's another one over here," J.D. observed. "Hell, there is a whole row of them. What do you suppose they're for?"

"Well, I'd say they tied somethin' down with them. No tellin' what. Maybe they tied stuff down to keep it from bein' stolen," Donny speculated.

Looking out a doorway that had no door left at all, Dak said, "Hey the rain stopped. Are you all ready to go?" The boys scurried across the field to the road, laughing about the big scare and telling stories they had heard of people encountering real ghosts.

Chapter 6

The Coffins

Dak woke up to a clear sunny Saturday morning thinking about two things: Melodie and the find on the Uppers. Of those two, right at the moment, Melodie seemed most important. He found himself wishing she were there right now, in his bed with him. Was he beginning to get fantasies like J.D.'s, he asked himself. He hoped not. Mr. Lerner had said he was not to see Melodie for a month, and it had been 27 days. Dak began thinking about setting up a date. Of course, he had been talking with Melodie at school anyway. It would be easy enough to set up a date anytime, just so long as the actual date didn't happen before a month had elapsed. He decided he would see if Johnnie David could get the car for a double date the following Saturday. If so, there was a rodeo in Marion. They could go there and have some fun. He had six dollars and fifty cents which he had earned helping Mary Webster's father build a picket fence. If he gave J.D. a dollar for gas, he'd still have plenty for a fun day.

"Mom, Mr. Jordan told me yesterday he's been talkin' to the admissions guys at the college and they think my admission and a small cash scholarship are pretty much a done deal," Dak offered during breakfast. "He said we should find out next week for sure. Also, the GI Bill application was approved." He took a big bite of bacon followed by another of jellied toast.

"That's great, Dak! Why didn't you tell me yesterday? That is really good news. I just know you'll get the scholarship." Eleanor got excited every time they talked about it. "Once you get official notice, we need to go back and talk with Mr. Savoy again. And we need to celebrate."

Dak got a dark look on his face. "Well, I'm not too anxious to talk to Mr. Savoy because he's going to bring up that stuff about me takin' Judy to the prom. And, if Mr. Lerner will let her, Melodie is goin' with me, not Judy."

"Oh, Dak, I understand how you feel about that, but you have to admit that it would be a small price to pay to get a college loan," Eleanor replied.

"The price of blackmail is never small," Dak said, obviously pleased that he had uttered such a sage remark. "Hey, I have to run over to see Johnnie. Be back a little later." He stuck the last bite of toast in his mouth and took a big drink of milk as he was scooting his chair back from the table.

When Dak reached Johnnie's house, he could see the old Western Flyer bicycle sitting upside down with both wheels off. "What are you doin'?" Dak inquired.

"Mornin' to you too, Dak. As I understand, you're the man who had so much fun the other night at Ellsworth Place, is that right?" J.D. was in one of those moods.

"No thanks to you, I actually did have quite a bit of fun...and I can tell you, those frog legs were delicious. Boy, were they delicious. I mean I've had some frog legs in my time, but..."

"Yeah, yeah, I know," J.D. interrupted. "If you must know, I'm actually cleanin' the combs of my axle and greasin' it up so it runs real smooth like. Also, I had a little leak in my front tube, so I patched it. Now, I'm puttin' this little leather strip from an old belt around my axles. Man, will those babies shine."

"Like polished mercury," Dak replied. "J.D., what are you doin' next Saturday?"

"Oh, I've got three or four different bee-utiful women been wantin' my body real bad...guess I better accommodate them," replied J.D. "Won't take long though. Something else you wanted to do?"

"Boy, do I have a deal for you," Dak parried. "There is a rodeo and music show over at Marion. Not only that, but there are these two beautiful women, name of Melodie and Marie, who would probably like to accompany us over to it. Maybe in a certain black Ford I know of. And the good news is that I have a dollar or two for gas."

"Que será. Sounds pretty good. Thing is, though, I'll have to put my life in hock to get the car again, and who knows when

Nancy might fall in the river or something just when the magic moment comes. These things happen." J.D. had all the plays this morning.

Dak knew that meant yes, so he decided to press the next subject. "Johnnie, what say we go up to the Uppers and check on our treasure? The water has gone down some."

"Oh, yeah, let's do," replied J.D., as he flipped his bicycle back to its upright position. It somehow looked much newer than it had before.

When the boys reached the Uppers, they could see that the water was low enough that they should be able to see their find. Of course, they realized it may have washed out and floated down the river. They scampered over the creek and hurried to the place where they had seen it before. It wasn't as easy to see the planks as they were expecting.

"There it is. It's hardly washed at all!" shouted J.D.

"Yeah," cried Dak. "Hallelujah! It didn't wash away."

They climbed on the cottonwood roots to see it closer and noted that there was less soil on top of the planks than before, but none of the planks was missing. The soil was still very wet. It was a sort of sticky, heavy clay that didn't look easy to deal with, at least not until it dried out a bit.

"Looks like we'll need a hatchet or saw to get the roots out of the way," said Dak.

"And then we could probably use a spade to get the biggest part of the dirt off the top. That will take a while." Johnnie added. "After that, if the dirt is dry enough, we can brush the rest of it off with our hands or a broom maybe."

"If it is a coffin, these planks go back into the embankment pretty far, so it's a bit of diggin'," Dak continued. "When we get the top all cleaned off, we'll need to take the top planks off. We may need a crowbar or somethin'."

"Probably not," J.D. countered. "I'd guess the planks are rotten enough that we can take them off real easy."

"Then the real fun starts," Dak said excitedly. "Then we need finer tools, like spoons, whisk brooms, and toothpicks. It would be good to have some paper and a pencil for notes and sketches. You know what? We also need some kind of box or bag to put things in...something to hold whatever we find."

Johnnie moved over for a better view. "I have a question though. Once we get started, how are we going to protect it from rain and all? And how are we going to make it so nobody else sees it?"

"Hadn't thought of that, J.D. Maybe we'll bring a tarp with us, and before we leave for the day, we spread the tarp over it. Then we could put some leaves and debris over that so it looks natural."

After a little more discussion, the boys felt they understood what tools they needed and how they would go about doing the job. They agreed to do it as soon as the soil was sufficiently dry.

• • •

On Monday morning, Dak was walking toward Gene's Grocery to catch the bus, in deep thought about the yearbook and all the work that remained to be done. In particular, he was thinking he still needed to talk with a few people about their finest moments and work up some spreads to try to capture the essence of them.

Just as he had arranged in his mind how he was going to do this, a loud horn blared just behind and to his left. Startled, he jumped slightly to his right while looking over his left shoulder to see what it was. There he saw a shiny new turquoise and white Pontiac convertible with its top down. Behind the wheel was Judy Savoy.

She motioned Dak over to the car, yelling, "Hi, Dak! Goin' down to the bus stop?"

Surprised, Dak said, "Yeah, got a new car?"

"Sure do," Judy said. "Get in. I'll give you a ride to Gene's."

Dak walked over, opened the door to the impressive car, and slid smoothly into the white leather seat. Judy looked over at him proudly and said, "Daddy got me this for my birthday. It's a '56 model. Like it?"

"It's beautiful, Judy. It's yours?" Dak had never even ridden in such a luxurious car.

"Yeah, it's a Pontiac Chieftain V-8 316," she said nonchalantly. "It has hydramatic transmission, because I'm not too good at shifting. You want to try it out?"

"Try it out?" Dak was puzzled.

"Drive it, silly! You want to drive the rest of the way?"

"Oh, no, that's fine." Dak replied. "I don't actually have a Driver's License because we don't have a car." Dak wondered why he didn't feel embarrassed at all to tell her that.

"Dak, my mom said she thought my left rear tire looked a little low. I just don't know what I'd do if I got half way to the high school, and it went flat. Why, I'd probably just break down in tears and...would you consider riding with me, all the way out there, in case it goes flat? I'm just scared that..."

Dak, as usual, was unable to refuse anyone requesting help. "Sure," he said. "I'll ride out with you, and maybe you can take it by Jimmy's Garage out by the high school before you come back home this afternoon."

"Oh, thanks, Dak," she said. As she drove past Gene's Grocery, several people, including Melodie and J.D., were out waiting for the bus. Judy picked up the speed a little and honked the horn all the way past the bus stop, waving and smiling at the other students. Dak was very uncomfortable with this but didn't know what to say or do. He just sat there like he was made of stone and thought how silly he must look to the students at the bus stop. On the other hand, he very much enjoyed the luxury of the car. It was so clean, so shiny, so quiet, and its radio had such a clear sound. He even loved the smell of it. As they approached the high school, he daydreamed a bit about how wonderful it would be to have one of his own.

At lunchtime, Dak and Melodie took their lunch out to the baseball field and sat on a bench to eat. It was a sunny day, and they enjoyed hearing the birds that frequented that area of the grounds.

Melodie's expression let Dak know that she had something on her mind. "Dak, Judy Savoy told some people over the weekend that you were probably goin' to take her to the prom. When my friend Annie told me about this, I didn't know what to say. I just told her that you had already asked me, and I planned to go with you. But then when I saw you ridin' to school with her this morning, I...."

"Oh, no, no, no...I'm not takin' Judy to the prom," Dak said as he reached out for her hand. "Some things have happened, Melodie, which I guess I've got to tell you about. I was hoping this would all just fade away."

Dak explained to Melodie what Mr. Savoy had said at the bank. Then he told her how it happened that he was riding to school with Judy.

"I had to tell you about that, Melodie, but I don't want that spread around. It wouldn't do anybody any good, and it might hurt the chances for my college loan," he explained.

Melodie understood, and she trusted Dak. They talked with excitement about the planned trip to the rodeo on Saturday. "My Dad wasn't too happy about lettin' me go," she said. "Especially with you." She laughed as she gave him a little shove.

• • •

At the Tuesday after-school yearbook session with Miss Hurd, Dak was full of enthusiasm. "I talked to Kay Walters yesterday. You know about that bake sale she organized after the Crandall family's house caught on fire? Well, she got more than sixty people to bake cakes for that, and she and her friends sold all of them at the ball game. She made over $200 for that family to buy clothes. Almost all their clothes had burned. Anyway, it was a pretty big deal, and we have some good pictures of the sale. How's that for a fine moment?"

Miss Hurd smiled and seemed very pleased, but before she could say anything, Dak continued. "And there is a real good thing for Ray Shorter. You know, he won second place at state for his Science Fair project. You saw it. It was the one where he got ol' Sid Snyder to take him around in the boat, and he measured river currents at all these different locations during flood stage. Then he figured out where they should strengthen the levee. That was a big hit. They say the Corps of Engineers is lookin' at what he learned. Hey, it could turn out he saves the town!"

Miss Hurd had forgotten about that. "Oh, yes," she said. "That's great, Dak! I guess that could be pretty important."

"And then there's Jennie Mae Newbury. The best thing for Jennie Mae is what she did in that poetry fair. She went to district and got a blue ribbon. Here's a piece of her winnin' poem. I thought it was real good, and we could actually spread that in light fading letters over the pictures of her gettin' the ribbon. Of course, we wouldn't cover her face."

Miss Hurd looked at the words Dak handed her and read them aloud:

"People rarely see the need...
for folks like them to take the lead
To do the things that must be done...
to help the orphans have some fun
To catch a dream, to plant a seed...
no, people rarely see the need."

"There was a lot more to it," Dak said. "But that kind of captures the heart of the thing."

Dak went through several others that he had been working on. Miss Hurd was astounded by how much he had done and, even more, by what a feel he had for what was important in the lives of the various students. She actually was aware of most of the stories Dak outlined but had not understood their significance. She had not realized how important they were to the students involved. She knew all of this would have been lost without Dak. She thought to herself, "The gods have kept the best for last in my teaching career. But that will make the end even harder."

• • •

The next morning before school, Johnnie David came by Dak's house in the old Ford, arriving just as Dak was coming out the door.

"What, you've got the car again?" Dak asked, rhetorically. "Hey, your pappy might as well turn the ol' beast over to you."

"I been tellin' him that, but he doesn't get it," J.D. replied. "Hell, he thinks I have to sign away future rights to breathin' before I get the danged ol' thing at all. Wish I had that car Judy Savoy got. Man, couldn't I have some fun? Can you imagine how many girls I'd have chasin' me? Have to beat them off!"

"As it is, you have to beat yourself off." Dak was pleased with his little bit of humor and laughed noisily. Getting no reaction other than a silly smile from J.D., he continued. "Well, hey, if you were Judy's boyfriend, you could drive that Pontiac all the time. And I bet she'd buy all the gas. Ever thought of that? You and Judy could have the front seat. Melodie, Marie and me--well, we could have the back seat, me in the middle." Dak was smiling.

"Not worth it. Besides, you're the one who rides around with Judy. That was quite an appearance you two made the other mornin'." With that, J.D. turned up the radio. It was his favorite song, so all conversation stopped. The Platters filled the air:

> Oh, yes, I'm the great pretender,
> Pretending I'm doing well.
> My need is such I pretend too much.
> I'm lonely, but no one can tell.

At school that day, Mr. Jordan called Dak to his office and told him that he had been admitted to the college and had been awarded a scholarship of $30 a month toward room and board in addition to the GI Bill. He explained that Dak would probably need another $60 a month or so to get by.

"If you don't have funds available from other sources, I'd recommend you check with the bank and see if you can't get a loan for the remaining amount," Mr. Jordan said. "The interest rates are pretty low for that kind of loan. Of course, you can pay it back over time when you graduate and have a good income. With your aptitude, I'd really recommend you make every effort to attend college."

Dak was pleased but dreaded facing Mr. Savoy. He certainly did not plan to pander to get the money. He decided to put it on the back burner for now.

• • •

After school, Dak and Johnnie David were sitting on the seawall at the top of the levee, facing the river and dangling their feet.

"Johnnie David, this is goin' to be some outstandin' weekend for us, provided it don't rain. The rodeo in Marion on Saturday and perhaps a little makin' out, and then...ta-duh...a genuine archaeological dig with all kinds of possibilities on Sunday. What think you of that?"

"Sounds wonderful. I mean, you'd think things don't get much better than that, but...well, I don't know."

"Don't know? What don't you know? What else could you ask for, J.D.? Hey, man, there are a few times in a person's life when it all seems to line up right...when you couldn't have made it better if you were in charge of the Universe. This is one of those times," Dak said dramatically. Then, he sensed that something serious was bothering J.D., and he felt a bit silly about his little speech.

Johnnie just sat there looking out over the river. Dak had a sinking feeling. After a few seconds pause, he said, "What is it, Johnnie?"

"Dak, I'm going to tell you something, and I don't want it out. So, this is for you to hear and nobody else,"

"Well, I'm sure you know you can count on that, J.D. What's the problem?"

"Okay, how can I say this? My mom has a problem. I think she has a mental problem. Hell, I don't know. My dad says I don't know what I'm talkin' about, but she ain't actin' right." J.D. was clearly pained. "I think my dad doesn't want it to be...just can't face it, won't admit it. I just don't know what to do."

"Well, Johnnie, you know if there's anything I can do to help, you just let me know. If you need to cancel this weekend, don't give it a second thought. How is it that this ...uh, manifests itself? I mean, what are the symptoms?"

"Lots of things. I walked in last night and made a little joke with her like I do sometimes, and she says, 'You no good scum. How dare you talk to me like that?' I was just doin' a little joke. Then, she says, 'You get your slimy butt out of this house. I don't ever want to see you again'." Johnnie's eyes were welling up with tears. He quickly wiped his sleeve across his face and looked the other way, hoping to hide his anguish from Dak.

"Oh, Johnnie, she doesn't mean it. She just has a problem of some kind right now. I'd think she needs some help from somebody who does that sort of thing. Some doctor."

"Thing is...when I go home tonight, she may be huggin' all over me. It just changes from day to day, even hour to hour. Oh, hell, Dak, I don't know what to do. My dad won't even admit there's a problem. Says she'll be okay. She just needs a little rest. I know better than that."

"Hey, J.D., I've got something for you to think about. You know that buildin' on the square in Harrisburg? The one with the radio tower on it? Well, I noticed when we were over there on that field trip, there's a sign that says, 'Doctor somebody or other, Psychiatric Disorders, Fourth Floor.' Why don't you see if you can get your dad to go see him and talk about it? And if he won't go, let's you and I go. I bet we could get some help for your mom."

"Well, how'd I be supposed to pay for that? I don't have enough money to hire a doctor like that. He's not goin' to talk to us without some money. Even if my dad goes, he wouldn't have that kind of money. Dak, I don't know what we'll do."

"No, Johnnie, I bet he'd talk to us about it for free. He'd probably make some suggestions about what we ought to do. You know, what we ought to do considerin' the money situation. There might be a state program or something." Dak was pretty convincing.

"Dak, you got a point there," J.D. said. Then he paused for a few seconds before continuing. "I'll see what my dad says about that. Dak, sometimes you're worth your weight in gold. Maybe there's a solution to this." Johnnie David went home feeling some better, but he hadn't answered Dak's suggestion that he may want to cancel the rodeo trip.

On his way home from their talk on the seawall, Dak was feeling pretty down about J.D.'s Mom. He was walking along slowly, reflecting back on what he had said about it being one of those times when everything lines up right. "What bad timing," he thought. Glancing down the street, he saw Judy Savoy heading his direction in her Pontiac. He hurried across the street, but she was there in just seconds. "Hi, Dak!" she said cheerfully.

"Hello, Judy." Dak replied, as he walked over to the car and leaned on her door. "What's up?"

"Oh, Norman Jacey just asked me to go to the prom with him, but I told him I'd have to get my daddy's permission first. Really, I just didn't have the heart to tell him 'No!' I'm waiting to decide who to go with because some others have asked me, too. I don't think it's that I'm so popular so much as it is that they want to go in my car. Don't you think?"

Dak saw his opportunity. "Well, Judy, I'm glad Norman asked you. He's really a neat guy. I'm sure a lot of other girls would like to go with him. You two would make a nice couple. I can just see it now... you and Norman, all dressed for the prom and drivin' along in your new Pontiac. I'm sure Melodie and I will see you all there. Melodie was like you. She had to ask her Dad. Fortunately for me, he agreed, but I still don't think I'm his favorite person."

They talked awhile, and as Judy pulled away, Dak thought to himself that he might have taken care of this problem. He couldn't help wondering, though, how Mr. Savoy would respond to this. Maybe if Judy told him she actually wanted to go with Norman, it would be okay.

The next morning, Johnnie David told Dak that he had talked with his dad about the man in Harrisburg. He said his dad had told him that the problem is alcoholism.

"When she drinks too much, her mind doesn't work the way it should," he said. "That's all."

"Can he make sure she doesn't get any alcohol?" Dak asked.

"Well, my dad said she sneaks and gets vodka and hides it around the house. Then from time to time, when she's feelin' down, she drinks. And then she gets crazy in the head. Anyway, it's a problem, but not as bad as I thought. Hell, I thought she was losin' her mind. I had no idea she drank like that. It's a worry, but nothin' that should stop us from doing our thing this weekend. That's what my dad says."

Dak couldn't help noticing how J.D. relied on his dad. How nice it must be, he thought, to have a dad to talk with, to provide you a car, to teach you to drive, and to do a hundred other things. When Dak arrived home that evening, he went to his room and looked at the picture of his dad for several minutes. "I wish you were here," he whispered.

On Saturday morning, J.D. herded the old Ford first by Marie's house and then to Melodie's to pick up everyone for the rodeo trip. Dak had already arrived at Melodie's, where he got a none-to-friendly reception from her parents. The four of them were quickly on their way, but J.D. had the radio turned so loud that conversation was next to impossible. As Don Cherry was charming them with *Band of Gold*, Dak, in the back seat with Melodie, asked if they could turn it down a little. Marie said, "Just a minute, Dak. Ready Johnnie?" Without answering, Johnnie and Marie together joined the song, overpowering even the radio as they sang along:

> I've never wanted wealth untold....
> but till the end of time
> There'll be a little band of gold....
> to prove that you are mine.

Then, Marie turned the radio completely off while Dak and Melodie clapped and hooted. "Hey, I didn't know you had such talent, J.D. Of course, maybe Marie's voice had something to do with it," Dak said. They all knew that Marie had a great voice. In fact, Dak had a layout for the yearbook that featured Marie singing *To Know You* in the school musical.

As they arrived at the rodeo grounds, clouds of dust were rising from the unpaved parking lot. The smell of horses, cattle, and hay was everywhere. There was a large crowd, and there wasn't much time until the show began, so they hurried to get their tickets. The rodeo was fast moving, loud, and brutal to both man and beast. Melodie held her hands over her eyes as a bull trampled and gored one poor cowboy when the rodeo clown was unable to attract the animal's attention quickly enough.

Following the rodeo, the music produced even more noise. It was, of course, country and western and featured Kitty Wells and Marty Robbins. While it wasn't their favorite music, it was the first time any of them had seen famous performers live, so they were thrilled with the show. The grand finale was Marty and Kitty together doing a stirring version of Marty's *Singing the Blues*.

> Well, I never felt more like singin' the blues
> 'Cause I never thought that I'd ever lose
> Your love, dear. Why'd you do me this way?

It was about 9 PM when they arrived back in town and parked down by the icehouse. The conversation about the day's events was cut short when J.D. got out of the car, opened the trunk and brought everyone a cold beer from a cooler. They were all four delighted with that, although Melodie was worried that her parents might smell the beer when she got home. After a second beer, J.D. reached over gently and kissed Marie on the cheek. She moved over closer, and before long, all four of them were engaged in heavy petting. The thing about a foursome, though, was that it kept things from going too far. After about an hour, Melodie said she needed to be getting home. It had been a wonderful day.

• • •

Dak and J.D. started early Sunday morning getting things ready for the "big dig," as they had been calling it. They placed the small tools in two grass sacks and each of them carried a spade.

As they walked up the street and onto the levee with all these supplies, they were fully loaded. Dak worried that anyone who saw them might ask what they were doing. As it turned out, only old Katy Shirkens had noticed them at all. Fortunately, she was sitting in her porch swing reading a romance novel. When she was doing that, little else actually registered in her mind.

Arriving at the site, Dak and Johnnie David looked around to see if there was anyone hunting or boating who might observe their activity. Concluding there was not, they began.

They removed all their equipment from the grass sacks and placed it in a row on the ground at the site.

"That's a nice camera you've got there, Dak," J.D. said. "Must have cost you a bunch."

"No, didn't cost me anything," Dak replied. "It belonged to Mrs. Scroggins' husband before he died. She my mom's good friend, and she gave it to me. Gave me lots of equipment with it too, flashbulbs and everything. She has a dark room for developin' pictures in her basement. She doesn't ever use it, but told me to use it whenever I wanted. She even taught me how to do it."

"Man, you are lucky," J.D. said.

"I guess," Dak said. "But you're even luckier to have a dad and a car to use."

J.D. chose to ignore that input. "Good we brought two hatchets because there are lots of these roots," he said.

"Yeah, but the cottonwood is pretty soft, not too hard to hack out," Dak replied, as he pulled a piece of root out of the way.

After clearing the visible roots, they decided that they needed to remove some of the dirt before they could proceed. As J.D. climbed up the embankment to do so, he noticed that there was a large flat stone on the ground.

"Hey, Dak, look at this big stone. Looks like somebody marked this spot." J.D. said, as he turned the stone on its end.

"How about that? Is there any writing on it?" Dak asked.

Johnnie turned the rock over and scraped the dirt off thoroughly. "Nope, no markings. I guess it just let them know the location."

J.D. proceeded to scoop the dirt off in a pile while Dak spread it around in a way that wouldn't be too visible to anyone who might pass through the area. Then they hacked some more roots and continued digging. After repeating this cycle for nearly three hours, they were down to the tops of the wooden boxes.

"What do you think, Dak? Does it look like coffins to you?" J.D. asked, looking at the rectangular-shaped tops.

"They do! It's two coffins, ain't it? They are spaced real close together, though." Dak said slowly as he put his hand on his chin. "They're just rectangular boxes. Not wider in the center like some of the old coffins were. I guess there's still a chance they are somethin' else."

Johnnie took the broom and began to clean the smaller pieces of dirt off the wood. The dark gray wood was moist and partially rotted, but still intact enough that they could see the grain. There was no evidence that there had ever been a cloth or leather covering on the wood.

"If they are coffins, they weren't very good ones," Dak noted. "If they were, they would've been covered in leather or copper or, at least, some cloth like velvet." Dak made some entries in his notebook.

Having cleaned everything off the top, J.D. smiled in anticipation. He held out his hands toward the two silent boxes, and said, "Well, Dak, here we are. We'll be the first ones in a long, long time to see what's in these ol' boxes. Let's do the one on the left first."

Dak took some pictures, and then they began on the board on the left edge of the left box. It was about six inches wide and was apparently nailed to the sides of the box with small square nails and not too many of those. "I think if we just wiggle this a little bit, it might come loose with not much force. It's a bit rotten," J.D. suggested. As he pulled on one end, the board pulled through its nails and broke in two.

"Gosh, what is it?" asked Dak. "Looks like just mud. Let's get the second board off." They pulled on the second board and it broke into three pieces. They carefully removed the three pieces.

"Look at that!" cried J.D. "That's teeth and...skull bones!"

"Yeah, the head's been broken! Wow!" Dak was thrilled to see the remains of a real body, or at least the head of a real body.

J.D. lowered his voice to something like a deep baritone, "Whoooooo, whooo," he said and then made his voice even deeper. "I'm going to haunt you guys for messing with my head. Whoooo, whooo."

"J.D., this is serious archaeological work," Dak said. "Do you think ol' Carter said that when he found King Tut?"

As the boys removed the other boards, they could see just the teeth and broken skull bones near the head end of the coffin. As their eyes moved toward the foot end of the box, they saw only muddy dirt. It was clear that the last few inches at the foot end had washed away. Again, Dak took pictures and made notes and sketches.

"Wow! J.D., can you believe this is happenin'? I wonder if we should tell the sheriff or somebody."

"Naaaa, it's ours," J.D. replied excitedly. "Why tell anybody?"

"So, it looks like with all those years of floodin', the body and whatever else was in here have decayed a lot. Some dirt may have washed up into the box from the foot end. And it looks like we're going to have to dig in the box to see what else is in here. We'll have to dig real careful like."

"Yeah," J.D. said. "And part of what you will be diggin' up is this man's rotted liver and stuff."

Dak ignored this input. He took a spoon and the box of toothpicks. "Let's start up here by the head and just gently remove the dirt. We'll see what we find," he said.

As they dug around the skull, they concluded that it would have been intact except for the forces of the water and decay. The bone pieces seemed to all be there, and they saw no damage to any piece. It was just that the pieces of the skull had separated from each other.

"What's this?" J.D. asked. He picked up a small metallic object with a bit of dirt stuck to it.

"I don't know. It's not iron. There's no rust," Dak observed. "Let's take it down to the water and wash it off."

As they washed off the object, they could see that it was a silvery piece of metal with a ring on one end.

J.D. used a toothpick to clean the mud out of the crevices. "It looks like a rough pendant with some sort of symbol on it and a loop attached to it."

"Let's make note of exactly where we found it," Dak said, trying to be as scientific as he could about all this.

They walked back up to the box, and J.D. pointed out the indentation in the dirt where he had found the pendant. "Right here," he said. Dak made some notes.

"Okay," replied Dak. "That would be the right side of his head, just behind where the jaw bone met the skull. That would be...that would be at about the bottom of the ear. Hey, that's it...an earring! It's an earring!"

J.D. looked closely at the object again. "Well, it was a pretty rough earring," he said. "Not a very smooth thing. No jewels or anything. And I wonder what this symbol on it is." He handed it to Dak.

"Yeah, it wasn't a very classy earring, was it? Still, must have been some good metal not to rust or get that white oxidation like aluminum does. This is a funny symbol. It's like three vertical lines, the middle one bein' twice as long as the first one and the third one. The third line is lowered so that the top of it is the same level as the bottom of the first one. Then it's got two horizontal lines, one at the center of the first line and one at the center of the third line." Dak had a good technical description but had no idea what it meant.

"Almost looks like the letter H twice, one set down from the other," Johnnie observed.

"Might be. I have no clue. Let's look at the earring from the other ear. Maybe it'll be clearer," Dak said.

As they dug carefully on the other side of the skull, they expected to find another earring in the corresponding location. There was none. They then assumed the second earring must have drifted in the mud toward the bottom of the coffin, so they dug deeper. There was still no earring.

"Well, hell," J.D. said, perplexed. "Surely, they didn't wear an earring on just one side."

"I think this person did, for whatever reason." Dak was writing in the notebook and then took a picture of the earring and a second of the area around the skull.

"What say we dig the area from the skull up to the head end of the coffin?" Dak asked.

Johnnie and Dak moved rapidly through that area, not expecting anything. "Nothing here, Dak," said J.D.

Looking more closely at the teeth, Dak handed the lower jawbone to J.D. "The teeth are in pretty good shape. I bet this person was not too old. How tall do you think?"

They reached for their yardstick and measured the distance from the top of the head down to the ankles. The feet had washed away, but they estimated the person was five foot, eleven inches tall. "Probably a male," Dak speculated. "People were smaller then. Very few females would be that tall. It's interestin' that a male would be wearin' an earring." He made more entries in his notebook.

As they moved down into the chest area, they found all the expected bones. In fact, everything was intact except for two rib bones that looked like they had been shattered. There was one in front and one in a corresponding location in the back. "Maybe he was shot," J.D. observed, as he took pictures of the bones. "Hey, what is this little thing?"

"Dang, you're havin' all the luck, Johnnie. That's the second thing you found. It looks like it's made of steel, quite rusty."

When they looked closely at the second piece of metal, they concluded that it was a piece from a suspender. "Has to be another one over here," Dak forecast as he dug on the other side. "Yep, here it is. So, he wore suspenders. Let's take these down to the water and clean them off."

With the dirt removed, they could see that there were some raised letters on the metal, but the rust prevented them from being able to read it. Dak took one of the spoons and scraped it a bit, causing shiny letters to protrude through the rust. It read, "Patented June 21, 1851."

Dak was thrilled. He took a close up photo in the sunshine and made some more notes.

It was J.D. who first heard the noise of a motorboat coming up the river. "Hey, Dak, we need to take cover quickly," he yelled, as he ran to the top of the embankment to hide behind some brush.

Dak was right behind. "Oh, man, I hope they don't see the area all dug up like that," he whispered to Johnnie.

The boat moved on up the river past their location with no apparent notice of their excavation. The two men in the boat were talking loudly above the motor noise, joking about some fish story, and drinking beer.

The boys at first thought the fishermen were going much further up the river, but then they stopped the engine and began fishing from the boat, letting it drift downstream. Though they were pretty far away, the boys could see that they would eventually drift right by their site.

Quickly agreeing to cover the site and leave for the day, the boys hid their supplies and tools, used their tarp to cover the excavated area, and then spread leaves and small debris over the whole thing. In a little bag, they took the earring and suspender buckles with them as they left.

"Oh, it's nearly five o'clock," Johnnie said. "It's been a sweet day."

Chapter 7

Their Finest Moment

As the school year entered into its final months, Dak was thinking about "the dig" but was also feeling pressure to complete the yearbook. In his after-school session with Miss Hurd, he showed her his last two layouts.

"How do you like this one, Miss Hurd?" he asked as he pulled out the display for Julia Hannig. "You know that history project Julia did? She read about that famous case where the Union soldier at Gettysburg died on the battlefield holdin' in his hand a tintype picture of his three young children. You remember, his identification had been lost, and there was no one who could recognize his body, so it became a national cause to find out who the man was."

"Oh, yes," Miss Hurd said. "It was a moving story."

Some magazine...I don't know if it was *Harper's Weekly* or some other one...spread this photo of the children all over the country and prizes were offered for the best poem about the incident and such. Well, the mother of the children eventually saw the picture and came forward, poor lady. Turned out the soldier was Sergeant Amos Humiston of the 154th New York Infantry. Anyway, it was a big thing, a real emotional thing...children of the battlefield and all. So, Julia, she investigated all this, found out who the living descendants are, wrote them letters, found out what ever happened to the children, got a copy of the winning poem. She really did a nice piece of research. Well, I've tried to capture her finest moment, the principal givin' her this award for her work, superimposed over a copy of the tintype picture of the children."

"That's a great layout, Dak. I knew she did this and helped her get started, but I didn't realize she had done so much." Miss Hurd was even more pleased because it was a history project.

"And here's my last one," Dak continued. "Or nearly my last one...there's one more idea I'll discuss with you later. But this one is for Ben Flores. In the wood workin' class this year, they got into carvin' a little, and they invited everyone to carve anything they wanted and bring it to class. Well, Ben carved this head of Ike, and, man, you wouldn't believe it. It looks exactly like the President. So everybody made over that, and they put a picture in the paper. Some man offered him $50 for it, but Ben wanted to donate it to the school, so they got it in the wood workin' classroom in a glass case. You ought to go see it. We got a picture of Ben, chisel in hand, Ike and a pile of shavin's on the table, and the whole class standin' in the background. The neat thing is that somebody got a bunch of 'I LIKE IKE' pins, and everybody in the class is wearin' that pin in the picture."

"I like that, Dak, and I like Ike, too," she said with a smile. "I guess we're about ready to finalize the yearbook, don't you think?" Miss Hurd felt a sense of urgency that Dak didn't seem to share.

"Well, there is one other thing, Miss Hurd. You know Charlie Johnson, Erma's twin brother? Charlie has really had a hard time in high school. He was sick quite a bit, and then, well, he had to stay home a lot with his mom ever since she got cancer. She's still alive, but his dad took off work and is stayin' with her during her final days. So, he got really behind at school, and he doesn't have much in the way of finest moments here. But he's been studyin' real hard for the history test comin' up on the depression era. I've been workin' with him to make sure he knows his stuff from start to finish. You are going to be really surprised what he knows about the depression, Roosevelt's approach, WPA, CCC, the plight of the farmers and all.

"Charlie said it would be the high point of his life if he was ever to make 100 on one of your tests, and he could take it home and show it to his mom before she goes. Says she would be so proud. The high point of his life, Miss Hurd. We're still workin' on it, and my goal is for Charlie to make 100 on this test next Friday. I know you don't usually give 100's, and you wouldn't give him credit if he didn't know his stuff, but he does know it all. And we really don't have any other moment to celebrate for

Charlie. Anyway, I sure hope you'll keep that in mind when you're gradin' his test paper. Sometimes, something is more important than strict gradin' standards. It's about dreams and hope, Miss Hurd. Dreams that come true, even little ones, give hope. That's what makes all the difference."

There was a pause. Then, Dak added, "I'll never tell anybody I said this to you."

Miss Hurd had a serious look on her face as she stood there, thinking about what Dak had just said. It went against everything she had ever believed about achieving excellence, enforcing tough performance standards, and adhering to the rules, no matter what. But there was something that rang true about Dak's message. Years of rigid rules said Dak was wrong, but her intuition was telling her that he was right, that sometimes things are best determined by the heart, and that, in the end, it is hopes and dreams that count. Why had she not seen that before?

Finally, she said, "You know, Dak, if one is to have any chance of making a 100 on this test, they should probably have a very good appreciation of Roosevelt's First Inaugural Address and, specifically, the line, 'The only thing we have to fear is fear itself.' and what that meant to the American people."

Dak's face lit up with a broad smile, but he said no more about it.

That afternoon in study hall, Dak sat by Charlie and went through Roosevelt's First Inaugural Address over and over. Then, Dak talked about the significance of the address and the importance of the line about 'fear itself,' why the American people were scared, how people listened to it on their radios, and what it had meant to them. Dak then wrote a paragraph on the significance of the address, in general, and the line about fear, in particular, and suggested to Charlie that he know this by heart. Charlie was becoming an expert on this speech.

After school, Dak jumped on his bike and rode to Melodie's house. As he entered the driveway and leaned his bike on a tree, he noticed that the family car was missing. He hoped it was Mr.

Lerner who was gone. Melodie opened the door, and as Dak walked in, she said her parents were gone to Harrisburg to have some dental work done and wouldn't be back for a few hours. Melodie popped some popcorn and opened two Pepsis. As they sat on the red plastic sofa and talked, Dak told Melodie all about the visit to Ellsworth Place after he and Donnie had gone frogging. Melodie was fascinated by the story and by the old house.

"How old is it anyway?" she asked.

"Not sure. I'd guess maybe 120 years, something like that. The place has such a ghostly presence about it. I just love it because it was so elegant, so beautiful, such an architectural marvel, so lavish. You look at it, and you imagine these genteel people arrivin' in their polished carriages drawn by four white horses, steppin' out in their colorful long dresses and topcoats, walkin' past azaleas along the walkway, then up the steps to the huge white columns, where the master of the house greets them and serves them a mint julep. But now the grandeur is long since gone. In decay, it looks like a bygone age...like shattered dreams...so lonesome, so sorrowful, so ruined, so haunted. You can almost hear the music and the laughter, but you know all the people who listened to the music and laughed are long since dead. I think it should be preserved for future generations." Dak wondered if he was boring her.

Melodie took Dak's hand in hers and said, "I want to go there with you sometime." That's what she said, but what she thought was, "Maybe what I love most about Dak is his imaginative, romantic mind."

"Sure, that would be fun," Dak replied. Then he got a whimsical look. "So, you're just arrivin' at Ellsworth Place, and I'm the master of the house," Dak said, as he stood in front of her, bowed, and gently kissed her hand. Then, he pulled her up and began kissing her arm repeatedly, making each kiss a little higher up her arm than the previous one.

"It would be rude to stop the host when he is giving you a cordial greeting," he said, as the kisses reached her shoulder and then her neck. Melodie liked what was happening.

"Well, Suh, I've just arrived from Mississippi, and I do like a proper greeting," she smiled.

Dak continued the kisses until he reached her mouth, and then the whole mood changed. It was a soft warm kiss with full body contact, and it was much more enjoyable than either of them were expecting. It went on for some time, and then Melodie took a deep breath and said, "Well, y'all certainly know how to welcome a Southern Belle, but I'm not sure I feel totally welcome yet."

"Ahh, I am sometimes inadequate. My apologies, Ma'am. Here, let me try again," Dak replied, as he kissed her again, this time with a partially opened mouth. Melodie reached under his shirt and rubbed his bare back as he kissed her.

They sat on the couch and kissed several more times, enjoying each one more than the last. They finally gave up on the Southern Belle bit and just enjoyed each other. Dak loved running his hands through her long honey-colored hair as they kissed, while Melodie found rubbing Dak's muscular back intoxicating. Dak began moving his hand tenderly under her blouse. She moved her hand to his right thigh.

Then there was the slam of a car door, and they knew it was over. They quickly straightened their clothes and picked up their Pepsis. By the time Melodie's parents walked in the door, Dak had a mouthful of popcorn.

"Good evenin', Mr. and Mrs. Lerner," Dak said, using his most courteous tone. "It is good to see you both." Dak didn't usually lie, but he thought the circumstances justified it this time.

• • •

Dak went to bed early, and before he was asleep, he heard a familiar noise. Occasionally, when a big barge was moving down the river, the vibration from the boat's propellers would cause one of the windows in the house to take on a high-frequency rattle. The rattling had just begun when he heard a second noise that sounded like a clock striking in the attic above his bed. Since he had never heard this striking noise before, he ran down the steps to ask Eleanor if she knew what that could be.

"Yes, I think there is an old clock stored away in the attic, Dak," she said. "Been there for many years, I guess. I think your grandfather Leventhal left several things up there when he used this as a town house, before your father and I were even married. I haven't been up there to look around because it's so hard to get to. But your father went up there once, and I remember him saying there were several things up there, including an old clock."

"But why would it strike now?" Dak asked.

Eleanor yawned. "Well, I don't know. It has done it before, but it has been a long time. Maybe the vibrations from the river boats set it off."

Dak walked slowly back to his bedroom thinking he needed to explore this stuff in the attic. He wondered what his dad would say about the clock. He would have liked to discuss it with him.

The next day was a scheduled Teacher's Meeting. For the students, this meant a day off school. Dak first thought about continuing "the dig," but he remembered Buck Watson saying that the Corps of Engineers were dredging just above town. He decided to go have a look, and sure enough, there were several large boats with workmen on them just offshore from the graves. "This is not a good day for digging," he said to himself.

As Dak thought more about Ellsworth Place and the graves on the river, he began to wonder if there was any connection between the two. It occurred to him that the two were not very far apart and were probably of the same time period. The more he thought about the possibilities, the more intrigued he became. He decided he needed to go to Ellsworth Place by himself and look the house over thoroughly to see what he could learn.

Dak jumped on his bicycle and rode over the levee to the vicinity of the bar pits with his notebook and camera in the basket attached to his handlebars. He quickly found a place to hide his bike under some brush beside the road and started walking over to Ellsworth Place. There had been a roadway to it many years ago, but fences had long since been placed across it, and brush had grown first next to the fence and then entirely across the roadway. So Dak was walking across a field to the house.

As he got closer, he was impressed again with the sheer size of the house and its architectural beauty. He decided to go to the back door this time, but when he reached the steps, he could see that they were not made of stone like those in the front of the house. The wooden steps had rotted over the years, and some were missing. He didn't think it would be safe to walk up them. As he turned to go to the front of the house, he stumbled on something. Kneeling to see what it was, he could see that it was bricks that edged a walkway that went from the steps out to the rear of the house. Since the bricks were not visible because of the weeds and rotted debris, Dak used his foot as a guide against the bricks and followed them to the foundation of a building that had been torn down long ago. He speculated that it had been the kitchen. He made a sketch in his notebook showing the walk and the foundation with approximate dimensions.

Dak then went to the front entrance to the house, the one he and Donny had entered after their frogging trip. He walked slowly through the main floor, again observing the dogtrot hall-way and the large rooms on either side of the hallway with their oversize marble fireplace mantels. In the tablet carved in the center of the mantle, he saw the letters DPL. It looked like this carving was original to the mantel, or at least very old. He thought, "That will be easy to remember. It's my initials." Just to make sure, he took a photo. After examining the other three rooms on the main floor, Dak headed up the broad spiral stair-case, being careful not to lean against the tenuous railing. Upstairs, Dak found that there was nearly nothing left of any furniture in the grand hallway. There were the remains of a harp with the frame broken and most of the strings gone. Also, there was what was left of a fine marble-topped mahogany dresser. The marble was lying on the floor, broken into five pieces, while the dresser was turned over and broken in several places. One drawer was missing altogether.

Going into the first of the four bedrooms, Dak found a good many beer bottles, some of them broken, and what appeared to be the headboard of a grand rosewood bed. The back of the headboard was stamped, "Belter and Sons 1852". Someone had hacked pieces off it and attempted to burn them in the fireplace, but most pieces didn't burn. The scenes in the other bedrooms were similar.

As Dak was pondering the huge doorway from the bedroom to the hallway, he thought he heard voices. He stood very still for a moment to listen intently, and then he was sure he heard voices. He quietly walked over to an uncovered window and peeped outside. Across the field maybe 100 yards, he could see two men walking toward the mansion. He could hear their voices, but not well enough to tell what they were saying. As they got closer, he could see that it was Mr. Savoy and some other man whom he did not know.

Dak decided that it would definitely not be a good idea for Mr. Savoy to see him in the mansion. For one thing, he was trespassing. For another, he wanted to see if he could learn why Mr. Savoy was at the mansion, and he certainly didn't want to get caught eavesdropping. In a stealth mode now, he ran back into the hallway and considered whether to go into the attic, to try to hide in one of the bedrooms, or to try to make it to the basement. Deciding on the attic, he gingerly made his way across the hallway and up the attic steps.

Fortunately, the attic was floored, though it was quite dark. Dak opened a heavy door, walked maybe 10 feet into the attic and heard the door swing nearly shut. He stood silently, waiting to become dark-adapted. It seemed to take forever. Seeing that there were some boxes and other items in various locations, he was afraid that if he moved, he would trip on something or knock something over. The resulting noise might give him away.

For a while, he heard no voices. He speculated that they were examining some item or had walked on past the house. Then, he heard them again, and it sounded like they were on the main floor. Now, he could hear snippets of conversation, pieces of sentences, or isolated words.

Mr. Savoy said something like "make sure it doesn't get in the way" and "thorn out of my side." The other man's voice didn't carry as well, but it sounded like he said, "We can do it pretty quickly..." and "around $500." Dak heard steps on the stairway and knew they were getting closer, coming to the second floor. Fortunately, he had become pretty well dark adapted now, and he moved very slowly across the attic and behind a large crate. He clearly heard Mr. Savoy say, "It's a shame in a way, but I think it's necessary." The other man asked, "Does everything have to disappear or can it be left?" Then Savoy said, "If anyone gets in the way". It was all mumbling for a while until Dak heard the other man say, "see the attic".

Dak's heart was pumping much too fast as he heard the two men coming up the attic steps. He crouched down as low as he could in a space created by three large, crumbling crates. He began trying to think what he was going to do if they saw him.

As the two men came in the door to the attic, they propped it open with a brick that happened to be there. This made a little more light in the whole attic area. The other man said, "Look at those timbers. It was really built, wasn't it?"

"Oh, yes, I would have liked to restore it one day if it weren't for this." Mr. Savoy said calmly. "At one time, I tried to get the state government interested in buying it and restoring it for visitors, but that was then, this is now." He chuckled.

"Is that right? Tell me, does all this stuff have to be removed?" asked the other man.

"I'll take care of that separately," Mr. Savoy said, as he walked further into the attic.

The other man walked even deeper into the attic and circled around the area where Dak was crouched, pausing just about a foot from Dak. *Calm down! Calm down!* Dak hoped the man couldn't hear his heart beating.

The man then walked on, saying, "Well, no problem. Let me give it some thought and get back to you with a good cost estimate." They walked back down the attic steps. Dak was very uncomfortable in his crouched position, so he stood up, banging his head on something sticking out of one of the crates. It made a loud noise, and he heard the other man say, "What the hell was that?"

"No telling," Mr. Savoy replied. "Always some strange noise in these old houses."

The two men walked on down the stairs and out of the house. Dak came down to the second floor and watched them walking back across the field to the road.

With all the adrenaline that had flowed into his veins in the last few minutes, Dak felt a little weak. He decided to sit for a minute in an upstairs bedroom.

When he had recovered, Dak went to the cellar level of the house. First, he wanted to examine in daylight the rings that he had discovered with J.D. and Donny the night they had visited the mansion. There they were, ten steel rings in a row, each attached to the stone floor by a large steel pin. They were about three feet apart. They had rusted but were still in reasonably good condition. He made notes and took pictures.

When Dak walked to the other end of the cellar, he found a wooden barrel. It looked like it had dirt in it. Dak wondered why. He grabbed the upper ring of the barrel and tilted it a bit toward him. The barrel was partially rotted but had something in it that was heavier than he would have expected dirt to be. As he turned the barrel on its side, it came apart, and a large iron ball rolled out of the dirt. It was attached to a chain about four feet long. "Wow!" he thought to himself as he took some pictures. "This is a real ball and chain; wait till I show it to J.D."

He knelt to push the dirt in a heap by the barrel, not wanting to make too big a mess. As he did that, a small object stuck between two of the floor stones caught his attention. He tried to pry it loose with his fingernail with no success, so he took out his pocket knife and forced it out. Scraping the dirt off it, he was astonished to see a metal earring with three vertical lines and two horizontal ones. It appeared to be identical to the one they had found in the coffin by the river. Dak sat back on the stone floor and looked at the earring for several seconds, trying to decipher the implications of this discovery. Totally baffled, he put the earring in his pocket, made some notes, and walked across the field to his bicycle.

The next morning, Johnnie David had the car again and stopped at Dak's house to give him a ride to school. The radio was blaring as usual, this time with Gale Storm's melodic voice.

> Take one fresh and tender kiss...
> add one night of stolen bliss
> One girl, one boy...some grief, some joy
> Memories are made of this.

Dak seized the moment and turned the volume much lower as the song ended. Then he filled Johnnie in on his trip to the mansion, with emphasis on the attic bit and the earring.

"Hey, what's going on?" J.D. asked. "What kind of earrings are these that they show up in the grave and at the mansion?"

"I can't figure it out right now, but I'm going to ask Miss Mattie when I get a chance. Maybe she'd know. But we need to go to the mansion again and see what else we can find. And we need to finish the archaeological work on the coffins, too." Dak wanted some answers.

• • •

In Miss Hurd's American History class, she passed out the test and instructed the class that they had 45 minutes to finish their work. She called their attention to the essay question and pointed out that 60% of their grade would be determined by their response to it. "Hold up your hand if you have any questions before we get started," she said.

Dak quickly flipped past the multiple choice and true/false questions to the essay instructions.

"Provide a discussion of Franklin Roosevelt's First Inaugural Address, specifically explaining why it was important, what tone it set for the people, and how it was received by the people.

Also, referring to the line, 'the only thing we have to fear is fear itself,' explain what fear the President was talking about, why he thought it was the only thing the people had to fear, the impact the line had on popular thought, and how it may have contributed to reducing the impact of the depression."

Dak tried to look like business as usual, but he found himself glancing over at Miss Hurd, and when they made eye contact, he gave her a broad smile. Charlie Johnson was also smiling.

• • •

On Saturday, Dak made an early bicycle trip over the levee to see Miss Mattie. As usual, it took her a while to get to the door. When she did, she had just taken a bath and was still clad in a pink fuzzy robe. She gave Dak a warm welcome and seemed so glad to see him. "Dak, would you like a couple cookies and a glass of buttermilk? I made pecan cookies last night."

"That sounds great, Miss Mattie!" Following her into the kitchen, he said, "I was wonderin' if you need anything, Miss Mattie, and also I wanted to tell you some things that have happened." Dak figured she was going to be short on supplies by now.

She handed Dak the cookies and buttermilk and said, "Why, I do need a few little things to eat, Dakkie, but let's sit and talk first." She walked out on the porch and sat in a big rocker, motioning for him to sit in the swing. "I'd rather gossip than eat," she added with a chuckle.

Between bites of the cookies, Dak explained the progress that he and Johnnie had made on the graves and what they had found. Then, he went over the events at the old mansion in a fair amount of detail. Finally, he got down to his questions.

"Do you have any idea who would've worn the earrings and what the earrings would've meant? I can't figure out why there was an earring on just one ear...and also why there would be the same kind of earring in the coffin and at the mansion. It would be just too weird if the two earrings are a pair-- one lost at the mansion, one taken to the grave."

Miss Mattie stared at her apron string and said nothing. Dak wondered if she had been listening. He thought maybe he should ask, but on the other hand, he didn't want to push her too fast if she was thinking about it. Eventually, she leaned forward in her chair, adjusted the pillow she was sitting on and said, "Dakkie, could I see one of the earrings?"

He took the earring from his pocket and handed it to her. "I'm sorry," he said. "I'd planned to show you this when I was tellin' you about it, but I forgot."

She held the earring in her hand and turned it over several times. "Well, I'm not sure, but I'm thinkin' I've seen an earring like this sometime. I'm thinkin' maybe there's a person in one of Aunt Mariah's pictures...you know, the ones you've got...that has an earring like this. I hope I'm not rememberin' wrong. Sure as I say it, it won't be that way. But you might look and see. Yes, I think so."

"Oh, I'll sure look and see. Miss Mattie, do you know what the earring might have meant?"

"No idea...I think maybe it was a darkie that wore it in the picture. Just have to see what you find. If it was a darkie, well, they used to enjoy most any kind of decoration, so might not have meant anything."

"Yeah, I guess," Dak agreed. "Let me ask you this. Do you know when Ellsworth Place was built and who lived there?"

"Why, you might check with your own family on that, but I always heard your great granddaddy built it, but then it went to the Ellsworths pretty early. I don't know if it's true, but that's what folks would say years ago. Have you ever heard that?" Mattie was a great source of information today.

Dak was surprised that anyone ever thought his great grand-father built that place. "No, no, I never heard that! Really, my great grandfather Leventhal might have built the place? Wow, I have to look into that. Wouldn't that be somethin'? Maybe that's the ol' home place, but I doubt it. I'd have heard about that."

"Why don't you ask your mama? She might know somethin' about it."

They talked a while longer and Dak thanked her for the cook-ies and buttermilk. Then, she unzipped her small coin purse and dumped the contents into her lap. Sorting out some coins from among buttons and tokens, she finally found enough for Dak to buy what she needed. When he returned from the store, Mattie took the groceries and gave him two dimes for his effort. "I'll sure be waitin' to hear what you find in the other grave," she said as she turned to go into the house.

Chapter 8

Hickory Hill

Upon passing Dak in the hall, Miss Hurd said, "Dak, I'll be handing out the results of the test on the depression years in today's class." She gave no hint as to what the results might be, but Dak was playing it safe. He carried some yearbook materials with him as camouflage, and, as though it were a part of that, he had his camera. In the event Charlie did get a grade of 100, he wanted the event captured for all time.

When the class had all arrived, but had not yet stopped their animated conversation, Miss Hurd tapped her pointer sharply on her desk to get everyone's attention.

"We have the results of the test, and I will hand them out in a few minutes. Before I do, I want to mention that most of you, in response to the essay question, showed a deeper appreciation of these years than for any of the previous periods we have studied. I attribute that to the fact that your parents, for the most part, lived as young adults during this period and felt it first hand. I suspect they passed down their views, wittingly or not, to you and your siblings."

At this point, Larry Lambert sneezed with such force that Amy Morrison, sitting in front of him, jumped and shrieked. This, in turn, caused guffaws throughout the room and momentarily ruined Miss Hurd's little speech.

"Bless you, Larry," she continued. "Now, if I might have your attention again."

"It was an important period, with great challenges. Perhaps no generation, with the possible exception of the one that fought the Civil War, did so much to get our country through very dark times. You all know, I'm sure, that the next topic we will study is World War II. Well, the same generation that led us through the great depression also pulled us through that terrible war. Some historians believe this was our country's greatest generation."

Dak looked at her impatiently and raised his camera a little so she could see that he had it, but she totally ignored him and continued her monolog.

"What they have done for your generation is invaluable. They have left their sweat on the handles of plows that tilled ground too dry, too poor to produce. They have left their tears on the deeds of farms that were no longer theirs. They have left their blood on places like Utah Beach, Salerno, and Okinawa when hope seemed an unrealistic expectation. The widows or mothers of 250,000 dead bravely received nicely folded flags taken from military-issue caskets. They gave you a continuation of liberty, guaranteed freedoms no matter what your heritage, a bastion from which you can pursue your happiness, dream your dreams, hope your hopes, whatever they may be."

Dak was no longer impatient. Instead, he was fascinated by what she was saying. When she said "Okinawa," he wondered if she had picked that specifically for his benefit, for the memory of his own dad. His eyes were misting over. And he loved it that she had talked of hopes and dreams.

"Today, we can do what we do because of them. We should all recognize that we stand on the shoulders of this great generation. Perhaps the best thing we can do to show our appreciation for what they did is to demonstrate that we understand what they did, that we know what events occurred, that we appreciate the sacrifices they made, and that none of it is forgotten."

Dak noticed that Miss Hurd had the class spellbound. *This ain't happenin'*, he thought to himself. *When did a class ever pay such rapt attention to anything in this high school?*

Miss Hurd continued. "A great example of demonstrating that we truly understand what this great generation did... is one of your responses to the essay question in our test. Let me read that response to you."

She picked up the paper on top of her stack and read, word-for-word, Charlie's response to the test, not mentioning whose paper it was. As she did this, Charlie leaned forward in his desk. He felt his heart rate increasing and his hands shaking.

When she had finished reading it, Miss Hurd said, "The same person who wrote this essay also answered every single multiple choice and true/false question correctly. It is rare in a career of teaching that I have seen such exemplary work, and as you know, it is rare that I give a grade of 100. Today, we have both."

At this point, all eyes turned to Dak. Everyone but Dak and Charlie was expecting that Miss Hurd was talking about Dak. Then she said, "Charlie Johnson, would you please come forward and get your paper?"

Shock and silence gripped the class for a few seconds. Then, things began to happen.

Charlie produced the grandest smile of his lifetime. He stood, and, though he was having trouble breathing normally, he walked up to Miss Hurd's desk and turned to face the class. His face was a little flushed.

It was J.D. who started it. He held his hands up in a clapping position and then very slowly did one loud clap, then another, and then a third. Other class members began to join the applause. The whole class soon followed suit. Then hoots and yells and whistles began. At that point, Dak stood, and everyone else followed. Some stood in their seats, hands over their heads, clapping, yelling and whistling. It was pandemonium, and Dak was capturing it all on film.

After a while, Miss Hurd held her hands up, palms out, to ask the class to stop the noise. Then she handed the test paper, with a large black 100 across the top, to Charlie. He held it over his head with both hands, the grade facing the students, a tear running down his cheek, while the class went into hoots and applause all over again. Miss Hurd turned to Charlie and said, "Congratulations!" No one heard, but Charlie didn't care. He knew his mother would be happy beyond belief, and that's what mattered most to him.

• • •

In gym class the following day, Dak and Donny Branch were involved in a basketball game, Dak being on the skins team and Donny the shirts. Dak was in the process of trying to block

Donny's beautifully executed jump shot, when somebody yelled, "What's that smell?"

"It's not me. I didn't do it! It was Donny!" shouted Arnie Randolph, trying to inject a little humor.

"Smells like a fire," Donny said as he held his nose higher. It was as if he thought another inch of altitude would surely solve the mystery.

Coach Jarsico stopped the ball and held it under one arm. A short round of discussion resulted in general agreement that there really was the smell of smoke. He ordered all the students to leave the building immediately and assemble on the parking lot. Then he stepped onto the stage to see if he could find the source. When he opened the door to the holding room to the rear and left of the stage, smoke and flames rolled out. The startled coach fell backwards momentarily but recovered quickly and ran out the door nearest the main building, yelling, "Call the fire truck! Run in and have someone call the fire truck!"

The volunteer fire department took about twenty minutes to get to the fire station and then another five minutes to get from there to the high school gymnasium. It was an easy fire to extinguish once they arrived, but considerable damage had been done to the stage end of the gym. This was all repairable, but the layer of greasy smoke residue meant the year's remaining physical education classes would have to be held outside. That was no big problem, but the gym was the only facility they had that was large enough for the graduation ceremony. The principal had gotten acceptance from the Lieutenant Governor to speak at the graduation, and he didn't want to schedule that outdoors and risk it being rained out after the speaker traveled from Springfield to do it. He made a quick decision to try to get the gym cleaned and repaired in time for graduation.

• • •

On Saturday morning, Dak and Johnnie David decided to continue their dig. As they walked to the site, Dak sensed that J.D. was a little down, so he asked how it was going with his mother.

"Well, she had another flare up, just about like what she had before. She was real hostile with me and with my dad, Dak... it's just real hard to deal with." J.D. said quietly.

"Oh, I'm sure it's hard, Johnnie," Dak replied. "I don't know how you cope with it as well as you do."

J.D. sighed. "I mean...it seems like I could just tell myself it's only this problem she has... don't get worked up about it. It's not her real self. But then when she does it, it's just so...it hurts too much. It doesn't work like it seems it would."

"Did your dad ever go talk to that guy at Harrisburg?"

"No, but I'm still pushin' him to do that. Maybe he will."

Dak thought for a minute. "Didn't you say your dad was goin' over to Harrisburg with you to get you a suit for graduation? Why don't you get him to go by that doctor's office while you're there?"

J.D. wasn't sure. "If I push too hard, he'll tell me to bug off," he said.

"Yeah, right, so just wait 'til you're on the way over there and say, 'Hey, Dad, why don't we stop in and see that guy I was tellin' you about. Maybe that could help Mom.' You could see what he'd say. I bet he'd do it." Dak had the ability to convince J.D. of most anything.

Finally, J.D. said, "Hell, I'll do it!" After that, he seemed to feel better.

The two boys found their archaeological site just as they had left it. They took off the debris and the tarp and recovered the tools from their hiding place. Then they continued digging at what they thought was about waist level on the skeleton. They immediately uncovered a leather braid or rope, which they judged had been used by the man as a belt. It was soft and mostly rotted, but intact enough that they could tell that it was leather.

"Seems like if it was a belt, there'd be a buckle," said J.D.

"Unless he just tied it," Dak replied, "and didn't need a buckle. It looks like it was just tied. See how this loops here?" Dak took some notes and a picture.

Just below the waist, Dak was taking one little spoonful of dirt after another when he heard a clink. Digging a little deeper, he saw something shiny.

J.D. saw it also. "Hey, Dak, there's something there!"

"I know. Let's get it out real careful like...don't want to break anything."

Dak pulled it out and brushed the loose dirt off it. His eyes grew large as he viewed the thing.

"Holy shit!" J.D. exclaimed, "It's a gold ring with some jewel in it."

They ran to the river to wash it off and were even more excited when they saw the glittering beauty of the red jewel.

"Is it a ruby?" J.D. asked.

"Gee, I don't know. It sure looks like it!" Dak was thrilled.

Returning to the grave, Dak said, "You know, this wasn't on a finger. See, his arm bones go down to his sides. Here's his elbow. The humerus is up here, the radius and ulna here...so his wrist and hand are down there."

"Hell, Dak, speak English to me. I thought a radius was part of a circle."

"Okay, okay. Thing is, J.D., this was more in his abdomen area. What do you make of that?"

"Beats the crap out of me," J.D. replied. "Maybe it was just laid on top of his body when he was put to rest."

Dak didn't think so. He took pictures from various angles of the site where they found the ring and wrote some notes about it.

They proceeded down the body, but found nothing else unusual until they got into the thigh area. There Dak saw an irregular area on the bone. "Look at this! Looks like he had a broken femur...uh, thigh bone...right at the neck of the femur, but it was healed before he died. See that, J.D.?"

"Know what?" answered J.D. "I'll be ready to practice medicine by the time we get through here."

Then, they went outward to the right hand. Near the hand, they noted a black thorny stem. It was almost as if it were petrified, hard and brittle, but clearly a thorny stem.

"Remains of a rose?" asked J.D.

"Maybe so. Wow! I bet it is!" Dak was trying to picture the scene that this all came from.

Near the other hand, but not in it, they found yet another item. This one was a small decorative cross. It was a verdi color, and Dak thought it must be oxidized copper. They washed it off and marveled over its elegance.

They could find nothing else unusual. It turned out that the legs terminated at the ankle because the end of the coffin had washed away and the feet had gone with it.

After taking more notes and photos, Dak and Johnnie took the thorny stem and tied it to a stick that acted as a splint to keep it from getting broken. Then they put the ring, the cross, and the thorny stem in a little bag to take with them. After some discussion of their options, they returned to their original configuration any bones that they had moved.

"That seems most respectful of the deceased," Dak mumbled. Then they moved the dirt back over the bones and replaced the rotting wooden plank pieces to their initial positions, as best they could.

Once again, the boys hid their tools, spread their tarp and covered it all with leaves and brushy debris.

As they walked back along the river toward town, J.D. took the gold ring out of the bag and examined it closely. "Hey, Dak," he said, "I don't think there is a chip or scratch on this jewel, ain't that something?"

"It's beautiful," Dak said. "You might look inside the band and see if it says it's 24 karat gold or something."

J.D. looked carefully and then stopped walking. "Hey, look at this. It says something inside. There's writin' in here." He handed the ring to Dak.

"Well, I'll be dipped in stuff, J.D. Know what this is? It's Latin. It says 'Semper Fidelis, Semper Amemus.' Know what that means?"

J.D. smirked. "I don't think you had to ask me that. No, butt hole, I don't know what that means. I bet I know somebody who does, though."

"Right. You are right about that. It means...are you ready for this, Johnnie David? Prepare yourself for romance. Drum roll, please. It means, 'Forever faithful, forever in love'. Hey, this is gettin' really good...we even have a love affair woven into our archaeological investigation."

"Forever in love, huh," said J.D. "Well, all that love didn't keep him from gettin' shot, did it?"

"No, it didn't. That's a big hole through his ribs, I'd say. Could even be that she shot him."

As the boys continued their walk back to town, J.D. said he'd like to go to Cave-in-Rock for a picnic with the girls. Dak thought that was a great idea, so they agreed do it on Sunday if the girls consented.

• • •

Early on Sunday morning, J.D. came by in the old Ford. Dak didn't hear the radio at first and thought it must have broken. Then Johnnie cranked down the window, and the whole neighborhood could hear Joe Turner singing, *Corina, Corina*. J.D. held up an unopened bottle of beer for Dak to see.

"Your ears will never be the same," Dak yelled.

"Yeah, this beer is a little lame," replied J.D., verifying Dak's assumption, "but it's the best I could afford."

Dak and J.D. had decided to tell the girls about their find on the river provided they could successfully swear them to secrecy. They thought this would be a good time to do it.

"Ladies," Dak began, "we have something interestin' to tell you, but it is such that we want it kept secret."

"Oh, Dak, what could ya'll know that could be so secretive?" Marie asked.

"Shut yo' mouf and lissen, girl!" J.D. exclaimed, mimicking some movie character he'd seen.

"So, do ya'll agree to keep it secret if we tell you...agree not to tell anyone, not even your mom or your close friends?" Dak asked.

The girls looked at each other. Melodie grinned and shook her head back and forth a little. Marie rolled her eyes and sighed.

"I don't know if I want to do that or not. Trouble is, I might slip and tell somebody, and you'd be all mad...and it's probably not that interestin' anyway." Marie was in a bargaining mood.

"What will you do for us if we do agree?" asked Melodie.

"Ahhhh, this evenin' we'll let the fire burn low, provide love songs on the radio, and kiss you till you beg for mercy," said Dak. "You can rub your lovely hands through my flat top and giggle. Believe me; we'll make it worth your while."

"Okay, silly," replied Melodie. "I'll keep it a secret. What is it?"

"Marie, my dear, your decision please. Must we ask you to wait outside while we inform Melodie?"

"Oh, I give up! Tell us the stupid secret." Marie would have bargained further, but without the support of Melodie, it seemed hopeless.

J.D. started the story, and Dak joined in. Before they stopped, they had told all the details of the graves, the mansion, and the conversations with Miss Mattie.

"Oh my God, you touched that stuff?" asked Marie. "I hope you washed real well. Yecht! Don't get that ring near me. No telling what kind of disease is on that stuff, not to mention that it might be haunted."

"No, no," Dak said. "This is very old. It's like an archaeological dig. It's just dirt and bones, but there is a mystery to be solved."

"Well, keep it away from me," Marie said. "I don't want to touch that stuff."

Melodie was more interested in the story. "What do you think the connection is between the mansion and the graves?" she asked..

"Who knows? But the same kind of earring bein' both places tells us there is a connection." J.D. responded.

They passed a sign saying, "You are entering Cave-in-Rock, the Best-Kept Secret in America!"

"No, no," said Marie. "The best kept secret in America is the graves on the Uppers, right?"

At Cave-in-Rock, there is a park area on a wooded bluff overlooking the Ohio River. Across the river is Kentucky farmland at a lower elevation, green as far as the eye can see, with cornfields interspersed with forested areas. On the river, a ferry struggles in a z-shaped path to cross the river and fight the current, adding to the beauty and quaintness of the scene.

The cave's mouth, which is under the bluff facing the river, is accessible by stairs made in the stone. Forming a gaping hole in the 120-foot cliff, the opening is perhaps forty feet high and sixty feet wide. The large part of the cave trails back under the bluff for a couple hundred feet, and no one seems to know how far beyond that the smaller subterranean opening traverses the limestone.

J.D. drove the car up onto the bluff and parked near a picnic table and fire ring. As they all walked over to the cliff's edge to see the river view, they noticed a circular stone railing surrounding a vertical hole perhaps twenty feet in diameter. Looking 120 feet down, they could see light that came from the cave opening. The hole was covered with rebar topped with something that looked like chain-link fencing. Dak jumped up on the fencing and started walking across the opening. Melodie, horrified that he would do such a thing when a rebar failure would mean certain death, screamed, "Dak, get off that right now! Hurry, Dak! Dak! Please!" She was feeling panicked and didn't know anything she could do but scream. "Oh, please, Dak, get off that!"

Dak quickly jumped off, saying, "Sorry, Melodie. I didn't realize it would upset you. Sorry."

They walked down the stone steps to the water's edge, and there was the huge cave, yawning at the river. "Wow, that's impressive! Look at that!" said Marie.

"Took me a long time to dig all that out," J.D. said, smiling. Then he looked over at Dak. "Hey Dak, weren't there pirates or something that operated out of this cave?"

"Yeah, there were. There were several pirate gangs. I think Sam Mason was the most famous. He had been a militia captain and a judge, but he turned to crime at some point. He converted the cave into a tavern and gathered a gang of men to help him with the pirate business."

"Pirate business, like Blackbeard, where he'd have his ship attack some other ship, draw their swords, kill the people, and steal the ship?" asked Marie, waving an imaginary sword in the air.

"No, it wasn't like that," replied Dak. "There were a lot of flat boats with families comin' down the river to go to Arkansas or Missouri or somewhere to settle. They would bring their belongin's with them, of course...all their valuables. Mason would have gang members posted up river in Shawneetown. When a flat boat would stop in Shawneetown, the gang member would make friends with the people on the flat boat...maybe help them get supplies, tell them some jokes. Then the gang member would ask to hitch a ride down river with them on their flat boat. When they got to Cave-in-Rock, he would talk them into stopping for a rest or a drink. When they did, the other gang members would show up and...well, they'd kill the family. Then, they would take the belongin's for their own."

"Why wouldn't the sheriff or somebody stop them?" asked J.D.

"Well, it was the frontier, and there weren't many lawmen runnin' around enforcin' the laws."

"I bet that was a big surprise. You come in to rest and get a drink, and a bunch of people come out and start shooting at you and your family," said Melodie.

"Yeah, I suppose it was...you can just imagine all the screamin' and panic," Dak said thoughtfully. "These were vicious people. And they got by with it for a long time because the travelers would just disappear... nobody knew what happened to them. Maybe they wouldn't show up in Natchez or some place where they were expected two weeks later. But, anything could have happened to them on the river, and nobody had any way of knowin' that it happened at Cave-in-Rock."

"So, whatever happened to Sam Mason?" Marie asked.

"Well, as the area got more settled, the law officers became more numerous, and Mason left Cave-in-Rock to go somewhere down the Mississippi. He still preyed on river travelers, though. Eventually, they captured him. Tried to claim he was just a settler comin' down river, but they found a big roll of money and a bunch of scalps. He was jailed, but he escaped."

"Man, this was one tricky guy!" said J.D. "So, was he ever heard from again?"

"Yeah, they put out a reward for him, and two of his own men killed him for the reward money."

"At least he wasn't capturin' freed slaves like ol' Crenshaw over at Hickory Hill," J.D. said.

"Yeah, but there were some other gangs doin' that," Dak countered. "Black people escapin' from the South had the problem that they had to cross the river some way. There weren't any bridges, so they'd find a ferry if they could. They say one of the gangs captured black people when they crossed the ferry and then sold them to Crenshaw up at Hickory Hill, not too far away. There was apparently a connection between Crenshaw and one of the gangs here."

They walked back into the cave until it got much smaller and darker, looking for some remnant of the pirate era, but they saw none. As they exited the cave, Johnnie David said, "Hey, let's go eat something."

Before long, they had a fire built and roasted hot dogs and marshmallows. J.D. opened the trunk and handed everyone a beer, while Marie suggested a sing-along. They attempted a few of J.D.'s favorites, but Marie was the only one of the four who had any sort of voice for it. J.D. cut loose with his version of *Heartbreak Hotel* to everyone's dismay. Finally, they decided to get out some blankets and just sit on the ground and talk.

After they sat awhile, Marie stretched out on the blanket with her head in J.D.'s lap. This caused J.D. to bend over and lightly kiss her. After a few more kisses, J.D. asked Marie if she would like to sit in the car and listen to some soft music. She said she would. Dak and Melodie, left on the blanket next to the dying fire, looked into each other's eyes, caressed, and thought what a magic moment it was.

• • •

On Monday evening, Eleanor planned to attend a Ladies' Aid meeting at the church and asked Nancy if she would like to go along. Nancy had gone to two previous meetings and proclaimed them both "very boring." "Even so," she said, "they will have some cookies, so I guess I'll go." For his part, Dak was happy to see them both gone because it gave him an opportunity to look at Aunt Mariah's papers. Dak pulled the box out from under his bed as soon as they were gone.

He began thumbing through the box and thought, *Wow, there's a huge amount of stuff here. I've only looked at about a tenth of this. It'll take me a long time to get through it all.*

The box contained many letters, both to Aunt Mariah and to other family members, from a variety of people. Surprisingly, it also contained what appeared to be letters that Aunt Mariah had written to others, but never sent. Then, there were loose notes that were dated. Some of these went into detail about not only what was happening, but also how she felt about it. They were like diary entries, except that there was no notebook or cover that attached them one to another. Finally, there were photographs, some of these enclosed in letters, some attached to notes, and some loose in the box. Most of the pictures had dates and notes written on the back.

Dak thought the first thing he should do is get the material in date order. When he started that process, he found that it was already in date order with only a few exceptions. "I guess she put it into the box as she acquired it," he thought. Apparently, whenever Miss Mattie had looked at any pictures, she was careful to put them back just where she found them.

Dak began thumbing through the material to see if anything stood out as being particularly interesting. He picked up one of the loose diary entries and thought, "She had such beautiful handwriting." As he scanned the page, it looked interesting, so he decided to read it all.

It told of one late night in the summer of 1856 when Crenshaw and one of his men had arrived at Hickory Hill with two other men in a wagon pulled by two horses. Mariah was in a front upstairs bedroom sleeping but was awakened by the noise. She went to her open window to watch and listen without lighting a lamp or candle. In the moonlit night, she could see that the two men in the wagon were black. They were both tied, and one of them seemed to be hurt. Crenshaw had called his wife out to help treat the injured man. He was clearly upset, cursing and yelling loudly. When things settled down a little, Crenshaw called the man stupid and said, "He acted up, and I had to hit him across the head a few times with my pistol." He asked his wife to bandage the man's wounds, said he would put the rings on the two men, and then they could stay in the attic for the night. He added that the one who was hurt might have to stay in the attic for a few days until he was well enough to go down to the salt springs. He said he didn't want to lose the man because he was worth a lot. Mariah added that as Crenshaw brought the men through the upstairs to the attic, she cracked open her door just slightly and watched them. She said she was very upset by the sight, that the injured black man was young and handsome, but his head was dripping blood. That ended Aunt Mariah's entry for that day.

Dak was fascinated by this story and began looking at the following entries to see what else he could learn. What he found was that about two days later, Crenshaw asked Mariah to treat the man's wounds. Both Crenshaw and the injured man told Mariah that the he had taken a fall from a horse while trying to move a log. Of course, Mariah knew better. She would go to the attic with a wash pan and cloths and clean the wounds, which were severe, and replace the bandages. After a few days of doing this, Mariah had gotten the man to admit to her privately that he was a freed man and that Crenshaw and his assistant had captured him at gunpoint. Crenshaw called the slave Georgie because he was born in Georgia. The man had been given his freedom in the will of a plantation owner who had no descendants. He and the other black man came from the same plantation and made their way together up through the South with papers verifying that they were free men. They had had some close calls but hadn't been captured until they arrived in Illinois and let their guard down. When he described Crenshaw holding a cigar to their freedom papers and burning them, he broke down in tears.

The most interesting thing to Dak was that Mariah was clearly sympathetic to Georgie's plight, increasingly so as time passed. By three weeks after the men had arrived, Mariah seemed to be more than sympathetic. It was reading more like he was a good friend. She would describe not only his progress in healing, but his personality traits and virtues as well. He was apparently a bright young man and by her description was strikingly handsome. Mariah seemed to think he was wonderful, but there he was, in leg chains in the attic of her relatives.

Dak would like to have gone further with this developing story, but he heard Eleanor and Nancy coming in the door downstairs. He replaced the papers in the box and slid the box under his bed.

• • •

At breakfast the next morning, Eleanor asked Dak if the suit he had was okay for the prom, or if he would need a new one. Dak said the one he had would be fine. Then Eleanor said she wanted to meet with Mr. Savoy and make sure everything was okay with the college loan. At that, Dak felt the pain run down his body, the pain that always struck when he heard unusually bad news.

"Okay," Dak answered, "but I'm going to the prom with Melodie, and Judy Savoy knows that. I think she has arranged to go with someone else, but I'm not sure."

"Well, if he is not going to give us the loan for that reason, or for any reason, we need to know it. We'll have to make other arrangements if that's the case." Eleanor seemed no longer to feel it was important for Dak to take Judy Savoy to the prom.

The next day, Dak took the afternoon off at school so he and his mother could meet with Mr. Savoy. They arrived a little early for their 2:30 PM appointment, but Mr. Savoy kept them waiting until 3:05PM. When he asked them into his office, he remained seated and the two other chairs in the room had books lying in them. As they stood facing him, he gave them a frosty greeting and said, "What can I do to help you?"

"We had talked with you earlier about a college loan for Dak, and it was left open," Eleanor said. "Dak has been accepted by the college and has been granted a scholarship, so he's all prepared to attend in the fall, provided the loan is approved. So, we thought we'd better get back with you and see where we stand."

"Where you stand, huh?" Mr. Savoy said. "Well, where you stand is out in the cold, I think, because money for college loans is a little short this year."

"That's fine, we'll..." Dak was responding, but Eleanor broke in with, "Oh, is money that tight, Mr. Savoy? I hadn't expected that because Brenda Paulson's mother had told me that you had approved a loan for her. She was quite surprised because she said Brenda's grades were not that good, and she was unable to get a scholarship."

"Mom, I don't want to do this. Let's go."

"No, no... just a minute, Dak. I just wondered why your loan wasn't approved. I'm sure Mr. Savoy will be gracious enough to tell us that."

"Mrs. Leventhal, it is sometimes hard to have a neat little package of reasons for our decisions on loans. It is a complex process that takes many things into account."

"I'm sure of that, Mr. Savoy," said Dak. "We thank you for..." Again, Eleanor interrupted.

"Things like what, Mr. Savoy? What kinds of things does your process take into account, and which of these were not favorable for Dak? Was it grades, was it character, was it what he does in the community, was it a poor recommendation by the school principal or a teacher, or was it his relationship with the other students? Just what was it, Mr. Savoy? What was it that made you think Dak is not a good risk? What was it, Mr. Savoy?"

Dak took Eleanor by the arm. "Mom, he has given us his answer. We'd better go." Eleanor turned toward the door, and Dak helped her with her coat.

Mr. Savoy leaned back in his chair and took off his glasses. "Well, Mrs. Leventhal, I'd have to say that my assessment is that Dak doesn't always use the best judgment, doesn't always make the best decisions, could have better considered what forces lead to success in life and which ones do not."

"Mr. Savoy, you have made yourself quite clear," Dak said, "and my Mother and I will not burden you further with questions on your rationale. We all have our own criteria for makin' our decisions, don't we, and yours is... what it is. Our decisions are our own business. In the end, time and events will tell whether we have made good decisions or not. I invite you to look at me twenty years from now, Mr. Savoy...to look at what I've been able to do in twenty years and decide for yourself whether I would have been a good risk. I will tell you this: I am going to college with or without your loan. Good day, Sir."

When they arrived home, Dak told Eleanor she should not beg for help for him, that he did not want that, and that he would somehow make it through college without a loan from Mr. Savoy's bank. "So, please, Mom," he said, "you don't have to beg from anyone, you don't have to look up to anyone, you can hold your head high... because you have done your job so very well... you have made Nancy and me into confident, happy people who have great dreams and hopes and that...that... is the very best any mother can do for her kids. Without that, Mom, not many kids can have a good life...and with it, no kid can fail."

Eleanor's eyes were misting over as she hugged Dak. She beamed with pride as she, for the first time, fully realized the truth of what Dak had just said.

Chapter 9

The Secret Room

Nancy had an important test coming up the next day, so Eleanor suggested she go to bed early. As soon as he thought Nancy was asleep, Dak yawned and said, "Think I'll turn in a little early, too." He went up to his bedroom and quietly pulled Aunt Mariah's letterbox into the middle of the room. He knew he didn't have much time but thought he might find something of interest even in a short time. He randomly selected a paper and began reading it.

Mariah's diary-like entry for that particular day seemed rather innocuous at first. It told of going for a walk into the apple orchard and finding James, a black man, in the process of picking apples for the family. Mariah had stopped to talk with James, who said he was a carpenter by trade, but since Master Crenshaw didn't have any carpentry to do today, he was told to pick the apples. Mariah asked how long he had been at Hickory Hill. James explained he had been there since two summers ago when he, as a freed slave, had made his way across the ferry at Cave-in-Rock, showing his freedom papers. When he was barely across the ferry, a small group of white men on horses surrounded him and, at gunpoint, took his freedom papers from him. They then tied him and placed him on a horse. After some discussion about whether to put a gag in his mouth, three of the men led the horse through a backwoods trail to Hickory Hill.

Mariah made no note of any concern about the way in which they had captured James and brought him to Hickory Hill. Rather, she wrote about asking James what kinds of carpentry he had done. He replied that he had worked in this part of the country before. He related that before he was freed, his master in Kentucky had leased him to a Master Leventhal to help with finish carpentry on a mansion near Shawneetown. He said it was a beautiful place and even had a secret room.

Fascinated by this entry, Dak read several more pages but found no further reference to the mansion or the secret room. He reread the part about Master Leventhal, hoping to glean some additional tidbit that he might have missed.

Dak had wondered who took all the photographs in the box. He thought most people wouldn't have had a camera in those days. Then he saw Mariah's comment about Mr. Crenshaw having a visiting photographer come once a month and take photos around the home, in the fields and orchards, and at the salt springs. *So, all these photos were taken by a professional,* he thought.

As Dak pondered what he had learned from Aunt Mariah's papers, he considered discussing it with Miss Mattie. He knew she would be okay with the discussion about James, but he wondered if the discussion of Aunt Mariah's relationship with Georgie might be a sensitive topic with her. After all, in her generation, relationships involving a white woman and a black man were not just taboo, they were scandalous. If Miss Mattie thought he was being impertinent in suggesting such a possibility, it might result in ruining the good relationship he had with her. If she were even mildly unhappy with him, she might ask him to return Aunt Mariah's papers. He decided to talk with her but to approach it carefully and feel his way along.

The next day, he went to her house. When he leaned his bike on a fence post in the front, he could hear the clanking of a cowbell in a little pasture that she had at the bottom of the levee. He could see that she was leading her cow into the small barn next to the pasture. As he made his way down the rocky path to the barn, he whistled so she would see him coming. *Not a good idea to startle her*, he thought to himself. She looked up with a big smile. "Good morning, Dakkie. I'm down here. Come on down."

Miss Mattie had a blue speckled water bucket she used for milking the cow. The bucket and a three-legged stool that was just the right height was all she needed for her task. When Dak arrived at her side, she sat and began filling a small bowl with milk for the orange tabby cat she kept in her small barn.

"Good mornin,' Miss Mattie! You're hard at work, I see."

Miss Mattie looked up and nodded as she positioned the bucket under the cow's udder. "I'm just milking Matilda. Going to make a little fresh butter and some buttermilk biscuits. How are you, Dakkie?"

"I'm pretty good, Miss Mattie," Dak answered, "I had a chance to look at a little bit of Aunt Mariah's stuff." After he said it, he wished he had made some small talk for a while before bringing it up.

"Oh, you did? Well, I'm real interested to know what it says. You know, I often wondered, but I just never did feel good about showin' it to anybody because Aunt Mariah kept it hid away all her life. I know she thought it had a lot of secrets, but she didn't want it thrown away either, so she gave it to me."

"Well, she had beautiful handwritin'," Dak opened, "and wrote real well. She wrote about bein' at Hickory Hill one night when ol' man Crenshaw brought home a couple black men, one of them injured. The injured one, Crenshaw kept in the attic, and after a while, he had Aunt Mariah go up every day and tend his wounds. Did she ever mention that to you?"

"No, Dak, Can't say as I ever heard that." Mattie said thoughtfully.

"Well, she seemed to feel real sorry for this injured guy, chained in the attic and all."

"Why, yes, Dakkie, she was sympathetic to the darkies and always felt they were not treated right." She moved the bucket a little and kept milking.

"She seemed to like this injured guy. She said he was real smart, as smart as any white man." Dak was approaching the subject gradually.

The cat had finished its bowl of milk and was brushing against Mattie's leg, wanting more. "I think you had enough, Carrots," she said. "Now you go lay down."

Dak could see he would have to try again. "What did Aunt Mariah think of Crenshaw?" he asked.

"Oh, she didn't like the man. She often said he was a powerful man, but not a good man. I tell you, though...she always said he treated her well, and he didn't have to let her stay there."

"Did she ever say anything about any particular darkie?" Dak asked.

"Well, no, I don't think so." Mattie started to say something else, but then paused. Catching her fleeting thought, she said, "Oh, there was one called Georgie. She used to say how smart and good lookin' he was. She said he was a mix, that he for sure had some white blood, and that he must have been sculpted by God because no man could make anything that beautiful. Why, we would poke fun at her for sayin' that this darkie was good lookin', but she would just laugh and say, 'Well, if you'd seen him, you'd think so too.' And I bet he was good lookin'...for a darkie."

"She never mentioned a darkie named James that was a carpenter?" Dak asked.

She seemed to be concentrating. Finally, she said, "I don't remember anything about a James."

"What do you suppose ever happened to Georgie, Miss Mattie?"

"Oh...oh, I think he got traded. I could be wrong, but I think Aunt Mariah said he got traded to somebody in Mississippi." Miss Mattie was having a little trouble with her memories. "Come on, Matilda," she said to the cow. "Let's put you back out in the pasture."

• • •

The following day, Dak was thinking about Ellsworth Place again. He was thinking about Miss Mattie saying earlier that she had always heard that his great-grandfather, Dakston Paul Leventhal I, had originally built Ellsworth Place. "Maybe I should ask Eleanor about this," he mumbled to himself. He expected she wouldn't know anything about it because she really wasn't interested in that sort of thing, but why not ask?

He found Eleanor on the back porch, taking clothes out of the rinse tub, putting them through the wringer of the washer, and then tossing them into a basket to be taken to the clothesline.

"Mom, I have a question for you," said Dak.

"How unusual!" she said. Eleanor was in a good mood this morning. There was something about doing the wash that she found refreshing, like starting anew.

Dak ignored her little quip. "I was talking to Miss Mattie, and she said she had heard when she was a kid that Ellsworth Place was originally built by my Great Grandfather Leventhal. I would have thought that I'd have heard of that before... if it's true. Do you know if he did?"

"Well, Dak, I think your information is correct. I heard that once, too," replied Eleanor.

"Where'd you hear it...anybody that should really know?" he asked.

"Dak, you're stretching my memory, but let me see. It was before you were born. Your dad had never mentioned it, but we were at a church social once when Reverend Harliss was there. You remember him, don't you?"

"No, don't think I do," Dak said.

"Well, anyway, they were raffling a quilt, and it was really a fancy one. It was a modified wedding ring design, I remember, with real soft beige-on-off-white colors and this gold eagle appliquéd over the center. The eagle was holding red and blue ribbons. It was a beautiful thing."

"Yeah, Mom, but what about Ellsworth Place?" Dak was getting a little impatient with his Mom's tendency to ramble.

"Well, so your dad, he bought ten raffle tickets and Blaze Putnam was there. Blaze said something like your dad must think there was a million dollars sewn into the quilt's lining. Your dad, humoring Blaze, says, 'Well, I think so.' So Blaze... I think he'd been drinking or something. He says, 'What would you do with a million dollars if you had it?' Your dad just jokingly said he'd build a big mansion. Then, Blaze surprised me by saying something like, 'That's what your granddaddy did'."

"But that doesn't say his granddaddy built Ellsworth Place. He could have been referrin' to something else." Dak replied.

"Oh, but that wasn't all. When we got home, I asked your dad what Blaze meant by that. I thought that maybe he was just drinking too much. But your dad said, no, he was right about that. He said his grandpa had built Ellsworth Place but later traded it to Captain Ellsworth for one of his river boats, the *Queen of Egypt*."

Dak dropped his mouth open in total surprise. "You are razzin' me!"

"No, that's what he said," replied Eleanor matter-of-factly. "I don't think we ever talked about it again because neither your dad nor I were very interested in that sort of thing."

Dak was trying to soak up this information while he was pumping water to fill the reservoir on the stove. Just as he finished his pumping chore, Johnnie David showed up unexpectedly on his bicycle.

"What? No four wheeled vehicle today? It must be tough!" Dak was envious of Johnnie David having the car so much and even more envious of him having a dad.

"Well," said J.D., "I've run out of things to promise the ol' man, so I'm stuck on the bike. Thought we might make a little trip to the Uppers. What say you?"

"Sounds good, soon as I finish here," replied Dak.

Before long, the two of them were on their way, walking up the winding path through the willows and brush, anxious to see what they would find in the second coffin. They were talking about what Dak had just learned about Ellsworth Place and the secret room. Suddenly, they were face-to-face with Donny Branch.

"Shit, Donny, you startled me!" J.D. exclaimed. "What are you doin'?"

"I've just been fishin'. I didn't catch a thing, so I was goin' home. I had a giant mama on the line, but she got loose before I got her in. I saw her though. It was a buffalo."

"That's what they always say," said J. D, "only they usually say it was a catfish."

Dak was wondering what they could tell Donny they were doing. He certainly didn't want to give up the secret of the coffins. Just hiking? Taking a walk? He was having a hard time coming up with anything credible.

"What are y'all doin'?" Donny asked, before they were ready to answer.

"Ahhh, we were goin' up to the Uppers to take a little swim," said J.D. "Guess we better get on our way. See you later, Donny."

"Swimmin'? Ain't it a little cold for swimmin'?"

"Well, we thought it might be fun to try it out, might be in-vigoratin'." Dak answered.

"Sounds like fun, mind if I join y'all?" Donny asked. "I haven't been swimmin' since last fall."

Surprised, J.D. said, "Sure thing, if you don't think you'll freeze your fanny off. It's still pretty cold. You might want to swim when it's warmer."

While Dak was wondering how they were going to get out of this situation, J.D. didn't seem concerned. Dak took that as a sign that J.D. had a trick up his sleeve.

When they reached the beach area, J.D. said, "Hey, we forgot our swimmin' trunks, Dak. I knew we were forgettin' something. Guess we'll have to skip the swimmin' today."

"Who needs swimmin' trunks, Johnnie?" Donny replied. "Hey, we swim in our birthday suits all the time."

J.D. had relied on the absence of trunks to get them out of swimming, but Donny already had most of his clothes off. "Let's go!" he yelled.

Caught with no other option, Dak and J.D. began undressing. Within minutes, they were all three running naked into the cold water, screaming outrageously to offset the effects of the sudden cold. Once they were in for a few minutes, it didn't feel so cold, but they certainly did find it invigorating. Dak suggested they go up river a little piece and see if they could find a log to roll into the water. He liked to try to stand on a floating log and also to sit on it and ride it downstream in the current.

They found a log soon enough because there was a big pile of driftwood deposited about a mile upstream. It took a while to get it into the water. Once there, they all tried standing on the log and rolling it, the objective being to be the last man standing. It turned out that J.D. was best at that sport, so he was most of-ten standing, while the other two were trying to get back on the tricky log.

Dak heard a motor boat and then spotted it downstream coming toward the Uppers. They couldn't tell who it was at first, but they could see that it was a man, so they weren't concerned about their nude condition. As the boat moved closer, they could see that the man was slowing the boat's motion. Then, he stopped the boat about 200 yards downstream from them and tossed out an anchor.

"Know who that is?" asked Donny. "It's Savoy, you know, the man that runs the bank. He just got that new boat about a month ago. I'd recognize it anywhere."

They all three quit what they were doing and looked uncertainly toward Savoy. Johnnie was still standing on the log, and the log was still drifting downstream toward Savoy. Savoy now had a pair of binoculars, looking at the boys.

"Hell, what's he doin'?" asked J.D.

"Lookin at us, best I can tell." Dak said. "Have no idea why he's doin' that. Are we breakin' some law or something? Or does he own the river too?"

"No, don't think so," said Donny. "Maybe he just likes looking at naked boys."

"I don't know what he's expectin' to see," joked Dak, "but he's gonna need somethin' stronger than binoculars if he's going to see J.D.'s micro-equipment." As he said that, he put his foot on a limb sticking out from the log and quickly rolled the log. J.D. couldn't maintain his footing, so he was in the water, and both Dak and Donny were on the log, battling it out.

"I hope he's takin' pictures of you two guys all naked!" J.D. said, laughing loudly.

As they drifted downstream, they came within 20 yards of Savoy's boat. He appeared to be fishing but kept looking in the direction of the boys. He didn't say anything as they passed, but changed his position in the boat so that he was always facing them. Donny started to hold up his middle finger, but Dak rolled the log before it was entirely obvious what Donny was doing. Eventually, the boys got far enough downstream that they ignored the boat but continued the log game until they reached their starting point. Then, they all got off the log and went to shore to get dressed.

"That log will be in New Orleans in a couple weeks," said Dak.

Dak and Johnnie could think of no suitable ruse to allow them to go look at the coffin while Donny went back to town. Besides, it was getting too late to get into the archaeology work today. So, off they went back to town, the three of them, talking about Savoy's weird actions and speculating about what he was really doing.

• • •

On Monday morning, Johnnie David once again talked his father into letting him use the old Ford. He picked Dak up at the usual time with the radio volume at its maximum level. This time, it was Kay Starr doing the *Rock and Roll Waltz*.

> And while they danced, only one thing was wrong
> They were trying to waltz to a rock and roll song
> a-one, two, and then rock.
> a-one, two and then roll.

To Dak's surprise, J.D. actually reached over and lowered the volume himself. This probably means he has something on his mind, Dak thought.

"Dak," said J.D., "you're goin' off to college next year, Marie is applyin' for a music scholarship, Donny is going to start workin' in his uncle's machine shop up in Peoria, and I don't know what the hell I'm going to do."

Dak thought for a few seconds. "Yeah, I'm goin' to college, but I don't know where I'm going to get the money because I didn't get a loan. Ol' Savoy won't give me one. Why don't you go to college with me? We all know you're smart enough to do it...and I'm sure your dad would help you with expenses." As he said that, Dak thought once again how nice it would be to have a dad.

"I don't think I'm cut out for it, Dak," replied J.D. "I just don't like to study as much as I'd have to. For me, it's hard to sit down for hours at a time and read stuff, and I hear that there would be work to do every night...I know it's easy for you, but I just don't think I could do it."

"Yeah, I know." Dak said quietly. He was a little saddened by the subject. He knew he could talk J.D. into going to college if he really tried but felt J.D. was actually right about his own personality. "I wish you liked that kind of thing because we could have some fun together. Ugly as you are, I'll still miss you if you aren't there. But, since studyin' is not your thing, maybe the Navy would be something you'd like. I hear they teach you real practical stuff like electronics that you could use to get a good job when you get out. Of course, you'd miss Marie."

As usual, Dak could easily sway J.D. "Do you really think the Navy would be right for me?" he asked.

Dak didn't hesitate. "I do," he said. "I think the Navy or the Marines, but it seems to me the Navy is better suited to your personality."

"I think I'll talk to the Navy guys and see what they tell me about it." With that, J.D. turned the radio volume up again and sank into deep thought until he was entering the doors to the high school.

"Don't forget, we're meeting Melodie and Marie at noon to go get lunch at Rudy's," Dak said, as he nudged J.D. on the shoulder.

At lunchtime, the four of them were walking the few hundred yards over to Rudy's Barbecue, and Dak was joking as usual. This time, he was telling the girls about the episode when J.D. ran from the addled squirrel. J.D. denied some of the details and threw his car keys at Dak. Dak caught the keys and said, "Hey, looks like I'm drivin' home."

When J.D. lunged for his keys, Dak threw them to Marie, who in turn threw them to Melodie as J.D. chased after them. Then, Melodie, under pressure from J.D., threw the keys much too hard. They landed on the hood of a shiny new black Packard that was sitting in front of Rudy's place.

"Uh oh," said Melodie, as she put her hands over her mouth, "I hope I didn't make a scratch on that car." Dak ran over and retrieved the keys just as Mr. Savoy came out of Rudy's Cafe.

"Hey, Leventhal, what the hell are you doing to my car?" he yelled. "Look at this. You've put a scratch on the hood. I just bought this car last week. Damn it! Young man, I have about had enough of your brashness. You're going to hear about this."

"Sorry, Mr. Savoy," Dak pleaded. "Let me assure you it wasn't intentional. We were just playin' around and..."

"I don't want to hear that stuff," Mr. Savoy said. "You'll be hearing more about this." With that, he strutted around to the driver's door and was gone.

"Oh, my gosh," said Melodie. "It was my fault. I'm sorry, Dak."

"No, no," said Dak. "You were just doin' what the rest of us were doin'. It's not your fault."

As they ate their lunch, Dak kept thinking, "What is it about Savoy? I can't get away from this man. What does he mean when he says I'm going to hear about this?"

After school, Dak said, "Know what, J.D.? Since Ellsworth Place probably has a secret room, maybe we should check it out. I'm feelin' more and more that the ol' mansion might reveal some of its secrets to us. What say we go explorin' out there again?"

"Sounds like a plan to me, Sherlock Leventhal. Maybe we'll get to the bottom of some of this stuff."

They went on their bikes early on Saturday morning, taking along a notepad and pencil, camera, flashlight, and a large screwdriver. The screwdriver's purpose was to help them get into the secret room if they happened to find it. They hid their bikes well so as to leave no hint that they were in the mansion.

"Seems to me," Dak said, "that the secret room shouldn't be too hard to find. It'd have to be pretty hard to hide a room in a floor plan without it being apparent that there's some space that's not accounted for."

"Yeah, I suppose so, depending on how big this secret room is. We should have brought a measuring tape." J.D. wasn't sure it would be so easy.

As they started across the field, Dak pointed over to their right and said, "Look at that!" It was a new and larger sign warn-

ing intruders that the area is posted. It had large red letters on a
yellow background:

POSTED
NO TRESPASSING
NO HUNTING, FISHING, OR NUTTING
VIOLATORS WILL BE PROSECUTED
PERCY SAVOY PROPERTIES

Dak was puzzled. "Why do you suppose he put up a new
sign, J.D.? There's been a small sign here for a long time."

"Maybe it's because of what Donny told Judy Savoy," replied
J.D.

"Uhhh, what would you be talkin' about? What Donny told
Judy?" replied Dak.

J.D. put his hands on his forehead. "Oh, maybe I forgot to tell
you. Donny and I were talkin' the other day, and he said he'd
told Judy about the time you and Donny went froggin' and
ended up in the mansion. Donny said he was just tellin' it to her
as a funny story and wasn't even thinkin' about it bein' her dad's
property. But, the next day at school, Judy saw Donny and said
she had mentioned it to her dad. She said he was steamin' mad."

"Oh, crap! That's not good!" Dak almost yelled. "Man, I can't
stay out of trouble with Savoy. I just get in deeper all the time. He's
going to have my butt one of these days. He already thinks I'm
brash and has promised I'll be hearing from him. I probably will!"

"Think we shouldn't go over to the mansion?" asked J.D.
"Wonder what he'd do if he caught us."

"Probably prosecute us," replied Dak. "I don't know what that
would amount to. Maybe he would shoot at us. I don't know.
Anyway, there's no way he'll catch us today if we're careful. If
we see him coming toward the mansion, we can run out the
other direction toward the woods and come back later to get our
bikes."

As they walked up to the barbed wire fence and prepared to
climb over it, J.D. pushed down on the wire to make it easier to

step over. "Yowieeeee!" he screamed. "Oh, crap, he's electrified the wire. Man, I really got a shock out of that. Be careful crossin' it."

"You know, there must be somethin' that doesn't meet the eye here. Ol' Savoy is takin' strong steps to keep people away from the mansion. Makes me wonder if he had somethin' to do with the warnings I got. Maybe he had Alex killed. All the more reason why we need to go check it out!" said Dak.

They carefully crossed the fence without touching it and made their way over the field to the mansion. They went in the front door and began looking at the room layout to see if they could see any suspicious looking arrangements that might hide a secret room.

Dak walked back to the front door to look out toward the road to make sure no one was coming. "We need to check every few minutes, so we would have a chance to run toward the woods if anyone is threatenin' from the road," he said.

J.D. agreed. "I think that it would take about 10 minutes at normal walkin' speed to get from the road to the house. So we need to check a little oftener than that."

As they walked around in the house, they didn't see any obvious space that was missing, but they realized that it wouldn't be a very good secret room if it were that easy to spot.

"Maybe the secret room is really just a secret space," said J.D. "Maybe these very thick walls hide a cavity that they refer to as a secret room."

"Probably not. I don't think most people would call a cavity a secret room." Dak was looking carefully at room sizes.

After a while on the main floor, they decided there was really no space where a secret room could be hidden. As they made their way up the rickety spiral stairs, J.D. said, "Hey, we don't really have any evidence there is a secret room. That slave, James or whoever, might have just been blowin'.

"Yeah, might have been, but probably not," Dak concluded.

On the second floor, they looked closely at the room arrangement, which was a near copy of the downstairs plan. Then, Dak spotted something he thought wasn't quite right.

"It seems to me that this room is not as deep, front to back, as the one on the other side. What do you think?"

J.D. looked at both the front rooms of the house and said, "It does look that way, but the bookcase built in across the back of this one would make it look shorter."

"I suppose," Dak said, "but the back room looks like it's not quite as deep, front to back, either. Of course, it also has that bookcase all the way across."

"Well, we can see how deep the bookcases are," J.D. suggested. "Let's walk off the length of the rooms and see whether the bookcases make up the difference."

It didn't take long for the boys to conclude that there were about three feet missing. "Okay then," Dak said, "Unless this wall is several feet thick, this must be where the secret room is located. Now we just need to figure out how to get into it."

It occurred to Dak that they had not been checking the view toward the road as often as they had planned. "Let's take a look at the road," he said.

"Oh, hell, there's a car parked over on the road!" J.D. said. "Is that Savoy's car?"

"I can't tell," replied Dak. "It is black, but I can't tell if it's his Packard."

"I don't think it is," said J.D. "Looks like an older car. Probably just somebody goin' to the bar pits. Just in case, though, maybe we better figure out how we exit this place without bein' seen."

"If we see somebody comin', let's quickly go to the first floor and down the inside steps to the basement level. From there, we can go out the basement door on the side opposite the road and then off into the woods to make our way over to the river. We can get our bikes later." Dak felt comfortable with that plan.

"Okay, Dak. In the meantime, let's see if we can get into the secret room."

"I think there is most likely some part of the bookcases in one of the two rooms that releases a secret door, or at least a secret panel," said Dak. "Wherever that part is, we should be able to see some wear on this ol' paint from repeated use, assuming they used it."

"I don't see any unusual wear here," J.D. said as he examined the bookcase in the front room.

Dak at first thought he saw an unusual area of wear, but upon closer examination, he could see it was not. "Let's try liftin', twistin', and pullin' each of the shelf supports," he suggested. "Here are a couple pieces of wood on this wall panel that look like they could be handles, but they won't move any direction, so I guess not. Wonder why they're here?"

Try as they would, they could find no movable part on the bookcases in the front room. Then they went to the back room and began the same process. Eventually, Dak lifted a bookshelf and tried to pull outward on the support strip under the shelf.

"Bingo!" he yelled. "Come look at this, J.D. This may be it!"

The support was clearly designed to pull out about two inches and click into place in that extended position.

"Okay, that probably released something," J.D. said. "Let's see if we can find a panel that will move now."

Again, they had no luck. They tried every panel in each of the two rooms, pushing, twisting, and lifting. Then they tried to move whole sections of the bookcase. Nothing worked.

"Maybe there is another support that also has to be repositioned at the same time to make this work," Dak suggested. They tried every support in both rooms, all to no avail. It was one of a kind.

"Has to be something else that acts in combination with this to release something," said J.D.

"I suppose, but it doesn't seem to be here," Dak agreed. "Maybe there is something on the ceiling downstairs or in the floor of the attic."

They went downstairs and looked at the ceiling to see if they could find anything that might be a handle or knob that could release a latch. Dak looked around the fireplace, even though he thought that was too far away from the bookcase to be a likely place for a latch. Nothing.

"Let's try the attic," J.D. suggested.

Grabbing the flashlight and camera, they ran up the stairs. In the attic, they tried to walk off the space to make sure they were above the secret room. "Should be in a strip along about here," Dak said, as he gestured with his arms to show where he thought the borders would be.

"Don't see anything," said J.D. "Let's move this ol' wooden box out of the way. Maybe the release is under it."

They pushed on the box but were unable to move it. "Hell, what's in it? Gold?" asked J.D. "Look at how this box is built. It's a heavy mother."

"Or, maybe it doesn't move at all," said Dak. "Maybe it's secured to the floor for a reason. Maybe you go through a trap door in the bottom of this box to get into the secret room."

The top surface of the box was apparently a lid, because there were hinges on one side. There was no handle for opening the lid, but there was hardware for securing it with a padlock. The padlock was on the floor with what looked like a large caliber shot through it.

"Look at this," Dak said. "Someone has torn this lock open with a gun and I guess no one ever put a new lock on it." He opened the box lid by pulling on the locking hardware.

Shining the flashlight in the box, J.D. said, "Nothing much in it, of course. If there ever was, whoever shot the lock took it. There is just some rope in it and only a few feet of that."

Dak climbed on the edge of the box and picked up the rope. "Yeah, but look at this. The rope goes through a hole in the floor, so maybe the floor lifts to become a door."

"Hey, that's it! This rope must open a door down into the room!" yelled J.D.

Dak pulled up on the rope. "The rope doesn't seem to be attached to the floor, and the planks don't appear to be cut at the edges of the box. Also, I don't see any hinges on the floor. It's not a door."

"Listen!" said J.D. "I hear a little click as you pull that rope. Be quiet and try it again."

Dak pulled the rope gently. Nothing happened. He pulled harder, and the rope came up about six inches. There was an accompanying noise below.

"Alright!" said Dak. "I bet that was the second release. Man, I really had to pull hard. I thought this ol' rope was going to break."

"It looks a hundred years old," said J.D.

"Probably is, maybe more." replied Dak, as he released the rope, causing another noise below.

"Hey, I bet that went back into the closed position. What, then? Maybe somebody has to hold the rope in position to release the secret door." Dak was guessing.

"Well, okay. Let me pull on the rope until I hear the noise, and then I'll hold it in that position while you go to the second floor and see if you can open some panel or door or something," said J.D.

Dak ran down the stairs to the second floor and made sure the bookshelf support was in its extended position. Then he began searching for something that would move. Nothing in the back room would move in any direction.

Dak went to the front room and began the same procedure. He grasped the two pieces of wood that he had noticed earlier and tried to move them. When he lifted upward, there seemed to be a little movement. He pulled harder and felt the panel moving upward.

"Hey, J.D.," he yelled excitedly. "I think I've found it...but don't release the rope yet."

Dak continued to lift the panel until it went up four feet or a little less. There, it seemed to snap into place. Dak was thrilled as he looked into the secret room. The first thing he noticed was a musty smell. He moved the bookshelf boards out of the way and stepped into the room but couldn't see much because the flashlight was in the attic.

"J.D., can you hear me?" asked Dak.

"Yeah, I hear. Did you get something to open?"

"A panel opened in the front bookcase and I'm in the secret room. Bring the flashlight!"

Excited by this news, J.D. released the rope and heard a loud thud as he ran for the steps. Reaching the front room on the second floor, he saw no open panel but could hear Dak screaming, "Hey, J.D.! Hey, when you released the rope, the panel fell shut. The panel must be an inch thick. Scared the crap out of me! It's dark as midnight in here!"

"Ohhh, no! What do I do now?" J.D. yelled loud enough to make sure Dak heard it.

"See those wooden handles on one of the bookcase panels? Lift them up!" said Dak.

Struggling, J.D. said, "They won't move!"

"Awww...that's right! You have to go back and pull the rope up and then, while it is held up, pull up on the handles on this panel."

"But...how can I hold the rope in the attic and pull up on these handles at the same time?"

Dak was feeling a little panicky but was trying to remain calm. "You'll have to pull up on the rope and attach it to something to hold it up. Maybe tie it to something. Then, come back down and lift up on these handles."

J.D. ran back to the attic and grabbed the rope. He pulled on it, but nothing seemed to be happening, so he jerked very hard. When he did, the rope broke, and a few feet of it whizzed through the hole in the floor.

"My God!" J.D. exclaimed, as he held the piece of rope in his hands. "What else could happen?"

He started back down the attic steps to talk with Dak when he heard a voice that definitely was not Dak's.

"Somebody in there?" the voice asked.

J.D. ran to the top of the stairs to the first floor, and there he was at the bottom of the steps looking up. It was Mr. Savoy.

"Why, hello, Mr. Savoy." J.D. yelled much louder than necessary, hoping to give Dak warning to keep still.

"Hello, my ass! What would cause you to come in here on posted property and just make your self at home, young man? I mean, damn, if you missed those signs over by the road you must be totally blind! This is not a playground for all the crazy teenagers who want to go out and destroy some property." Savoy said.

"No, no. Was just out hiking, started out over on the river...nice day for just gettin' out and seein' things. I haven't been over by the road yet. Anyway, I came upon this ol' abandoned mansion. Thought I'd look through it. How nice to meet you here."

"Well, this place is posted, and I don't know how you got here without seeing the signs. I have signs over on that side, too. I'm half a mind to prosecute you. You've got no business on my property." Savoy replied.

"Oh, well, I'm very sorry, Sir. Don't know how I missed your signs. Guess I just happened to come in between a couple of them. It won't happen again," J.D. replied.

"You're Hampton Robinson's son aren't you?" inquired Savoy.

"Why, yes I am. My dad speaks very highly of you." J.D. extended his hand and said, "I guess we've never really met. I'm J.D. Robinson, very nice to meet you."

To J.D.'s amazement, Savoy not only shook his hand but also put his arm around J.D.'s shoulder and said, "Son, I don't want to prosecute you for this. I think I have your word you won't trespass on this property again. You said you won't, and I believe you. You're a nice looking boy and I don't want to see anything bad happen out of this."

"Well, thank you very much, Sir. I really appreciate that. I don't want any trouble. Just out hiking."

"Yes, I understand. Out hiking. A young man's fancy turns to nature this time of year. You know what? You'd be a good match for my Judy. You know her?"

"Oh, yes, sure, yeah, yeah...sure do. I know Judy quite well. We have some classes together. Nice girl, Judy. I've always thought she was a nice girl."

Savoy smiled broadly. "Well, she likes hiking, too. I don't know if you noticed, but she has a new Pontiac. Nice vehicle. She told me she just broke up with her boyfriend and is looking for someone to go to Harrisburg next week to see a movie. How about it? Would you like to do that? I understand that you didn't intend to trespass and don't want to be prosecuted. No problem."

"Harrisburg? For a movie? Why...uh, sure, Mr. Savoy. Sure thing. Yeah, Judy is a nice girl. Oh, and that's a nice car, real nice car. Tell you what, I'll talk to Judy and make some arrangements, okay?"

Savoy rubbed his hand up and down J.D.'s back several times and said, "Okay, sure thing. Come on over to the car, and I'll give you a ride back to town, J.D. I just know you and Judy will hit it off." Then he got a big smile and said, "Have fun and enjoy yourself with her, you know. Do the things that young people do, just as long as she doesn't end up pregnant or something. Know what I mean?"

"Oh sure, Mr. Savoy. Sure thing. No, I don't need a ride. I left some of my gear hidden over by the river, so I'll just hike back over this direction if it's okay with you. You tell Judy hello for me until I'm able to see her, okay?" J.D. was a master at this kind of thing.

"Okay, sure," Savoy said. "Just one other thing. When I was coming across the field, I thought I heard voices. Is there some one with you?"

"Oh, no, no...I was singin', I guess that's what you heard. Sorry about that. Don't have a very good voice...didn't know anyone was listenin'."

"See you later then," Savoy said, as he started back across the field. "And you tell all your friends to stay off this property. I'm definitely going to be prosecuting people, whether they got here accidentally or not."

J.D. breathed a sigh of relief as he ambled slowly the other di-rection and into the woods, singing a few lines from *The Great Pretender* to add credibility. He positioned himself so he could see Savoy's car and stayed there until the car was gone.

Running back into the mansion, J.D. was trying to figure out how he would get Dak out of the secret room and how he'd deal with his agreement to take Judy to the movie. He felt over-whelmed with problems.

"Dak, can you hear me?" J.D. said, as he reentered the front upstairs room.

"Yeah! God, I didn't know what happened, but I heard you say hello to Savoy, so I just kept quiet. Did he leave?"

"Yes, he left, but let me tell you how I got him to leave,"

"Spare me the details right now and get me out of here!" Dak replied.

"I know the rope broke when you were pulling on it. I felt my way around in here and figured out that I can pull the rope up from in here."

"Great! Do it and I'll raise this panel."

Dak pulled the rope and heard the noise. "Okay. Now, pull up on the handles!" Dak watched as J.D. gradually pulled the panel to its full-open position.

Dak tied the rope to a large hook on the wall. "We better get out of here quickly. Savoy may circle back and come in again. First, I want to show you something real quick." He held up a beautiful sword covered with a heavy layer of dust.

"Wow! Man, wonder why they left that here?" J.D. said.

"I don't know. Quick! Get the camera and take a picture!" Dak replied.

They took the photo, replaced the sword to its original loca-tion, left the rope tied to the hook in case they wanted to come in again, and closed the panel. Then they went into the back room and returned the shelf support to its normal position.

"Now, let's get all these shelves back in place and gather up our equipment," said Dak. "We need to get out of here!"

They ran into the woods for safety but then circled a wide loop back to their bicycles. As they rode home, J.D. said, "I'm in deep trouble with Savoy. What am I going to do about taking Judy to a movie Sunday?"

"Well, I'm in trouble with him too," said Dak. "But I have a really good idea!"

Mariah's Love

The next day, a Sunday, was bright and sunny and had the fragrance of springtime. Both Dak and Johnnie David were out early on their bicycles, and it didn't take them long to find each other. Dak rode up the graveled road that goes over the levee at Main Street, stopped at the levee's peak, and straddled his bicycle while taking in the river view. The people on the two fish docks below were cleaning off their decks with river water while a large boat named *The Mississippi Queen* was moving gently downstream. On the riverbank a few hundred feet upstream, Ramblin' Rudy, a local folk hero, barbecue connoisseur, and water ski acrobat, was cleaning his boat. Two dogs, a large orange one with white paws and a small white one with a tail that curled up over his back, were making their way down the levee, stopping along the way to smell several patches of weeds. J.D. was riding down Main Street at that time and, spotting Dak on the levee, rode up and stopped next to him.

"I wish I was on that boat," J.D. said, with no other greeting at all.

"Well, J.D., I don't think you could have any more fun on *The Mississippi Queen* than you're havin' right here," Dak joked. "Outwittin' ol' Savoy is about the most fun you can have unless you get better lookin'."

"Actually, I can think of a lot of things that are more fun. Hey, this thing has got me worried, Dak. If you do have a good idea about how I get out of this mess, I need to hear it. I need some miracle right now. What is Marie going to think when she hears I've agreed to take Judy to a movie?"

"I know J.D. It could be a problem, but tell me what you think of this idea. First, you talk with Marie and tell her of your predicament. Tell her ol' Savoy was going to prosecute you, and you didn't want to go to jail. She'll be sympathetic. Explain to her that you need her help. Tell her you need to arrange for four of you to go to a movie without it being like a date, you and her along with Norman Jacey and Judy Savoy."

"Norman Jacey? Hey, a double date with me taking Marie is definitely not what Savoy had in mind, Dak," J.D. said.

"I know, I know! It's not like a double date. Explain that to Marie. Then, when Marie agrees to the plan, you go to Norman and tell him that you need his help. Tell him the whole story. Norman doesn't have a girl friend right now, and he seems to like you pretty well, so he'll do it."

"Yeah, Norman would do it, especially if I pay his way into the movie," J.D. admitted.

"Of course he will. Just tell Norman that you'll pick up Marie and him and that the three of you will go to Judy's house to pick her up. Tell him you'll arrange it with Judy and that you expect to go in her new Pontiac. He'll like that."

"Yeah, okay, that's smooth, but what will I tell Judy?"

Dak could see that J.D. was considering his proposal. "Talk with Judy at school," he continued. "Tell her that you and some others are going to a movie at Harrisburg next Friday night. Ask if she'd like to go. She will agree to go, of course, and will no doubt offer to let you drive her Pontiac. Accept her offer."

"Yeah, I might actually enjoy driving the Pontiac if the circumstances were different."

"You'll love it!" Dak said. "Be sure to mention Marie's name and Norman's to Judy in no particular order so as to leave the subject a little fuzzy. Then tell her you will pick up the others and be by her place at such and such a time to switch to the Pontiac. Explain that it's just the four of you going for fun, not as dates. Instruct Norman ahead of time that when you get to Judy's house, he is to take the back seat. Tell Marie she is to get in the front passenger's seat. That only leaves one place for Judy. It'll work out fine."

"I don't know, Dak," J.D. said. "She may feel she is being tricked and get really mad."

"Well, what's to get mad about? Don't make it like two dates. Make it like four people going to a movie together. Hey, Judy

knows you and Marie are a steady thing; she is not going to expect you to romance her with Marie sitting there. The only
person being tricked is ol' Savoy, and he'll never know it because
Judy's not going to go home and say, 'Know what Dad? J.D.
tricked me. He didn't even make out with me at the movie.' No, I
don't think so. Do it, J.D.! But while you're with Judy, don't be
too cozy with Marie either. Just make it like four neutral people
having a good time."

"I think I will," J.D. said confidently, "although it may be difficult for me to act like a neutral person because I'm anything but
neutral!"

"Well, you can have a hormone explosion later," Dak said.
"For now, we have got to get you out of this problem. Oh, and
one more thing."

J.D. sighed. "There's always a catch, and here it comes."

"No, no," said Dak. "I just want to remind you to keep the
speed down to something less than Indianapolis 500 standards.
Savoy might get pretty upset if you wrecked Judy's new Pontiac.
Those cars tend to look kind of bad when they have their fronts
all smashed in. Not to mention that somebody might be killed or
something. We don't need that."

"Yeah, yeah," J.D. said. "We'll try to keep the car all in one
piece. Don't worry about it."

The boys rode to Dak's house with the idea that they would
pick up a couple things there and proceed to the Uppers to work
on the second grave. As they neared the house, Savoy's Packard
was speeding away and Eleanor was still standing on the porch,
her arms folded. Dak got that shooting pain that he occasionally
experienced when something ominous occurred.

"Awww, man. Savoy has been here. This is not goin' to be
good."

"Don't worry about it, Dak," J.D. said in a comforting tone.
"It's probably nothing."

As the boys leaned their bikes on the front porch, Eleanor
walked toward them with a very worried look on her face. "Dak,
Mr. Savoy was here," she said. "He's pretty angry. Says he hears

you recently trespassed on his property and damaged some things. He also said you maliciously used some keys to scratch his new Packard."

"Well, he's right. I did trespass. I went in the ol' mansion out by the bar pits, but I didn't damage anything. And I guess it's fair to say I put a scratch on his car, but it wasn't intentional. Is he threatenin' any legal action?"

J.D. spoke up quickly. "Hey, Dak, it wasn't even you who threw the keys that landed on his Packard."

"True," Dak said, "but I was involved in the horseplay just like all of us were, so I'm as responsible as anybody."

"Well, he is very upset," Eleanor said nervously, "and he said he was going to talk with the sheriff about this. Said he was going to ask Sheriff Summers to watch his property and to keep an eye on you and Donny. Oh, and he said if he catches any of the teenage vandals around here on his property again, he will prosecute them to the full extent of the law. He was so angry! Said he would have called me if we had a telephone like normal people. He was right in my face, wagging his finger and shouting profanities. I was getting a little scared."

"Well, Mrs. Leventhal, I wouldn't worry much about this," J.D. said. "Savoy is an evil ol' thing, but he doesn't have much to go on here. How bad is it to walk through an ol' abandoned mansion? And we got four people who can verify that the scratch on the Packard was an accident, and it wasn't even Dak who had that accident."

"I'm sure glad to hear that," Eleanor said.

Dak noticed that she was dabbing her eyes with a handkerchief and still looked very worried. He put his arm around her and said, "Mom, don't worry about it. We'll be careful. He yells a lot, but there's not much he can do." Then the thought crossed his mind that the graves were probably on Savoy's property, too.

As Dak and J.D. walked over the levee and down the path to the Uppers, they considered whether the graves were on Savoy's property. Dak pointed out that people go to the Uppers all the time without a problem.

"True," J.D. said, "and there are not any posted signs near the Uppers, so I guess we're okay."

They uncovered the second grave and began carefully taking the rotted planks off the top of the pine box.

"This one looks just about the same as the other one," Dak noted.

"Yeah, full of dirt and all," noted J.D., "but look at this. The area around the skull doesn't have much dirt. There must have been an air bubble or something."

"Well, maybe so," Dak replied. "Look at these nice white teeth. I bet this person was young."

"His skull is in pretty good shape," J.D. said. "And guess what? Here is another earring. I think it's the same as the one the other guy had."

They washed the earring in the river, and sure enough, the symbol found on the other earring was on this one as well.

"Fancy that," Dak said. "So these guys had something in common other than just bein' buried in the same place."

As they continued their dig, they found suspender buckles just like those in the first grave, but one thing was different. There was a large hole through the breastbone, and the rib bones near it were broken, apparently from the force of a bullet hitting the breastbone.

"So both of these people were shot," said J.D.

"Yeah," Dak agreed. "And I think they were both male from their size. This guy looks about the same size as the other one. In fact, their bone structure is remarkably alike. Also, they wore the same kind of belt."

"Where's the gold?" asked J.D. "Shouldn't we find a gold ring and a little cross?"

"Well, it seems like it. If it is here, it doesn't seem to be in the same place as on the other guy." Dak was puzzled.

As the dig continued, the boys were a little frustrated that they were not finding the same relics as in the first grave. As a result, they dug more thoroughly around the skeletal remains. Having exhausted the possibilities, J.D. picked up the spade and dug on the far side of the pine box, just to see if there might be any clue there.

"Hold it!" Dak said. "Look at this. There is a rope here."

J.D. pulled a little on the rope, but remembering how he had broken the rope to the secret room in the mansion, he did so very gently.

"Maybe this is the rope they used to lower the pine boxes into the grave," Dak said.

"But it doesn't go under the box," J.D. replied, as he took a trowel and dug around the rotten rope to see where it led.

"Look at that, J.D.! This rope goes out away from the box. You must have dug about a foot and a half, and it is still goin' that direction. Ain't that curious?"

"I'd say so," J.D. replied, "but we can't dig very far that direction without takin' all the top dirt off like we did for these two boxes. That's several feet of diggin' again. We could tunnel under another foot or so. Let's do that."

J.D. handed the trowel to Dak. Digging carefully to avoid triggering a collapse of their little tunnel or breaking the rope, Dak was able to go another foot or so.

"I ran into somethin'," Dak said. "Feels like some sort of coarse rotten cloth. It may be wool or somethin' like that."

J.D. reached into the tunnel and felt the cloth.

"So, I'm guessin' we've got somethin' else there," J.D. said, "but not another coffin...unless it is covered with this cloth and maybe some paddin' under that."

Dak just sat there for a few seconds. Finally, he said, "Funny thing, J.D. I wonder why the clothes on these two men all rotted away, but that cloth, whatever it is, is somewhat intact?"

"Maybe it's a different kind of cloth," J.D. speculated.

"Yeah, or maybe it was buried later," Dak said.

The boys scoped out the job of uncovering the third item, whatever it was, and decided it was a project for another day. They took pictures and notes on everything they had done and carefully replaced everything except the earring, which they took with them.

On the way back from the Uppers, the boys discussed the possibility of going back to the old mansion within a few days. J.D. felt it was a dangerous venture considering Savoy's attitude, but Dak thought that if they approached it from the river side, they were very unlikely to be seen. Further, he felt they hadn't done a good job last time of watching for cars on the road by the bar pits. With a little more vigilance, he thought they would be completely safe. J.D. was skeptical.

"But J.D.," Dak insisted, "If we don't get some more information, we may never know what these graves are about. There is clearly a connection with the ol' mansion. Remember the earring I found in its cellar? We need more time to explore the secret room and see what other clues we can find."

Still not getting a favorable reaction from J.D., Dak thought to himself that it would be better to wait and approach J.D. on this subject a little later, when Savoy's visit to Eleanor wasn't so fresh in his mind.

When they reached Dak's house, J.D. explained that he had promised Marie he would go to her house in the evening to play Monopoly, so he had to leave. Since Melodie and her family were spending the weekend with an uncle in Evansville, Dak considered what he could productively do and decided that after dinner he would make some excuse and go to his room to read some more of Mariah's papers.

At dinner, Eleanor was still a little unnerved by Savoy's visit, although she seemed less worried than she had been immediately after the visit. She had prepared a dinner of fried chicken, mashed potatoes and milk gravy, corn, and hot rolls. Eleanor made this meal about once a month, and it was one of Dak's favorites, although there was always the problem that both he and Nancy preferred a drumstick to any other piece of the chicken.

When Eleanor and Nancy sat down to watch *I Love Lucy* on the little television set, Dak retired to his room and closed his door. He pulled out the box with Mariah's papers and began looking carefully at each of the photographs in order without reading the notes accompanying each one. After a while, he came across a picture of two black men carrying a tub full of pears. He noticed that the two men were dressed alike in what appeared to be dark cotton pants and lighter-colored cotton shirts. Upon closer inspection of the photo, he could see that one of the men had an earring in his right ear. The other man did not have an earring that Dak could see, but his head was turned so that his right ear was not visible.

The granularity of the photo was such that it was difficult to determine whether the earring was the same as the ones that he and J.D. had found in the graves. Dak went downstairs to get a small magnifying glass that Eleanor kept in the top left drawer of the China cabinet. With it, he looked more closely at the earring. He could see that the shape of the earring was roughly the same as the ones from the graves, but he could not tell whether there was a symbol on it.

Dak turned the photo over. On the back, in Mariah's handwriting was the caption, "Georgie (left) and his brother bringing in the pear crop."

"So Georgie wore an earring!" Dak mumbled to himself.

Dak hurried through the other photos to see if there were any others that showed black men with earrings. He reached the last photo but found no more of black men except a couple where the object of the photo was obviously something else, and black men were incidentally in the scene. In these photos, the black men were at such a distance that little could be discerned other than their color.

Disappointed, Dak went back to the front of the chronologically arranged materials to make sure he had not missed any. When he did, he found one photo that had slid down between the vertically stacked papers and was lying flat on the bottom of the box. It was a close-up photo of two black men, each with an earring in their right ear. The earrings looked like the ones they had found at the graves. Dak noticed that his heartbeat was accelerating as he grabbed the magnifying glass and studied the earring with the clearest image. Bingo! There it was, the same symbol found on the earrings from the graves.

Dak was actually trembling with excitement. He turned the
photo over and, again, in Mariah's elegant handwriting, was the
caption, "Georgie and his brother with their new Hickory Hill
earrings all dressed up for the darkie church service."

"Hickory Hill earrings?" Dak thought. "What does that mean?"

He pulled out one of the actual earrings from the graves and
inspected it again. "So, is this a Hickory Hill earring?" he asked
himself. And then, it came to him. "Awww, yes! How could I be
so dumb? This is two symbols of the letter H with the second
one set so that the right side of the first H and the left side of the
second H make one line, with the remainder of the second H
lower than the first."

Dak was thrilled to have finally identified the earrings as being from Hickory Hill, the Old Slave House. He suspected that
they were put on the slaves to identify them as Hickory Hill
property if they ran away or were kidnapped or lost, but he did-
n't know.

Pulling out some diary entries, Dak almost felt guilty reading
Mariah's description of her relationship with Georgie. It seemed
very private. Still, since none of the players was alive, he felt it
was historical material and therefore was okay to read.

Mariah told of Georgie gradually recovering in the attic as
she cared for his wounds. As he was recovering, she had become
more and more taken with him to the point that she would make
excuses to go to the attic just so she might have a few moments
with Georgie. One morning, she had gone to the attic to attend
his wounds, and after changing his bandages, she decided to
embrace him. She described how her heart pounded as she satis-
fied her urge to hold him in her arms, not knowing how much of
her excitement was due to fulfilling her desire to hold Georgie
and how much was due to the fear that someone might see her.

As the days went by and Georgie's wounds healed, Mariah
found that Georgie was constantly on her mind. She wrote that
she could think of little else.

Finally, Mr. Crenshaw determined that Georgie was well
enough to go to the salt springs and work like the other slaves.

At that point, Mariah had petitioned to get more time for Georgie to recover from his wounds. She had said, "I wouldn't risk re-infection and the loss of a valuable slave by being too quick about it. He must be worth a lot on any plantation." What she thought was, *If they take Georgie to the salt springs, how will I be able to see him?* Crenshaw thought the risk of re-infection was past and said he would take him the next morning and start him maintaining the fires under the salt kettles.

That evening, Mariah waited until everyone was asleep. Then she quietly made her way to the attic and gently touched Georgie on the face. He woke immediately, and she explained in whispers what was to happen the next morning. They both understood that this might be the last time they would be able to talk and embrace. They kissed and cried, and eventually, Mariah took off Georgie's shirt. He opened her blouse and began kissing her breasts.

Mariah and Georgie were holding each other tightly when he heard someone coming up the stairs to the attic. Immediately, he nudged Mariah and told her to hide quickly in the empty cell at the end of the row.

Mariah jumped up and, buttoning her blouse as she ran, leaped into the cell. It was Mr. Crenshaw. Holding a lantern, he began looking around in the attic as Georgie lay still, pretending to be asleep. Crenshaw walked from end to end but did not see Mariah. He kicked Georgie, who jumped as though he was startled, but faked grogginess and shut his eyes again. Eventually, Crenshaw went back down the stairs.

Mariah was afraid to move for a long time. After about an hour, she carefully made her way back down the attic stairs and into her room. Her mind whirled with a mixture of fear and sadness.

The next morning at breakfast, Mr. Crenshaw mentioned to Mariah that Mrs. Crenshaw had been sick in the night, and he had come to get her to help. That's all he said. She hesitated because she wasn't sure what Crenshaw was thinking. Had he just knocked on her door or had he opened the door and noticed that she wasn't in bed? Eventually she said, "Oh, I guess that was when I couldn't sleep and went out for a walk in the fresh air. I'm sorry I missed you. I assume, Auntie, you are okay this morning?" Crenshaw looked at Mariah with an expression of something between disgust and disdain, but he said no more.

Right after breakfast, Crenshaw moved Georgie to the salt springs while Mariah looked out her window and cried.

Three days later, Mariah felt she must see Georgie, even if only from a distance. She told her aunt that she was going for a horseback ride and went off on Bonaparte, her favorite horse, toward the salt springs.

As she got near the kettles, the foreman saw her and, removing his hat, said, "Miss Mariah, the darkies are all loose right now doing their jobs, so it is not advisable that you be here. Never know when one of them might act up."

Mariah nodded, giving recognition that she had heard him, but kept riding slowly down the row of kettles until she spotted Georgie. When she reached the kettle where he was working, she stopped her horse for a minute and watched. He looked up but gave no indication he had ever seen Mariah before. Mariah, thinking she was out of view of everyone but Georgie, threw him a kiss just as the foreman stepped out from behind a tall stack of firewood. Highly embarrassed and shocked that he had seen her, she spurred the horse quickly forward and went immediately back to the plantation house. She was shaking as she walked in the door to the house. Mrs. Crenshaw, seeing that she was upset, asked if she was okay. Mariah said that a snake had spooked her horse, giving her a bad scare, but that she was okay now.

The following day, Mrs. Crenshaw told Mariah that her uncle had gone into town to arrange the sale of a couple of the slaves. Mariah wanted to ask but was afraid of drawing attention to her situation.

At this point, Dak heard Nancy coming up the stairs, so he quickly returned Mariah's writings to the box and slid the box under his bed. Picking up a Captain Marvel comic book, he leaned back on his bed and opened it to a page near the center.

"Dak, can I come in?" Nancy said as she gave a light knock on his door.

"Sure," Dak said. "Enter my Kingdom!"

Nancy opened the door and said, "Dak, you missed a really good *I Love Lucy* show." She began recounting the details of the show and who said what. Dak listened patiently for a few minutes and then yawned and said, "Know what, Nance-girl, I'm a bit sleepy. Maybe you could fill me in on the rest of it tomorrow."

Nancy sighed and said, "Okay, but it was really a good one. Your loss." She ambled off to her room, closing the door behind her.

Chapter 11

Death on the River

As Johnnie David's car rolled up in front of Dak's house, the brakes made a screeching noise that drowned out the voices of The Penguins, which otherwise could have easily been heard through his open windows:

> Earth angel, earth angel, will you be mine?
> My darling dear, love you all the time.
> I'm just a fool, a fool in love, with you.

Dak, in a trick he had perfected through many attempts, actually went through the open window on the passenger side head first and landed with his legs over the back of the seat and his torso and head front-side-up, crumpled in the bottom of the seat.

"Show off," J.D. said stiffly, as *Earth Angel* came to a gooey end that somehow seemed to depress him a little. He turned the radio off as Fats Domino was just warming up to the next song.

Dak, rotating around to a normal sitting position, said, "Hey, J.D., I know all about the earrings we found in the graves."

"Que será," J.D. said, leaving Dak even more puzzled than usual. Dak had tried to follow the evolving meaning of this expression and had finally concluded that J.D. occasionally used it for the sole purpose of baffling the listener.

"Yeah," Dak said, just as though he knew exactly what J.D. meant. "Wait till you hear this story!"

Dak went through all he had learned and described the pictures showing the earrings. "So, it's pretty clear that the bodies in the graves are slaves from Hickory Hill," he concluded, as they rolled into the high school parking lot.

J.D.'s mood seemed to have improved, and he had gotten into the story. "Hey, I'd like to see those pictures when we get a chance," he said. "This is pretty amazing, ain't it? We actually have a romance coming out of the grave. Marie will love it."

The boys went their separate ways to their classes. Before lunch break, Mr. Jordan came on the public announcement system to explain that he was canceling the prom for the year because of the fire in the gym and the lack of a suitable alternate facility for the event. This caused a furor among the students, many of whom felt this cheated them of something very meaningful.

As Dak and Melodie were walking to the ball field to eat their bagged lunches, Melodie said, "That really stinks. The prom is one of the great memories of high school, and we don't even get to do it. I already have my dress and everything. Why didn't they tell us sooner?"

Dak was also disappointed but felt he needed to focus on consoling Melodie. "I know. They should at least have told us sooner. Everyone was really lookin' forward to it. It's once-in-a-lifetime. But let's don't let it get us down. Let's pick a night and do something else, something unusual, something that would also leave us with great memories."

"Maybe," Melodie said, still dejected, "but what could we do?"

"I have an idea," he said. "We could dress in our prom clothes one night, go out to eat somewhere nice, and then go somewhere with a bottle of wine and a blanket. We could ponder the stars, talk about what a beautiful person you are, foretell what the future holds, and make up poems about our love."

"Dak, you make that sound so romantic, and with you, it probably would be. Let's do it. That actually sounds like more fun than the prom. But don't tell my parents about the wine! Do you think J.D. and Marie would like to join us?"

"I think so," Dak said, happy that Melodie was cheered a bit. "We'll call it 'Our Special Night,' and we'll make it the most special night of our lives. We'll get photos, and we can remember it forever."

Still thinking about how to arrange their special night and how he could earn some money for it, Dak went to the literature class that afternoon a bit distracted. Miss Hurd explained a poem called "The Psalm of Life." She had written a stanza from the poem on the blackboard:

In the world's broad field of battle,
In the bivouac of life,
Be not like dumb, driven cattle!
Be a hero in the strife!

Being in great form that day, she involved the students in interpreting the stanza and giving their opinion of it. After thorough discussion, she noted that there are people who have adopted those lines as a guide to their lives. "What would that mean?" she asked no one in particular. "Would it be a good guide for your life?" Then, recognizing that she was taking some risk, she asked Larry Lambert if he thought the stanza would be a good guide for his life.

Before answering, Larry belched loudly, clasped his hands and stretched his arms forward, palms out, cracking his knuckles. Then he slumped down into his seat. "Well," he said, clearing his throat, "I think Rocky Marciano would be a good guide for my life. I'd really like to be the heavyweight boxing champion of the whole world. Ever notice on TV how all those chicks follow him around?" Then, he belched again for emphasis and put his finger in his mouth, apparently trying to pick something out of a back tooth.

This unusual combination of intentional crudeness and naiveté somehow struck Dak as the funniest thing he had ever observed. Despite trying to control himself, he launched into hysterical laughter that turned out to be highly contagious. With the whole class in gales of guffaws, Larry surveyed the room with a puzzled look, removed his finger from his mouth, and loudly said, "What?" Miss Hurd could only smile lamely, shake her head, and let the thing die a natural death.

On the way home that day, J.D. told Dak that he had completed arrangements for taking Judy Savoy to a movie in Harrisburg on Sunday afternoon.

"Was it difficult to arrange?" Dak asked.

"No. Marie understood my situation and even laughed about the whole thing," J.D. said. "She'll go along with it, but she doesn't want to hurt Judy Savoy's feelings. Norman Jacey also agreed to go and didn't even ask me to pay his way. Judy, bless her heart, seemed real happy about it and said she thought that would be fun. So, it's a done deal, Dak my boy." J.D. seemed greatly relieved that arrangements were complete. "Hopefully, this will get ol' Savoy off my back, and I won't be prosecuted."

J.D. drove the old Ford up Main Street and parked in front of Ann's Cafe, saying, "Let's have a coke while I teach you the fundamentals of pinball." As they were walking into the cafe, Sheriff Summers and one of his deputies were coming out. When the sheriff saw the boys, he grabbed Dak by the shirt collar and said, "Step out here for a minute, boy. I need to talk to you." He looked over at J.D., who had stopped and was looking at the sheriff, and said, "What are you looking at? You go on about your business." With that, the sheriff tugged on Dak's collar as he walked to his squad car and told Dak to face the car, put his hands on top of the car and spread his feet. Dak nervously complied while several people in the cafe stood at the window watching the action. The deputy then frisked Dak and pulled on his collar again to turn him back around, facing the sheriff.

The sheriff had a nightstick in his right hand that he repeatedly slapped into his left palm. He leaned into Dak's face. "Hey, boy," he said loudly, "I've been hearing about some of the vandalism you've been committing around town, and I want you to understand that I won't tolerate it. It is just by the charity of Mr. Savoy that I haven't picked you up for a little time in the brig while we sort out what you've been doing. I don't think you would find that to be as much fun as what you've been doing. Mr. Savoy hasn't pressed any charges, but I'm telling you that if I hear of any more incidents, you and I are going to tangle."

Dak wanted to say, "Is that rotten fish on your breath, or is there something else that smells that foul?" Deciding that wasn't wise, he said, "What vandalism?"

"I don't think I have to tell you what vandalism you've done. I'm sure you know very well. I don't want any more smart talk from you, either. You remember what I just told you. You've had your last warning, boy. You'd better walk a narrow line, or we're going to have trouble." With that, the deputy released Dak's collar, and the sheriff pushed him so forcefully that Dak nearly fell. "Go on, now," he said, "and I'd better not hear a pip out of you."

Dak, a little shocked by all this, walked into the cafe, where J.D. was standing by the pinball machine with two cokes. He handed one to Dak and said, "That fat ol' bag of crap must be on Savoy's payroll."

"I don't know," Dak said, "but either somebody has told him some lies or he's just trying to do what he's been told to do. In any case, Savoy must be more upset with me than I thought. It's crazy."

The boys drank their cokes, and J.D. played a little pinball. Dak, distracted by what had happened, watched without really paying attention. Donny Branch walked in the cafe and came over to talk with Dak and J.D.

"Did you hear what happened to Charlie Johnson?" asked Donny.

"Not another accident, I hope," Dak said.

"It wasn't an accident. It was intentional. That lard butt sheriff and his deputy caught Charlie five miles over the speed limit and insisted that Charlie give up his driver's license. Charlie said he wasn't supposed to give up his license, so they began beating him up with their nightsticks. They gave him some bad blows to the head and he's over at Eldorado in the hospital. He was on his way to the drug store to get a prescription for his mom when it happened. Charlie's sister said the doctor told them that their mom only has a couple weeks left."

"What an SOB Summers is," J.D. said. "Charlie Johnson wouldn't hurt anybody, and he is really down about his mom and the cancer and all."

"He'll get his one day," Donny said, as J.D. and Dak were leaving. "One day, he'll get it."

J.D. dropped Dak off at home, saying, "Don't worry about it, Dak. Everything will be okay. They're just bluffing. You haven't done anything."

Dak decided not to worry Eleanor by telling her about the sheriff's warning or about Charlie Johnson, as much as he wanted to talk about it and get it out of his mind. He went upstairs to his room and held the picture of his dad. "Dad, I would really like to have you here to talk about this," he whispered.

When Dak went downstairs, Eleanor explained to him that she and Nancy were going to a Home Bureau meeting at Mrs. Scroggins' house. She said they were going to make some aluminum trays. "There is some beef stew in the pot on the stove, still warm," she said, "and I know you'll like it."

After eating a big bowl of stew, Dak was all alone and was still having some difficulty getting the sheriff off his mind. "I know what I'll do," he mumbled. "I'll look at some of Mariah's stuff. I need a good distraction."

Dak slid the box holding Mariah's materials from under his bed and found the place where he had been reading a few nights ago when Nancy interrupted him. *Ah, here we are*, he said to himself, as he began reading her beautiful script.

Dak found the story fascinating. Mr. Crenshaw arranged to sell eleven slaves to a Mississippi plantation owner named Colonel James Dabney. The eleven slaves, composed of six males and five females, were selected and a description provided to Col. Dabney in an earlier letter. After that, Mr. Crenshaw's foreman at the salt springs told Crenshaw that he had seen Mariah throw a kiss to Georgie. Although Crenshaw had already suspected that a relationship was developing between Mariah and Georgie, he was furious with this confirmation of it. When he confronted Mariah about the accusation, she denied everything. Nonetheless, Crenshaw decided he must get rid of Georgie to stop any possibility of an affair involving Mariah and a slave. It would just be scandalous for the family, and he could not let it happen. He immediately substituted Georgie and his brother for two of the slaves previously selected for sale.

While Crenshaw's decision to sell Georgie devastated Mariah, she told Crenshaw she was happy that Georgie was going. "It will stop the vicious lies," she told him. Later, as she was sitting in her room sobbing about the coming loss of her lover, she thought of the ruby ring she had bought for her fiancé some years ago. She had been deeply in love with him, and, on a trip to Philadelphia, she had bought an expensive ruby ring and had it engraved with the words "Semper fidelis, Semper amemus." Her plan to give the ring to her fiancé came to a devastating end when he was killed in a duel before their marriage. It took her years to recover, and she had never had another lover until Georgie. Now she was losing him also. She decided that she would give Georgie the ruby ring before he left for Mississippi.

Mr. Crenshaw had worked closely with the Ellsworths over the years, using their facilities for holding slaves and their access to the river for loading slaves on boats to go downstream into the South. As compensation for this, Crenshaw gave Ellsworth a percentage of the profits on all sales of slaves. This time, Mr. Ellsworth and his family were touring Europe, but Ellsworth had told Crenshaw to work with his foreman and use the facilities as much as he needed. He had even suggested that if Crenshaw needed to entertain, he should feel free to use the mansion and its house staff to serve dinner.

To enable the sale of the eleven slaves to Col. Dabney, Crenshaw had arranged to have the group of slaves transported at night from Hickory Hill to Ellsworth Place, where he had them chained to rings on the cellar floor. Mr. Dabney's son, a dapper and arrogant young man named John, was to arrive by a chartered boat at the river landing near Ellsworth Place and, after paying Crenshaw, was to bring the slaves back to the boat and return them down the river to their plantation near Natchez.

When Mariah rode down to the salt springs to try to give Georgie the ruby ring, she found that he and the other ten had already been transported to Ellsworth Place. She was heartbroken that she wasn't at least able to have this parting moment.

Her anguish turned out to be premature. An hour later, Mr. Crenshaw told her that he needed her to go with him the next day. He explained that he would be entertaining young John Dabney at Ellsworth Place the following evening, and since Mrs. Crenshaw was indisposed, he would like Mariah to act as hostess. There would be a big dinner and an evening of social activities.

Because of the possibility of seeing Georgie one more time, Mariah was thrilled by this development. She set about putting her two prettiest dresses along with jewelry and other accessories into a trunk. She made sure she brought the ruby ring.

The following evening, Mr. Crenshaw and Mariah hosted a grand dinner at Ellsworth Place for James Dabney and some of his aides as well as a few of Crenshaw's aides. Mr. Crenshaw toasted the Dabney's health and prosperity and rambled on about states rights and the possibility of secession if the government went too far with abolition. Young Dabney responded with a gracious toast to the Crenshaws and their beautiful cousin Mariah. A lot of Ellsworth's fine wine was served at dinner. After dinner, they first listened to Mariah play *The Monastery Bells* and *Darling Nellie Gray* on the pianoforte. Then they retired into the gentlemen's room to smoke. There the house slaves served several glasses of Ellsworth's fine Kentucky bourbon.

At some point in the evening, it was apparent that young Dabney was drunk. Crenshaw, taking advantage of this situation, brought forth the contract for the sale of the slaves and entered a higher price than had previously been discussed. Dabney signed with a flourish and mumbled about Crenshaw being one of his very best friends.

During the night, Mariah tried desperately to get the ring to Georgie, but it was not possible because Crenshaw's foreman kept a sentinel posted at the cellar doors all night long.

The next morning, Dabney awoke with a headache and a bit of nausea and proceeded to begin arrangements for loading the slaves. Crenshaw gave Dabney one of the two copies of the signed contract. Dabney, seeing the price, objected strenuously.

Crenshaw claimed that he had substituted two higher-quality male slaves, namely Georgie and his brother, and had raised the price accordingly. He said that he had explained this to Dabney the previous evening before they had both signed the contract. Dabney grudgingly accepted that explanation and paid in gold coins, with aides from both sides witnessing the transaction. Crenshaw signed a receipt for the gold.

Crenshaw's aides then released the eleven slaves from the cellar floor and chained them to each other. Joining Dabney and his aides on the river side of the house, they presented the slaves and said they were ready to march them to the river for loading. Dabney expressed disappointment with the apparent frail condition of one of the male slaves. Although it was obvious that the man was sick, Crenshaw explained that the slave looked frail, but was, in fact, a first-rate worker.

The group proceeded down the narrow brushy trail to the river. As they neared the loading area, Dabney asked the slave women which three of them were pregnant. Only two answered. Dabney asked the other three individually if they were pregnant. Each one answered, "No suh, Massa." He became furious and yelled that the agreement was that three of the women were pregnant. Crenshaw made a joke of it and said Georgie could take care of that little detail on the boat.

Dabney had had enough of Crenshaw's deceptions. The accumulation of one-sided changes to the deal that had been agreed upon was upsetting him terribly. He began yelling at Crenshaw, and it was clear that a confrontation was shaping up. Crenshaw directed his aides to fall back to the rear of the group of slaves. Dabney and his men were between the slaves and the river. One of Dabney's men went onboard their boat and returned with several pistols, giving one to Dabney. Crenshaw and three of his men were also armed with pistols that they routinely wore. Dabney yelled a profanity at Crenshaw and called him a scoundrel and a liar. Crenshaw immediately drew and fired his pistol in the air as a warning to Dabney's men. Dabney became highly enraged and began firing indiscriminately toward

Crenshaw and his men. Crenshaw and his men returned fire, and one of Dabney's men yelled, "Cease fire. Dabney is hit!"

While Crenshaw kept his men back, Dabney's aides carried the young man onto the boat and loaded all the slaves except for two who had been hit and apparently killed in the crossfire. They cut the chains on these two and left them lying on the ground. Then they boarded the boat, pulled up the anchor and headed downstream as quickly as they could.

When Crenshaw sensed that the danger had passed, he ordered his men forward where they found Georgie and his brother lying dead in large puddles of blood.

Dak could see in the larger, scribbled script that Mariah was very upset as she wrote these lines. Even so, she continued to tell her story.

After hearing the shooting, she ran down the trail toward the river. Arriving there, she found Crenshaw and his men standing around the bodies of Georgie and his brother. Crenshaw was saying something about the shooting of Dabney being self-defense and the shooting of these slaves being an accident. He ordered his men to prepare two pine boxes. He said the thing to do was to bury them right there by the river and put some large chunk of stone there, so he could show Ellsworth when he returned from Europe. Then he walked back to the mansion.

Mariah no longer cared what anyone thought about her loving Georgie. She sat on the ground by the bodies and put Georgie's head in her lap. She stayed with him and sobbed for hours until they returned with the pine boxes. One of the men, who actually liked Georgie and his brother, brought a couple roses out of Ellsworth's garden to put on the graves. The men put the bodies in the pine boxes but forgot to bring the hammer to nail down the lid. As they went back for the hammer, Mariah pushed the lid to the side and put the ruby ring in Georgie's pocket. Then she took off the necklace she was wearing, removed the cross pendant and placed it in Georgie's hand. Finally, she picked up one of the roses and placed it in the coffin with him.

Soon, the men returned and nailed the lids on the coffins. One of the men escorted Mariah back to the mansion while the others stayed and buried the two pine boxes.

Mariah wrote that she would never love another man.

Dak found himself wiping a few tears on his sleeve as he pushed the box back under his bed. *How extraordinary,* he thought, *that all these years later, I'd not only find Georgie, but also his sad story.*

Chapter 12

The Lady's Bones

Dak was off to Gene's Grocery early the next morning to catch the bus to school. He was very anxious to tell J.D. that the graves held Georgie and his brother, but there was no way to do that discreetly with so many students there. Giving up on that, he entered into the banter and horseplay that was underway. Norman Jacey walked up to Dak, tugged on his collar, leaned into his face, and said, "Hey boy, I understand you're some kind of vandal."

It hadn't occurred to Dak that everyone would know about his encounter with the sheriff, so he was a little taken aback. "Eat crap, Norman," he said. "Who told you about that?"

"Oh, I dunno. I don't think there's anybody in town who doesn't know about that," Norman said. "Ol' Lard Butt does that kind of thing. He is Savoy's dog, and he barks when he's told. I don't know if he's fatter or Savoy's uglier. Savoy is some kind of relative of mine, and I still can't stand him."

Dak, adjusting his mind to the situation, smiled and said, "Yeah, just call me Dak the Vandal. It's kinda like Jack the Ripper."

A couple of the other students overheard "Dak the Vandal" and took it a step further. "Hey, everybody, here's Dak the Vandal!"

Marie heard this and said in mock horror, "Oh gosh, it's Dak the Vandal! Let's get out of here!"

As Dak was getting on the bus, Buck Dawson put his hand on Dak's shoulder and added his touch. "It's vandal man! My bus will never make it to the high school in one piece."

Dak smiled tolerantly at all the attention and, after a while, began ignoring it.

During study hall, Mr. Jordan's secretary came to Dak and asked him to come to the office. Dak immediately started to the office but thought, *This is not good.* He wondered if the sheriff had talked to Mr. Jordan. He could just hear the sheriff saying, "Jordan, one of your students is involved in vandalizing the property of one of our outstanding citizens." Dak felt one of those pains that sometimes ran through his body when something bad happened.

As Dak walked into the principal's office, Mr. Jordan stood and extended his hand. "Congratulations," he said, "You are to be the valedictorian for the Class of '56. I know it has been a lot of hard work and extra time, but I hope you feel that it was worth it."

Greatly relieved, Dak took a deep breath and smiled broadly. "Well, Mr. Jordan, it has been a happy time for me, these last four years. I don't think bein' the valedictorian is so significant, but I feel I have learned a lot, and that is important."

"In my opinion, being valedictorian is very significant," Mr. Jordan said. "And I want to ask you to make some brief comments at the graduation ceremony...say five or ten minutes. Would you be willing to do that?"

"Oh, I hadn't thought of that," Dak said. "Sure, I would like to do that if I don't get stage fright. I don't have much experience speakin' before a crowd, you know."

"You'll do fine," Mr. Jordan said. "During the ceremony, I'll introduce you and look forward to hearing what you have to say. I do have some sample speeches which you can draw from if you'd like."

"No, I don't think I want to do that," Dak said. "It might cause me to say something that was not truly my thoughts. But I'll figure it out and practice it ahead of time so maybe I won't get stage fright."

"Fine," Mr. Jordan said. "I would like to ask you to keep this confidential because we want to have some suspense at the ceremony. Is that okay?"

"Sure," Dak said. "I won't tell a soul."

After school, as soon as Dak and J.D. were out of earshot of the other students, Dak started explaining what he learned about Georgie and Mariah. J.D. stopped him, saying, "Hold a minute. Here comes Marie. I want her to hear this because she is nuts about a good love story. Where's Melodie?"

"She's gone to the dentist," replied Dak. "I'll tell her later."

When Marie caught up with them, Dak relayed the whole story of the love affair and how it ended, finally explaining that the graves were of Georgie and his brother and that the ruby ring from the grave was the one Mariah had tearfully left in Georgie's pocket. Marie was fascinated and saddened at the same time. Even J.D. seemed moved by the story. He said, "We really ought to have a little service and put everything back in place, including the ring, after we finish up."

"I agree," Dak replied, "and I guess we're about finished up. We just have to check out that rope that seems to go to something else." Dak then explained that he had to hurry along because he needed to tell Miss Mattie about all this.

As soon as Dak was able to get home, greet Eleanor and Nancy, and change his clothes, he was off to Mattie's on his bicycle. When he arrived at Mattie's, he saw no sign of activity, so he knocked on the door. No one answered, but he heard some faint noises. Putting his hands beside his eyes to stop the glare, he leaned against the window and looked inside. There was no one in the front room, but he could see Mattie on the floor in the next room, moving her hand to try to get his attention.

Dak rushed through the unlocked door and kneeled next to Mattie. "What happened?" he asked. "Are you okay?"

Mattie was very weak and asked for some water. Dak quickly got some water for her and gently held her head up a bit, so she could drink.

"Tripped over Carrots," she whispered. "Happened yesterday, and I've had a lot of pain. Not able to get up." The orange cat put her tail high in the air and rubbed against Dak's leg as he supported Mattie.

"Let me get some cushions for you," Dak said, "and get you more comfortable. You'll be okay, Miss Mattie. I'll get the doctor. We'll take care of you."

Dak did his best to make her more comfortable but could tell that she was suffering. After reassuring her that he'd be right back, he ran to his bicycle and hurried to tell Eleanor about

Mattie's situation. Eleanor told Dak to ride down to Gene's Grocery and call the doctor while she went to comfort Mattie.

After the doctor examined Mattie and gave her an injection to relax her, he said, "I believe she has a broken hip, and aside from that, she is very weak and must go into the hospital. I'll arrange for an ambulance to take her over to Eldorado. She is very lucky that Dak came along." Dak was worried about her because she was so old and frail.

"Don't worry about Miss Mattie," Eleanor said. "I'll get Mrs. Scroggins to take me over to the hospital to visit her tomorrow. She'll be there for quite a while."

• • •

On Friday night, J.D. was to take Judy and the others to Harrisburg to a movie as he had promised Savoy. Since Dak and Melodie were not involved in that activity, Dak suggested to Melodie that they meet on the seawall and enjoy the view.

"That sounds like fun, Dak," Melodie said, "but I have an even better idea. My parents are going to play Bingo at the church hall tonight. If you could come over about seven, we could make popcorn balls and have the house to ourselves."

"Oh, wow! I'll be there. It's our lucky day."

Dak arrived at Melodie's place a little early so he could say hello to her parents. Having consumed a glass or two of wine, they were in a great mood. "Don't do anything I wouldn't do," Mr. Lerner said. "And keep in mind that we may be back at any time. Sometimes, we don't stay long at Bingo." After a little lighthearted discussion, Mr. Lerner told an old joke and then repeated the punch line twice as he walked out the door.

Dak dutifully laughed and said, "Have a good time at the Bingo."

As the door closed, Melodie said, "Hey, Dak, I have a good idea for our special night. You know that my parents have that cabin at Big Lake?"

"Yeah, right next door to J.D.'s parent's cabin, right?"

"Right," Melodie replied. "We could have our special night in our cabin."

"Your parents would never allow that," Dak said.

"Well, I asked them what they thought of that and my Mom said we'd have to have a chaperone," Melodie said.

"Wouldn't that ruin it all? How could we talk and dance and have fun with some parent sitting right beside us?" Dak asked.

"Well, it would depend on who the parent was and how much they hovered over us," Melodie said. "One advantage is that with a chaperone, we could stay all night if we wanted. When we got sleepy, you guys could go to the Robinson's cabin and Marie and I could sleep in ours."

"Let me talk with J.D. about that idea," Dak replied. "I think it has promise."

It didn't take Dak and Melodie long to make the popcorn balls and eat a couple of them. Then, they went to the living room sofa and sat down to talk. Melodie spread her body over the couch with her head in Dak's lap. As they talked, he stroked her hair. Knowing that Melodie was going into a nursing program in Evansville next year, he kept thinking about how much he was going to miss her.

"I wish we were going to the same college in the fall," he said. "How will we see each other? It'll be so lonesome without you."

"I know," replied Melodie, "but my parents insist that it is the best program for me, and I do like the idea of nursing. I just wish...well, that we could at least see each other every weekend."

Dak sighed. "I don't even have a car. There is no way we can see each other that often."

"Well, Dak, I'll wait till the end of time for you if necessary," Melodie said. He leaned over and kissed her passionately.

After a while, Melodie put a 45 rpm single on her record player. "I wish I had a nicer record player like Judy Savoy's Collaro Conquest, but I'm afraid this is it, Dak," she said. "Judy Savoy has a better record player. I have you."

As Johnnie Ace began the song, *Pledging My Love*, they stood and danced slowly and intimately. The music rolled through their psyche and created the sublime feeling that comes only with young love.

Forever my darling,
Our love will be true.
Always and forever,
I'll love only you.
Just promise me darling
Your love in return.
May this fire in my soul dear
Forever burn.

Half way through the song, Dak began a kiss that lasted until the end of it. As it ended, their embrace continued, and the song began again. Dak realized that it would repeat until they stopped it. The two of them became one as Melodie reached under his shirt to place her left hand on his bare back and her face against his flannel shirt. Dak nuzzled his face into her golden hair and dreamed that this would never end. Melodie was listening intently to the words, thinking how appropriate they were for her and Dak. She wanted to forget that the two of them would be in separate places next fall and concentrate on the here and now. Dak murmured in her ear, "You are such a beautiful person, so perfect."

They let the song repeat nine times and seemed to get closer, more intimate each time. Then the doorbell rang.

"Awww, who would that be?" asked Dak.

"I don't know, but their timing is awful," replied Melodie, as she went to the door. It was Mrs. Staley, the next-door neighbor, wanting to use the phone.

"Sorry to bother you," she said. "We really should get a telephone, but they cost so much. I sure appreciate..."

"Think nothing of it," Melodie said. "Glad to help."

Mrs. Staley talked on the phone for about 25 minutes. By then, it was only about 10 minutes until the Bingo was to end.

"Well, it was a wonderful evening, Melodie," Dak said, as he took the last bite of another popcorn ball and opened the door to leave. "I wish we had more time alone together, but I'm thankful for what we had."

• • •

Dak woke to a bright Saturday morning and could hear the birds singing in the trees outside his open window. Eleanor had saved some fried mush and scrambled eggs for him and gone on with her work. As Dak made his way down the steps, he could see her sweeping the front walk. He was not even finished with breakfast when J.D. walked in the back door.

"J.D., have a piece of fried mush and tell me about how it went with Judy," Dak said.

"Oh, it didn't go exactly as planned," replied J.D. "When we got to Savoy's house to pick up Judy, she came walkin' out all spiffed up wearin' new clothes, and ol' Savoy was right behind her. So, we walk over to her Pontiac, and Savoy says, 'Young man, you drive carefully.' I say, 'Sure thing, Mr. Savoy.' He says, 'I see you have another couple to go with you.' "

"Oh, no," Dak interrupted. "He didn't."

"Yeah, that's what he said. So, I'm feeling a little heat and tryin' to figure out what to do. Then, Marie puts her arm around Norman and says, 'I guess we get the back seat, Norman.' And she looks up at him like he's the sweetest thing she's ever seen and says, 'I don't think we'll need more than half of it though, if you know what I mean.' "

"You're razzin' me...she didn't say that," Dak said, laughing.

"No, that's exactly what happened. So Norman took advantage of the situation and leaned over and kissed Marie and whispered something in her ear. So, Marie, she giggles like he must have said something real sexy. Ol' Savoy got this silly little smile on his face like he was really enjoying all this affection between Marie and Norman. I think he was hoping for more. So Judy plays along with it and says, 'Now, don't you all go too far back there. We have a rear-view mirror, you know.' "

"What did Savoy do then?" Dak asked.

"Well, Judy sat in the front with me, and he went back in the house. I don't know. He was probably disappointed that Judy and I didn't jump in the car and start taking our clothes off or something. The man is nuts!"

"What about the rest of the evening?" Dak asked.

"Oh, it was pretty uneventful. We all sat together in the movie. It was me, then Marie, then Judy, and Norman. It was a little strained because we all knew Judy must be embarrassed, but she didn't act like it. If she was, it didn't keep her from braggin' about her new clothes and her car and exactly how much everything cost. After the movie, we went to some little place and had a shake and came home."

"Hey, sounds like to me Marie kinda likes Norman," Dak joked. "Guess you're a has-been."

"Yeah, guess so. So are we gonna go to the Uppers and figure out what that rope goes to, or are you gonna eat mush all day?" J.D. said.

"I might eat mush all day," Dak said, trying to look serious. "Have you tried this stuff with a little butter and jelly on it?"

The boys reached the site of the graves a short time later and uncovered the work site. For a while, they discussed whether there was any way to resolve what was at the end of the rope without removing all the dirt from the top of that area. Eventually, they determined that they would have to move the dirt, so they each picked up a spade and went to work. A little more than two hours later, they had finished the job.

"We need to be careful now," Dak said. "We're about to the level of the other graves."

"Yeah, but I don't see anything here. Let's start at the rope and dig along it now to see where it goes."

"Right," Dak said. "That should be the quickest way."

J.D. kept carefully removing a little dirt from just above the rope, while Dak took the trowel and gently dug around the rope, being careful not to break it.

"This rope is pretty rotten, so we'll just have to go slow with it," Dak said.

"Hold it! I think I just dug into something," J.D. said.

"Okay, let me just use the trowel," Dak said. "What is this stuff? It looks like a blanket, or at least a piece of one, don't you think?"

"Yeah, is that rotted wool? That's what it looks like to me."

"It probably is. Partially rotted, I'd say. Let's just take all the dirt off this blanket as far as it goes and see what we have," Dak said.

A half hour later, the boys had uncovered the remains of what appeared to be a wool blanket that ran about five and a half feet end-to-end. The rope was around the blanket near the center. In addition, two other pieces of rope enclosed the blanket a little more than a foot from each end.

"Let's measure this," Dak said, placing the yardstick across it. "It looks like whatever is inside is about fifteen inches wide."

The boys took some photos, leaving the yardstick in place for reference. Then they discussed how to proceed.

"We need to get the blanket off and see what we have," J.D. said.

"I know, but if we try to remove the blanket, it will just come to pieces, won't it?

"It will, but I don't know any way around it," said J.D. "It's just too rotten to remove in one piece or even two pieces. Let's just cut squares of it and remove them one at a time. We can keep them in order so we will know which piece goes where."

As they took off the first piece, they found there was another layer of the blanket.

"Okay," Dak said. "This blanket has been wrapped around something, and you know what? It's about the right size for another body."

"Probably so, but I'm hoping for gold ingots or something," J.D. said.

They began at one end removing the second layer of the blanket. As they removed the first piece, they could see a skull and hair mixed with settled dirt.

"Wow!" Dak exclaimed. "Look at this! This skull has not been in the ground as long as Georgie's. It's not nearly as old. This skull is whiter and still has its hair intact."

"Oh, man! Well, there went the gold. Look at those nice teeth. Let's hurry and take the rest of the blanket off," said J.D.

With the blanket entirely removed, what they saw was mostly dirt, but clothing fragments were visible and at the foot end, the remains of leather shoes.

"Look at these ol' shoes," Dak said. "They're not even so rotten. Know what? These are women's shoes. These are the remains of a woman."

"Well, let's take our trowel and spoons and carefully dig down to the level of the clothing," J.D. said.

As they attempted to take the dirt off the clothing fragments, they found the cloth so rotten that it was impossible to end up with a somewhat fully clothed skeleton. What they had, instead, was patches of clothing here and there. In other areas, there were just the tops of bones. The rib bones were visible on the right side, but on the left side, several patches of cloth covered most of the ribs. They took several photos.

"Interesting," Dak said. "You can even make out the pattern in the cloth. It was a flowered dress. See that?"

"Oh, yeah, hadn't noticed that," replied J.D.

"Let's dig around the skull and see if there is a hole from a gunshot or something," said Dak.

As they progressed around the skull, they found no holes. What they did find was a large indention in the back of the head.

"Oh, look at that," J.D. said. "Somebody hit her really hard in the back of the head."

"Wow!" Dak said. "I guess that makes it very likely that this was murder."

The other thing they found was a lot of hair. "Can you believe all this reddish hair?" J.D. said. "It's all mixed with the dirt, but there's lots of it here. It goes on down under the rib cage. Really long."

"Wouldn't think there would be this much dirt," Dak said. "I thought the dirt was just decomposed flesh and organs and stuff, but maybe some dirt washed into the blanket when this area flooded year after year."

As they continued to dig, they found no other evidence of violence. The bones seemed to be intact. Also, there were no rings, watches, or pendants. There were some buttons from the dress the woman had worn and there was a belt buckle that seemed to be made of bone. They found hair all the way to the waist.

"Who do you suppose this woman was?" J.D. asked.

"Anybody's guess," Dak replied, "but she hasn't been there nearly as long as Georgie and his brother. Let's see. They've been here about a hundred years. We know that. Her bones are hard and solid and lighter colored, whereas Georgie's skull was brown and almost crumbly. Georgie's clothing was totally rotted away, whereas there are many fragments of hers remaining."

"So, what do you think...about a fourth as long, maybe twenty-five years?" J.D. asked.

"Well, I don't know much about forensics, but I think that would be a reasonable guess," Dak said. "Let's cover this all up for now. Maybe we can find some other clues to this. We could take a shoe or the belt buckle to try to see how old they are, but I don't know what we could tell people about where we got them."

"Let's take both," J.D. replied. "Who knows what trickery we might come up with to get some answers?"

Chapter 13

Shoes from 1935

As the boys were returning from the Uppers with the shoe and belt buckle in a bag, it occurred to them that the third grave had implications that the first two didn't have.

"You know," J.D. said, "since the lady's grave is much newer than the other two and looks like murder, it's more likely to be of interest to the law enforcement people."

"Yeah, it could be a fairly recent murder for all we know," Dak replied. "I don't have a good feel for how long it takes to rot. We could go tell the sheriff except that the ol' bag is lame in the head and would probably ignore the skeleton and try to convict us of trespassin' or vandalism or somethin'."

"True," J.D. said. "Let's just keep it quiet and see if we can figure out when she was buried and who she is. I think maybe we shouldn't even tell the girls about this until we know what this is all about."

"Yeah, I agree. Why don't we go home and clean up a little and then go up to the clothing store and see if they know how old the shoe is?"

"Come on, Dak!" J.D. responded. "What do we do? Go into the store and say, 'Hey, we just dug up a woman's grave, and we were wondering if you could tell us anything about this shoe she was wearin'?"

"Don't be silly. It's Mrs. Staley, Melodie's neighbor. We could tell her we were diggin' a flower garden, and we came upon this shoe. How about sayin' that?"

J.D. thought for a minute. "Okay," he said. "You do most of the talkin'. I'll meet you in front of the store in an hour."

As they were going into the store, Dak said, "Just follow along, sort of reinforcin' whatever I say. That will make it more believable."

"Sure thing," replied J.D.

"Oh, hello, Mrs. Staley," Dak said. "I haven't seen you since the other night at Melodie's."

"It is so good to see you, Dak," Mrs. Staley said, "and you, too, J.D. What can I do for you boys today? We have a new shipment of short-sleeve shirts that I'm sure you would like. Make you look like Charles Atlas."

"Uh, well, we just have a question, Mrs. Staley," Dak said. "J.D. and I were diggin' a flower garden, and we came across an ol' shoe. I say it's from the 1920s, and J.D. says it's from the 1940s. So we made a bet on it, and we were wonderin' if you could tell us how old it really is so we can settle our bet."

"I might be able to," Mrs. Staley said. "Here, let me see it."

Mrs. Staley took the dirty shoe in her hand and turned it over a couple times. Then, she looked at the insole, rubbed it a bit with a dust cloth, and positioned the shoe to get the best light reflection.

"Oh, yes, if you look carefully, the words 'Revette Creation' are stamped into the insole," she said. "That's a shoe we carried back in the thirties. Oh, I'd say about 1935. It was a black suede pump with an open toe and cut-outs at the sides, as you can see. It was top stitched across the vamp and was a very good shoe, but a little expensive. Where did you say you found it?"

"J.D. and I were diggin' up a flower garden, and there it was," Dak offered.

"Yeah," J.D. added, "my parents wanted some flowers planted in the back yard, so Dak and I made this huge bed for them, all the way across the back line."

"Oh, how nice," said Mrs. Staley. "I'll have to stop by and see it when I'm over that way."

Dak opened the door as he said, "Thank you very much, Mrs. Staley. I guess we don't either one win the bet."

As they walked down the sidewalk, Dak said, "You might have made the flower bed a little smaller, J.D. That way, you could've actually dug one to show her in case she comes over to your house to see it."

"Oh, crap," J.D. said. "I didn't think of that. I doubt she will really come to see it, but what if she does? I'll just say, 'Oh, no,

Mrs. Staley, it was Dak's back yard, not mine. You should really go see it.' She'll probably come over to your house."

"I better start diggin'," Dak replied.

"Hey, Dak, I have to go," J.D. said. "Here, take this bag and put it with our other stuff from the graves. I'll see you tomorrow."

• • •

As Dak was walking home, he was thinking about what he was going to do with the rest of his day. "Melodie is off on a band field trip. J.D. has a hot date with Marie. So I'm on my own," he thought to himself.

He knew he should read that book on the Battle of Austerlitz that he had checked out from the library. He thought this battle was the crown jewel of Napoleon's career and that Napoleon was the crown jewel of European history, so it should be very interesting. In addition, he had already turned in that battle as the topic for his book report that was due in a few days. The trouble was that all the facts that he and J.D. had gleaned in the last few weeks kept haunting him. He felt a strong urge to press the subject to completion.

When Dak arrived home, Eleanor had dinner just about ready. She had cooked pork chops. She served them with some wilted lettuce covered with a bacon dressing and some buttered carrots that she had canned last summer. She had also made biscuits because she knew Dak liked them so much.

"Ahh, you make a nice meal, Mom," Dak said, as he started counting the biscuits. "Well, let's see, Nance-baby, you get one biscuit, Mom gets two and I get three. Now that we've settled that, pass the pork chops."

Nancy just grinned and put a big blob of butter on the biscuit she had just cut open.

"Mom, you remember you told me one time about Josephine, Savoy's first wife?" Dak asked. He took a big bite of the wilted lettuce.

"Why, yes. She was a good friend of mine," Eleanor replied. "Josephine Ingres was her maiden name. What made you think of her?"

"Oh, I read somethin' about Lafayette the other day, and it reminded me that you said she descended from him," Dak said. "Did she look anything like Lafayette?" He pretended to slap Nancy's hand as she reached for a second biscuit.

"Oh, I'm not sure I know what Layfayette looked like," Eleanor replied. "She was medium height or a little shorter and had a petite build, a very pretty face and very long reddish-brown hair. Part of what made her look so good is that she always dressed so well."

"When was it that she went back to France?"

"Mid thirties," Eleanor said. "It was a year or two before the '37 flood. I'd guess '36, but it may have been '35."

"It would be real interestin' to talk with her and hear all the family stories about Lafayette and the famous painter named Ingres. Lafayette actually visited Shawneetown in 1825, you know."

"Yes," Eleanor said, "and I think that was one thing that attracted Josephine to our little town. She liked the thought that her ancestor was here a long time ago."

"What do you know about Ingres, the painter?" Dak asked.

"Not too much, actually," Eleanor said. "I just know what Josephine told me. I think she said his name was Jean-Auguste Ingres. I remember she said he was a pupil of David, the most celebrated French painter of his time. David did that painting I'm sure you've seen of Napoleon crossing the Alps...the one where he is on the rearing stallion and has this red cape blowing in the wind. Anyway, she always went on about Ingres' great sense of color and mastery of line and such. I hardly even knew what that meant, but I gather he was extraordinary."

"You saw some originals of his paintings, didn't you?" Dak asked.

"No, I only ever saw one," Eleanor said. "I think I told you before that she had one large original of his. As far as I know, it was the only one she had. It was beautiful."

"I think you said it was of a sitting lady?"

"Yes, it was," Eleanor replied. "The lady was a Rothschild, a baroness I think. She was a beautiful woman and had a pink satiny gown with lace and jewels. I remember that the painting had the name 'Rothschild' and a miniature coat of arms in the upper right corner. It was very nice."

"Yeah, I suppose. Hey, that was a good meal. Let's have it again tomorrow. Think I'll go read my book on the Battle of Austerlitz. I think Nance-baby volunteered to do the dishes. Hopefully, she doesn't drop the whole stack like she did one time." Dak smiled at Nancy but didn't notice that she rolled her eyes as she scooted back from the table.

Dak was already gone when Eleanor said, "I had planned to have left-over mincemeat pie for dessert, but I guess Dak doesn't want dessert tonight."

Dak went into his room, closed the door and arranged his pillows on his bed to form a comfortable place to sit and read. He read one paragraph, but he couldn't get his mind off the graves, especially the third one. He closed the book, picked up a pencil and a sheet of notebook paper, and leaned back on his pillows. Using the Austerlitz book as a writing surface, he began writing his thoughts on the paper.

Savoy meets Josephine Ingres in France
Josephine visits here
They get married
They don't get along very well
Josephine returned to France in 1936 without saying goodbye
Eleanor asked for Josephine's address
Eleanor writes letter to Josephine at that address
No response to that letter
Josephine had long reddish hair
Lady in the grave has long reddish hair
Josephine here in 1935
Lady in the grave had shoes from 1935
She had two heirloom possessions
A sword from Lafayette
A painting of Rothschild lady by Ingres
There is a sword in the Secret Room at Ellsworth Place

Is it the Lafayette sword?
Is there a painting in the Secret Room?
Is the third grave really Josephine?
If so, why would she be buried with old graves?

Dak felt a surge of adrenaline as these thoughts raced through his mind. He wondered if he was seeing ghosts. He wondered what it meant. He warned himself that this stuff can get in your head, and you can start drawing conclusions that aren't valid.

"Does it mean that Savoy murdered his first wife?" he asked himself.

Dak reread the thoughts on the notebook paper again, asking himself what other rational explanation might account for all this. Other questions were streaming into his mind. *If it looks like murder, who can I tell? I certainly can't tell Sheriff Summers. What about J.D.? Is this scary enough that he might panic? Should I tell Mom? No, she would insist on going to the sheriff. Is Savoy actually capable of murder? He's a butt hole, yes, but I don't know about murder.*

He picked up the paper with his notes and added one more line:

Did Savoy murder Josephine?

Dak decided he needed more information. He retrieved the photos he had taken in the mansion and looked at the photo of the sword in the secret room. It was apparent from the photo that it had a heavy layer of dust on it. Even though he could see what appeared to be some engraving on it, he couldn't make it out because of the dust and the poor picture quality.

Having thought it all through, Dak was convinced that he needed to go back to the mansion. He needed to determine what engraving was actually on the sword for one thing. Also, he wanted to look for the Ingres painting. Further, he decided that J.D. could be trusted with this information. J.D. was overly cautious sometimes, but he would not panic. Dak had a course of action. He would see J.D. about going back to the mansion tomorrow.

Dak sat aside his paper and opened the Austerlitz book again. He thumbed to a page near the end of the book. It was Napoleon's message to his soldiers after the battle: "It will be enough for you to say, 'I was at Austerlitz,' to hear the reply, 'There is a brave man'!" "Fascinating man, fascinating battle. I'm going to enjoy this book," he told himself.

Then he heard the windows start rattling. "Another big barge on the river," he thought to himself. The rattling grew louder, and then he heard the clock in the attic strike three times. It was the second time this school year that he had heard the old clock. It was as though it was saying, "I've been shut away in this attic for eighty years. Won't someone come and wind me up again?"

Dak went to his closet and pulled out the stepladder they used when changing light bulbs. As he was positioning it under the panel in the ceiling that led to the attic, he heard a knock on the front door downstairs. Speeding down the steps, he opened the door to find J.D. standing there.

"Well, what a surprise," Dak said. "I thought you were out on a date."

"I was,"J.D. said dejectedly, "but Marie got sick and wanted to go home. Probably that chili dog she had earlier."

"Oh, sorry," Dak said. "And what caused you to knock instead of just walkin' in like usual?"

"My X-ray vision told me the door was locked." J.D.'s attempt at humor seemed to cheer him up a bit, even if it didn't seem very funny to Dak.

Eleanor stuck her head through the sliding doors. "Oh, hello, J.D.," she said.

"Good evenin', Mrs. Leventhal," J.D. said. "It's just me."

"Come on up to my room, J.D. I've got something to show you, plus I need some help with something," Dak said. Eleanor disappeared behind the sliding doors as they closed.

"Here's the thing, J.D.," Dak said, as he handed J.D. the sheet of paper on which he had put all his notes. "We have to be very quiet about this until we figure out for sure what has happened, but this could be murder by somebody we know."

"By somebody we know?" J.D. said loudly.

"Shhhh...Yeah, by somebody we know."

"You're razzin' me," he said quietly, as he read the notes. Then, with an alarmed expression on his face, he went back to the top and slowly read them again. "Holy crap!" he said. "Oh, my God, do you suppose? Would ol' Savoy do such a thing?'

"I'm not sure," Dak said. "We really need to go back to the mansion to learn more..."

"Oh, this is getting deep, Dak," J.D. interrupted. "Maybe we should drop this whole subject and forget it all. Hey, we couldn't even tell the sheriff. That butt hole would have us behind bars or worse. Besides, we don't know that Savoy did anything."

"I know, I know," Dak said. "But, we're in a spot. If he did do it, we should do whatever is required to bring him to justice. Nobody else knows what we know, so we do it, or nobody does it. We've figured out a lot of things. We can't quit now. I don't know exactly how we deal with the sheriff, but we need to find out the truth first. We need to go back to the mansion."

"Oh, man, I don't think I'm up to goin' back to the mansion," J.D. said. "This was fun for awhile, but it's gettin' scary. If Savoy knew about this, there is no tellin' what he might do. Why don't we just back out of all this and enjoy the ladies? We don't have to mess up our lives like this. Besides, if they catch us in the mansion again, we're hamburger."

"J.D., we have here on a small scale the same thing as the great decisions of history. Lincoln didn't have to push so hard against slavery. It would have been a lot easier to back off and forget about it. They didn't have to do the Declaration of Independence. It would have been a lot easier to back off and put up with the King. We didn't..."

"Yeah, yeah, Dak, I get your point," J.D. said, "but I ain't Lincoln or Washington. Besides, Lincoln ended up with a hole in his head, which is exactly what I don't want. This history stuff only goes so far. We could get in big trouble. I don't know."

"It's about courage, J.D. The question is whether we have enough courage to do what's right."

"Hey, it's not my obligation to figure out who did what crime around here," J.D. said. "That's what ol' lard butt is supposed to be doin'."

"It's not your obligation, that's true. But I'm talkin' right and wrong. It's the right thing to do. We will be very ordinary people if we go through life doin' only what's our obligation and not what's right."

"Dak, what makes you think I want to be anything but ordinary?" J.D. said with a smile. "For me, the good life is makin' out with Marie. Not riskin' my life tryin' to right a wrong."

"Okay, I know you're going to say yes when you start smilin'," Dak said. "So how about tomorrow morning while everyone is at church?"

"Dak, it's sometimes disgustin' how persistent you can be," J.D. said. "Okay, one more trip to the mansion, and that's it babe. So you better get what you need. I ain't goin' back."

"Well, now that you volunteered to do it, how about 8 AM?"

"Que será," said J.D. "Now what was it you wanted me to help you with?"

"Oh, I almost forgot," said Dak. "A big boat went by on the river, and the vibration caused the clock in the attic to strike. I got out the stepladder to go see what kind of ghostly clock this is and what else is up there. As far as I can tell, nobody has been up there in eons. Maybe even a hundred years."

Dak had two flashlights. They each took one and climbed up the ladder and into the dark, dusty attic. Shining their lights into the south end, they didn't see much.

"What is that thing, an ol' bookcase?" asked J.D.

"It could be, or more likely, it's a set of shelves to put canned goods on. It looks like there are some ol' cannin' jars on it. Hey, they could be full of tomatoes from 1860 or something, for all I know."

"I pass," said J.D., as they turned their lights toward the north end of the attic.

"Okay, we have several things up there," Dak said. "We even have boards to walk on so we won't fall through the lathes and plaster."

"I'm not crazy about all these spider webs," J.D. said. "And look at all the mud dauber nests."

It turned out that the old clock was the first thing they reached.

"Look at this clock," Dak said. "I imagined it was a grandfather clock, but it's only, what, 30 inches high."

J.D. shined his flashlight on the front surface. "Look how that mud dauber built right on the front of the clock," he said.

"Yeah," Dak said, "it has a door on the front that opens if I unlatch this little hook. There's its pendulum, and look at that scene painted on the lower part of the glass in the door."

"What's it say on the face?" asked J.D.

"Nothing that I see other than the numbers," Dak responded, "but there is something on the back of the inside, behind the pendulum."

"Ahh, yes. It says 'Riley Whiting, Winchester, Connecticut, 1825,' right there."

"How about that? Here, I'll put it over by the opening so we can take it down when we go," Dak said. "Maybe I can get it to run."

When Dak returned, he opened an old box. It had what appeared to be Christmas tree ornaments from another age. "Wow," he said, as he retrieved a wooden ornament of a manger with a star on top and handed it to J.D. "This is really old. I'll have to tell Mom about this."

The next thing was a carved Victorian walnut marble-topped table, without the marble. "The marble must be around here someplace," said Dak, "but I don't see it."

"I bet they put it up here because the marble broke," J.D. suggested.

As they were looking at a wicker baby buggy filled with dusty, rotted cushions, J.D. bumped against a small metal box. "What's this?" he said, focusing his light on it.

"It's a box full of gold," Dak said, as he tested the lid. The box was not locked and readily opened. It had several papers in it.

"What, no gold?" J.D. asked.

"No, just papers from long ago, Dak said, as he picked up a couple of them. "This is a receipt for the sale of lumber from Leventhal farms dated May 14, 1861. I think I'll take this box down and look through it when I have time."

As the boys climbed down the ladder, J.D. said he really had to go.

"You don't like all my spiders and mud daubers?" Dak asked.

"It's not that," J.D. replied. "This is good stuff; it's just that I want to go back by Marie's and see if she's feelin' better. She was pretty sick."

"Okay, I'll see you in the morning, then," Dak said.

"Que será."

Chapter 14

The Wreck on Route 13

D ak looked again at the piece of paper that held his notes on a possible murder, folded it, and inserted it into a slot in his wallet. He considered whether to go to bed because it had been a very busy day, but he felt keyed up by the developments and knew he would not be able to sleep. Thinking that he needed to read the book on the Battle of Austerlitz, he picked it up again and started to thumb through it when he heard Eleanor and Nancy coming up the stairs. Eleanor was carrying a basket of clothes.

"Get your pajamas on, Nancy, while I put these clothes away," Eleanor said. Nancy, who already had her pajamas on, gave Eleanor a puzzled look and yawned.

Dak tossed his book aside and picked up the old clock from the attic. As he did, he heard a rattling noise inside. "Not a good sign," he mumbled.

"Good night, sleep tight," Eleanor said to Nancy, as she pulled the bedroom door shut. Nancy apparently didn't have the energy to respond.

Eleanor picked up her half-full basket of clothes and walked into Dak's room. "What have you found now, Dak?" she said, as she began putting his folded clothes into a large orange-colored chest that stood between the front windows of his room.

"You know the ol' clock we have heard from time to time in the attic?" Dak asked. "Well, this is it. It's not as big as I expected."

"What an attractive old clock," replied Eleanor. "Why, look at those three brass spheres on top of it. I'll bet the Leventhals used that for a lot of years."

Dak opened the door to investigate the rattling noise. "Ahh, here's the key to it," he said. "It was rattling around loose inside."

Positioning the clock across his knees over his wastebasket, he used his pocketknife to scrape the mud dauber's nest off and then used a pair of dirty socks to wipe off the heavy layer of dust. Positioning the old clock on his table, he set the time to match Eleanor's watch and wound it until it became hard to turn. Giving the pendulum a little swing, he said, "We'll see if it keeps good time."

"What else did you find up there?" Eleanor asked.

"Well, one thing was a box of Christmas ornaments," Dak said. "They were made out of wood and looked really old."

"Oh," said Eleanor, "we should get them out at Christmastime and put them on the tree."

"Yeah, and we found this metal box with old papers in it," Dak said. "Sit down, and we'll go through them."

Dak picked up a yellowed paper and handed it to Eleanor. "This one is a receipt for lumber sold from Leventhal Farms in 1861," he said, "and look at this. It's a receipt for the purchase of a carriage called a 'Town Phaeton.' I guess it was pretty fancy."

Eleanor retrieved an old stiff paper that had been folded into thirds. Opening it carefully, she said, "This is a Land Grant. I don't recognize the people the land was granted to, but the thing was signed by Andrew Jackson Donelson, Secretary for Andrew Jackson, who was President of the United States at the time. It's dated March 5, 1833."

"Dak picked up another document. This one says 'Lease Agreement'," he said, as he studied the document. "Let's see if I can figure it out."

Eleanor, still enamored with the Jackson Land Grant, didn't acknowledge Dak's comment.

"Hey, this is pretty interestin'," he said. "This is an agreement between Colonel John Ellsworth and Dakston P. Leventhal, my great grandfather. Leventhal agrees to provide a 100-year lease on a certain 800 acres of land and all facilities on that land, including the Leventhal Mansion and all barns, out buildings, smokehouses, and even a distillery. All this is in exchange for the permanent possession of the riverboat *Queen of Egypt* and all equipment related to it."

"A 100-year lease?" asked Eleanor.

"Yeah, that's what it says. The lease includes all lumber rights, use of all croplands and pasturelands, and use of all loading docks on the river. It specifically says Ellsworth accepts full liability for any damage or injury to the person or property of others on the land during that 100-year period and is to pay all taxes and fees. At the end of 100 years, the property is to return to Leventhal and any direct descendants forever, to be equally divided among them."

"Well, can you beat that?" Eleanor said. "I thought Ellsworth bought the property. I don't think your Dad ever mentioned anything about a lease."

"The Lease Agreement is dated January 11, 1856," Dak said. "And here's a note on the front. The note says, 'This is the Lease Agreement with Ellsworth for the mansion and surrounding property for whatever it is worth. The County has agreed to forward all tax bills directly to Ellsworth and successors. For all practical purposes, the property is his. We probably should keep this somewhere, in case there is any question about liability or terms. Also, of course, it can be passed to any heirs for eventually reclaiming the property, but that will be long after we're dead.' It is signed with the initials D. P. L. and dated October 10, 1871."

"How interesting," Eleanor said. "I suppose that sometime down through the years, the Ellsworths or the Savoys, as their heirs, bought permanent rights to the property."

Dak thought a minute. "It is likely, although I don't think they bought it in the last 20 years or so. You would have heard about that. And if a person still had 50 years to go on a 100-year lease, he probably wouldn't bother to buy it. So it's possible that they never bought it."

"Oh, my," Eleanor said. "Wouldn't that be something? The hundred years were up last January."

"If it should turn out that way, are there any heirs other than Nancy and me?" Dak asked.

"Well, let's see," Eleanor said. "Your Grandfather Leventhal was an only child and your Dad only had one sibling, your Aunt

Katherine. Of course, she never married, and then she died in that car wreck up in Indiana a few years ago. So you and Nancy are the only Leventhal heirs."

"This is fascinating," Dak said. "We need to check into this in case the Ellsworths never bought permanent rights. The problem is that we need to do that without anyone knowing about it, because if Savoy gets wind of this, he will be madder than a pregnant grandma."

Eleanor thought for a minute and yawned. "Maybe I can figure out a way of doing that. Let's go to bed for now, and we'll find the answer in a few days." She walked down the stairs, and Dak noticed that it was 11:30 PM.

This time, he went to bed.

• • •

Dak slept so late on Sunday morning that he was still asleep when J.D. arrived. Eleanor opened the sliding doors and yelled, "Dak, get up. J.D. is here." Dak quickly made it down the stairs and greeted J.D.

"Here are your waffles, Dak," she said. Then, noticing that Dak was off washing his face, she said, "J.D., won't you have some waffles? We have plenty, and they are flavored with some pecans that Dak picked up last winter."

"Now you've done twisted my arm, Mrs. Leventhal," he said. "Don't mind if I do."

Even Eleanor was surprised at how many waffles the two boys ate and how much milk they drank with them. "Here's the last one. Won't you split it?" she said. When they finally declined, she nibbled on it while they got their gear together for their project.

The gear included, among other things, a camera and two flashlights. Noticing this, Eleanor said, "For heaven's sake, what use could you make of two flashlights on a sunny day like this?"

"It's a secret, Mom," Dak said as he stashed the items into a grass bag, "but, don't worry. We're not going down in a cave."

"Well, that's a small relief anyway," she said with resignation. "Whatever you're doing, be careful."

The two boys hurried over the north levee, choosing to approach the mansion from the river side. If anyone were there, this approach would allow them to get closer to the mansion without being seen. It didn't take long to get to the vicinity, and then they moved cautiously from one clump of brush or bushes to another, stopping at each one to see if they could see any evidence of anyone being there. They reached the clump of bushes closest to the mansion and could see no sign of anyone.

"Let's run for the door to the cellar and then pause just inside," Dak said. Once inside the door, they stopped and listened for a full minute. Hearing nothing, they proceeded quietly up the steps from the cellar to the first floor. The door, which was warped and tended to stick, was propped open.

Just inside the door, there were two steel animal traps. Both were set and placed directly in the path of anyone walking through the door.

"Oh, man, look at this! Be careful!" Dak said loudly and then put his hand over his mouth.

"Hey, the man is crazy!" J.D. replied. "Dak, I don't think we should be here. I know that Savoy has the sheriff watching the place, and he would kill us if he caught us here."

"We've got to spring these traps," Dak said. "There's an old broom over there."

J.D. grabbed the broomstick and sprang the two traps. Then, he shut the door to the cellar. "Dak, we'd better get out of here," he said.

"It won't take us long," Dak countered. "Let's move quickly." He practically ran for the stairs but noticed two additional loaded traps on the first stair.

J.D. used the broomstick to spring them and then noticed some more just inside the front door. "This is really dangerous. These traps are everywhere," he complained.

They went up the stairs and into the front room. "Maybe we better go to the other side and look to see if there's a car on the bar pits road, just to be safe," Dak said. J. D went to do that while Dak began moving shelves from the bookcase.

When J.D. returned, he seemed to feel a little better. "There are no cars over on the road," he said. "We need to check every few minutes so we don't get caught."

"Yeah," Dak said. "We need time to get out of here if somebody shows up. Okay, now we will have to remove these shelves. Then, if you'll go into the back room and pull the shelf support into position, I should be able to raise this panel. We shouldn't have to do anything with the rope because the last time we were here, I left it tied in the open position."

J.D. left to go to the back room to pull the shelf support into position, and Dak heard a yell. When he ran to the back room to see what was wrong, he found J.D. going for the broomstick. "More traps," he said disgustedly. "Dak, it's dangerous as anything in here."

"I know, I know," Dak said. "Let's just be careful and make sure we don't get hurt."

In another minute, J.D. was back in the front room, saying, "Okay, the shelf support is in position. Let's get into the secret room and get our business done."

Dak grasped the handles on the panel and pulled upward. At first, he thought it was not going to move, but then it began to open. "Ahh, here it comes," he said.

Dak turned on his flashlight and went into the room, while J.D. crouched at the entrance holding the second flashlight. "Here's the sword," Dak said excitedly. "It's not in the scabbard, but the scabbard is here also. Let's see if I can make out the inscription. No, see, the dust is too heavy."

Dak took the tail of his shirt and swiped it down the sword a couple times. "Now," he said, "hold your light right on the sword, and I'll see if I can read what it says." With J.D. dutifully positioning the light, Dak turned the sword to best position it. "Okay, it says, 'Presented to the Marquis de Lafayette in grateful appreciation by the People of the United States of America.' That's it! It's Lafayette's sword! Here, let me get some pictures."

J.D. smiled weakly. "Isn't that something?" he said.

"Okay, we need to see if we can find the Ingres painting," Dak said, as he scanned the walls with his flashlight. Seeing none on the walls, he began searching through the things sitting on the floor. "Here are some books called *Record of Deeds, Gallatin County, Illinois*," he said.

"Dak, we need to hurry. Skip the books. Let's go!"

"Well, I don't see the painting," Dak said. "Do you see anything I might be missing?" he asked.

"There are some things rolled up over there. Maybe one of those is the painting."

Dak picked up the largest roll and untied some ribbons that were around it. As he pulled the top end open, he could see a brownish background and then, in small letters, the words, 'Betty de Rothschild.' "This is it!" Dak yelled. "It's the Ingres painting. Here's the Coat of Arms."

J.D. was impressed but was more concerned about getting out of there. "Okay, get a photo, and we're out of here."

As Dak unrolled the painting, the beautiful lady in the pink satin dress and jewels came into view. "What a great painting," he said. "J.D., this thing keeps trying to roll up again. Here... hold this end down, and I'll put these deed books on the other end to hold it down so I can get a photo."

Dak took several photos and then carefully rolled the painting and tied the ribbons back in place. "J.D.," he said, "maybe we better check the view out on the bar pits road again."

While J.D. was gone, Dak quickly looked through the other things in the room. He opened a small roll that appeared to be a map of the farm showing gravesites. As he was studying the map, J.D. returned. "Still no cars," he said.

"Look at this," Dak said. "Here's a map of the farm showing several sites where slaves are buried. It even has the spot marked where Georgie and his brother are."

"Dak, would you quit looking through all that crap and get finished?" J.D. said in a panicky voice. "I'm out of here in a few minutes. Let's go!"

"Okay, okay," Dak said. "Let me just get a couple photos." He took several more shots, including one of the deed books, one of the map, and a couple of the general view of the room. Then, he backed out of the room, making sure he had the camera and flashlight. With J.D. urging him on, he pulled down on the handles on the panel until it was closed. "Okay," he said. "If you'll go return the shelf support in the back room to its closed position, I'll get all these shelves back in place," Dak said.

The boys quickly stuffed their equipment into the grass sack and ran into the hallway, sack in hand. Dak, thinking he heard something, said, "I heard a noise. Let me go look at the road again." He ran over and, seeing no car, almost stepped on a trap as he returned. This caused a surge of adrenaline as he quickly retrieved the broomstick and sprang the trap. Then he ran for the stairs and could see that J.D. was already down them. As he was bounding down the steps, he saw, through the fanlight window above the main door to the house, the figure of a person coming up the stairs to the front porch. He quickly motioned to J.D. and pointed to the front porch. J.D. easily got the point, and they both ran for the door to the cellar.

As they reached the door to the cellar, J.D. grabbed the doorknob and pulled. The warped door was stuck. He jerked the knob several times, as they heard footsteps on the front porch. Then, both boys got their hands on the knob and simultaneously jerked as hard as they could. This time, the door popped open, and Dak fell backward. J.D. ran down the steps to the cellar as Dak was getting back on his feet. Now, Dak heard footsteps in the hallway. He lunged forward and took the steps three at a time. J.D. briefly considered hiding in a dark area of the cellar but rejected that and ran out the door. "Run for the clump of bushes!" Dak said. It was barely loud enough for J.D. to hear.

Hiding behind the bushes, the boys could see the river side of the house, including the door which came out of the cellar, but did not see the person who Dak had glimpsed on the front steps. "Let's just sit tight for a minute," J.D. said. "If it's the sheriff, he'll be coming out of the cellar before long."

"Who knows," Dak whispered. "Maybe it is just Donny playing a trick on us."

J.D. proved to be prescient. The cellar door opened, and Sheriff Summers peeped out. Apparently convinced that no one had a gun pointed toward him, he came through the door and walked in a stalking posture with his pistol held in front of him with both hands. He moved close to the house and walked quickly to the back corner of the building. There, he kneeled and peeped around the corner into the back yard.

While he was looking toward the back, Dak picked up a small rock and threw it toward an upstairs window that was covered with rusty corrugated steel. The noise seemed to startle the sheriff and apparently convinced him that someone was inside the mansion. He turned, still in his crouched position and went back through the cellar door.

The boys decided this was a good time to move further away from the mansion. This time, their target was a pile of brush which someone had apparently stacked for burning. They ran for it as fast as they could and slid in behind the brush. "Should we go for those bushes back there?" J.D. asked. Before Dak could answer, they heard a faint noise and then saw the sheriff on the front porch. "Maybe we should stay put until he's out of sight," Dak whispered.

The sheriff came down the front stairs, and, still walking in a crouched posture with his pistol held in front of him with both hands, he seemed to be circling the house on the river side again. However, it was clear that he was moving further from the house than he had the first time. "What is he doing?" J.D. whispered.

Dak said, "He may be heading for us." The sheriff seemed to be trying to move toward them without making it obvious he knew where they were. Then, he started running directly toward the pile of brush. "Run for it!" Dak said. They ran as if their lives depended on it toward the next clump of bushes.

The sheriff yelled, "Halt! Halt or I'll shoot!" If anything, that added to their speed.

"Zigzag!" Dak screamed. It wasn't much of a message, but J.D. instantly understood that Dak meant to go back and forth so as to make a more difficult target.

With that, the sheriff stopped and shot several times toward them without effect. Then he started running toward them again. When the boys were behind the next clump of bushes, they paused to see what the sheriff was doing. They were both breathing hard, and they could see that the sheriff was still coming. Surprised by the obese man's stamina, they immediately darted toward the next clump back and continued to zigzag.

Stopping again, with the bushes to provide them some shield, they could see that the sheriff had also stopped and leaned forward with his hands on his knees. In a few seconds, the sheriff unloaded whatever he last ate. Then, he stood erect and put his right hand on his chest. Finally, he sat down in the grass and began holding his chest with both hands.

"Oh, God, we could have been shot!" J.D. said, trying to keep his voice low.

"I know! Why would he actually shoot at us? Man, I hope he doesn't have a heart attack," Dak said.

"Why?" J.D. replied.

"Because he seems to be having problems. He could be having an attack."

"No," J.D. said. "I mean, why do you hope he doesn't have one?"

"You've got a point," Dak said. "Look, I think he's gettin' up. Yeah, he is walking back toward the mansion."

"Boys, one," J.D. said. "Sheriff, zero."

"Do you think he could see us well enough to recognize us?" Dak asked.

"Probably not," J.D. answered, "we're quite a piece away, but he may suspect us."

"I wonder why we didn't see a car parked on the bar pits road," Dak said.

"Maybe the sheriff had his deputy drop him off and then drive on," J.D. replied. "That way, we couldn't see a car parked on the road. Maybe he was expecting us to look for a parked car."

"Maybe so," Dak said. "If he's thinking like that, we should probably walk over to the Uppers and wait awhile before we go back into town. I'm guessing the sheriff will go to the road over the north levee and wait to see who comes back into town."

"Yeah, I agree," J.D. said.

The boys soon reached the river. It seemed to Dak that, no matter what happened, he always came back to the river. They found a log and sat on it.

"I've been meaning to tell you about what ol' lard butt did to my Mom," J.D. said.

"What he did to your Mom?"

"Yeah, he caught her walkin' home from the store the other mornin', and he pulled the squad car over by where she was walking," J.D. said. "He actually turned on his siren. That scared the stuff out of my mom, of course. She thought at first that he was after somebody else and that she was just caught in the middle. Then, he got out of the car and walked over by her and said, 'I hear you been drinkin' a lot, and I want you to know I won't tolerate drunkenness on my streets.' He grabbed her bag of groceries and went through them. I guess he thought she had alcohol, but she only had a box of macaroni and a loaf of bread. He told her to get on home, and he better not catch her drunk on his streets."

"The man is a disgrace," Dak said. "He shouldn't be a sheriff."

"Hey, he shouldn't be a human," J.D. replied. "When Mom got home, she was cryin' and at first wouldn't tell me what happened. Then she told me but made me promise not to tell Dad. She was a nervous wreck all evening. I hate that butt hole. I hope he did have a heart attack."

"That's an awful thing for him to do," Dak said. "How is your mom doin' other than that?"

"Oh, well, that's what I was goin' to tell you. This guy in Harrisburg has been a big help to her, and she's really improvin'. I hope this thing with the sheriff doesn't set her back too much."

"How did the sheriff know she's been drinkin'?"

"I don't know that. I don't think word has gotten around town, do you?"

"No, I don't think so."

After a while, J.D. said, "Let's take a quick swim so we won't be so sweaty when we get back to town." In minutes, they shed their clothes and were in the water but there was no frolicking this time. Their hands were still shaking from the excitement of the chase.

"It's hard to believe that somebody was actually shooting at us just a half hour ago," Dak said.

"Yeah, we could be dead by now," J.D. said.

"It might be a good idea if we went back to town separately," Dak said, as they got out of the water. "That way, if he sees one of us, he won't be so likely to associate us with what just happened at the mansion."

"Yeah, I agree," J.D. said. "Also, it might be a good idea to hide the camera and flashlights and pick them up later. If lard butt stops one of us and takes the camera, the photos would prove we've been in the mansion. That wouldn't be good."

They carefully hid the grass sack containing their equipment. Then J.D. headed for the fish docks where he would go over the levee onto Main Street, while Dak headed over the levee at the north end of town.

Dak was walking along, deep into a thought, when he came to the top of the levee. Too late, he realized that the sheriff's car was parked just over the peak with the sheriff sitting in it. He decided to keep on walking and act like nothing was wrong. As he passed the sheriff's car, he heard the sheriff say, "Where have you been, Leventhal?"

"I've been to the Uppers and had a good swim," Dak said confidently. "As hot as it is, it felt good." He kept walking.

The sheriff could see that Dak's hair was wet. Also, he was alone and not carrying anything, whereas one of the two men at the mansion had been carrying something in a sack. Still, he had his doubts. "Come back here, boy," he yelled loudly. Dak turned around and walked toward the sheriff's car. The sheriff stepped out of the car, grabbed Dak by the collar and said, "Where else have you been? Now you had better not lie to me, boy, or somebody's going to get hurt."

Dak did not hesitate. "Have I ever lied to you?" he said. "I already told you. I've been swimmin' over on the Uppers. Before that, I walked way up the river to get a log so I could float downstream. I do that all the time." Dak noticed the smell of vomit on the sheriff and could see a wet spot on his shirt.

"Did you see a couple of men out that way anywhere? A couple of thin men carrying something in a sack?" The sheriff made the question sound like an accusation.

"No," Dak said thoughtfully. "I don't think I saw a soul other than some people on a big barge that went downstream a while ago." Dak could tell that the sheriff believed his story. Even so, the man clearly liked harassing people, so he continued.

He jerked Dak's collar sharply toward him until there were only inches between their faces. Then he yelled, "Boy, I'm going to accept your story this time, and if I find out it's a lie, your life won't be worth living. Do you understand?" At this point, a fisherman named Cliff Burney and his brother came walking over the levee laughing and talking loudly. Cliff had a grass sack with something in it that Dak assumed to be fish. The sheriff looked suspiciously at the two men and said, "Well, look what we got here." He released Dak's collar and walked up the levee toward the other two men. Dak started whistling and walked on home.

When Dak walked in the back door of his house, J.D. was sitting at the kitchen table having a glass of ice water. "Where have you been, Dak?" he asked.

Eleanor was at the cabinet opening a quart jar of canned cherries, obviously in the midst of making a cobbler. Dak didn't think it was a good idea for Eleanor to know that the sheriff was harassing him, so he said, "Oh, I stopped up on the levee and was talking to some people. Cliff Burney was up there with his brother. They were full of stories."

"Did you boys have fun?" Eleanor asked.

"We sure did," Dak answered. "I don't know when we've had more thrills. It's still a secret, but I'll tell you all about it one day." Eleanor rolled her eyes as Dak added, "What've you been doin'?"

"Before I decided to make this cobbler," she said, "I went over and visited with Ann Scroggins a while."

"Mrs. Scroggins always knows all the news," Dak said. "What good stuff did she tell you?""Actually," Eleanor said, "she told me something pretty interesting. She said that Savoy is going to build a big warehouse and loading area above town. It's supposed to be a big deal with new roads, truck scales, a large turning area, big wharf and some storage bins. It will handle grain, coal and some other things. I don't know much about it, but she said he is going to start on it soon and will be tearing down the mansion to make way."

"So, that's what he was talking about when I was out there," Dak said. Before he had even finished the sentence, he realized he shouldn't have said that, but it was too late now.

"Since you were out where?" Eleanor asked.

"Well, I was out hiking a while back and passed the ol' mansion, so I thought I'd go in and look around. While I was in the building, I heard voices and realized Savoy was there along with someone else. I hid in the attic to keep from gettin' in trouble, and I could hear them sayin' somethin' about doin' the job for $500. I could only catch snatches of conversation. At the time, I didn't make any sense of it, but I'm pretty sure that's what they were talkin' about."

"Dak, you shouldn't be trespassing on Mr. Savoy's property," Eleanor said. "Why, I bet he wouldn't like it at all if he knew you were eavesdropping on him. Besides, you could get hurt. I bet that place is really rotten and very dangerous."

"No, it's not really rotten inside," Dak said as if that were the issue at hand.

"Dak, I swear. I hope I can get you to 21 years of age," Eleanor said, as J.D. got up to leave.

"I won't have the car tomorrow," J.D. said. "My dad will be using the ol' buggy. He promised me I could have it on Tuesday, though."

"Okay. See you at the bus stop in the morning," Dak said

With J.D. out the door, Dak asked more about Mrs. Scroggins' report that Savoy would tear down the mansion. Eleanor went through all Mrs. Scroggins had said again but had no additional information.

"We really need to find out quickly if this ol' lease agreement has any validity," Dak said. "We need some discreet way of findin' out. If we start openly diggin' into that, Savoy will go to any length to stop us."

"Oh, I don't think Mr. Savoy is that bad, Dak. He is a little obnoxious, yes, but you make it sound like he would resort to violence."

"Yeah, that's right, Mom," Dak said. "I think he would. I think he has the sheriff do his dirty work, and I know the sheriff beat up Charlie Johnson. I sure wish there was some way we could stop him from demolishin' the mansion. It's one of a kind. It's a historical ol' building, and it was built by Leventhals."

"Well, anyway, I was thinking about how we might find out more about the lease agreement." Eleanor said. "You know, Ann Scroggins works in the County Clerk's Office at the Courthouse. She's a good friend, and I could ask her to quietly check into it. I thought about doing that yesterday but thought I should talk with you first."

"Yes, I think we should do that," Dak said. "I know that Mrs. Scroggins talks to a lot of people and likes to spread news around, so be sure to emphasize how important it is to be discreet."

The next morning, Dak was up early and off to Gene's Grocery to catch the bus. He went a little earlier than he normally would because he wanted to talk with Melodie.

When he arrived, she was sitting on a bench in front of the store, yawning. *God, she's beautiful,* he thought, but what he said was, "Is it a little too early for you?"

Melodie held her arms out in front of her, clasped her hands, tilted her head back and stretched. Then she yawned again and said, "I guess it is."

"I hope you get rested up because graduation is Friday, and our special night is Saturday," Dak said.

"Oh, yes," Melodie said. "Count on it. I'll be rested up for that. And I have some good news. My dad said last night that we could use his cabin up at Big Lake for our special night and we can stay all night as long as we have a chaperone and there's no hanky panky."

"He did?" Dak asked, excitedly. "That's great! That'll be a lot of fun." Then he thought for a minute. "But, what is the definition of 'hanky panky'? What is wrong with hanky panky? Hanky panky, properly conceived and executed, is a wonderful thing. Among all the things that are available to people on this ol' Earth, hanky panky is probably the most fun. In fact, if I ever run for president, my platform will promote the regular practice of hanky panky."

Melodie was laughing. "Yes, well, don't tell my dad. He thinks hanky panky is awful."

"Anyway," Dak said, "I talked with J.D. about it and he said he's sure his mom would be our chaperone if we want her to," Dak said. "He says he can talk her into being considerate of us and not sittin' right in the middle of our party."

"Great!" Melodie said. "Mom will want to talk with her about it."

"Yeah, I suppose," Dak said. "Is there a record player at the cabin?" One needs good music to practice hanky panky."

"Yes, there is, and it is actually pretty good, Dak. I'll take all my records, so it will be dreamy." "You're dreamy," Dak said. "Is there some kind of fire pit in the back yard where we could fry some fish? That would be even more fun than going to a restaurant. It's more private."

"There are some flat stones arranged in a circle. My dad had some rebar welded and put over the top so you can put a skillet on it. He uses it to fry crappie."

"Perfect," Dak said. "What say we get some fiddlers, and I'll get Mom to make us some hush puppies to fry with our fish?"

"Sounds good," Melodie replied. "I can't wait, Dak."

The bus pulled into position, and the door opened just in front of them. "Come on, love birds. It's time to go to school," Buck Dawson yelled, with a big smile.

Buck was eating a donut, one of several that were missing from a six-pack he had bought the night before. "Buck, aren't you getting a little big around the middle?" Melodie joked.

"Just heavy enough to look good in my clothes," he replied, as he wiped his sugary hand on a handkerchief.

• • •

The PE class that morning met in the gym even though not all the repairs were completed. It was a bit messy, but no one seemed to care. The coach was doing some individual tumbling instruction, leaving most of the class idle. Dak noticed that Charlie Johnson was back. He walked over and put his arm around Charlie's shoulders. "Good to see you back, Charlie. That was an awful thing ol' lard butt did to you, but it looks like you're as good as new."

"Yeah, I am," Charlie said, "but I was stuck in the hospital most of my Mom's last two weeks. She's gone now, so I'll never see her again. One day, he will pay for that."

"Yeah, I was so sorry to hear about your Mom. I know you'll miss her a lot, Charlie, but she suffered so much in her last few months. Now it has stopped. So there is some good in everything. She was a courageous lady."

"You're right. It is better for her, but I hate it that I missed her final days," Charlie said. "I'll get that man one day."

The coach blew his whistle, and everyone ran for the showers.

Miss Hurd had asked Dak to meet with her briefly at lunchtime, so he told Melodie he would not be able to join her for lunch. She said, "Okay, just don't forget this Saturday."

"How could I ever forget that?" Dak asked. "Could Ike forget D-Day? Could Julius Caesar forget the Ides of March? Could the Pope..."

"Okay, Dak. You won't forget," she said with a big smile.

When Dak entered Miss Hurd's room, she closed the door behind him. "Dak, the yearbooks will be out next week. I just want to thank you for all your work making them so special," she said. "The seniors are going to love their 'finest moments,' and the overall quality is very high. It is easily the best we have ever done since I've been here."

"Oh, thanks, Miss Hurd. It was really a lot of fun. I don't know of anything I could have done that would have been more fun." Then it occurred to him what he had told Melodie earlier about hanky panky, and he realized that there are things more fun than the yearbook.

"Oh, and I wanted to let you know that I will be moving back to Moline after classes are over," she said. "I haven't taken a job there yet, so I'm not sure what I'll do, but I won't be here."

"Miss Hurd, I wish you wouldn't do that," Dak said. "You're the one who makes these classes so alive. With you, we don't study history. We live it. We don't study literature or poetry. We experience it. This town won't be the same without you. The town really needs you."

"I do appreciate your comments, Dak. They mean a lot to me. I'd better let you go, or you won't have time for lunch," she said as she opened the door.

Dak walked out the door with his head down and slowly made his way down the steps.

After school, Dak and J.D. got off the bus and walked to-gether up to Ann's Cafe to get a coke, when Dak brought up the subject of Josephine Savoy. "You know," he said quietly, "we really need to talk to somebody about it, but there is no way we can talk with Sheriff Summers. So, we need to figure out what else to do. We can't just let Savoy get away with murder."

"We sure can't talk about it in the cafe with all the people there," J.D. said. "Let's just get our drink and go to my house. My mom and dad went to Harrisburg today, so we can sit on the back porch and figure it out."

When they arrived at J.D.'s back porch and were comfortably seated in the back porch swing, Dak said, "I went to the library at lunch and looked up the address and phone number for the state trooper, the county judge, and the state's attorney. I don't know if we could trust any of them. I'm afraid the county people might talk with Sheriff Summers if we tell them."

"Yeah, Dak. We can't go to the county guys,"J.D. said. "It is too dangerous. They might go to the sheriff, and if the sheriff knew we had information showing Savoy murdered his first wife, he would try to do us in. Really, he would."

"He probably would," Dak agreed. "Well then, how about the state trooper? His name is Lew Evans. He lives in Equality. That's not very far."

"I don't know, Dak," J.D. said. "We don't know him at all. There is also some chance he would go to the sheriff. Maybe we should just tell our parents."

Dak thought for a minute. "I'm afraid they might tell somebody else or insist on going to the county judge or doin' something we wouldn't want to do," he said. "I don't think they understand how bad these guys are."

"Maybe we should just keep it quiet and not tell anyone," J.D. said. "That's the only way to be sure the sheriff doesn't come after us."

"I don't think that would be right," Dak said. "We can't just keep evidence to ourselves when we think somebody has committed a murder, but right now I don't know a good solution. Maybe we..."

At that point, J.D.'s mother came walking out the back door with two glasses of lemonade. "I bet you boys could use a glass of lemonade," she said. "Here, Dak. These glasses aren't very big, but you can refill if you like."

J.D. was astonished. "I thought you and Dad went to Harrisburg," he said.

"Oh, we did," she replied, "but we got everything done much quicker than we thought, so we got back early. Your Dad went up to get a haircut."

She was slurring her words just slightly, and J.D. knew that she often mixed lemonade with vodka. He noticed that the kitchen window that looked out onto the back porch was open and wondered how much his mom had heard through the screen.

"Well, thanks for the drink," J.D. said.

"Sure," Mrs. Robinson said. "It sounds like you boys are discussing serious stuff, so I won't bother you. Let me know if you want a refill."

When she went back into the house, J.D. motioned Dak to follow him as he walked to the end of the house. "Dak, I think she might have heard us," he said nervously. "God, I hope not, because she's drinking. Hey, she might call the sheriff. She can get real aggressive when she drinks too much."

"Oh, man, that's scary," Dak said. "Maybe the best thing for you to do is to stay close to her this evenin' and stop her if you see her callin' anybody."

"Yeah, I guess, although I was plannin' to go for a little drive with Marie," J.D. said. "I guess I'll just have to cancel that. We can't take a chance on this."

"We'll decide later what to do," Dak said. "You're drivin' in the mornin', right?"

"Yeah. See you then," J.D. said.

When Dak arrived home, Eleanor told him she had talked with Ann Scroggins about the lease agreement. "Ann promised me she wouldn't mention it to anyone," she said. "She is going to discreetly check to see what the courthouse records show about ownership of the area around the mansion."

"Great. That's very nice of her," Dak said. "Had she ever heard of that land being leased?"

"No," Eleanor replied, "but she said she wouldn't necessarily have heard anything about it. She just does clerk duties."

Even the remote chance that the mansion might be his was very exciting to Dak. However, deep down, he believed it was not going to happen and to ward off future disappointment, he told himself that there was no chance at all. As a result, he regarded it as something of a history project to find out exactly what had happened. Even that was secondary to the problem of what to do about the information they had about Josephine Savoy. He could not get his mind off what he strongly believed was murder.

After dinner, Dak walked to the Uppers and retrieved the equipment that he and J.D. had hidden after their visit to the mansion. *I need to get this stuff to make sure no one else finds it*, he thought to himself.

• • •

The next morning, J.D.'s arrival at Dak's house was a little earlier than usual. Fortunately, Dak was also running early and was out on the sidewalk waiting. Dak immediately noticed that J.D. didn't have the radio turned to maximum volume like usual. In fact, it wasn't turned on at all. "Something is wrong," Dak thought to himself.

"What happened to your radio?" Dak asked, as he slid into the car the customary way.

"I didn't turn it on," J.D. said impatiently. "Dak, we have a problem. Man, I hate to tell you this, but my Mom talked with Donny's mother last night and told her what she had overheard us talkin' about."

"Oh, no, J.D.," Dak said. "I thought you were going to stay with her to prevent that."

"That's right. I was, but Marie came by and honked," J.D. said, "and I went out to see what she wanted. We talked for a few minutes, and when I went back in the house, Mom was on the phone. I heard her say something about us thinking Percy Savoy had murdered his first wife Josephine. I hurried over and grabbed the phone, but it was too late. The worst part is that Donny's mother is Harriet Savoy's first cousin."

"Hey, J.D., it's not your fault," Dak said confidently. "Don't worry about it. We'll figure out how to deal with it. It could be that Donny's mother won't tell the Savoys what she heard. But if she does and worst comes to worst, we will have to go to the state trooper with the whole story and ask for protection."

"My mom got to drinkin' more after you were there, and when she drinks, she does this kind of thing." J.D. couldn't get it off his mind.

"It'll be okay, J.D. We'll figure out what to do," Dak said.

As they were driving out the highway to the high school, Dak said he would try to get to the phone at the high school and talk to the state trooper to see if they could meet with him. While they were discussing this, J.D. looked in his rear view mirror and saw flashing lights. Then the siren started.

"Oh, crap," J.D. said. "It's lard butt and his deputy."

"Let's just pull over and be calm," Dak suggested.

When J.D. had pulled off the side of the road, he could see the sheriff's car stop a few feet behind him. He rolled his window down.

Sheriff Summers came to J.D.'s window and said loudly, "Well if it's not Robinson. Hey, Robinson, isn't it a little early for 90 miles per hour?"

"Yes, it is," J.D. said. "I was only goin' about 45. What's the problem?"

"Hey, boy," the sheriff practically screamed, "I'll tell you how fast you were going, and you will keep your mouth shut until I ask you a question."

"Okay," J.D. replied.

"Who's that you got with you? Looks like Leventhal. Well, you boys just can't quit doing the criminal bit, can you?"

"We didn't commit any crime," J.D. protested.

"That's not the way I heard it," the sheriff said as he wrote a ticket. "What I heard is that you've been telling malicious lies about our most respected citizen. It's called slander. It's also called trouble."

"No, we have not been..."

"Hey, boy, I thought I told you to keep your mouth shut until I ask you a question," the sheriff yelled, as he reached in the window and grabbed J.D.'s throat.

Dak could see that the sheriff might get violent and was trying very hard to figure out what to do in that event. He knew both the sheriff and the deputy were armed, and he couldn't see any good options for dealing with them.

As the sheriff released his grip on J.D.'s throat, there was a startlingly loud noise in the back of the car. Both J.D. and Dak instinctively jumped forward in their seats.

"What was that?" J.D. screamed in astonishment, as he turned to look back. His rear window was smashed, and the deputy was walking back to the squad car with a baseball bat in his hand.

"Not a problem," the sheriff said, as he handed the ticket to J.D. "Not a problem at all. Just a little accident, you see. He's just not very good with a baseball bat. Oh, he can sometimes hit something as small as a human head, but so much of the time, he accidentally hits something he didn't intend to hit."

Both J.D. and Dak were so angry they could hardly contain themselves, but their fear helped them maintain self-control.

"Now, let me tell you boys something," the sheriff said, still yelling. "The next time I have to stop you, I'm not going to be as friendly as I was this time. I'm thinking somebody will get hurt. The baseball bat might hit something other than your window. That doesn't feel very good. If you don't believe that, you should check with your friend Charlie Johnson. So, I'd suggest you not say anything at all to anyone about our distinguished citizen, Mr. Savoy. You understand that?"

"Yes." It was all J.D. could manage.

"What about you, Leventhal? That handsome face of yours wouldn't look very good with a lot of scars on it, would it? All the girls think you're hot stuff. Yeah, they think you're a pretty boy, but you wouldn't be so pretty. You understand what I'm saying to you?"

"Yes." Dak was shaking and decided to follow J.D.'s lead on how to respond.

"Okay," the sheriff continued. "You boys run on to school now before I get in a bad mood. The only thing you are to report about this incident is that you were stopped for speeding. You accidentally broke your back window while playing ball. Now, get your butts out of here!"

J.D. drove off. Both boys just seethed for a few seconds. Then Dak said, "J.D., it's clear now what we have to do. We have to go to the state trooper. Otherwise, the sheriff will kill us."

To Dak's surprise, J.D. agreed. "That's right. Let's do it. He's following us now, so we've got to go to school, but as soon as we can, we have to go to the state trooper."

"I'll get to a phone this morning," Dak said. "Miss Hurd has one in her room, and I'm sure she'll let me use it before classes. If I can arrange to meet the trooper, we can leave at noon. We don't have all the photo evidence with us, so we'll have to go back to my house and get the pictures before we head to Equality. Some of the film is still in the camera that we hid at the Uppers. Fortunately, last night I went back to the Uppers and got the camera.

So, we'll have everything we need, but some of the film isn't developed."

"Good, I'll meet you at the car at about a quarter till twelve, okay?" J.D. asked.

"Right," Dak replied. "A quarter till twelve."

The morning went quickly, and Dak was back in the car a few minutes early. J.D. was there only a couple minutes later. As J.D. jumped in the car, Dak said, "I was able to call the state trooper's home. He wasn't there, but I talked to his wife. I told her we needed to talk to her husband. I explained that we thought the sheriff was covering up a murder done by a man named Savoy. She said he would be home by noon and would be there until 6 PM unless there is an emergency. She suggested we come on over. Said she knew he'd be happy to talk with us."

"We're on our way," J.D. said.

"Right. But we have to go back to my house first and get the evidence," Dak said.

"Awww, Dak. Well, okay. But I hope he doesn't stop us again," J.D. said in a worried voice.

As J.D. stopped the car in front of Dak's house, Dak already had the door open. In three minutes flat, he was back out with a box full of photos, papers, the camera, and a separate box with the relics in it. "Okay, go," he said, as he closed the door.

"What did your Mom say?" J.D. asked.

"Nothin'. I don't think she saw me," Dak replied. "I think she's on the back porch doin' the wash today."

As J.D. drove the old Ford back past the high school, he noticed a large green car trailing behind him. Although it hadn't been behind him very long, he had the feeling it was following him.

"Dak, do you know who that is in the car behind us?" he asked.

Dak turned and looked. "No. I don't think I've seen that car before," Dak replied. "Why do you ask?"

"I have the feelin' that he is followin' us," J.D. replied.

"Oh, I doubt it," Dak said. "Why do you think so?"

"I don't know. It's just a feeling. He came out of the high school lane, and I've never seen that car at the high school."

"Well, if it bothers you, turn left up ahead, circle around the grain elevator, and come back out onto the highway," Dak said. "If he's not trailin' you, he won't be there when you get back."

J.D. circled the elevator and came back onto the highway. The green car was parked on the side of the road with the driver apparently looking at a map spread across his steering wheel. As J.D. drove by the car, it pulled back out onto the highway.

"Okay. It probably is following us," Dak said. "That isn't good. Wonder who it is?"

"I don't know, but I bet ol' lard butt knows," J.D. replied.

Dak watched the green car closely as J.D. continued out Route 13 toward Equality. "Now, there's a truck behind the car, but it's probably just waiting for an opportunity to pass," Dak said.

"Wonder what the guy in the green car has in mind," J.D. said. "If he is after us, he may try to pull up beside us and then shoot at us."

"J.D., maybe we should pull off at those mail boxes up ahead and see if he will pass us," Dak said.

J.D. immediately swerved off to the right side of the highway and positioned the car just to the left of the mailboxes. As Dak opened a mailbox and then closed it again, the green car did pass them but then turned into a farm lane up ahead. To Dak's surprise, the truck had also pulled off the road, but it was about a quarter of a mile behind them. J.D. moved his car back out onto the highway and hoped that the other two vehicles would not follow suit, but as he passed the farm lane, the green car resumed its position behind them. Not only that, but the truck was back on the highway behind the green car.

A few minutes later, the green car moved into the left lane and increased its speed. "I'll watch the man closely," Dak said. "If I see him raise his hand with a gun, I'll say duck."

"Oh, hell, here it comes," J.D. yelled.

The green car moved forward until the two cars were side by side, but the man did not raise a gun or even glance at the boys.

Instead, the car kept moving forward until its right rear wheel was beside J.D.'s left front wheel. Then it swerved sharply to the right. J.D. instinctively swerved to the right also but not soon enough to avoid a loud bang as the cars collided. J.D. momentarily lost control of the car.

"Ohhhh, crap...ohhhh, I almost lost it!" J.D. shouted. "Ohhh, I thought it was going to roll over. He's tryin' to roll us."

"He's tryin' to roll us, not shoot us," Dak said. "Oh, man, I hope we make it to Equality. We're almost there."

The green car moved ahead of J.D. and then off the road on the right side. J.D. continued down the highway past the green car and picked up speed in an attempt to get to Equality before the green car could make another attempt. The truck passed both cars on the left.

"That's a big ol' flat bed farm truck," Dak said. "Can you believe it has such acceleration?"

"What's that he's got on the bed? Anything he's goin' to use against us?" J.D. asked.

"Looks like oil-well weights. It's just slabs of steel to give the truck better traction when it doesn't have a load."

"Here's the green car," J.D. said. "He's comin' again."

"This time, when he gets all lined up and starts to swerve to the right, hit the brakes hard," said Dak. "It may cause him to lose control. I mean, because he's expectin' to hit you, but he'll be out in front of you."

The man in the green car seemed to have only one trick. He positioned it again and then swerved sharply to the right. "Now!" Dak shouted.

J.D. stomped the brakes. The green car missed J.D.'s car altogether and went off the road on the right side. It went back and forth like a snake slithering through the grass, throwing gravel and dust high in the air.

"Roll over, you piece of crap!" J.D. screamed, but the driver fought the steering wheel until he regained control. Then he moved back on the highway behind J.D.'s car.

"God, he's persistent," Dak said. "He'll do it again. This time, let's make him catch us."

J.D. mashed the accelerator to the floor, but the green car had better acceleration. It was gaining on J.D. Then, Dak noticed that the truck was moving over into the left lane in front of the green car.

"Look," Dak said. "The truck must be tryin' to slow the green car."

"Or maybe he's also goin' to try the swerving trick on me," J.D. said.

J.D. reached 85 miles per hour this time when the green car moved next to him in the left lane. The truck was also in the left lane and was only 50 feet or so in front of the green car.

"What the...what are the two of them tryin' to do?" J.D. asked.

Before Dak could answer, the truck driver suddenly slammed his brakes. White smoke rolled as the truck was coming to a screeching halt. The driver of the green car, focused on getting in position relative to J.D.'s car, seemed not to see the truck at all. The crash was earthshaking as the green car went all the way up under the flat bed. The car's smashed windshield went all the way to its back seat. The large rear wheels of the truck were now imbedded in the mid section of the car. The combined steel monster careened across the road as it rotated and continued to slide sideways down the highway, finally stopping off the right side facing the opposite direction. The truck driver jumped from the truck and ran. A split-second later, the stack of steel exploded and began burning.

It had been a challenge for J.D. to maneuver his car to avoid hitting the wrecked mass as it slid down the highway. When he managed to stop the car, he wasn't sure whether the truck driver was friend or foe. Even so, Dak ran toward the burning beast, determined to rescue the man. When he encountered the intense heat, he quickly realized that rescue was out of the question. By then, black smoke was billowing into the sky. Then the truck driver walked up beside him.

"Charlie Johnson!" Dak said in astonishment. "What the..."

"Hi, Dak. I know you didn't expect to see me here," Charlie replied.

"Did you just happen to be drivin' out here?" Dak asked.

"No, I thought somethin' was about to happen and thought I might be able to help. I'd do anything to get even with ol' lard butt."

"How did you know this was goin' to happen?" Dak asked.

"I didn't know what was goin' to happen, but I thought somethin' big was in the works," Charlie said.

Dak looked puzzled. "What made you think that?" he asked.

I was outside the door to Miss Hurd's room this mornin' when you called the state trooper," Charlie said. "Judy Savoy and several others were there too. The door was closed, but we could hear. When you said murder and Savoy in the same sentence, Judy ran down the steps and left in her car."

"Oh, man! She heard me?" Dak said.

"Yeah, she did. When I saw her leave, I knew Savoy would have the sheriff try to get you. I saw the sheriff talking to the guy in the green car a couple days ago, so I thought he was up to no good. I didn't know what he was plannin' to do, but I figured he was up to somethin' when I saw the green car pull in the lane to the high school late this mornin'."

"What did you do, go home at lunch and get your dad's truck?" Dak asked.

"No, I drove the truck to school this morning and I was sitting in the cab eating my lunch when I saw the green car pull out to follow you. I decided to trail along to see if I could help."

Dak's mouth fell open, and all he could say was, "Wow!" He stood there a few seconds soaking up the fact that Charlie had not only figured out what was happening, but had risked his own life to save the two of them. "Charlie, you are a genuine American hero," Dak finally said. "You saved our lives! Man, we will be forever indebted to you."

By then, J.D. was there. When he saw Charlie, he banged his own head with the base of his hand as if to clear his registers of obviously incorrect data. "Hey, Charlie," he said, "I couldn't be more surprised if it was Joe DiMaggio. Where did you come from?"

"Well," Charlie said in a whimsical tone, "I was just drivin' down the road, goin' over to Harrisburg to get my brakes serviced when I came upon you goin' real slow. So, I passed you, and while I was still in the left lane, my brakes locked up on me. I guess this guy was followin' too close. He was goin' too fast, obviously didn't have control of his car, and rear ended me. He had been drivin' erratically, as I'm sure you noticed. He was probably drinkin' or somethin'."

"Well, Charlie," said J.D., "you are a good man, and we thank you, thank you, and thank you. I know what you're sayin', though, about that man in the green car. You had a little brake problem, and he was passin' us at high speed, trailin' too close, didn't have control of his car. What a shame. I guess he was drinkin'."

"Yeah," said Charlie. "I hope his life insurance is as good as my dad's truck insurance. I can't wait to see what ol' lard butt thinks of this."

"Hey, Charlie," Dak said. "I just don't know how to thank you for savin' our lives, but I don't like your story. If the state trooper comes, let's tell him the whole truth. There is nothin' wrong with what you did. You stopped someone who was in the process of tryin' to murder some people. It makes you a hero, not a criminal. None of us did anything wrong. I don't think we ought to make up a story. I think we should be proud of what really happened. Especially, you should. I want people to know you are a real hero."

"No, I'm not a hero," Charlie said. "It's just that you guys are my friends, and I have sworn an oath to get even with the sheriff for preventin' me from bein' with my mom at the end. I will have his butt if it's the last act of my life. I mean it. Even if I die in the process, I will have his butt. Nothin' will stop me. You watch."

"Well, we've got to be careful with our story, Dak," J.D. said. "What if the sheriff gets here before the state trooper?"

"In that case, nothing will work," Dak answered. "We're just in deep stuff."

Chapter 15

The Sheriff Falls

At the scene of the fatal accident, Dak, J.D., and Charlie waited for the law enforcement officials to arrive. They needed to explain what had happened so Charlie could go home, and the other two could go to the state trooper's house in Equality.

"I guess we can't leave the scene," Dak said, "but, on the other hand, if it's Sheriff Summers who shows up, we'll wish we had." Several other people stopped to see if there was any help they could render, but there was nothing they could do. An uncle of Charlie's was waiting to drive him home.

Dak was thrilled and relieved to see a State Police car arrive. The trooper jumped out of his car and ran to the smoking wreck to see if there was anything he could do to help. Then, Dak overheard him arranging for an ambulance and two wreckers to come. As the trooper walked back into the group of people who were now there, he asked the driver or drivers involved in the collision to identify themselves. Charlie Johnson identified himself and pointed out that there were two other witnesses. The state trooper introduced himself as Trooper Lew Evans to the three boys and asked that they come over to his car one at a time to tell him what happened.

Dak went first to make sure the other two boys knew which story was operative, though they couldn't hear what Dak was saying. He started his story with the sheriff's stopping J.D. for speeding in the morning and the breaking of J.D.'s rear window. He explained that later, he had made the phone call and reached Mrs. Evans and how that had led to the current situation. He told in some detail how Charlie had saved their lives. Trooper Evans seemed very surprised with this story and asked many questions, taking notes as he talked. It wasn't clear whether the trooper believed Dak or not. Dak told him that he and J.D. feared for their lives and believed the sheriff would kill them if he could. "This is all related to the evidence of murder we have in our car," Dak said. "We would like to show you that evidence, if possible, after you have taken care of this collision."

Trooper Evans walked over to the highway and asked Dak to explain the skid marks and the sequence of events related to them. Then, he turned to Dak and said, "That will be all for you for now. Please ask your friend to come over to my car."

J.D. was the next to be questioned. The trooper went into the same detail with J.D. that he had with Dak and then asked him to send Charlie over to talk. As Trooper Evans was just finishing questioning Charlie, Sheriff Summers drove up and parked next to the trooper's car. "That's all I need for now, Charlie," the trooper said, "but please don't leave just yet."

The sheriff approached the trooper as he was writing some final notes on his pad. "What happened here, Trooper?" the sheriff said in a tone that seemed to blame the trooper for the whole thing.

"We had a pretty bad one," Trooper Evans said. "We have a man who died in the wreckage over there.

The sheriff shot a quick glance at the trooper. "There is just one man in the car?" he asked.

"Yes," the trooper answered. "As far as I can tell, there is just one person in the burned-out car."

The sheriff looked like someone had hit him in the chest with a tire tool. He ran over to the wreckage, obviously upset, and looked into the area where the man would be. When the trooper joined the sheriff at the site of the wreckage, the sheriff was breathing very rapidly and sweating profusely. He said, "What happened to the boys?"

Although the trooper realized that the sheriff should have no way of knowing that boys were involved in the crash, he didn't ask. "They are over there," he said, as he pointed to them. The sheriff looked over and saw them and, next to them, the old Ford with the back window broken out and a big dent in the front left fender. He also saw Charlie Johnson standing next to Dak.

"I will be taking all three of those boys into custody," the sheriff snorted. His face was beet red and his breathing, if any-

thing, was getting worse. "It's sure as hell good that you appre-
hended them for me. They've been nothing but trouble," he
gasped. Pausing for a minute to cough and wipe the sweat from
his forehead, the sheriff continued. "Also, if you don't mind, I'll
complete the reports and let you get on your way, Trooper."

Since the trooper had been recently transferred to the region
from a previous assignment upstate, he didn't know the sheriff,
and, of course, he didn't know the boys. He was getting two very
divergent views from them. Normally, he would lean heavily
toward what he heard from another law enforcement officer, but
right at the minute, he was finding the boys more credible. Not
only that, but he could see the sheriff was having an attack of
some kind.

"No, it's not a problem," the trooper said. "I'm actually pretty
far along with the paperwork. I'll just go ahead and finish it. Feel
free to get on back to the courthouse if you want. It's all under
control."

The sheriff obviously did not like that response. "No," he said
emphatically. "It is my county, and I'll take care of the prisoners
and the paperwork," he said.

"Prisoners?" the trooper asked. "Why would there be any
prisoners? We just need to get statements from the boys and any
other witnesses and then let them go. We'll ask them to stay
around town for a couple weeks and to be available in case we
need any further information from them. Listen, you seem to be
having a little trouble with your breathing. I'll handle this. Why
don't you go over and sit down."

This seemed to upset the sheriff even more. He bent forward a
little, put his right hand on the center of his chest, and began
breathing even harder as he moved his right hand to his left arm.
"This is my county, Trooper!" he screamed. "Get the hell out of
here. This is my county, and I'll take the entire case. The trouble
with you arrogant squad jockeys from Chicago is you think like Al
Capone, and you...you..." He hesitated and then seemed unable to
continue. His head bobbed back and forth a little, his face looked
like it might explode, and he slumped slowly to the ground.

As the sheriff lay on the ground, the trooper ran for the ambulance crew that was by now trying to extract the dead man from the wreckage. While the trooper motioned the ambulance crew, Charlie walked over and bent down over the sheriff, getting right into his face. "My, my," Charlie said. "Looks like you are having a little problem, Sheriff." The sheriff glared at Charlie but was unable to say a word. Charlie put on a big smile and said, "Gosh, you're lucky that when you die, you aren't goin' to the same place as my mom, because she would spit in your face." Then, he repeated it slowly, "She would spit in your face."

The ambulance crew quickly ran to the sheriff's side. In just a few minutes, they placed him on the gurney, rolled it into the ambulance, and sped off to the hospital, siren blaring. Trooper Evans asked if there were any more witnesses to the collision, and a farmer said he had seen one of the cars trying to run the other one off the road down the way apiece. The trooper took a statement from him on what he had seen. He then asked the crowd which had formed to move along, leaving only the wrecker crew and a second ambulance that had shown up to extract the dead man.

Charlie's uncle was waiting, and the trooper told Charlie it was okay for him to leave. "Just make sure to be around where you can be reached if there are any complications with the case," the trooper said. Charlie agreed to do that.

The trooper didn't want to leave the scene of the collision until the workers had removed the body and wreckage. However, he did ask Dak and J.D. to join him at J.D.'s car, which was completely out of earshot of the workers. "Let's see this evidence you were talking about," he said.

They went to the car and pulled out the box of photos and papers that Dak had assembled. Then J.D. removed another box with the earrings, the gold ring, the shoe, and the other relics from the graves, each carefully tagged with a description of which grave they came from and in what area of the grave.

"It's a fairly long story, sir," Dak said, "but let me go through the short version for now, and then, whenever you want, we can get into as much detail as you'd like."

Dak started by explaining all about Savoy and his marital history. He described Eleanor's relationship with Josephine Savoy
and mentioned Josephine's ancestors. He explained that Josephine had shown his mother her heirlooms, a sword and a
painting. Then, he explained the history of the old mansion and
the land surrounding it.

"Well, Dak, if this is the short version, how long will the ex-
panded one take?" the trooper asked.

"Sir, it is not a simple story, but it is true," Dak said. Then he
explained about the planks jutting out of the embankment up the
river and the archaeological project that he and J.D. had under-
taken. He pointed out that the first two graves were very old and
that they subsequently learned that they were slave graves from
prior to the Civil War. Showing photos as he went through the
story seemed to increase the trooper's tolerance level for its
length.

When Dak moved into the subject of the rope leading to the
third grave, the trooper asked several questions. Dak methodi-
cally, almost scientifically, answered each one. Sometimes, J.D.
joined in the explanation as they described the contents of the
third grave. Dak compared the long reddish hair to what his
mother had described as Josephine Savoy's hair. Then, he told
about the shoe and Mrs. Staley's comments on it. J.D. handed the
actual shoe to the trooper to examine.

Next, Dak told about the secret room in the mansion and
about finding the sword and the painting. Explaining that it took
more than one visit to get all the details, he showed the trooper
close-up photos of the engraving on the sword and the name on
the painting. The trooper seemed quite impressed with the de-
tailed information the boys provided.

"It doesn't prove a murder," Dak explained, "but if it was not
a murder, why didn't Josephine answer the letter, and who is the
lady in the grave? And why are the heirlooms in the ol' mansion
instead of bein' in France with Josephine? And why does the age
of the shoe fit so well with a murder at the time of Josephine's
disappearance? And why does the lady in the grave have not

only very long hair like Josephine, but also the right color? It all
fits. We think Percy Savoy murdered his first wife, Josephine."

"And you believe the sheriff is trying to have you killed to
prevent you from bringing the evidence of Savoy's crime to
other law enforcement officials?" the trooper asked.

"Yes," Dak said. "We were sittin' on J.D.'s back porch talkin'
about the evidence and were overheard by his mom. Then his
mom told a relative of Percy Savoy's. And everybody in town
seems to know that the sheriff is paid by Savoy to do his biddin'.
So, we believe the sheriff was tryin' to kill us because Savoy told
him to. We're pretty sure Savoy is capable of murder. Look what
happened to Josephine."

The trooper sighed and thought for a moment. Then, he said,
"Well, boys, I don't know any of the people involved with your
story, and you have more information than I can digest quickly,
but clearly this thing deserves investigation. I will need to take
the evidence with me and take this case up the line. I know the
State will want to dig into all this." He sighed again and paused
for a few seconds and then added, "I don't know if you realize it
or not, but you have broken a couple laws along the way too,
though they are not too serious. I don't know what the State will
do with that part of it."

The ambulance workers had transferred the bodily remains
from the wreckage to the ambulance and the wrecker drivers
had brought in a large truck and placed the wreckage on its flat
bed. As they were all leaving, Trooper Evans said, "Boys, I'm going to let you go for now. I want you to stay around town so that
you're reachable when the State folks get into this investigation.
They will want to see the gravesites and the mansion. Of course,
since you are not of age, they will have to talk with your parents
also."

"Well," J.D. said, "you can't get in to see the mansion very
easy because it's got an electric fence around it and 'No Trespassing' signs everywhere. Also, I bet ol' Savoy gets to the mansion
soon and removes all the evidence. If he has any idea we have
seen the stuff in the secret room, he will."

"Okay, guys, you may be right," the trooper said. "I don't know how much Savoy knows about what you've learned. We'll try to secure that area and the area of the graves as possible crime sites as soon as we can."

"Okay," Dak said. "Thanks very much."

"Yes, well there are just a couple more things. Don't discuss this case with anyone other than your parents. I don't know enough to know who else is involved in all this or who else may want you dead. I don't know what other means this man Savoy might have to try to kill you, if indeed he is trying to kill you. The point is that you need to be careful. Stay at home as much as possible, stay with your parents or other adults, and be observant. It's not a good time to revisit the possible crime sites or to go out on your own. Okay, you can go now."

In a half hour both boys were home, each trying to explain what had happened to their parents. "Mom," Dak said, "I need to tell you a story that Nancy shouldn't hear. Since she's off to her friend's house, this is probably a good time."

"Oh, Dak," Eleanor said. "I can't wait. Your stories are always so interesting."

It was not the kind of story Eleanor was expecting. It took him more than an hour to go through the whole thing with her, partially because she kept asking questions. When she had heard it all, she was overflowing with emotions. First, she could hardly believe or accept that this had happened. Also, her feelings were hurt that Dak hadn't told her more about events as they unfolded. She had prided herself on her close relationship with Dak, yet he hadn't even mentioned something as involved as all this. In addition, she felt worried and insecure about Dak's safety. Would someone make another attempt on his life? Further, she was sad that her friend Josephine Ingres had probably been murdered years ago. As all these emotions combined, she broke down in tears that she was unable to control for nearly a half hour. Dak tried to console her by explaining that the reason he hadn't told her before was that he loved her and wanted to avoid upsetting her. He told her the State Police would get involved now and that he thought their family would be safe. After a while, she grew calmer and seemed to accept the reality of these events. When it occurred to her that Nancy was not at home, she went immediately to get her, saying she would feel safer if everyone was at home.

When Eleanor returned with Nancy and recovered a bit more from what Dak had told her, she remembered that she had news for Dak. "Dak, Ann Scroggins checked into the deed situation on the Ellsworth property," she said.

Even though Dak had used all his adrenaline for one day, he was very interested in this. "Really?" he said. "She didn't waste any time. What did she find out?"

"Well, it seems that nothing having to do with the mansion is simple, and this is no exception," Eleanor said. "She says there is apparently a long-standing mix up on who owns the land."

"A mix up?" Dak frowned. "How can there be a mix up on who owns the land? Either Savoy owns it, or we do. What did the deed records show?"

"She looked first at the tax records," Eleanor said. "The Leventhals paid the taxes until 1856, but since then, for a hundred years, the Ellsworths or their descendants, the Savoys, have paid the taxes on the property. That's a long time."

"It is, but if they had a hundred-year lease that began in 1856, that is exactly what you would expect," Dak replied.

"Yes, I know," Eleanor said, "but when she went to look at the deed records, she found that there was a problem. There was a hand-written note attached to the deed file that said something about the ownership being uncertain since the 1884 flood, but that it was presumed to be owned by John Ellsworth and heirs. Well, we know that Savoy is his heir."

"How can the ownership be uncertain?" Dak asked. "There must be deed records that show who owns it."

"Well, she didn't know, either. The information was not in the file, so she asked me if it would be okay if she talked with old Mr. Harpton, who is 94 years old now. You know, he worked in that office for 40 years or so, starting back about the turn of the century.

I told her that would be okay. She knew we wanted her to be discreet, so she thought she should ask before she talked with him."

"Oh, yeah. I guess he should know almost everything that ever happened if his mind is still okay," Dak said.

"Ann said he is as sharp as if he were forty," Eleanor replied. "Anyway, she went by his home and took him a plate of cookies and sat with him a while. In the course of her conversation, she asked him about the deed uncertainty on the Ellsworth Place."

"Come on, Mom, you're leavin' me in suspense," Dak said.

"Okay. What he told her is an interesting story. He said that he was always told that in 1884, a big flood was shaping up, and at that time, the levee wasn't as high as it is now. The county officials were concerned that the courthouse would be flooded and the records destroyed. So, they asked various leading citizens who had homes on higher ground, or substantial three-story homes, to take portions of the county records and store them until the flood was over."

"I remember reading that there was a bad flood in 1884," Dak said.

"Yes, I guess the water was very high," Eleanor continued, "and portions of the records were turned over to each of the fourteen people who volunteered to take responsibility for some of them. It turns out that Ellsworth took part of the deed records, and the part he took included the records for Ellsworth Place. Then, he loaded these records on two small boats to take them to high ground, but one of the boats hit a sharp tree limb or something in the floodwater and sank before they could save the records. Apparently, it happened so quickly that it was all they could do to save the two guys who were in the boat that sank."

"This is weird," Dak said. "He happened to lose part of the deed records, and the part he lost happened to include those for Ellsworth Place."

"Yes, well...Ann said she commented to the old man about that being quite a coincidence. She said he just smiled and said Ellsworth may have chosen which records he took, and he may have chosen which part of those he lost."

"I see," Dak said. "In other words, it could be that the loss of the deed records was intentional."

"We don't know, but it is possible," Eleanor replied. "Anyway, after the flood, everyone returned the records except Ellsworth. He returned one group but just reported that the others were lost in a boat accident. They searched the property where the boat supposedly sank, but never found the records. So, they put public announcements in the newspaper explaining what had happened and describing all the property for which they no longer had records. They asked the owners to bring in their deeds to establish ownership, so a new set of records could be prepared."

"Well, I can just imagine how that went," Dak said. "Ellsworth didn't have a deed since he was only leasing the property, and Leaventhal didn't bother to take the deed in because he considered the property to be Ellsworth's for all practical purposes."

"That may be what happened," Eleanor said. "Anyway, no one ever brought in deeds to the property. Ellsworth told them that the property was his, but he had lost the deed. They checked with Leventhal. He told them it was his property, but that it didn't matter because Ellsworth had essentially a permanent lease on it. So it was left in limbo, but since Ellsworth claimed the property and paid the taxes, it was just treated as if it were his property."

"It would be good if we had the deed, but since it wasn't with the lease agreement, it's probably lost after a hundred years," Dak said. "Of course, Savoy doesn't have the deed either, and we do have the lease agreement."

"We might have enough of a case to take Savoy to court," Eleanor said, "if we had the money to do that. Unfortunately, we do not. I don't know how to proceed from here."

Then it hit him. "Oh, you know what?" Dak asked. "In the secret room at the mansion, there were some big, heavy books that had to do with deed records. I wonder if they could be the missing records. I wonder if there was never a boat accident at all. Maybe ol' Ellsworth took the records to the secret room but said they had been lost. That way, there would be no proof that Leventhals owned the property, unless Leventhal had the deed. It could even be that Ellsworth already knew that Leventhal had lost his deed."

"That is a lot of conjecture, Dak," Eleanor replied. "The other thing I wanted to tell you is that Harriet Savoy told Ann Scroggins that the mansion is to be demolished Saturday in preparation for that new facility they plan."

"Oh, man, I wish they wouldn't do that," Dak said. "But I don't know how to stop them. I wonder if they have taken the deed records and Josephine's heirlooms out of it yet."

"I haven't any idea," Eleanor replied.

"Well, at least, I have photos of those books," Dak said. "Oh, I don't anymore, because I gave them to the trooper, but he has them." It had been a long day, and Dak was feeling helpless and frustrated by the intractable problems that faced him. *I wish my dad were here,* he thought. *I bet he would know what to do.* He went to his room and looked at his dad's picture for a while. Then he went to bed wondering what the next few days would bring.

The next morning, J.D. arrived early again in the old Ford. As Dak jumped in the car, J.D. turned the radio off. "Dak," he said, "I told my parents all about what happened and all about the graves, the mansion, the sheriff, the trooper, everything. They weren't even mad at me for the broken window and the smashed fender. But, the thing is that they think the thing should be out in the open. My dad right away went up to the barber shop and told everybody there about it."

"He did?" Dak asked, wondering how that would affect the outcome of things. "Well, maybe at this point, that's not so bad. I bet most everybody knows about it anyway because Charlie said there were several people standing outside Miss Hurd's room when I called the trooper's house."

"Well, I hope it doesn't matter, because my mom was also hot on the phone tellin' her friends, and she wasn't even drinkin'. It was makin' me really nervous. It'll be all over town before long."

"Don't worry about it, J.D.," Dak said. "This is bigger than just you and me now. I guess they are going to tear down the mansion Saturday. At least, that's what Harriet Savoy told Mrs. Scroggins."

"It's not fair to the town to tear down a great ol' historic place like that," J.D. said.

"I know. It's like cutting an ancient tree," Dak said. "You can never get it back."

When they arrived at school, Dak looked for Judy Savoy to offer his support to her for what he knew would be a sad and stressful time as the story got around. When he could not find her, he asked Miss Hurd about it.

"Why, Dak, Judy left a couple days ago on a European vacation with her aunt. She doesn't plan to be here for graduation," she said. "Her mother is going to pick up her diploma after graduation."

"That's probably good," Dak said. "It would not be good if she was in school right now."

Miss Hurd knew what he meant. "Dak," she said, "I heard from Mrs. Scroggins all about the events yesterday and about the mansion and the river. Is that all true?"

"I don't know what all she told you, Miss Hurd, but there has been a lot of excitement." As Dak explained what had happened over the last few months, Miss Hurd sat quietly and listened.

When he had finally finished, she seemed a little shocked. She stood and took his hand in hers. "I had no idea, Dak." she said. "That is a most extraordinary story. Please let me know if I can do anything to help."

"Thanks," Dak replied. "I don't know of anything. The sheriff is in the hospital, so I don't think we're in any danger. Are the yearbooks going to be here tomorrow?"

"Yes, they should arrive late today. We will pass them out first thing tomorrow," she said. "And graduation is all set for Friday afternoon. You haven't forgotten that you will be asked to make a short speech after they announce that you are the valedictorian, have you?"

"No, no," Dak said. "I think I have it all in my mind. I went out in the laundry shed and said it real loud several times. It won't be very long."

"I look forward to hearing it," she said. "I should also tell you that Mr. Jordan will be announcing at the graduation ceremony that I will not return next year. I will make brief remarks in response."

"Awww, well, I do not look forward to that," Dak said.

Chapter 16

The Speeches

On Thursday morning, Miss Hurd passed out the yearbooks to the students. Dak looked over his copy and was thrilled with how it turned out. The printer had done a great job, and his "finest moments" shone through like the summer sun.

Mary Webster found Dak and was so thrilled with the photo of her playing the silver trumpet before a standing ovation that she gave him a big kiss on the cheek. Donny Slager, the kid who only got to play in the competitive basketball games for a few minutes all year, but ended up making the winning point in the biggest game of all, said, "Hey, Dak, how did you get that photo with the scoreboard in the background as I made the winning point? That's amazing. Now, maybe my grandma will believe it." In fact, the scoreboard had been superimposed over the famous shot.

Kay Walters, the girl who organized the highly successful cake sale for the poor family, jumped up and down several times and screamed with joy when she saw her picture. She was shown with both fists full of cash high over her head and a big smile on her face, as she jumped in the air with the "Cake Sale Benefit" sign in the background. Her friends began calling her, "The Jumper."

Ray Shorter was more subdued. He sat at a desk and looked for a long time at the photo of him receiving the state science fair ribbon from the lieutenant governor. It was against a backdrop of his drawing of the Shawneetown levee and his measurements that had shown how to strengthen it. When he saw Dak, he said simply, "Hey, Dak, you are fine."

"No, Ray," Dak responded, "As the picture shows, it's you who did the fine deed."

In Jenny Mae Newbury's winning poem, the big line was, "People rarely see the need...for folks like them to take the lead." These words were superimposed over a photo of her taken as she was awarded the blue ribbon. She gave Dak a big hug.

Julia Hannig's picture receiving the award for her history project was against a background of a blow-up of the tintype of the children of the battlefield. She walked up to Dak, swished her hand through his flattop and rubbed her cheek against his, her arm around his neck. She whispered, "I love it, Dak."

It was the woodcarving of Ike that was Ben Flores' finest moment. While Ben couldn't quit looking at his photo with the carving and all the classmates in the background, wearing "I like Ike" buttons, he felt a little embarrassed by all the attention it attracted, so he said nothing. Dak found a note in his history book from Ben that said, "Dak, I'm glad you like Ike too. Signed, Ben the Carver."

Several other students came to Dak to express their appreciation that the yearbook had indeed captured their finest moment, but the best was Charlie Johnson. The large photo of Charlie with his biggest smile, the history test held high over his head sporting the numerals 100 at the top, and the students standing on their desk seats, roaring their approval, was the ultimate. The caption was a direct quote from Miss Hurd: "We don't pretend to be perfect, and we can't expect ever to get 100." Miss Hurd had smiled wryly when she first saw that.

Thrilled as Dak was by the explosively successful yearbook, he was unable to keep his mind on it very long at a time. He kept thinking about the mansion, the murder, the lease and the deed books, the sheriff, his valedictory speech and perhaps most of all, the special night. It was very exciting to think of graduation on Friday afternoon and their special night on Saturday, but the feeling that his business with Savoy and the sheriff was not finished continued to haunt him.

Mr. Jordan had decided to hold the graduation ceremony outside this year because they could not complete the gymnasium repairs soon enough. Since there was no outdoor facility with lighting for evening activities, they held the ceremony in the afternoon with contingency dates in case of rain. A temporary platform had been set up in the ball field for speakers and dignitaries while steel folding chairs were arranged in neat rows to accommodate the graduates and those who came to view the

ceremony. Mr. Jordan had insisted on setting up a public announcement system to make sure everyone could hear the
speakers.

On Friday morning, J.D. came by as usual, and his mood was
definitely upbeat. The radio was at its loudest setting, and Gale
Storm could be heard a half block away pounding out *I Hear You
Knocking*.

> You better get to your use-to-be
> 'Cause your kind of love ain't good to me
> I hear you knocking
> But you can't come in
> I hear you knocking
> Go back where you've been.

As they went to school that morning, it didn't occur to either
boy that this was their last trip to high school as students, and
notwithstanding the problems before them, they felt like it was a
wonderful day. When they arrived at school, they began to enjoy
the festive feeling of graduation day.

The seniors made the rounds of the classes to say goodbye to
their teachers, signed silly autographs for each other, told jokes
about naive freshmen, emptied their lockers, turned in their
books, received their final report cards, and continued to talk
about their wonderful yearbook. At mid-morning, they were
treated to a skit by the juniors, who took over the platform that
had been set up for graduation ceremonies. The juniors poked
fun at the old-fashioned seniors and bid them farewell.

At lunchtime, Dak and Melodie went to the ball field, as they
had so often done, and had their lunch. "My mom went to the
cabin at Big Lake yesterday," Melodie said, "and cleaned it so it
will be perfect for us tomorrow night."

Dak smiled and said, "If you're there, it will be perfect. And
how about your dad? Is he still talking about hanky panky?"

"Naw," she replied. "He hasn't mentioned that for two days.
He is comfortable with the chaperone."

By two o'clock in the afternoon, the families occupied all the steel folding chairs, except the empty ones in front that had been reserved for the graduates. Eleanor and Nancy were sitting with Mrs. Scroggins, who had given them a ride to the ceremony.

The band, which had been seated to the side of the platform, struck up *Pomp and Circumstance*. The graduates in caps and gowns marched in to the music and took their seats while Mr. Jordan approached the podium. The various speakers talked of wonderful futures, of the importance of ethics, and said words like "this great country" and "our proud heritage," while Dak's mind whirled with thoughts about the mansion, the murder, and what to do about it all. Right in the middle of an idea about how to prevent the mansion from being demolished, he heard Mr. Jordan say, "It is my pleasure to introduce our valedictorian for the Class of 1956, Dakston Paul Leventhal."

Jumping back to the subject at hand, Dak rose and walked to the podium to loud applause and yells by his classmates. When he stood facing the crowd, it looked bigger than he had thought. He felt his heart pounding and his breaths getting shorter as he experienced his first bout of stage fright. He reassured himself by thinking, *I've got this talk memorized cold.* Fortunately, the applause was long enough to allow him a few deep breaths. Then, he began.

"Good afternoon classmates, teachers, and ladies and gentlemen. I promised Miss Hurd that I would try to make this talk pronouncing my verbs with the 'g' on the end, so if I say 'going' instead of 'goin', you will know why. I learned long ago that it is best to do what Miss Hurd asks, and I can tell you, I would follow her to the ends of the Earth. She is one great teacher."

Miss Hurd blushed as the crowd applauded wildly for her. Dak allowed a pause and then began again.

"Who am I to address all of you, to try to give you advice, to add to your knowledge or skills, or to affect your lives? You are already the world's finest classmates. Attending school with you has been sublime. You have all had your finest moments, and you have been my finest moment for four happy years."

There was light applause and Dak continued.

"I would just say to you that I hope you have big dreams for your life. I hope that when someone tells you that you are a dreamer, you will proudly say, 'Yes, I am.' I hope that you have great fun making your dreams come true. I know that when your dreams come true, it will be your finest moments.

"I hope that when you have children, you will recognize that making even their smallest dreams come true gives confidence and hope to them--and that this confidence and hope leads to bigger and better dreams, so that they may also have their finest moments. And I hope you realize that this cycle is what life is all about.

"I believe, classmates, that we will be a driving force for giving hope to those who have no hope and for giving dreams to those who cannot dream. I believe that, in this way, we will show our determination to make the world a better place.

"Dreams are not just for today or tomorrow. I hope that if you live to be 100, you will still have big dreams and that when you die, your successors will carry on these dreams. Your dreams must never die. Dreams are forever."

The crowd, many of whom had not fully comprehended what Dak had said, began with polite applause. The classmates, most of whom did fully understand what Dak had said, applauded loudly. Then, Charlie stood, followed by J.D., Melodie, and Marie. Mary Webster, the girl with the silver trumpet, then rose, turned to the crowd, and brought her arms upward, her palms facing the sky. With that, everyone stood and applauded, but as the general crowd tapered off and sat down, Ben Flores rammed his fists skyward and issued some loud yells, stimulating the classmates to continue for another full minute. Dak had not expected this reaction, and he had the unusual sensation of feeling overwhelmed. A tear ran down his cheek. *Why is this happening to me?*" he thought. Then he wiped his face with the arm of his gown and continued.

"Finally, I want to thank my mother, Eleanor Leventhal, for providing me an environment of hope. I love her dearly. And I want to honor my father, Paul Leventhal, who gave me life and then gave his life for our country. I have missed him so much, and I miss him more than ever today."

With that, Dak stepped down and returned to his seat as Mr. Jordan returned to the podium. The principal told the audience that Miss Hurd had made the decision to return to Moline next year. He raved about her accomplishments at the school and lamented her loss. He called her to the podium and presented her with a dozen red roses in appreciation for her service. Then, he offered her the podium.

Miss Hurd gazed out across the crowd and greeted them warmly. She explained that she loved the town and had so enjoyed the students in her years there. Then she said, "In fact, it is largely because I lose my senior students each year that I'm leaving. I find it difficult to part with those I hold in such high regard. I will seek a new life as something other than a teacher."

The crowd seemed puzzled by this and obviously found it hard to understand. Then Miss Hurd went on to another and even more controversial subject.

"I will seek my happiness at another place doing another thing. But, you all know that there is something very special about this little town. There is something very different about it. There is something that has to do with its ancient Indian heritage. There is something that has to do with its history as the oldest town in the state and a gateway to the west. There is something about its brushes with greatness--with Tecumseh, with Lafayette, with Posey, with Lincoln, with U. S. Grant, with James Harrison Wilson and Michael Lawler, and, yes, with Tom Sawyer. There is something that has to do with its never-give-up spirit, its will to survive in spite of great catastrophes. There is something that has to do with its beautiful river. You should not let these things be taken from you because they are the character, the backbone, the essence of your town. They are what make your town extraordinary. If they are lost, your town will be just another one of ten thousand run-of-the-mill small mid-western towns. If they survive, generations to come will celebrate them as I do today."

After pausing for applause, she continued, "In that regard, I have heard that you may lose the historic Ellsworth Place tomorrow as they raze the building to construct a warehouse. My advice to you is not to allow it. That building is part of what you are, of what you have been, and, hopefully, of what you will be. You should not, you cannot in good conscience, let it be taken from your town. Organize and march and protest, and if necessary, stand in front of the dozers, until a way can be found to save it. That is my advice."

She picked up her roses and left the podium. Mr. Jordan appeared unhappy that Miss Hurd had converted his graduation ceremony to a call to action. Many in the crowd were very surprised by what she had said. The students, however, were fully in tune with her. While the applause was abating, Dak got up and whispered into Melodie's ear. Melodie, in turn, ran over to two other girls and whispered to them. Then all three girls, who happened to be the school's lead cheerleaders, ran to the front and began chanting as their arms cranked the air, "Save Ellsworth Place, Save Ellsworth Place, Save Ellsworth Place!" Dak joined in the chant, and in seconds, the whole class was chanting, "Save Ellsworth Place!"

Mr. Jordan, at the podium, was saying, "Please, students, this is not the time. Students, please be seated. Students, please. Could we have order, please?"

The answer to his question was a resounding, "No!" By now, the general crowd had joined the students, and it seemed that everyone but Mr. Jordan was chanting along with the students. Finally, he seemed to get the point.

He turned up the volume on the mike and said, "Okay, okay. Can I have your attention? Please! Let me suggest a plan." The noise receded, and Mr. Jordan continued, "Let me suggest a plan. Immediately after this ceremony, let's meet here at the platform to organize our march on Ellsworth Place. Could we do that? Let's march on Ellsworth Place, but let's finish the graduation ceremony right now."

Everyone sat, and relative quiet was restored, although many people were still talking to those around them. Without waiting for full silence, Mr. Jordan quickly completed the ceremony. At the end, Dak ran over to Melodie, and they threw their caps high into the air together and kissed while their caps were descending. The band played *Ode to Joy*.

Chapter 17

The March on the Mansion

A t the end of the graduation ceremony, most of the attendees assembled around the platform to organize a march on Ellsworth Place. It wasn't as simple to organize as everyone at first assumed. There was the question of where the march should start and then whether it should proceed during the remainder of the afternoon or early Saturday morning. Some people asked what would keep Savoy's people from starting the demolition that night. Others asked what the legal situation was if they marched on posted private property.

Inevitably, there were a few people who felt that it was Savoy's property, and if he wanted to demolish it, he had that right. Some said it was their understanding that there was uncertainty about whether the Savoys or the Leventhals actually owned the property. Dak explained what the situation was with the 100-year lease and the lost deed book. A question was raised relative to how to handle law enforcement officials if they arrived, but it was pointed out that the sheriff was in the hospital, and that left only the deputy. Most people felt the deputy wouldn't be too difficult to handle. Debate and discussion continued for an hour and a half.

Finally, the few people who did not want to participate left to go home. For the others, agreement was reached that the first group, made up of about one-third of all those assembled, would drive immediately to the road by the bar pits and assemble near the mansion with the intent of staying all night and stopping any effort to raze the mansion. One man volunteered to go by his home and get a pair of insulated wire cutters to cut the electric fence.

The second group, comprising the other two-thirds of all those participating, would arrive at the same place at 8 AM Saturday to relieve the first group. Within each group, certain people were assigned to bring water and food for those who were staying at the site. Toilet accommodations consisted of some dense woods to the south of the mansion. J.D. decided he would take the Friday night session while Dak agreed to arrive at 8 AM Saturday morning.

Dak thought word about what had happened at the graduation ceremony must have gotten to Savoy. He thought Savoy would appear Friday night at the mansion and demand that everyone vacate his property. As it turned out, Savoy didn't show up at all on Friday night. The group of protesters cut the electrified fence and encircled the mansion. Since it was a very cloudy night, they built bonfires to make some light. When there was no attempt to destroy the mansion, they frolicked and told jokes. The only excitement of the night was when someone walked into the mansion, flashlight in hand, and nearly stepped on an animal trap. After that, the crowd got their excitement from ghost stories and stories of the murders that were rumored to have happened there. The story of Josephine Savoy was well known by then, and that, too, was a hot topic of conversation.

On Saturday morning, Dak arrived a little before 8 AM and talked with several people who had spent the night. Although it was very cloudy, they reported that it had not rained at all during the night. When Dak learned that Savoy had not been there, he was sure something big would happen soon. He walked around the mansion, expecting to see some evidence that the State Police had cordoned off the mansion as a crime scene. He had assumed they did that immediately after he and J.D. told Trooper Lew Evans about the possible murder. Suddenly, he realized that there was no yellow ribbon. With the sheriff in the hospital and Savoy nowhere to be seen, he thought, *I actually have a chance right now to try to retrieve the deed books from the secret room.*

Dak knew he would need a flashlight and wanted someone to go in with him. He noticed J.D. across the way putting some things in the old Ford, getting ready to leave. He ran over and borrowed J.D.'s flashlight but didn't explain why he needed it, because he knew J.D. would try to talk him out of going back into the mansion.

Then he found Charlie and asked him if he would be willing to go inside to try to retrieve the deed books. Charlie didn't hesitate. As they walked quickly toward the building, Dak explained about the animal traps inside. Charlie picked up a heavy stick that he could use to spring the traps without injury. When they had reached the front steps, they heard a roar from the crowd. Looking across the way, they could see the sheriff's car and Percy Savoy's pickup truck rolling in across the field.

Dak and Charlie stopped to see what was happening. With the sheriff's car in the lead, the two vehicles slowed as they approached the circle of people around the mansion.

"You don't suppose the sheriff is out of the hospital already, do you?" Dak asked.

"I wouldn't think so," Charlie replied. "It's probably the ol' dumb deputy."

The deputy got out of the sheriff's car and began shouting, "Okay, all of you get off this property. Go get in your cars and go home. It's over now. Go on home. Let's move!"

The crowd began shouting at the deputy and waving their fists in the air. Dak couldn't understand what they were saying because so many were yelling at once. However, it was clear that they weren't leaving, at least not yet. The deputy reached back in his car and grabbed a bullhorn. He repeated his call for everyone to leave, this time through the bullhorn. Still, no one budged, and the noise level of the crowd only increased.

The deputy was getting agitated. He picked up the bullhorn again and shouted, "If you don't leave immediately, I am going to have to start issuing citations. You are on private property. You must leave now, or you will be given a ticket for trespassing."

The crowd still did not move, and the high noise level continued. The deputy took his ticket book out of the car and walked over to old Mr. Harpton, the guy who had worked in the county clerk's office for so many years. As he asked Mr. Harpton for identification, the crowd booed loudly. Then J.D.'s mother, Mrs. Robinson, came out of the crowd, walked up to the deputy, and slapped him briskly in the face, making a loud popping noise. It was obvious Mrs. Robinson had been drinking and the crowd broke into laughter.

"Mr. Harpton is my friend," she yelled, "Don't even think about giving him a ticket." The deputy didn't think it was funny. He reached for his nightstick, but several men grabbed him and took both his nightstick and his weapon. Then Percy Savoy got out of his pickup truck, came forward, and grabbed the bullhorn. The crowd got quieter because everyone wanted to hear what Savoy had to say.

"It is okay for you folks to stay if you want," Savoy said, "but I've called off the bull dozers for today. Do you see any dozers? There are no dozers here. We aren't going to have any house wrecking today, so you might as well leave. You can feel free to stand around here, or you can go home where I'm sure you have something you need to do."

"We're going to stay a while!" someone shouted. The crowd roared their agreement.

"Well, okay, stay a while," Savoy said. "Enjoy yourselves. Just let me through with my pickup, so I can dump these cattle supplies. Then, I'll get out of here and you can enjoy your little get together. Maybe you want to do some fishing in the bar pits while you're here and have a couple beers. Make yourself at home." He chuckled.

The crowd could see that Savoy really did have some blue five-gallon buckets in the back of his truck. Assuming these were the supplies he had mentioned, they decided to let him through the line of people surrounding the mansion. The deputy moved his car forward until he was just past the rotten back steps to the mansion, and Savoy drove the truck in behind him. The deputy walked over to the truck, pulled the tailgate down, and carried the three buckets to the bottom of the steps. Savoy took the lids off each bucket as the crowd watched. Then, the deputy dumped the contents of the first bucket on the steps. The crowd, not knowing what was happening, started to run toward the steps. Savoy attempted to dump the second bucket, but it was apparently too heavy for him. He spilled most of it, including some on his shirtsleeves. The deputy quickly dumped the third bucket on the steps and threw a match after it. The crowd could smell gasoline.

The resulting explosive fire was obviously much bigger than the deputy expected. He had apparently felt panicked by the crowd rushing forward and had thrown the match on the gasoline prematurely. The explosion knocked both him and Savoy off their feet, and Savoy's shirt was on fire. The deputy, not noticing Savoy's problem, quickly got back to his feet and moved the sheriff's car away from the big fire. Savoy began screaming, and two men grabbed a tarp out of Savoy's truck and rolled it on him to put out the fire. Working in intense heat, they pulled him away from the fire, but by now, his pickup was also burning.

Percy Savoy had second-degree burns on both arms and lesser burns on his chest and face. He was loaded into Mr. Jordan's car, which left a trail of dust across the field as it headed out to take Savoy to the hospital.

The back steps to the mansion were burning furiously, and the fire was making its way into the back doors. The crowd found several buckets, including the three that had contained the gasoline, and formed a bucket brigade from the nearest bar pit, inadequate as it was. Some other men drove quickly back into town to get the fire truck.

"Charlie, we've got to do it," Dak shouted. "This may be the last chance to retrieve the stuff in the secret room."

"Let's go!" Charlie replied.

They ran in the front door of the mansion, and immediately Charlie barely missed stepping on an animal trap. "Oh, wow!" he yelled, using his large stick to release the trap. "Let's not get in too big a hurry, Dak. We have to be very careful."

"Right," Dak replied. "Charlie, we have to go upstairs and release a shelf support in the back room on the right. There are lots of traps up there too, so keep watchin'."

When they got to the back room upstairs, smoke was billowing into the hallway. Dak quickly moved the bookshelf and pulled the support into its extended position to release the panel to the secret room. Then, he went to the front room and moved the shelves out of the way so he could grip the handles of the movable panel. By now, smoke was streaming into all the rooms.

Dak pulled the handles upward, but the panel wouldn't move. He knew the panel fit tightly and was prone to stick, so he hammered on it with his fist.

"Better hurry, Dak," Charlie said. "The smoke is getting heavier all the time."

"I know," Dak said as he pulled on the handles again. "Ahh, it's coming now. Hand me the flashlight."

"Oh, crap!" Charlie said. "I think I left the flashlight downstairs when I stopped to release that trap. I'll run get it."

The smoke was getting so heavy that Dak decided he would have to proceed into the secret room even though it was dark. He had started coughing and knew he couldn't stay much longer. As he felt his way along the shelf, the thought crossed his mind that Savoy might have put an animal trap along the shelf. He moved his hand along the shelf, being careful to keep it flat on the surface so as not to set off any trap that might be there. Then, he felt the sword. He threw it out the door just as Charlie returned, missing him by only a couple of inches.

"Aarg," Charlie said as he jumped back. "Don't kill me with the sword. I'm preferrin' smoke as my way to go. Here's the flashlight."

"Sorry, Charlie," Dak said, as he grabbed the light. Dak coughed repeatedly, but retrieved the two large deed books and handed them to Charlie. Charlie had placed a handkerchief over his mouth, and that left him with only one hand for carrying.

"I'm taking the deed books and leaving," Charlie said. "Come on! We've got to get out of here."

Dak wanted to get the painting, too, but was having trouble finding it. He knew it was rolled and he thought it should be easy to see. But where was it? Then he realized that it wasn't on the lower shelf at all. He had put it on the back of the upper shelf, which was not visible from eye level. He quickly retrieved it and ran out of the room. Grabbing the sword, he started for the door but could see that the smoke was extremely heavy now. Charlie was gone.

Dak considered going to a window but thought there was probably no ladder available to reach him. On the other hand, he could see that the smoke was so heavy that he might not be able to see any animal trap that might be in his path. In addition, the thought occurred to him that he might collapse from inhaling the smoke. Coughing continuously now, he decided he had to chance it. Immediately, he kicked a trap across the room. It issued a loud clang as the impact with the wall released the spring. Running out of options, he slipped carefully down the stairs and sliding his feet instead of walking, he moved from the steps to the front door. As he ran out the front door with an upraised sword in his right hand and the rolled painting in his left, he looked like some classic warrior charging an entrenched enemy. The crowd saw him and began clapping and hooting. Dak sat down outside in the grass and coughed deeply for several minutes. Melodie, who had thought he might be caught in the mansion, ran over and embraced him. When he was feeling a little better, though still coughing, a loud thunderclap shook the area, and a drenching rain began pounding the ground around him. "How sweet it is," he thought. Melodie took the sword and painting to Charlie's car where the deed records had also been placed. Dak sat in the grass with his face pointing skyward and let the heavy rain flow over him for a long time. Soaked to the bone, he finally lay back in the flooded grass with one knee up and savored every drop that hit him. He could see that the rain was extinguishing the fire at the back of the mansion. The fire truck had arrived, but Mother Nature was outdoing it. Twenty minutes later, the rain was still coming down in cascades, and the smoke had turned white. After twenty more minutes, the smoke stopped altogether. The crowd, worried that their cars would be stuck in the mud, had almost all left the area.

Chapter 18

The Prom

Dak finally rose from the water and grass and walked to the back of the mansion. While there was some damage, he thought it was all repairable. It appeared that the interior damage was mostly confined to the back door area and the back end of the dogtrot. He was certain there was a heavy smoke film throughout the mansion. Melodie went home with her dad after Dak reminded her that he and J.D. would be by her house at 6 PM to pick her up for their special night.

As Charlie and Dak were leaving, Trooper Lew Evans and several state police officers arrived. The boys stopped long enough to talk with Trooper Evans. He told them the mansion and the area around the graves would be secured as possible crime sites.

"We've heard from several people everything that happened here today," the trooper said. "It's too bad we didn't do this yesterday. It would have prevented some unfortunate incidents, but I was unable to get the central office to move as quickly as I would have liked. We also have men over at the gravesite right now. Your friend J.D. Robinson showed us the location of the graves."

Dak turned over the sword and the painting to Trooper Evans. He explained that he and Charlie had retrieved them when it had appeared the mansion would burn to the ground. "Charlie and I decided to go in and retrieve the heirlooms and the deed books," Dak said. "We'll turn the heirlooms over to you now, and if it's okay, we will return the deed books to the county clerk."

"Actually," Trooper Evans said, "I think it would be better if we returned the deed books also."

"Well, here they are," Dak said. "Please don't lose them." With that, the boys went back into town where Charlie let Dak off at home.

Eleanor fixed Dak and Nancy a big lunch while Dak got into some dry clothes. After eating, he lay on the sofa and slept for more than two hours.

When Dak awoke, he had the special night on his mind. Eleanor assured him she would have the hush puppy dough ready for him to take. She had already walked to the fish dock, purchased four pounds of fiddlers for their fish fry and packed them in ice in a bucket. Dak reminded her that they were wearing their suits and formals for the special night and that he needed a flower for Melodie.

"Dak, why ever would you wear your suit to a fish fry at Big Lake?" Eleanor asked.

"It's because it's a substitute for the prom we didn't get to have," Dak replied. "We didn't want to give that up. This is our prom, our only prom. We want it to be special."

"Well, okay," Eleanor said. "But try not to get your suit messed up. Oh, and Dak, I know it will be just the four of you and Mrs. Robinson at the cabin. You're all young and, well, temptations are great sometimes. Please be careful."

Dak smiled. It was the first time Eleanor had ever said anything like that in all his seventeen years. "Okay, Mom," he said, "I think the way Mr. Lerner put it was, 'No hanky panky'."

"Actually, I didn't say that. I asked you to be careful. Even though you are young, you are a high school graduate now. I know you are mature enough to be responsible and make good decisions if you think about it. I'm just reminding you to think about it and be careful."

"Thanks, Mom. I like having your confidence."

"I'll call Ann Scroggins and see if I can get an orchid from her," Eleanor said. "She grows them, you know."

Dak pumped water for the bathtub in the laundry shed and scrubbed himself to pristine cleanliness. He spent some time with his flat top and made sure all his clothes were pressed and ready for the big night. By 5 PM, he was dressed, and Eleanor had prepared the orchid for Melodie.

J.D. came by in a new Plymouth Fury Special 8 that his uncle had graciously loaned him. Dak put the hush puppy dough and the bucket with the fiddlers in the trunk and jumped in the back seat. Already in the car, Marie looked like a movie star in a light blue strapless taffeta gown with a maroon orchid pinned to it. When they stopped at Melodie's house, Dak went to the front door. Melodie opened the door before he rang the bell. She was dressed in pale pink satin with netting around her shoulders and looked so beautiful to Dak. Mr. Lerner looked on as Dak pinned his orchid to Melodie's gown.

"What time will you be home, Melodie?" Mr. Lerner asked.

"Some time tomorrow morning, Daddy," Melodie said. "As you know, Mrs. Robinson will be our chaperone. She will be there with us, and when our party ends, Mrs. Robinson and the guys will go sleep in Mrs. Robinson's cabin. Marie and I will be fine in ours."

"Hrrrumph," was all Mr. Lerner could manage as she shut the door.

As they drove to Big Lake, J.D. said, "We have slaw, a green Jell-o salad, beer, and four bottles of wine in the trunk."

"And the pecan pie," Marie added.

"And the fiddlers and hush puppy dough," Dak said.

Marie suggested they sing along instead of listening to the radio on the way to the lake. She ran through the lyrics to *Rock and Roll Waltz* and then asked them all to sing on the count of three.

> And while they danced, only one thing was wrong
> They were trying to waltz to a rock and roll song!
> a-one, two, and then rock.
> a-one two and then roll.

It wasn't so good the first time because Dak was a little off key, and J.D. forgot the lyrics. Marie insisted they try again. It was better the second time, and by the fifth time, they had it iced. On the sixth time, they all sang to the top of their lungs and produced something that would have made Kay Starr proud.

Arriving at the lake, they noticed that J.D.'s mother was sitting in a yard chair on the back porch of the cabin next door. She appeared to be reading a book and, as instructed by J.D., she didn't seem to notice their arrival. "Keep a very low profile," J.D. had said to her earlier in the day. "Being our chaperone doesn't mean joining in the party."

They unloaded their food and started the fire in the stone ring. Dak put the big skillet from the cabin on the fire and scooped three inches of lard into it. Before long, he had the golden brown fiddlers and hush puppies ready to eat. Melodie had set the table beautifully. She even had candles.

Mrs. Robinson walked over while they were eating and told them how nice they looked. She told them she didn't want to interfere with their party and asked them to let her know if they needed anything. "I'll be next door reading and will check in from time to time," she said. "Have fun!"

Along with jokes and banter, the foursome tried at times to look forward. J.D. said, "Wouldn't it be interesting to know where we will be twenty years from now and what will have happened to the world?"

Marie thought a few seconds and said, "Twenty years from now? We'll probably have kids in high school and be caught up in the busy world of work and taking care of the house and such."

"It won't be the same,"J.D. said. "There will probably be people on the moon and Communists in Mexico and Canada."

"Hard to say," Dak added, "but I hope the old mansion is all restored, and people are tourin' it and marvelin' about its history. And maybe there will be another girl named Melodie II who just graduated high school and is off somewhere havin' a wonderful graduation party while her parents worry about chaperones and hanky panky."

Melodie couldn't resist. "Maybe there will be another boy named Dak Number Five who just graduated high school and has big dreams."

"Yeah," Dak said, "It would be too much to hope that he has friends as good as the three of you. But maybe he will have a dad at his graduation."

As the sun sank in the west, J.D. opened a bottle of wine and gave everyone a glass. Melodie turned on the record player and played several Elvis songs. Then she did "Earth Angel" by The Penguins. They danced cheek to cheek for several songs and sipped wine in between. When Marie asked for *Graduation Day*, Melodie dug in her stack and found it. "So appropriate for tonight," Marie said. As it played, she sang along softly.

> There's a time for joy
> A time for tears
> A time we'll treasure through the years
> We'll remember always
> Graduation Day
>
> At the senior prom
> We danced 'till three
> And there you gave your heart to me
> We'll remember always
> Graduation Day

The wine was adding to the ambiance of the occasion. "That's so sweet, Marie," Melodie said, as a tear ran down her face.

"Well," Dak said, "we will certainly remember graduation day, won't we. I don't think I could forget it if I reached 110." He took another sip.

"This is our prom, so we get to dance until three," J.D. said as he filled everyone's glass.

"J.D., I could dance with you forever," Marie said. "Maybe I will."

"Me too, J.D.," Dak said. "Let's dance."

J.D. got up, and Dak joined him for a few seconds of dancing to *A Tear Fell* while the girls roared with laughter.

"If I had to dance with you very long, a tear would fall," Dak said.

"I don't know," J.D. said. "Your after shave was kinda growin' on me. Or maybe it just rubbed off on me."

"Know what I like?" asked Melodie.

"I'm hoping it's the same thing I like," said Dak.

"No, no," Melodie said. "I mean what song lyric."

"I don't know, I guess," Dak replied.

"I bet I do," Marie countered.

"What? You do, and I don't?" Dak said. "Tell me it's not true."

"It is true," Marie said. "It's, 'Take one fresh and tender kiss... Add one stolen night of bliss.' Am I right?"

Melodie screamed with delight that Marie would know that.

"Okay. I didn't know, but I agree with the sentiment," Dak said, as he leaned over and gave her a particularly tender kiss.

"This being our prom..." Melodie said. "This is where you have to give your heart to me, Dak."

"I'm way ahead of the prom," Dak said. "You've had my heart for a long time. You just didn't know it."

As they drank more wine and expressed more sentiments, J.D. and Marie left the sofa to Dak and Melodie and scooted over to the daybed on the other side of the room. The next record that fell into place was Johnnie Ace's *Pledging My Love*. This song had ignited Dak's emotions. As the song played, he almost engulfed Melodie with his body and kissed her open lips for long times, running his fingers back and forth through her long hair and down her back.

Forever my darling,
Our love will be true
Always and forever,
I'll love only you

Just promise me darling
Your love in return
May this fire in my soul dear
Forever burn

J.D. turned off the overhead light, leaving only the light that came from some cheap nautical glass globe that bubbled as its

25-watt bulb heated some enclosed liquid. This led to a pro-
longed period of heavy petting on both sides of the room while
the records recycled. Dak finally pulled an afghan down over
Melodie and himself. While J.D. was up to fill the wine glasses
again, he noticed that his mother was walking up to the door.

"Is everything okay?" Mrs. Robinson asked.

J.D. stuck his head out the door and said, "We're fine, Mom.
There are some left over fiddlers and stuff on the table out there
if you want some. There's also other stuff in the refrigerator in
here."

"Oh, thanks," Mrs. Robinson said. "I'll take a couple fiddlers."
She went to the table and put two fiddlers in a napkin. She also
picked up one of the full wine bottles and took that along.

After another three love songs, Dak stood and emptied his half-
full glass of wine. "Why don't we ever hear *Unchained Melody* in
that stack?" Dak said to no one in particular. Marie moved off the
day bed, and he could hear the records sliding. Then, it started.

> Oh, my love, my darling
> I've hungered for your touch a long, lonely time
> Time goes by so slowly
> And time can mean so much
>
> Are you still mine?
> I need your love, I need your love
> God speed your love to me

Dak took off his jacket, tie, and shirt. Then he whispered in
her ear, "You are unchained tonight, Melodie. I love you." Their
kisses grew longer and more passionate, and their hands roamed
further as the evening went on. When Johnnie Ace came on the
next time, Dak was lost in love.

At some point in the evening, it occurred to J.D. that his
mother had not checked in for hours. Deciding that he should
investigate, he went to the family's cabin to find his mother
asleep in a lawn lounger with an empty wine bottle lying on the

porch floor. He carried her inside and laid her on the bed. She never stirred.

At about 2 AM, Marie said, "Oh, this is so wonderful. When do we have to go to our own cabins? I don't want this to end, but what will the little ol' ladies in town say?"

"I don't care what the little ol' ladies say," Melodie replied. "I just don't want my dad to be all upset. But we don't have to break up already, do we?"

"I want to stay as long as you're comfortable with it, Melodie," Dak said.

"Why don't we just stay the night?" J.D. asked. "What's the worst that could happen? My mom is asleep, but we're the only ones who know that. The thing is that life doesn't get any better than this. Think about it...really... life doesn't get any better than this, and we would interrupt it?"

"You've got a point, J.D.," Dak said. "Fifty years from now, do you think we'll look back at this and wish we had cut short such a glorious evenin' because the little ol' ladies might gossip? I don't think so. If we do cut it short, we'll look back fifty years from now and we'll say, 'Well, we had one brief shinin' moment when everything was perfect. One brief shinin' moment when everything was right. One magical evenin' when we were young and energetic and full of love and happiness. High school graduates, but still loose and carefree. No responsibility for college or job or family. Just the four of us enjoyin' a perfect night. It doesn't happen often in a lifetime, but it happened that night. And we cut it short because we didn't have the courage to live our lives the way we wanted. Then we went out into the rat race for the rest of our lives. For the rest of our lives, we got up and went to work and we came home and we mowed the grass and we washed the clothes and we cleaned the house. We never had another single moment so grand.' That's what we'll say."

Melodie and Marie smiled and clapped their hands while Dak bowed. "Let's get on with it," J.D. said. "Let's not waste another minute. Dak and I can go to the other cabin around six and all will be well. Mom probably won't wake before seven."

They took the pecan pie out of the refrigerator and had a snack as they took turns telling their favorite jokes and stories. Maybe it was the wine or maybe it was the late hour, but they had never laughed so hard. When Dak acted out the story about J.D. running from the addled squirrel, the girls simply lost it. They had to recover before they were able to listen to J.D. reenact the discussion he had with Mr. Savoy when Savoy caught him in the mansion. Dak covered some of Larry Lambert's more hilarious moments and made great fun of J.D.'s body movements in the moments following the baseball bat's smashing his rear car window.

Melodie played first herself and then her dad as she portrayed their discussion about hanky panky. The boys loved her version of Mr. Lerner fumbling through an explanation of the term as Melodie pressed further and further into its exact definition.

After a while, the record player cycled again to Johnnie Ace and Dak asked Melodie to dance again. This led to several more dances that felt erotic to Dak because he had taken his shirt off earlier and Melodie kept rubbing his thoroughly sun-tanned bare back. Actually, J.D. had taken his shirt off also, but in a concession to civility, he had kept his bright plaid tie firmly around his neck.

The magic hours disappeared and soon it was 6 AM. Dak said, "Well, I guess it's time for us to go to the other cabin, J.D."

"I suppose," J.D. replied.

"We'll cook breakfast as soon as everyone has had some rest," Dak added. "See you ladies in a little while. And thank you for the most wonderful evenin' of my life."

It was nearly 11 AM when Melodie was awakened by a knock at the cabin's door. She could see through the door's window that it was her dad. She slid into a bathrobe and opened the door with a yawn. "Good morning, Dad," she said.

Mr. Lerner seemed a little nervous. He said, "Good morning. Is everything okay here? We got a little worried when you weren't home yet."

"Everything is fine. The boys and Mrs. Robinson are in their cabin. We're going to have breakfast together in a while. I hope that's okay. I told you we'd be staying all night."

"Yeah, as long as Mrs. Robinson is here," he said. "Just a little worried about you, that's all. Sorry to bother you. There's some bacon and eggs in the refrigerator." As he turned around and headed for his car, he mumbled to himself, "Just a little worried..."

A few minutes later, Dak and J.D. were up. They each had a pair of J.D.'s old swimming trunks on and J.D. was chasing Dak down the bank toward the fishing pier. When Dak reached the end of the pier, he jumped into the water with J.D. just behind. After some jousting in the water, they noticed the girls were up and ran up to Melodie's cabin.

Dak built a new fire in the stone ring and fried bacon and eggs. Coffee would have been good, but they couldn't find any, so they had hot tea. Marie was decidedly sleepy, and J.D. had just a bit of a headache. Mrs. Robinson joined them as they ate breakfast, but seemed not to be feeling well. Dak hugged her and thanked her profusely for being their chaperone.

As much as they hated to leave, J.D. had promised his uncle that he would have the Plymouth back by noon. They slid into the car and rode along talking about what a memorable night it had been and how glad they were that Mr. Jordan had cancelled the other prom.

Chapter 19

Dreams are Forever

After arriving home that Sunday at noon, Dak sat on the sofa to read the paper and fell asleep. Two and a half hours later, he was startled when one of Nancy's friends rang the doorbell. He could hardly believe he had slept so long. He put his suit away, took a bath in the laundry shed, and donned his usual faded jeans and colorful shirt.

He was thinking about Miss Mattie Lott and decided to go see her at the hospital. Not wanting to bother J.D. when he had a headache, he decided to hitchhike. He walked down to Route 13, and his luck was good. In ten minutes, he was on his way to Eldorado. Arriving at the hospital, he asked at the desk for Miss Mattie's room number.

"Oh, Miss Mattie has been awfully sick," the receptionist said. "The doctor has been monitoring her closely. She slips in and out of consciousness. She is in Room 14, but please don't stay long. The doctor says she only has a few days left."

When Dak went to her room, he could see that she was very weak but she was conscious. She looked up at him and smiled wanly.

"How are you doin', Miss Mattie?" he asked.

"Not good, Dakkie," she whispered. "I think the Lord is goin' to take me soon. It's so good of you to come."

Dak told her the neighbor lady seemed to be taking good care of Carrots and the cow Matilda. Mattie said she had told the lady that she could have the animals "when I depart." She told Dak she wanted him to have Mariah's papers. She took his hand in hers and looked at him for a full minute as tears welled up in her eyes. He leaned over and hugged her as she lay in the bed. While he was bent over her, she put her mouth near his ear and whispered something about lilacs. Then she shut her eyes and didn't move again. Alarmed, Dak called the nurse. She assured him that Mattie was still alive and would probably be able to talk again in a while. Dak waited nearly two hours. When Mattie didn't wake, he finally left and hitchhiked home.

• • •

The next morning, when Dak came down to breakfast, Eleanor said, "Dak, Ann Scroggins told me this morning that Savoy has been arrested and charged with murder. How could they do that so quickly?"

"Wow!" Dak said. "The evidence that J.D. and I gave them is pretty convincin', and maybe they found more. I don't know. But I'm glad to hear he's in custody."

"Well, I don't know if 'custody' is the right word or not. He's in the hospital with his burns, but he has been arrested."

"Whatever," Dak said. He was suddenly much less interested in Percy Savoy. "She didn't say anything about the deed books?" he asked.

"No, but then it is too early for that," Eleanor responded.

• • •

Two days later, J.D. dropped by on his bicycle. "Guess what?" he said. "I've signed up with the Navy. I leave on the seventeenth of August, and I'll be getting a lot of electronics training."

Somehow, Dak was happy for J.D. and saddened that he would be leaving, all at the same time. He had once looked forward to going to college with J.D. but had realized for some time that the Navy was J.D.'s better choice. "Hey, that's great," Dak said, trying to hide the sad side of his emotions.

J.D. spent some time excitedly giving Dak the details of what the Navy man had told him. He explained where he would be going and what he would be doing. "I'll get to travel all over the world," he said. "And he told me that there are lots of jobs doin' electronics when I get out. He said they really pay a lot. Well, I have to go. I need to go tell Marie."

Dak and Eleanor decided to go to the County Clerk's Office and ask about their status regarding the deeds. Eleanor was a little concerned that there may be some sympathy there for Percy Savoy, or that he might have paid them to support his position, but she decided to risk it. She arranged a ride with Mrs. Staley, who was making the trip for another purpose. The county clerk, whose name was John Harrison, walked out to the counter. He said he knew the situation and had looked at the deed books as soon as he received them from the state trooper. Dak showed him the 100-year lease agreement and asked their position. Mr. Harrison said, "As long as Mr. Savoy doesn't come up with a deed, I'd have to say that the property belongs to the Leventhal heirs, because the long-lost deed book lists it that way and your lease agreement substantiates that the property was leased, not sold. Now, Mr. Savoy may take you to court, but I don't think his chances are good, and besides, he has much bigger problems to deal with."

Dak thrust his hands upward and yelled, "Oh, wow! Ohhh! Ohhh, God! Mom, did you hear that? The land is probably ours! Wow!" The startled county clerk stepped backward and stood speechless as Dak began laughing and then hugged Eleanor. Dak had never let himself think that the land and the mansion would actually be his and Nancy's. "Well, this should solve the college money problem," he said. "I'm sure we can lease the fields for more than I'll need for college."

Eleanor became weepy and said, "Dak, this is wonderful!"

"Mom," he said, "why do you always cry when you're happy?"

They went to the drug store and treated Mrs. Staley to a soda to celebrate the event. Then Dak asked that they drop him off at Miss Hurd's house near the high school, saying he wanted to say good-bye to her before she moved. He told Eleanor he would hitchhike home. He made his way up the walk and knocked on her door as the car drove away. Then he noticed a note attached to the door. It said, "I have moved to Moline, Illinois, and can be reached at the following address." Dak read no further. "Man," he mumbled to himself as his earlier elation turned to sadness, "I really wanted to say good-bye to her." As he walked toward the highway to hitchhike home, he thought that good-byes were very hard for Miss Hurd, and maybe it was best she was just gone. *She's probably right,* he thought. *She's probably gone forever. But even if I never see her again, there is a part of me that is always hers, a part of me that she has changed forever.*

After catching a ride down Route 13, Dak went by Melodie's house. Melodie answered the door and gave Dak a big kiss on the cheek. "What are you here for, hanky panky?" she said with a big smile.

"No," he said. "I just wanted to tell you about some developments."

"Good," she said. "Let's go sit in the back porch swing. Mom is vacuuming in here."

Dak told her what the county clerk had said, and Melodie squealed with delight. After discussing that a bit, he said, "J.D. has joined the Navy. Did Marie tell you?"

"No. Marie has some relatives in town, and I haven't talked with her," she said. "J.D. joined the Navy? When does he start?"

"He leaves on the seventeenth of August," Dak said.

"Really?" she said. "That's the same day I have to leave for nursing school."

"I know," he said. "I know." She could see that this saddened him.

When he got home, Eleanor was sitting in the porch swing with some papers in her lap, staring into space. "What you doin'?" Dak asked.

She didn't answer at all. She didn't even look up to acknowledge that he was there. Dak wondered if she was sick. Could she have had a stroke or something? He sat down in the swing beside her and gently put his hand on her arm. "Are you okay, Mom?" he said.

Still looking straight ahead, she handed him the papers. He leaned back in the swing and saw that he had an envelope and three pieces of paper. There was a brief note on a clean white card and two sheets of old, badly stained paper. Dak read the neatly penned note on the white card.

June 2, 1956

Mrs Eleanor Leventhal,

So sorry to bring sad letter, but thought you want to know. My grandson found a helmet when digging a flowerbed. In the helmet was a tobacco can with the two sheets of paper and piece of cloth. I send them to you.

Mamoru Kuribashi
Naha, Okinawa
Japan

Dak unfolded the first stained page, handling it very carefully since it seemed so fragile. The scrawled writing was faint, but readable.

ATTENTION
ANYONE WHO FINDS THIS
PLEASE SEND TO
MRS. ELEANOR LEVENTHAL
SHAWNEETOWN, ILLINOIS
UNITED STATES OF AMERICA

His heart was pounding as he opened the second soiled page.

Okinawa
April 9, 1945

Dearest Eleanor,

Afraid I've let you down. Promised to return w/o a scratch, but have bad leg wound. Will lose left leg. Trouble stopping the bleeding. By myself last few hours. This letter may never get to you, I pray it does.

Landed on this place on Easter. Easy for a while. My buddy Bobby & I doing fine for a couple days. Then had trouble. Japs all dug in. Big explosion near me & Bobby. Don't know what happened to Bobby. Gone. Think most our guys pulled back down the hill. Can't move. Yelled so much--no one answers.

May not make it, Love. Remember, love you more than anything. Tell Dak will always be my special boy. Love to baby too. May die, but spirit will be with you, my dreams are forever. God bless all.

Love

Paul
Dakston Paul Leventhal III
Pfc U S Army
77th Infantry Division

Dak was stunned. Nothing in his lifetime had moved him so deeply. As his eyes filled with tears, he turned away from Eleanor. Then, unable to control the sobs and no longer caring if she saw him, he turned back. He saw circular spots on the soiled pages that he thought were stains from his dad's tears. He moved the fragile letter up to his face and let his own tears join those of his dad. There was silence for two or three minutes. Then Dak spoke softly to Eleanor. "Did you notice what my dad said? He said, 'my dreams are forever'."

"Yes, he did, Dak," she said, putting her arm around him. "If only he knew. Oh, if only he knew about you."

The words from the letter tumbled through his mind for days. It was not a long letter, but it was enough. Dak thought about every sentence and filled in the abbreviated prose with words of his own. He thought about why his dad had written each of the sentences. He imagined how his dad felt as he was writing. He visualized how the surroundings looked, thought about how the foxhole smelled, and fantasized about how loud the noise of battle must have been. As he reconstructed the scenario in his mind, he concluded that writing the letter under such desperate and painful circumstances showed how much his dad cared. Dak memorized the text of the letter. Now he felt he knew more, much more, about his dad. And although he still missed him, the letter brought some closure which Dak had never felt before.

• • •

Miss Mattie died four days later. Dak was one of the pallbearers at her simple funeral. The minister followed Miss Mattie's request that his talk at her funeral be based on Ecclesiastes Chapter 7, first verse: "A good name is better than precious ointment; and the day of death than the day of one's birth." Only a few people attended the funeral, and Dak wondered how the passing of the wonderful old lady could get such scant attention. He tried to find some lilacs for her grave, but it was too late in the year.

The boys frolicked the summer away. Dak and J.D., and sometimes Charlie and Donny, swam in the river and rode logs downstream. They pedaled their bicycles far into the countryside looking for more adventure. On one of these events, Donny was coasting downhill on a steep gravel road when the front wheel fell off his bicycle. Donny ended up in the ditch with maybe a pound of moist clay stuck to his head, but with no injury other than his pride. They dug for relics in Indian mounds, climbed fire patrol towers, explored caves, and picked blackberries in the hot mornings. They went frogging during the dark nights, marveled at the size of the snakes, and told ghost stories. They visited the mansion one more time and talked about Mariah, Georgie, Crenshaw, and Savoy. They talked about girls and sex. They speculated about the future, the changes they would see, and when man would go to the moon. It all went very quickly.

Melodie and Dak wrote some love poems that summer. Whenever her parents went out for the evening, they listened to Johnnie Ace and talked about their future. They had some intimate evenings with J.D., Marie, and a couple beers in the old Ford parked down by the icehouse. One night, the four of them sat on the seawall and sang *Beautiful Ohio* under Marie's direction. But through it all, there was not to be another evening in the cabin at Big Lake. It was the prom, the only prom, and nothing ever again matched its perfection.

Dak and J.D. were allowed to return the relics that had come from the graves. They put them as nearly as possible in their original location and replaced the dirt that they had removed. After the dirt was thoroughly compacted, they repositioned the large flat stone to mark the place. Then the two of them held a short service. "God, please bless these three poor murdered people," Dak said. "And from this point forward, may their bodies and their souls rest in peace."

"Amen," J.D. added. Then he sighed and said, "Hey, Dak, it seems like a shame to put that ruby ring back in the ground, doesn't it?"

"J.D., have some respect," Dak said as he grabbed J.D. in a headlock. A tussle followed which ended with J.D. on top of Dak and Dak yelling, "I give up, be disrespectful if you want!"

For a while, the boys worried about the sheriff returning and using his nightstick on them or maybe even shooting one of them. It was not to be. The sheriff died of complications following a second major heart attack while still in the hospital. The folks in the barbershop talked about how he had prostituted himself, even to the point of attempting murder, for a few dollars from Percy Savoy. No one seemed to know anything about his funeral service or where his body was interred.

The new sheriff fired the deputy and brought charges against him for some of his blundering crimes. Before his trial date, he disappeared and they never saw him again. Rumors were that he left for eastern Kentucky where he had previously lived.

Trooper Lew Evans learned that the former sheriff had, at Savoy's request, hired the man driving the green car. The man was from Memphis and was a professional hit man but not a very smart one. Apparently, Savoy's idea was to have him handy in case lesser measures did not silence the boys. When Judy told her dad about overhearing Dak talking on the phone about a Savoy murder, he put the man to work.

Percy Savoy maintained his innocence for a long time, but finally broke. Under intense interrogation two weeks after his arrest, he admitted that he murdered Josephine. He spilled the whole sordid story. He told authorities that he asked her to go on a picnic along the riverbank north of town one October day in 1935. His intent was to kill her with one well-placed smashing blow to the back of her head at an opportune moment during the picnic. For his weapon, he chose a two-foot long lead pipe. He carefully filled the pipe with buckshot to add weight before capping off the ends. Then he hid the pipe behind a tree where he planned to hold the picnic. His thought was that he would bury her body next to the bodies of a couple slaves from long ago so that if the bones were ever uncovered many years later, it would appear that there were three graves of a kind. He thought no one would guess that one of the three was Josephine. He had dug the grave in advance next to the slave graves, which were marked by the large flat stone. Also, he had hidden a blanket and rope ahead of time to contain the body for burial. He thought it unlikely that the graves would be disturbed for many years.

Savoy's plan worked almost perfectly. He explained that he temporarily lost his nerve the first time he walked over to the tree to pick up the pipe. But he had another sandwich with Josephine and tried again. This time, he did it. He caught her in the middle of a sentence with a massive blow to the back of the head. She slumped to the ground and never moved again. He was prepared to strike a second blow, but it was not necessary. He wrapped the body in the blanket and used the three pieces of rope to tie around it all. He encountered only two difficulties. The first was that he had chosen the picnic spot too far from the grave site and found it exhausting to drag her body that distance. The second was that he had neglected to plan for the disposal of the lead pipe. He ended up hiding it under a pile of fresh-fallen cottonwood leaves the day of the murder. Later, he returned in a boat, retrieved the pipe, took it to the center of the river, and dropped it overboard.

Savoy was asked why he kept the sword and painting in the secret room at the mansion. He replied that they had great value, but he thought it unsafe to sell them on the open market until at least 20 years after the murder. He thought the secret room was the perfect hiding place in the meantime. His plan had always been eventually to take them to an upscale antique auction in New York or London. In fact, he was going to do that before the building was demolished, but gave up on that idea after the march on the mansion. There were just too many people around. His next best option was to destroy them before someone else saw them. He also wanted the deed books destroyed, so burning the mansion seemed like a good solution.

The defense attorney and the prosecutor spent the summer preparing for Savoy's murder trial. It was to begin in September, and it was considered likely that he would get life in prison. Charlie and J.D. hoped for a death sentence, but Dak thought that would be too hard for Judy. After finally locating Josephine Savoy's relatives in France, the State Police returned the sword and painting to them.

Savoy was very surprised that there was a surviving copy of the document for the 100-year lease. When confronted with it, he proclaimed that the Ellsworths had probably purchased the property in a cash transaction that was never recorded. In view of his other problems, he eventually decided not to legally challenge the ownership of Ellsworth Place by the Leventhal heirs.

Dak never heard from Miss Hurd again, nor did he try to contact her. Even so, he thought of her every day and, other than his mother, he considered her the person who had most influenced his life. He occasionally wondered whether she was happy with her new life, and he often replayed in his mind scenes from her class such as the day Charlie received the grade of 100 on his test.

And then there was the day of good-byes, the seventeenth of August.

Dak went by J.D.'s house as his parents were preparing to take him to Eldorado to the train station. J.D. had already said his good-byes to Marie. He put his arm around Dak's shoulders and said, "Well, this is farewell for a while, Dak. I don't have the words." He looked down and paused. Then, he said, "Have fun at college."

"No need for words, J.D.," Dak said. "But we've done some things, haven't we?"

"Que será," J. D said as he squeezed Dak's hand. He slid into the driver's seat. As the car rolled away, J.D. stuck his head out the window and waved. Dak could hear the radio, "...down at the end of Lonely Street at Heartbreak Hotel."

"Que será," Dak whispered.

Dak hopped on his bicycle and rode to Melodie's house. She had finished packing everything into the car and was walking in the backyard when he arrived. He walked up behind her and put his chin on her shoulder. "I'm not sure I've sufficiently welcomed the lady to my plantation," he said.

"Why, Suh, I don't believe you have," she replied. He gave her a kiss on the neck. Just as she started to say she still didn't feel really welcome, Mr. Lerner stuck his head out the back door and said, "Come on, Melodie, we're ready to go."

Dak walked Melodie to the car. As he gave her a long hug, she said, "Don't forget to listen to Johnnie Ace. Remember it's always and forever."

"Don't forget to write me at college," he said. "I love you."

She stepped into the back seat of the car, but left the door open and held Dak's hand until Mr. Lerner started the engine. Then she shut the door and threw kisses through the window as they drove off. Dak threw kisses back and waved until the car was a spec on the horizon.

When J.D. and Melodie were both gone, it seemed to Dak that there was a strange quietness about the town. Everything seemed somehow different now. As he rode his bike slowly along the top of the levee, he could hear the muted sound of some worn-out honky-tonk song coming from a jukebox in one of the old taverns on Main Street. At some point, he stopped his bike and stood on the levee looking over the town. It seemed so small now and felt like something from an earlier time. He walked slowly down the dusty trail to the Uppers, the path that he and his friends had so joyfully descended on all those carefree summer afternoons. Reaching the beach, he sat on a big log and looked at the still water. There was no one there, no boats on the river. In his mind, he could hear echoes of boisterous banter left over from the thousand times they had jumped into the cold water or flipped a floating log. But now it was so quiet. After a while, he heard a single dog bark far off in the distance. For the first time in his life, he felt terribly lonely. There was something about him that desperately wanted things to continue as they had been before J.D. and Melodie left. He kept thinking about what Miss Hurd had said. "You always think, 'Well, we'll stay in contact'...but, Dak, that's not the way it works. They are gone. They are gone for good." As he tried to get his mind around this, he faintly heard the forlorn whistle of a train as it passed some crossing many miles away. *Those people are going somewhere else, leaving here,* he thought. A little later, he heard the town clock strike, its sound muffled by distance and the levee. He didn't need that reminder that time was moving on. He kept trying to tell himself that things would be the same, that nothing had really changed, but it didn't work. Deep down, he knew that things would not--could not--ever be the same again. He wept for more than two hours in long, anguished sobs as he mourned what he knew he had lost. Finally, he walked down to the water and washed his face in the river.

When Dak went home, he explained to Eleanor that he had been for a swim and had gotten soap in his eyes. She understood. She patted him on the back and suggested he get some rest. "Tomorrow, we need to start getting together the things you will be taking to college next week," she said.

Dak went to his room and stared at the picture of his dad. "Well, Dad," he whispered, "I've just finished the first big dream of my life. I know the second one will be okay once I get into it, but right now I'm havin' such a hard time giving up the first one. Can't I get an extension or somethin'? Oh, man. Help me with this, Dad." The tears came again, and then he fell asleep.

On the eighteenth of August, Dak sat on the seawall, looking at the river and pondering his future. *It is always me and the river,* he thought. *It's me and the river and my dreams.*